HAND IN GLOVE

The death of a young English poet in the Spanish Civil
War casts a shadow forward over half a century.

'Cliff-hanging entertainment'
GUARDIAN

CLOSED CIRCLE

1931, and two English fraudsters on a transatlantic liner stumble
into deep trouble when they target a young heiress.

*'Full of thuggery and skulduggery, cross and
doublecross, plot and counter-plot'*
INDEPENDENT

BORROWED TIME

A brief encounter with a stranger who is murdered soon afterwards draws
Robin Timariot into the complex relationships and motives of the dead
woman's family and friends.

*'An atmosphere of taut menace...heightened
by shadows of betrayal and revenge'*
DAILY TELEGRAPH

OUT OF THE SUN

Harry Barnett becomes entangled in a sinister conspiracy
when he learns that the son he never knew he had is languishing
in hospital in a coma.

'Brilliantly plotted, full of good, traditional storytelling values'
MAIL ON SUNDAY

BEYOND RECALL

The scion of a wealthy Cornish dynasty reinvestigates a 1947 murder
and begins to doubt the official version of events.

'Satisfyingly complex...finishes in a rollercoaster of twists'
DAILY TELEGRAPH

CAUGHT IN THE LIGHT

A photographer's obsession with a femme fatale
leads him into a web of double jeopardy.

*'A spellbinding foray into the real-life game
of truth and consequences'*
THE TIMES

SET IN STONE

A strange house links past and present, a murder,
a political scandal and an unexplained tragedy.

'A heady blend of mystery and adventure'
OXFORD TIMES

SEA CHANGE

A spell-binding mystery involving a mysterious package, murder and
financial scandal, set in 18th-century London, Amsterdam and Rome.

'Engrossing, storytelling of a very high order'
OBSERVER

DYING TO TELL

A missing document, a forty-year-old murder and the Great Train
Robbery all seem to have connections with a modern-day disappearance.

*'Gripping...woven together with more
twists than a country lane'*
DAILY MAIL

DAYS WITHOUT NUMBER

Once Nick Paleologus has excavated a terrible secret from his
archaeologist father's career, nothing will ever be the same again.

*'Fuses history with crime, guilty consciences and human fallibility...
an intelligent escapist delight'*
THE TIMES

LONG TIME COMING

For thirty-six years they thought he was dead...
They were wrong.

'When it comes to duplicity and intrigue,
Goddard is second to none'
DAILY MAIL

BLOOD COUNT

There's no such thing as easy money.
As surgeon Edward Hammond is about to find out.

'Mysterious, dramatic, intricate,
fascinating and unputdownable...
The crime writers' crime writer'
DAILY MIRROR

SET IN STONE

Robert Goddard

CORGI BOOKS

TRANSWORLD PUBLISHERS
61–63 Uxbridge Road, London W5 5SA
A Random House Group Company
www.rbooks.co.uk

SET IN STONE
A CORGI BOOK: 9780552164160

First published in Great Britain
in 1999 by Bantam Press
an imprint of Transworld Publishers
Corgi edition published 2000
Corgi edition reissued 2011

Addresses for Random House Group Ltd companies outside the UK
can be found at: www.randomhouse.co.uk
The Random House Group Ltd Reg. No. 954009

The Random House Group Limited supports The Forest Stewardship
Council (FSC), the leading international forest certification organisation.
All our titles that are printed on Greenpeace approved FSC certified
paper carry the FSC logo. Our paper procurement policy can
be found at www.rbooks.co.uk/environment

Typeset in 11/13pt Giovanni Book by
Kestrel Data, Exeter, Devon.
Printed in the UK by
CPI Cox & Wyman, Reading, RG1 8EX.

2 4 6 8 10 9 7 5 3 1

SET IN STONE

Prologue

Maybe you already know what I'm going to tell you. Maybe death isn't the slammed-shut, sealed-tight doorway we reckon it is. I've seen enough these past few months to doubt it. If it isn't, maybe you've been watching me all this time, wondering when I'd turn round and look at you and speak.

I can't see you, Marina. I can't hear you. But that doesn't matter. And then again it does. More than anything. I love you. I will always love you. I never expected to feel as much for another person as I feel for you. I never even wanted to. Because dependency is dangerous. And dependency on the dead is halfway to madness. But still I love you. It's as simple and as desolate as that. I don't need to chase your ghost. It's here, at every moment, beside me. It's almost tangible. But not quite. You'll always be just out of reach. I can't touch you. Ever again.

But I can talk to you. And maybe, just maybe, you can listen. I wish I could tell you a different story, though. I wish I could tell you your death was just a single outbreak of meaningless misfortune. I wish I could wipe away the events it set in motion and have you back,

11

alive and contented, to love and be loved. But wishing is all it comes to. It changes nothing. There is only one story I can tell you. And this is it.

Chapter One

I never wanted to leave London. You know that. The simpler, purer country life was your dream, not mine. You'd always talked about it and I'd gone along with the idea to keep you happy, silently banking on a solid set of practical objections to fend it off. Then Matt and Lucy moved to Leicestershire, and every weekend we visited them gave you an extra ounce of determination to turn your dream into a reality. Suddenly Lucy had something you wanted more than you reckoned she did. And you and your sister always were a competitive pair.

The difference was that Matt was already making a success of Pizza Prego by then. He could afford the country-squire act. We weren't so free and easy. Whatever my career amounted to, it wasn't the prototype for home-based working in the sticks. And your client list was all corporate metropolitan. But fortieth birthdays do strange things to people. I let you persuade me that London was choking me as well as you, and that you could earn enough as a rural solicitor to tide us over until I sold the concept of professional recruitment services to local employers. Then you threw yourself into the search for a suitable opportunity and, before

I'd done more than flirt with the implications of what we were embarking on, you found one.

It was everything you wanted. A cosy little practice over a pharmacy in the centre of a genuine Devon market town. Real people with real problems, not sharp-faced men in suits demanding contracts by yesterday. I remember driving down to Holsworthy with you for the first time and walking round the square on a quiet, sunny Saturday afternoon. There was a gleam in your eye that told me this place was our future. Well, yours, anyway. I'd be moving, whereas you'd be going home. You belonged there, instantly and completely, whereas for me . . . it was where I had to be to stay close to you.

Not that I was blind to its attractions. The pace of life was slower, the surrounding countryside was a picture postcard succession of winding lanes and rolling hills. And the air was like champagne. The back of beyond had its own allure. And Stanacombe was beautiful. 'A cob-and-slate whitewashed farmhouse just over the Cornish border, in need of some renovation.' That's what the estate agent's blurb said. But I saw in it what you saw: a private patch of heaven, nestling in green fields, beneath the last westward swell of the land before Cornwall hit the Atlantic in a jagged line of high granite cliffs.

You thought I was reluctant to take on the work that needed doing on Stanacombe. And so I was at the outset. But after we'd moved down I really began to enjoy it. It was a lot more rewarding than headhunting high-flyers in London, even if nobody was paying me to do it. Besides, we had a comforting slab of capital to fall back on after selling the house in Chiswick, and you charmed most of your predecessor's clients in Holsworthy into staying with you, so I didn't need to rush into making any money. Three months of renovation stretched into six. Spring came in, clean and fresh and new, scattering flowers round the high-banked lanes in a way I'd have thought belonged to some remote, rustic past. That's when I knew what you'd known all along: moving to the country was going to be the best move we'd ever made.

Contentment crept up on us during those months. We didn't seem to miss our London friends. The isolation I'd feared became a privacy I cherished. We never even visited Matt and Lucy as promised at Easter, to see the new house they'd moved into. We would have done, of course, sooner or later. There just didn't seem to be any urgency about it. Not when there was so much to be enjoyed in our own new home. It could be an illusion, bred by the loss of you, but I don't think so. Last winter and spring at Stanacombe, we fell in love all over again. It seems so clear now, the memory of you lying beside me in our bedroom beneath the eaves. So clear, yet so fragile. More fragile than I knew.

What was the last thing you said to me? I've been trying to remember, but the words won't come. It was nothing. Just a run-of-the-mill farewell, a leave-taking for a few inconsequential hours. You'd said you'd be home early, to make a start on the garden. And I'd said I might not be there when you got back. It depended on whether there were any useful lots in a furniture auction at Bideford I was driving over to at lunchtime. You nodded and called something back to me over your shoulder as you walked out to the garage. I heard the car start and pull out into the lane. I went to the window and waved. I think you waved back, but the sun was in my eyes and I didn't glimpse much more than a flicker of movement through the glare. Then you were gone. And already, though I didn't know it, as the sound of the car faded into the softness of the morning, you were a memory.

I bought a gateleg table at the auction. I reckoned it would go well in the hall. I was confident you'd like it. I phoned the office to tell you. But Carol said you'd already left. Two hours since, apparently. I tried you at home, but there was no answer. Busy in the garden, I assumed. I started back an hour or so later and made it to Kilkhampton about six. I stopped at the New Inn for a drink and phoned you again from there, thinking you might want to join me. The sun had been hot enough to give you a thirst, but now there was the first cooling hint of evening in the air – our favourite time of the day. Still no answer, though. I finished my drink and left.

You weren't in the garden. You weren't at home at all. But your car was in the garage and your briefcase was in the study. And it looked as if you'd brewed some tea. The pot was standing upside down on the draining board in the kitchen, the way you used to leave it to dry. There was a rubbish sack full of prunings outside the kitchen door, so some gardening had been done. But that was it – no other sign of you. Not that you ever left many signs. You always were meticulously tidy. There was a time that used to annoy me. But that time was long gone.

I decided you must have gone for a walk. I had another beer, read the paper and waited. When you weren't back by seven thirty, I began to worry. Nothing concrete, nothing desperate, just low-level anxiety. I headed out, down the lane, and tried the footpath to Stowe Woods, your favourite after-work stroll. It would have been a swiftly forgotten relief to see you emerging from the trees ahead of me, but you didn't.

I turned back then, knowing you could have taken one of several routes through the woods. Besides, you might just as easily have gone the other way, down to Duckpool Beach. It made more sense to return home.

I saw the police car as I turned into the drive. In that instant, anxiety became alarm. I hesitated, then strode towards the car. A policeman was sitting in the driving seat, talking on his radio. I could hear what he was saying through the open window. 'No reply at the house. I'm going to—' He broke off, catching sight of me in the wing mirror. Then he climbed out, the setting sun flashing at me in the mirror as the door opened and closed. He was young and burly, built like a rugby player. He pursed his lips and said, 'Mr Sheridan?'

'Yes.'

'Mr Anthony Sheridan?'

'Yes.'

'Husband of Marina Sheridan?'

'What's going on?'

'I'm afraid there's been—'

'What's happened to her?'

'An accident, sir. We think the victim is your wife.'

'What kind of accident? How badly hurt is she?'

'I'm very sorry to say, sir, that she's—'

'Dead.' That's what he said. Dead. The full stop in the middle of a sentence. The end before you've properly begun. You can talk about it, envisage it, acknowledge it, but you can't prepare for it. Not when neither you nor the one you love most in all the world is ill or old. Not when everything you've done assumes a future.

They must have told me what had happened several

17

times before it sank in. I didn't want to believe it and so, at first, I couldn't bring myself to. So much fear hides beneath our everyday concerns, Marina, so much dark, lurking dread. We bury it deep. We pretend it isn't there. And then, in a sickening instant, it surges to the surface. And consumes us. I was shocked. Of course I was. But most of all I was frightened. Of every hour and day and week and year I was going to spend without you.

A couple of walkers had found your handbag, discarded at the top of Henna Cliff, near Morwenstow. They'd followed the footpath down towards the stream to the south and gone out onto the landslip halfway to get a view of the beach at the foot of the cliff. From there they'd spotted you lying among the rocks, the incoming tide crashing around you. To them you were no more than a crumpled shape against the black rocks and foaming white surf. Your life crushed, and mine smashed, beneath the soaring cliff face and the wind-stirred clumps of gorse.

I think now of the times I saw you in death, at the mortuary and the chapel of rest. It wasn't you, really, not any more. But that didn't stop me dreaming of you slowly sitting up and smiling at me and making everything right again. Only a dream is all it was. You were gone, and you weren't coming back.

The police thought you'd killed yourself. I could tell that by the way they cleared their throats and avoided my gaze. I knew better, of course, but there was no way of convincing them of that. It was an unaccountable accident, after all. The cliff top is fenced off, the danger obvious. And you knew the area. Then there was the handbag. Why put it down unless you meant it to be found, to ease identification and save me some suspense? It didn't make any sense.

18

Except to me. I went to the cliff top two days later, when I was beginning to be capable of logical thought and action. The sunlight was dazzlingly bright, the blue of the sea and sky sweepingly vast, the clarity of the air almost intoxicating. You loved the cliffs, didn't you? Perhaps you loved them too much. I've known you cross the fence in that very spot to get closer to the edge, while I've waited for you on the bench near the stile, back up the path. The wild flowers delighted you. You could reel off all their names and recognize them at a glance, whilst I still can't tell a thrift from a campion. That's what I decided must have happened. You noticed an interesting specimen clinging to the edge, put your handbag down so that it didn't flap around your shoulder in the breeze, stooped for a closer look, either slipped or momentarily lost your bearings and took a step in the wrong direction, then . . .

A sheer plummeting drop of 400 feet or more. Standing there, buffeted by the wind, confused by grief and the out-of-scale wonder of that high green corner of cliff, I saw the whole event as a sudden scrambling mishap, neither more nor less. I saw it and felt the loss of you, there in the pure yawning chasm of air. It wouldn't have taken much, except the courage I didn't possess, to step after you into the void. But if onlys clung to me like restraining hands. I still couldn't quite bring myself to believe it was true, so I turned and ducked back beneath the fence.

Matt and Lucy arrived later that day. It was a bleak reunion. Matt offered me what comfort he could in his gentle, understated way, while Lucy was clearly as shocked and bewildered as me. You'd always been a part of her life. In that sense, I was just a newcomer. She'd been expecting to see you again soon and now she never would. You were closer than a lot of sisters. More like twins, you used to say, despite the two-year gap. And she looked even more like you than usual on account of a recent diet. To see her smile, and to be reminded instantly and acutely of your smile, was hard to bear. Not that she did smile much. Or cry, come to that. Her grief was a kind of paralysis, through which she seemed to fumble for meaning as much as consolation.

But there was no meaning. That was the worst of it. I could show them Stanacombe and describe the plans we'd had for it. I could take them to Morwenstow and up onto Henna Cliff. I could drive them down to Bodmin and wait outside the chapel of rest, while they went in to say goodbye to you. But I couldn't explain what had happened in any way that seemed either fitting or appropriate. I sensed that Lucy blamed me for your death, blamed me, that is, for not taking better care of you. She didn't say so, of course. She knew it wasn't rational or reasonable. You'd have resented any hint of protectiveness, just like her. But it was there nonetheless. In me as well as her.

They stayed on for the funeral and handled a lot of the arrangements, thank God. Well, Matt did, to be honest. Lucy and I weren't up to much, beyond talking about you. We drove to Bournemouth to see your mother, but she didn't show the slightest understanding of what we were telling her. Maybe senility does have its blessings after all.

You'd specified cremation in your will, of course, like the model solicitor you were. I'd have preferred burial. It would have meant I could visit you. But you always were suspicious of markers and memorials, weren't you? Or perhaps you wouldn't have wanted me moping at a graveside. I never asked what your reasoning was. I didn't want to think about your death, even as a remote contingency. But now it was neither remote nor contingent. It was here and now. It was what I had to live with. And to live through.

A lot of our friends from London came down for the funeral. I was glad they were there, though I probably didn't show it, glad for your sake as much as mine. Kilkhampton Church was nearly full. I had no idea there were so many people who were going to miss you. You liked that church. I remember you saying so. I was glad of that too. It was just Matt, Lucy and me at the crematorium in Bodmin, though. There's nothing I can say about those final moments. They passed and it was done. I tried to register them in my mind, but all I could think of was you alive and laughing. It was nothing to do with you, that clinical consignment to the flames. You weren't there at all.

But you were nowhere else either. Your clothes still hung in the wardrobe. Your creams and perfumes still stood in the bathroom cabinet. Your lists of useful things still lay in the kitchen drawer. Yet all they amounted to was physical proof of your absence. I'd wake at night, believing for a fraction of a second that your death was a dream. But it wasn't. I was alone.

Matt and Lucy went home two days after the funeral. They urged me to accompany them, but I insisted I was better off learning to cope without you. Not that I think I'll ever learn how to do that.

'You can't mean to stay here,' said Lucy. 'It's not you, Tony. This place is all Marina.' She was right. It might have been different if we'd lived at Stanacombe for a few years. As it was, we'd hardly finished moving in. And without you I felt like a stranger there. But then, where wouldn't I? 'Let us take care of you for a while,' Lucy urged. 'This is going to take a lot of getting over.'

I promised to think about it. Lucy wrote, repeating the offer, a few days later. By then I'd been notified of a date for the inquest, so I suggested visiting them after that. I wasn't sure I'd want to, even then. Stanacombe was as close as I could be to you. It wasn't my home, but it was still yours. I helped Carol close down the practice in Holsworthy and carried on with the renovation work, between long cliff-top walks. I tired myself out, one way or another. I got through the days and looked forward to the nights, when I could sleep and forget you weren't sleeping beside me.

But it was only a short-term survival strategy. Sooner or later I had to make a break. And I suppose the inquest made it for me. Lucy came down on her own to attend. It was a brief, low-key affair at the courts in Bodmin. The coroner was businesslike but sympathetic. He asked me to describe your state of mind in the days before your death, giving me the opportunity to scotch the idea of suicide.

'My wife was sometimes impulsive,' I said. 'I'm afraid that probably explains what happened as well as it can be explained. She must have got bored with gardening and gone for a walk. I've known her to walk much further along the cliff path than she intended, just because the scenery's so magical. That would be why she went as far as Morwenstow. She was probably glorying in the spring flowers. Neither of us had realized how colourful they'd be when we moved down here. I'm sure that's why she was so close to the edge. No other reason. It must just have been . . . a misjudgement, an accident; a terrible, terrible accident.'

They let me have my way, Marina. Accidental death

was the official verdict. 'There is absolutely no reason to suppose', said the coroner, 'that Mrs Sheridan was minded to take her own life.' Exactly. No reason at all. And therefore an accident was the only possible explanation.

'That is what you truly believe, isn't it?' Lucy asked on the way back to Stanacombe. 'I mean, I'd understand, really I would, if you were keeping quiet about a . . . possible motive . . . for suicide.'

'Marina was no more suicidal than you are. She wasn't the type.'

'True enough. But a terminal disease, something like that.'

'She hadn't seen a doctor in months. We hadn't even got round to registering with one down here.'

'Good. I mean, I just wanted to be sure. I hadn't seen her for quite a while and I, well, I wish I had, I suppose. We were hoping you'd come up for Easter, you know.'

'I'm sorry we never made it, Lucy. There was a lot to do here. You've just moved yourselves. You know what it's like.'

'Yes. But we've settled in now. Are you going to come up? You need to get away, Tony. Put things into some kind of perspective.'

'You're probably right.'

'It's what Marina would have recommended.'

And it was, wasn't it? Precisely what you'd have recommended. You were always realistic, as well as sensitive, more of both than me. I was going to have to start thinking about money soon. I was going to have to start thinking about a lot of things. And Stanacombe was no place to do it. So I went along with what everybody seemed to reckon was best for me.

I took Lucy out to a pub in a village south of Bude for

a meal that evening. You and I had never been there. That's why I chose it. It was strange to be alone with her. I couldn't remember ever being so before. With Matt, yes, mostly before I met you. But never Lucy. I knew her as your sister, as much from stories of your childhood as from my own experience. I knew her as another version of you, with similar mannerisms and gestures, but different moods and opinions. She was always shorter-tempered than you, shallower as I saw it, less mature. But I was beginning to think she'd changed without me noticing. There was a gravity to her now that couldn't all be down to grief.

'Tell me to mind my own business, if you like, Tony,' she said, as we lingered over a last drink after the meal, 'but do you wish now you and Marina had had children? Or would that make all this so much worse?'

'I don't know. I haven't thought about it.' That was true. We hadn't talked about having children, had we? Not in years. 'I suppose it would give me somebody to . . . share the loss with.'

'You can share it with me, you know. And with Matt. We met at your wedding, remember.'

'I haven't forgotten.'

'What I mean is that it ties us together closer than the average pair of sisters and their husbands. The four of us. That's the way it's been for fifteen years. Now it's changed. And I reckon we need to help each other deal with the change.'

I tried to listen to what she was saying, but her reference to our wedding had thrown my thoughts back in time. Even though I'd been sure marrying you was what I wanted to do, I'd still been frightened, not by the commitment to you it represented, but by pledging the rest of my life in any particular way. I'd talked to Matt

24

about it the night before and he'd given me some good advice. 'As long as you're sure it's the right thing to do *now*, you can let the rest of your life look after itself.' I'd reminded him of that six months later, the night before his own wedding. And now here I was, fifteen years on, facing the kind of future I'd never imagined, sure of nothing, except that it wasn't going to look after itself.

'Are you with me, Tony?'

'Sorry. I seem to have had trouble concentrating since it happened. Tell me about the new house. We were surprised you moved. What was wrong with the old place?'

'Nothing. But Otherways has a magic all of its own.' Some of the sparkle that had been missing from her eyes since your death returned as she spoke. 'The moment we saw it, it cast its spell on us.'

'Otherways. Unusual name.'

'Unusual house. It dates from just before the First World War. The architect designed it to be full of surprises. And the biggest surprise of all is how homely it feels. As if it's the place I've been looking for all my life, without knowing it.'

'I'm looking forward to seeing it.'

'No need to wait. I have a photograph.' She opened her bag and slid an envelope out of a zipped compartment. I remember thinking how odd it was to carry a picture of your house around like that, as if it were a loved one, but I supposed she'd only brought it to show me. She took the photograph out of the envelope and handed it to me. 'What do you think?'

What I thought was that I'd never seen a house like it before. It was the height and breadth of a smallish manor house, set in its own wooded and lawned grounds. But it was completely circular. The roof was a cone of brown slate, its line broken by dormer windows and chimneys that still preserved the circular shape. There were no gables or bays. The lower windows all followed the curve of the grey-pink stone walls, while the front door was recessed in a porch, with steps leading up to it set within. The angle of the photograph made it difficult to judge, but the house appeared to be surrounded by a moat, a circle of water around a circle of stone. The only straight line visible seemed to be the bridge leading across the moat to the porch, although even this looked narrower at the end closer to the house, exaggerating the width of the moat in the process. There were two other bridges as well, and presumably a fourth, out of sight behind the house, all equally spaced around the perimeter. The overall effect was of geometrical symmetry and architectural bizarrerie. It drew the eye and confused the brain with its contradictory solidity. It was patently there, yet somehow, at the same time, not there, like a stage set or a projection: a mellow old stone house that threatened to dissolve even as you looked at it.

'Different, isn't it?' Lucy asked with a smile.

'It's certainly that.'

'You'll love it there. We do.'

'How did you find it?'

'Pure chance. Or fate, maybe. If you believe in fate.'

'I'm not sure I do.'

I wasn't sure. Not then. But now is different. Now even fate seems too weak a word to describe the way that house and the secrets within it had coiled themselves unseen around us. Lucy. And Matt. And me. And you too, Marina. I hadn't even set eyes on it then. And you never will. But already it had begun to reel us in.

26

Lucy left next morning, taking with her my promise to follow within a couple of days. She also took some of your clothes, after I'd talked her into choosing those that would be useful to her. What was the point of hoarding them or donating them to Oxfam when you and Lucy were the same size and had swapped skirts and blouses often enough in the past? It seemed only sensible. You wouldn't have been sentimental about my clothes in such circumstances, would you?

The eerie thing was, though, that Lucy's selections were my particular favourites: the purple frock coat; the cerise jacket; the crisp, white oversized shirt with the coral trim; the clotted-cream summer trousers; the pale-blue silk scarf I gave you on our first wedding anniversary. I didn't know whether to be glad or sorry. But I let her take them, knowing I'd always think of you when I saw her wearing them, knowing I could always dream it was still you wearing them – if I wanted to.

After Lucy had gone, I drove to Holsworthy and asked the estate agent we'd bought Stanacombe through eight months before to put the house back on the market. Then I drove to Morwenstow, walked out past the rectory to the top of Henna Cliff and sat on the bench there, as the wind ripped at the surf below and shower clouds moved in and away, trailing scraps of rainbow and broken pillars of light. The air was clear and moist, glass-like and gleaming.

I ran my hand across my chin and realized I hadn't shaved that morning. I'd simply forgotten to, and Lucy had been too kind to mention it. Grief had made me untidy and forgetful. You'd have told me to smarten myself up. You were never one for slovenly chic. 'Move on,' I could almost hear you say. 'Don't linger now I'm no longer here.' You'd have been so much better at this than me, Marina, so much more certain of what to do.

I stayed there for a couple of hours, staring at the wire strand of the fence you'd crossed as it sagged and tautened in the gusts of wind. It all seemed so brutally pointless, so arbitrary, so bloody-minded of whoever or whatever ordained such things. Why let me have you at all if I was to lose you like this?

It was then, for the very first time, that I felt a stirring of anger at you for leaving me in such a stupid fashion. A fatal fall while admiring the spring flowers. 'For God's sake,' I said aloud, 'why couldn't you just have been more careful?' There was no answer, of course. From you or anywhere else.

I started packing as soon as I got back to Stanacombe. I had no clear idea how long I'd be gone, or if I'd ever return, other than to clear the house for a buyer. When I drove away next morning, my instincts told me I was leaving for good.

I stopped at Holsworthy, to drop the keys off at the estate agent, and bumped into Carol crossing the square. She'd found a job at the golf club and was in a hurry to finish some shopping before starting work for the day. I told her I was going away and that Stanacombe was up for sale.

'I hope things work out for you, Mr Sheridan,' she said.

'Me too.'

'I'm sure they will,' she added as we parted.

I wasn't sure, of course. But I'm blessed with an

optimistic nature, so you always said. Part of me reckoned this had to be as bad as it could get. And that part of me was right. I just didn't know how bad it really was. But I was going to find out. Whether I wanted to or not. At Otherways.

Chapter Two

Matt and Lucy's reason for moving to Leicestershire seemed logical enough to me. With Pizza Prego expanding into a nationwide chain of franchises, it made sense for Matt to find a base from which he could readily travel to any part of the country. You suggested, not entirely tongue-in-cheek, that it was more to indulge his passion for fox-hunting, though you must have known that really blossomed after they'd moved. A general enthusiasm for country squiredom was there from the start, however. But you always doubted whether Lucy shared that enthusiasm. You'd come away from sisterly heart-to-hearts implying she was bored with life at Market Bosworth. You suspected the move to Rutland, which they announced in the middle of our preparations to leave London, was meant to keep her busy with another round of designing and decorating. She'd admitted to frustrated maternal longings as well, though whether there was a physical problem or not was never made clear, and I know you didn't probe too hard in case a painful contrast with our own voluntary childlessness became apparent.

They were both strangely coy about the new place when they came down to Stanacombe at Christmas, if you remember, saying only that we'd be surprised when we saw it. Now I knew why. Otherways was nothing like the standard pile of manorial gabling I'd vaguely imagined. It existed entirely on its own terms.

Quite apart from its design, it was oddly located, though that at least was no doing of the architect. Rutland Water was created twenty years ago, when a couple of valleys east of Oakham, the county town, were flooded to form a reservoir. The crest of land between the two valleys survives as a peninsula, stretching out from the western shore most of the way across the lake. I drove onto it from Oakham on the afternoon of my arrival through patches of woodland and sparkling watery vistas. I came to the village of Hambleton – an achingly picturesque cluster of mellow stone houses – and followed Lucy's directions east, along a lane between fields of sheep and random glimpses of lake, until I reached the turning for Otherways.

It stood concealed from its surroundings behind a spinney-clad fold of land. The photograph had prepared me for what I'd see, but it still came as something of a shock, sitting there in the Rutland countryside like some kind of *trompe-l'œil* whose most artful deception was that it was no deception at all. The wedge of lake visible between the trees framing the house somehow got in on the act. The lake looked genuine, but wasn't. The house looked as if it wasn't there, but it was.

Matt was waiting to greet me, guessing I'd arrive before Lucy got back from a tennis lesson. He looked worried, it seemed to me, or distracted, perhaps by the prospect of an open-ended visit from me. But I didn't really think that was the cause. The roots of our friendship went too deep for that. I wondered if he had business problems. If so, he probably didn't want to burden me with them.

At first, we talked as if everything was as it had always been, as if you were still alive and the past few weeks had never happened. He showed me round the outside, enjoying the opportunity to unveil the oddities of the place to a first-time visitor, though he was disappointed by my lack of obvious astonishment. It soon emerged that he didn't know Lucy had shown me a photograph of it. I had the impression he didn't even know she carried one around with her.

'Lucy's playground more than mine,' he said, by way of explanation, as we circled the lichen-patched wall around the moat. 'I'm not sure I'd have bought it, but she insisted. I've had to switch hunts, you know.'

'Life can be a bugger, can't it?'

He grinned at me. Then the grin froze. 'But it has been for you. Lucy's cut up about it, of course. So am I. But for you . . .'

'Tell me about the house, Matt. It's made me curious. And curiosity takes my mind off Marina – for a while.'

'All right. It's the only known work of some oddball Anglo-French architect active just before the First World War. Emile Posnan. He built it for a wealthy recluse called Basil Oates. Oates died in the Thirties. Several owners since then, of whom yours truly is the latest. Everything really is as you see it. Circular. Or part-circular. The rooms narrow towards the centre. Every window is slightly convex, most of the internal doors slightly concave. Must have cost a fortune to build. Certainly costs a small one to maintain. But worth it, I suppose.'

'Because Lucy likes it?'

'Exactly. I try to keep her happy.'

'I wish I could still try to keep Marina happy.'

'I'll bet you do.' He squeezed my shoulder. 'If there's anything . . . Well, treat this as your home, Tony. Stay as long as you like. There's bags of room. We want to help, you know.'

'I do know. And knowing does help.'

'Want to see inside?' He winked. 'Weirder still.'

We retraced our steps to the entrance bridge and crossed the moat. As Matt opened the front door, I saw what he meant about convexity and concavity. The curvature of the door was so slight it only became apparent as it swung on its hinges. But it fitted perfectly, as it had to, obedient to the overall concept. The same went for the frame, presumably. Posnan must have driven his carpenters to the brink of madness.

Inside, perspective was immediately distorted by the circularity of the whole design. A short passage, which looked longer because it narrowed *en route*, led to a central hall, from which a staircase wound, like a single elegant circuit of a screw's thread, up to the galleried first-floor landing, then wound round another circuit to the second floor. Doors at the other quarter-points of the hall led to a drawing room on the left, a dining room straight ahead and a library to the right, converted into Matt's study-cum-office. Each of these large rooms, identically shaped and proportioned and fitted with French windows to access their private bridges across the moat, commanded broad, curving views of the garden, supplemented, in the case of the dining room, with the late addition of Rutland Water. The kitchen lay below this room, served by a spiral staircase and a dumb waiter. A short tunnel linked the kitchen with a circular cobbled yard beyond the moat, to which the entrance drive had led me on arrival. Beyond this, concealed by curving walls and coiling rhododendrons, stood a garage and stable block, where circularity had given way to utilitarian rectangles. Matt's theory was that Oates's patience or pocket, or both, had worn thin before Posnan's concept could run away with itself into every nook and corner of the property.

That still left the house itself, however, as a tribute to his curvilinear imagination. There were three bedrooms on the first floor, each equipped with its own dressing room and bathroom – an unheard-of extravagance in its day. Oates was evidently fastidious as well as reclusive. But an Edwardian recluse still needed servants, hence the small dormer-windowed rooms on the second floor, currently filled with the possessions Matt and Lucy still hadn't got round to unpacking, and some complimentary clutter left behind by the previous owner.

'Duncan Strathallan, a prickly old Scot,' said Matt as we peered at a dusty roomful of steamer trunks and assorted household junk. 'I've asked him to clear it out, but it looks like we'll have to do it for him.'

'Did he live here alone?'

'Another recluse, you mean? Not exactly. It was his family home for years, as far as I can gather. But he ended up on his tod. Seemed happy to go back north of the border.'

The top rooms had the widest-ranging views, out between the elms and oaks that looked as if they'd been there long before the house was even dreamed of, and across Rutland Water on either side towards gentle, rolling countryside.

'Oates owned quite a few acres to the north,' said Matt. 'Strathallan sold them and they've since been flooded, leaving the house high and dry. The lake cuts us off, of course. It's six miles to the A1 as the crow flies, nearer twenty by car. But that gives us privacy *and* fishing on the doorstep.'

'Huntin'. Now fishin'. It'll be shootin' next.'

'Think I've sold out to the squirearchy, do you?'

'Oh, I think that happened years ago. Even as a student, you had a suspicious penchant for tweed.'

'What I had, Tony, was good taste. How you ever persuaded Marina to overlook your charity-shop wardrobe I'll never—' He broke off, and we looked at each other, both shocked, I think, by our momentary lapse into old jokes and easy assumptions.

'Don't worry about it, Matt. I don't want you watching your every word.'

'Even so . . .'

'I have to come to terms with what's happened. I'm on my own now. Like poor old Strathallan.'

'Nothing like him, I assure you.'

'Good. Let's try to keep it that way.'

We swapped a tentative smile and headed downstairs, the phrase I'd used echoing in my mind as we went. Coming to terms implied negotiation. But just who was I supposed to negotiate with?

When Lucy came home, we had tea in the garden, as the warm afternoon mellowed into a sultry evening. Then we walked into Hambleton for a drink and a bite to eat at the pub. I can't remember what we talked about. I suppose we were all feeling our way towards a restoration of casualness and ease. Neither Matt nor Lucy avoided mentioning you. But they mentioned other things as well. The ordinariness of life in the face of death is both banal and comforting. It goes on, even when you can't believe it will. Even when you don't want it to.

35

* * *

That night, a strange thing happened. When I woke the following morning, to sunlight nudging through the curtains of my bedroom and a shrill dawn chorus in which the screech of seagulls didn't feature, I realized that, for the first time since your death, I hadn't dreamed of you. It was only then that I realized how much I *had* been dreaming of you. Was this part of letting go? I wondered. Was this one of many milestones on the road that led me away from you? If so, I didn't want it to be. But what I wanted was irrelevant. Time is a road on which there's no slowing down, let alone turning back. You'd left the road, but I was still on it.

Nesta Worthington, the housekeeper, had been mentioned to me the previous day. I encountered her for the first time that morning. She didn't turn out to be the stereotype I'd envisaged. Plummily accented and smartly kitted out, she looked more like the mistress of the house than the hired help. Matt had gone into the Pizza Prego office in Leicester and Lucy was in the bath after a morning run, so it was Mrs Worthington who kept me company over breakfast in the kitchen. And she was evidently no believer in silent breakfasts.

'My husband died last year,' she volunteered. 'That's when I found out how poor I really was and how futile it is to avoid uncomfortable facts. Lucy tells me you were very happily married. You have my genuine condolences on your loss.'

'Were you very happily married, Mrs Worthington?'

'I was once, but not by the end. All the love got worn out along the way. Maybe you're lucky in that sense.'

'You think so?'

'I only said maybe. Don't take too much notice of the

36

things I say. Lucy will tell you I converse the way I keep house: thoroughly but heavy-handedly. I'm not allowed near the porcelain. I'll say one thing you could do worse than bear in mind, though. The death of someone close to you acquaints you with how things really are. And they aren't necessarily as you'd thought. Bereavement can be cruel, but enlightenment can be crueller still.'

Lucy had planned a tour of the neighbourhood for me that day and I raised no objection. It was warm and she was wearing the white shirt and cream trousers of yours she'd taken from Stanacombe. She said nothing about it, though she must have known I'd notice.

She drove me round Rutland Water, stopping to see Normanton Church, preserved and marooned on a promontory in the lake, before we headed south, through quiet farming country, to Kirby Hall, a vast and derelict Elizabethan manor house, where we wandered through roofless halls and empty courtyards, accompanied by the mournful cry of peacocks.

'This is your way of cheering me up, is it?' I asked as we walked out across the lawns and looked back at the stone skeleton of chimney stacks and gable ends.

'Actually, yes,' Lucy replied, with an ironic smile. 'I always come here if I need to remind myself what's important in life.'

'And how does it do that?'

'Well, it's all gone, hasn't it? The people. The power. Even the plaster. They probably thought it would last for ever, but this is what it comes down to. A ruin, maintained by English Heritage to remind us of the futility of planning ahead.'

'I'm not sure that's English Heritage's remit.'

'Then it should be. Live for the moment. That's the

lesson, Tony. Doesn't Marina's death underline that? Aren't there things you and she put off till another day, another year, that you wish now, with all your heart, you'd gone ahead and done – before it was too late?'

'Lots of things.' I looked away, afraid she'd see the tears well up in my eyes.

'I'm not saying this to hurt you.' She hugged me, and we stood together, gazing at the hollow shell of Kirby Hall. 'I'm saying it because it's true. Matt and I have an existence most people would envy: affluence, leisure and security. But sometimes I think it's too safe, too risk-free. One of the last things Marina said to me – talking about your move to the West Country – was that she was trying to be more spontaneous. Don't we lose that as we grow older: spontaneity?'

'I suppose we do.'

'But we don't have to.' She kissed me on the cheek. 'Do we?' Then she set off at a smart pace across the lawn, back towards the house.

I followed, walking slowly, letting her march on ahead, watching her grow more similar to you as the distance stretched between us, watching and wondering just what had happened inside her because of your death. It was almost, though I could hardly allow myself to think it, as if something had been released, something freed that was previously captive. And it had just begun to take flight.

The next stop on Lucy's tour was Stamford, just the other side of the A1, a lovely old town, apparently untouched by time – or at least the last couple of hundred years of it. Walking round, I found it easy to imagine you enthusing over its cobbled streets and Georgian shopfronts. Seeing new places was, in that sense, worse than clinging to old haunts. I wanted to share the joy of discovering them with you. But I couldn't. And without the sharing, where was the joy?

We had lunch in one of the town's old coaching inns. A strange disorientation latched itself onto the beer I drank and made me begin to question my senses. Rutland Water, Otherways, Stamford, even Lucy herself all seemed to be so uncertain in their identity, looking like things they weren't or, in Lucy's case, people they couldn't be.

'We've been invited to tea by a friend I've made since moving here,' Lucy announced. 'You don't mind going, do you?'

'Of course not.'

'Her name's Daisy Temple. She lives in a gorgeous old house at Harringworth. We drove through it on our way to Kirby Hall, if you remember. The Welland Viaduct?'

'I remember.' It was actually the viaduct, an arrow-straight span of Victorian red-brick railway arches across a valley south of Rutland Water, that I remembered more than the village it overshadowed. 'How did you meet her?'

'Her sister used to live at Otherways before the war. I contacted her because I was curious about the history of the house. Nesta mentioned the connection. We've become friends, despite the age gap. Daisy's eighty odd, but up here' – Lucy tapped her forehead – 'ageless.'

'And has she told you anything interesting about Otherways?'

'You could say so. As a matter of fact, I ought to fore-warn you about that. Not that it'll crop up over tea. It's hardly . . . Well, it's still a painful subject for Daisy, even after all these years. Naturally.'

'What is?'

'Her sister was murdered there.'

'Murdered?' I put down my glass and looked at her. 'Really?'

'Yes. Really. Ann Milner, her name was. Killed by her husband, James Milner. He was hanged for it.'

'When did this happen?'

'The autumn of 1939. Nearly sixty years ago. When Daisy was just a bright young thing.'

'Did you know about this before you bought the place?'

'No. Matt got on his high horse about that. Said the agent should have told us. Ridiculous, really. Why would the agent say something likely to put the mockers on the sale?'

'Would it have?'

'I imagine Matt might have gone wobbly if he'd known.'

'But not you?'

'No. Why should I?'

'The usual reasons, I suppose: superstition, fear of ghosts.'

'I'm not afraid of them.'

It was an odd choice of phrase. *I'm not afraid of them.* As if they really did exist. But it didn't strike me as odd at the time.

'Besides,' Lucy went on, 'the murder didn't actually take place in the house.'

'Where, then?'

'In the gazebo.'

'I haven't seen a gazebo.'

'You wouldn't have. It was in a sunken garden north of the house, reached by a zigzag path down the rhododendron bank. The path's been allowed to grow over, on account of the fact that neither the garden nor the gazebo's there any more. The rhododendrons grow down to the water's edge now.'

'It really is a shifting landscape round here, isn't it?'

'Do you mean literally, or metaphorically?'

'Both, I suppose. But tell me, what was the background to the murder?'

'Marital strife, I believe. Look, if you want the salacious details, which aren't actually very salacious at all, I can let you have a magazine article about it. One of the Sunday supplements picked up on it when plans for the reservoir were announced back in the Seventies. "Murder scene to vanish underwater." That sort of thing. The Milners had exotic connections. They made the murder seem more interesting than it really was.'

'How did you come across the article?'

'I found it amongst the junk Strathallan left behind. His idea of a joke, maybe. To let us know he'd kept us in the dark. Do you want to see it?'

'Very much. You've whetted my appetite.'

'OK. I'll dig it out for you when we get home. On one condition.'

'That I say nothing to Daisy about it?'

'I assume you wouldn't anyway.'

'No. I wouldn't.'

'There you are. Then, that isn't the condition. It's Matt. He mustn't hear I've been through Strathallan's stuff. He's very old-fashioned about that kind of thing. About quite a lot of things, as a matter of fact.' She laughed. 'So, can I rely on your discretion?'

'If you think it's necessary.'

'I do.'

'All right, then. I won't breathe a word to Matt.'

'Good.'

And so, without thinking much about it, or weighing its significance, I became party to my friend's deception. The issue was minor enough, of course. But, as Matt himself would have said, what begins as minor doesn't necessarily stay that way.

Maydew House was a more conventionally elegant building than Otherways, though constructed from the same grey-pink stone and brownish slate. It was a squarish, modestly gabled country residence on the outskirts of Harringworth, where the village petered out into fields, fringed by massive old horse chestnuts. I think I'd expected manicured lawns and a raked-gravel drive, but actually the garden was a jungle and the house in need of painting. As for Daisy Temple, she wasn't exactly what I'd expected, either.

Getting no answer from the doorbell, Lucy led me round to the side of the house, where a ramshackle block of stables and outbuildings stood engulfed in ivy and wisteria. Music I vaguely recognized from your Shostakovich phase was billowing out of a sagging doorway. We entered a dusty workshop to see a small, gaunt woman with cropped iron-grey hair, dressed in dungarees and a check shirt, sitting at a stool in front of a bench, kneading thoughtfully at a clay bust.

'Daisy,' Lucy called.

The old woman looked round. She had startling cornflower-blue eyes and a placid, welcoming smile. 'Oh dear,' she said. 'You've come for tea.'

'Did you forget?'

'Absolutely not.' She turned off the cassette player, stood up and wiped the clay off her fingers with a cloth. 'I just got the day wrong. You must be Lucinda's brother-in-law,' she continued, advancing to greet me.

'I don't advise shaking my hand, but I *am* pleased to meet you.'

'Delighted to meet you, too, Miss Temple.' Her use of Lucy's full name had surprised me. No-one else bothered with it. But I was even more surprised by the bust standing on the table.

'Please call me Daisy. I feel as if we know each other, Tony, even though we've never met before. Lucinda's told me so much about you. And your late wife, of course. I was so very sorry to hear of her death.'

'Thank you.'

'I have the impression, judging by the look on your face, that Lucinda didn't tell you she was my latest subject.'

'No, she didn't. Nor even that you were a sculptress at all.'

'Good. That means you won't have turned up expecting a Michelangelo. My work is on a smaller scale than some people seem to imagine.'

'And none the worse for that. It's very good.'

'It is, isn't it?' said Lucy.

'Not finished yet, of course,' said Daisy, glancing back appraisingly at the bust. 'But shaping up nicely.'

The bust's unfinished state was probably why I found it so disturbing. Lucy seemed unaware of the effect, though it stared out clearly enough at me from the fashioned clay. It could just as easily have been you as her. That was the point. Daisy Temple had never met you. But in the likeness of Lucy she'd shaped she'd nonetheless found you.

We went indoors for tea. Lucy took charge of preparing it, while Daisy changed out of her sculpting clothes. 'Sorry I didn't tell you about the bust,' said

Lucy as we stood together in the kitchen. 'I wanted your unrehearsed reaction.'

'You got it. It really is very good.'

'That's what you genuinely think? You seemed, I don't know, distracted when you were looking at it.'

'Did I? Well, it didn't mean anything. What does Matt—'

'He doesn't know yet. I'm planning to surprise him.'

'Another secret?'

'Another *harmless* secret.'

'Yes. Of course.'

There were several busts in the drawing room, where we had tea, dotted around on plinths and window sills. Friends and relatives of Daisy's, I assumed, some living, some dead. I couldn't help wondering whether they included her sister or brother-in-law, but I had no intention of asking. Their plaster faces kept us an odd kind of company as we drank our tea and talked about the places Lucy had taken me to that day. Daisy had lived at Maydew House all her life, she told me, and knew the area intimately. The changes wrought by the coming of the reservoir couldn't be overestimated, though she thought most of them changes for the better. Lucy's ban on any mention of the murder threatened to make this a difficult subject to discuss, but the ban turned out to be unnecessary.

'I'm sure Lucinda will have told you about my sister, Tony, so I'll save you the trouble of mincing round the point. Her husband murdered her in a fit of unfounded jealousy at Otherways sixty years ago and was himself hanged for the crime. I have come to terms with those events long since.' There was that phrase again. *Come to terms*. 'People seem to find me interesting on account of that one ghastly episode in my family's past, which can be irritating, given that I believe I may claim to be interesting enough in my own right.'

'You certainly are,' said Lucy.

'Well, well, it's kind of you to say so.' Daisy smiled. 'Perhaps I shouldn't complain. I doubt you'd ever have contacted me but for hearing about the murder. And then I'd never have got closer to a racecourse than the columns of *Sporting Life*.'

'We've become a pair of racegoers, Tony,' said Lucy, seeing my quizzical look. 'Daisy's an excellent judge of form. We're off to Newmarket next week.'

'Are you coming, too, Tony?' Daisy asked.

'Well, I . . . haven't been invited.'

'You have now,' said Lucy.

'In that case, thank you. I'd be happy to.'

'We usually have a lot of fun,' said Daisy. 'It takes my mind off things to get away for a day. I find it therapeutic, even if scarcely profitable.'

What things she needed to take her mind off, I didn't like to ask. Seeking a change of subject, I gestured around at the busts. 'How long have you been doing these, Daisy?'

'Since my teens, off and on. There have been . . . intervals . . . for one reason or another. And more failures than successes. These represent the pick of an indifferent bunch.'

'Hardly that. I'm no expert, but you're obviously talented.'

She looked genuinely appreciative. 'Thank you.'

'What's the earliest piece of work you have here?'

'Over there.' She nodded towards it. 'By the window.'

It was the head of a young woman, cast in green-veined marble. Her chin was raised, emphasizing a

45

slender, swan-like neck. The face was clear-browed and high-cheeked, the hair swept back flatteringly. She was beautiful, but Daisy's sculpture revealed more than that. It revealed something approaching sadness within the awareness of her beauty.

I got up and crossed the room to admire the piece. As I stood beside it, I heard the sound of a car engine outside and glanced up to see an old grey Morris Minor pulling in through the gates. It came to a halt beside Lucy's car. 'Looks like you have another visitor,' I said, watching the driver clamber out. He was a paunchy, mop-haired man in early middle age, dressed casually in trainers, trousers, anorak and a sweatshirt. Our eyes met for an instant, but he neither smiled nor nodded, merely looked away and marched towards the front door.

'Not a visitor,' said Daisy from behind me. 'My lodger, Mr Rainbird.'

'He gives me the creeps,' murmured Lucy, as the front door closed behind him. There were footsteps in the hall, then on the stairs.

'Quite possibly,' said Daisy, as another door closed somewhere above us. 'But he gives me the money I need to buy clay and back leaden-hoofed racehorses, so we mustn't complain.' She smiled at me. 'Sculptresses don't get rich, Tony. Mr Rainbird subsidizes my art.'

'I should have thought your work would fetch a good price.'

'Alas, no. As a matter of fact, the only substantial sum I've ever been offered is for the bust you're standing next to. But I couldn't bring myself to sell it. You may have guessed the reason, which is also the reason why I was offered so much.'

'Because it's your sister?' I hadn't guessed till that

moment. And then it wasn't so much obvious as inevitable.

'Yes. It's Ann, as she was only a few months before her death. And now as she will always be.'

'A remarkable woman,' I said to Lucy as we drove back towards Rutland Water later that afternoon. 'And not at all reluctant to discuss the past.'

'That's what you think, is it?'

'She made it clear enough.'

'I suppose she did. But I ought to warn you, Tony. It's partly a pose. The murder affected Daisy more profoundly than she's willing to admit. She didn't just lose her sister.'

'What do you mean?'

'James Milner had a brother, Cedric. Daisy was engaged to him. But they never married.'

'Because of the murder?'

'Presumably. She never talks about it. In fact, she's never mentioned him to me.'

'Then how do you know?'

'It's in that article I found. Cedric Milner's quite a famous man. Or perhaps I should say infamous.'

'I've never heard of him.'

'Sure?'

'I think so. Cedric Milner? Means nothing.' But as I repeated the name it did begin to mean something. Not much, but something. 'Hold on . . .'

'Light dawning, is it?'

'I can't place him, but now you ask . . .' I snapped my fingers. 'A spy of some kind.'

'You've got him. A physicist. Betrayed atom-bomb secrets to Russia just after the war. What's more—'

'Yes?'

'At his trial, James Milner said he killed his wife because he believed she was having an affair . . . with his brother.'

Matt was already home when we reached Otherways. Complaining good-naturedly that Lucy had been monopolizing me, he proposed that the two of us visit the local pub before dinner. It was a soft June evening of gentle lakeside air. The Finches Arms was busying up for Friday night. We sat outside, where a boules match was underway, and drank our beer to the accompanying click of the boules and the sleepy cooing of doves.

'What did you make of Daisy?' he asked.

'Feisty old girl,' I replied. 'And a talented sculptress.'

'Lucy certainly likes her.'

'Don't you?'

'Oh, I like her well enough. It's just . . . well, the murder's something we could do without. You know? I don't want Lucy . . . dwelling on it.'

'What's there to dwell on?'

'A lot of people wouldn't like living in a house where somebody had been murdered.'

'But you don't mind, do you?'

'I don't let it affect me.'

'Neither does Lucy, as far as I can see.'

'No. That's right. As far as you can see.' He frowned. 'I don't know. It's nothing definite, Tony, nothing concrete. Lucy gets on with Daisy. That's all there is to it. At least, well, it would be, but . . . I have this feeling' – he shrugged – 'that slowly, bit by bit . . .' Then came a dismissive shake of the head. 'No. It's nothing. Nothing at all.'

'You don't look very sure about that.'

'Sorry. I don't know what I'm talking about.' He gave

a half-hearted laugh. 'Old house. Murder most foul. You can imagine anything if you try hard enough.'

'What kind of anything?'

'Oh, the supernatural kind, I suppose.'

'You're saying Otherways is haunted?'

'Good God, no.' He looked aghast at the suggestion. 'Absolutely not. I've seen nothing, heard nothing, the least bit spooky. But Lucy . . .'

'She has?'

'No. Well . . .' He lowered his voice and leaned closer. 'I'm not sure, Tony, to be honest. She spends a lot of time alone there. Probably too much. My fault, I dare say. She loves the place. She really does. She told me only recently that she couldn't bear to leave it. I suppose there's nothing wrong in that. But I worry that the . . . attachment . . . is too strong. Unnaturally strong. Do you know what I mean?'

'Not really, Matt, no.'

'That's understandable.' He smiled ruefully. 'I'm not sure I do myself.' He looked into the middle distance for a moment, then said, 'I don't want to burden you at a time like this, but, while you're here, I'd be really grateful if you'd keep an eye on her for me.' He stared on past me for another moment, then added, 'Just in case.'

So, within a day of my arrival at Otherways, I'd become a confidant for Matt and Lucy in a way I'd never been before. The friendship we'd had while you were alive was the friendship of two married couples. We'd always been at ease together, joking and relaxed. But I was beginning to see the superficiality of that now. It had left me unprepared for the insights into the ambivalence of their relationship that both Matt and Lucy seemed

49

determined to give me. Just as it had left me unprepared for almost everything that was happening to me.

There was an obvious explanation for my failure to have appreciated how turbulent Matt and Lucy's outwardly placid life in the Midlands countryside was, of course: Otherways. A bank of clouds had moved across the sun as we walked back towards the house that evening. The stonework had turned a flat, cold grey in the altered light, the convex windows throwing back at us faintly distorted reflections of the pallid skyline. The building suddenly looked hostile in its weirdness, keeplike and sullen. Had I really been so unobservant over the years? I wondered. Or had their move to Otherways been the catalyst for changes you and I had simply been too busy to notice?

Nothing more was said about the murder over dinner. Nor did Lucy refer, even obliquely, to the magazine article she'd promised to show me. I began to think she might have forgotten, though I could hardly remind her in Matt's presence. Nor did I much want to. Some instinct deterred me from seeming overeager.

Lucy hadn't forgotten, of course. As she went up to bed, leaving Matt and me to our whiskies, she airily remarked, 'I put that history of Stamford you asked about in your room, Tony.'

'Thanks.' I glanced across at Matt, but it was as if he hadn't even heard her.

'Good night, then.' She looked back at me as she closed the door behind her. Her expression was unreadable, amused almost, though at whose expense I couldn't imagine.

*   *   *

It was a *Sunday Times Magazine* dating from the summer of 1972. The heavy print, the fashions of my teens and a back-cover advertisement for Peter Stuyvesant cigarettes shocked me into realizing just how long ago that really was. The front-cover photograph was of the surrounding countryside as it had been before the excavation of what was referred to as Empingham Reservoir. Nobody seemed to have thought of Rutland Water as a name then. An article about the excavation and the impact on the lives of people moved out to make way for it filled several pages. What I was looking for was a less-prominent piece, tacked on as an afterthought it seemed, under the title RESERVOIR CLAIMS SCENE OF FORGOTTEN MURDER.

There was a photograph of what I took to be the sunken garden – an inevitably circular lawn, with a pond in the centre and a surrounding cluster of rose bushes, with larger rhododendrons above them on a bank. At the edge of the lawn, bowered in roses, stood the gazebo, a sort of wooden maquette of Otherways, in terms of shape and proportion, though it was open-fronted, of course, with a bench visible inside, which ran round the internal wall.

The photograph of the garden was in grainy black and white. It clearly wasn't contemporary. Though the caption didn't say so, I imagined it was an archive shot, dating from the time of the murder. What the caption did say was that Ann Milner was sitting in the gazebo on the evening of Saturday, 2 September 1939, when her husband, James Milner, shot her dead.

My attention was drawn to the writer of the article, Martin Fisher, by the simple fact that someone had underlined his name in red where it appeared beneath the title. Why I couldn't imagine. I assumed he was just a reporter assigned to the case. He certainly wrote as if he was. I lay on the bed and read the piece through.

They still talk about the Milner murder in Rutland, even though more than 30 years have passed since 27-year-old junior diplomat James Milner walked into the garden of his family home near Oakham and shot dead his beautiful 26-year-old wife, Ann, as she sat in a gazebo enjoying the evening sunshine. They talk about it not because there was any doubt about James Milner's guilt. He telephoned the police straight afterwards and admitted what he had done. They talk about it because circumstances have conspired to prevent them forgetting.

The latest of those circumstances is the destruction of the garden where the murder took place. It, along with 3,000 acres of surrounding farmland, is being bulldozed to create a huge new reservoir. The Milners' old home, Otherways, a strange circular moated house, built just before the First World War by an equally strange Anglo-French architect called Emile Posnan, now perches like some inland lighthouse over a muddy wasteland criss-crossed by the trackways of gigantic earth-moving equipment. The past has been swept away. But that seems only to have sharpened the memories of those who lived near by at the time.

Murder is not, as it happens, the only crime associated with the Milner family. Arguably, James Milner's brother, Cedric, who was living at Otherways in 1939, was guilty of something worse still. And he, unlike his brother, did not pay for it with his life. Cedric Milner would face a charge of treason if he ever returned to this country. But that is unlikely. He has lived in the Soviet Union since the summer of 1950, having fled there, fearing arrest as a spy.

The value of information he passed to the Soviet Union while working as a physicist at the Harwell Atomic Energy Research Establishment in the 1940s has never been disclosed. Some believe it was every bit as significant as that passed by the other more famous Harwell traitor, Klaus Fuchs, whose arrest and trial early in 1950 is thought to have triggered Milner's defection. It is probably just as well that James and Cedric Milner's father, Sir Clarence Milner, died in 1936, a year after their mother, Olga, Lady Milner.

Sir Clarence was a distinguished career diplomat, Lady Olga the Russian beauty he had met and married while serving at the British Embassy in St Petersburg during the last years of the Tsar. How they would have reacted to the execution of one son for the murder of his wife and the condemnation of another for betraying his country is hard to imagine.

Lady Milner's father was a prominent banker, assassinated by a revolutionary just before the outbreak of war in 1914. Naturally, she would have been no friend of the Bolshevik regime, which seized power in 1917. James Milner had been born in St Petersburg in 1912, and Lady Milner, plain Mrs Milner as she was then, was pregnant for a second time when the ambassador and most of his staff, along with their families, were evacuated from the country in January 1918. Cedric Milner was thus, by an apt irony, born in England, but conceived in Russia.

After the war, Clarence Milner was posted first to Belgium, then to Portugal, where he served as ambassador for the last few years of his career. It was in Lisbon that he met Emile Posnan, who had lived there since leaving England in 1914. Posnan aroused his curiosity with a description of the house he had built in Rutland. Milner took the opportunity to visit it during his next home leave and, finding it on the market, he bought it for his retirement.

Milner left the diplomatic service in 1933 with a knighthood and settled at Otherways. James Milner was by then an Oxford undergraduate. Cedric was a boarder at Harrow, already noted for his scientific brilliance. James followed his father into the diplomatic service in 1934 and married Ann Temple, daughter of a local doctor. He was soon posted to the British Embassy in Moscow – where the capital had moved since the Tsar's days – because of his fluency in Russian. Initially, Ann accompanied him, but eventually returned to England alone, presumably because of the dangers and difficulties of life in Moscow under Stalin. There was no suggestion at this time of marital strain.

The parting must have been hard on James, however. His parents were dead by then, but Ann had her own family to fall back on for company. She was especially close to her sister, Daisy, who still lives in the area but declined to discuss the murder with me. For James there was nothing but a tedious round of clerical work in a city where the local population lived in fear and the diplomatic community looked on helplessly as Stalin tightened his grip on society.

Cedric went up to Cambridge in 1937, and there he came under the influence of J. D. Bernal, the Marxist physicist. He must have seen the other side of Marxism, however, when he visited his brother in Moscow during the Easter vacation of 1938. The Bukharin show trial, which James had attended in an official capacity, had just ended. How Cedric was able to overlook Stalin's tyrannical excesses to the extent he obviously did is a mystery. But it is only one of several mysteries surrounding him and his brother.

During his vacations from Cambridge Cedric lived

mostly at Otherways with Ann. This was an inevitable but unnatural arrangement, throwing together the beautiful young grass widow and her handsome brother-in-law. Far away in Moscow, James must surely have feared the worst. If so, his fears would have been allayed by Cedric's announcement in the spring of 1939 of his engagement to Ann's younger sister, Daisy. James should have come home for an extended leave that summer in good spirits, but the extension had been granted because of nervous exhaustion. Perhaps the coming tragedy was already taking shape.

Exactly what happened at Otherways during the weeks between James's return from Moscow and the murder is unclear. Two of the four people who could tell us are dead, another is definitely unavailable for comment, and the fourth, Daisy Temple, declines to discuss the matter. All we are left with is what emerged at the trial.

The murder of Ann Milner, and the subsequent trial and execution of her husband, got little national coverage amidst the welter of war news. Great Britain declared war on Germany the day after the shooting at Otherways. The murder counted as sensational in Rutland, of course. Elsewhere, people had more important things to think about. Besides, James Milner was a member of the diplomatic service, a representative of his nation overseas. He had done a dreadful thing and must pay for it. To dwell upon the event could have been interpreted as unpatriotic.

The trial itself was brief and anti-climactic. James pleaded guilty and gave no direct evidence. It was explained, on his behalf, by his barrister, that he had become convinced, erroneously as he now accepted, that his wife was conducting a clandestine affair with his brother. He had held her, as the elder party, more to blame. Having failed to obtain assurances from her that she would end the relationship – impossible to give, since it did not in fact exist – he had killed her, using a revolver issued to him by the embassy in Moscow for his personal protection. It was not explained why he had become suspicious of his wife, nor how he had subsequently been persuaded of her innocence. Cedric did not give evidence. Nor did Miss Temple. The only witnesses were, in fact, the senior police officer called to the scene and the pathologist who had conducted the post-mortem. No reference was made to James's nervous state when sent home from Moscow. Nothing in the way of mitigation was even attempted. James Milner seems to have been intent on paying the ultimate penalty for his crime, and the court was content to oblige him. He was sentenced to death and hanged at Leicester Prison on 10 November 1939.

It sounds like a straightforward if poignant tale of domestic disaster. As such, it is surprisingly well remembered in the locality, where it is referred to as a tragedy, about which the full truth can never be known. Perhaps that is just as well. For all concerned, it may be best to assume that James Milner's suspicions of his wife and brother were groundless. Either way, by his own admission, he undoubtedly murdered Ann Milner. Except, of course, that admissions of guilt are often the hardest kind of evidence to test. Cedric Milner was present at Otherways on the day of the murder, even though he did not witness it. We must *assume* he did not witness it, anyway. The exact sequence of events at Otherways on 2 September 1939 did not emerge in court. In fact, very little emerged, apart from James Milner's determination to bear full responsibility for what had happened.

Whether he deserved to do so is not necessarily as impenetrable a mystery as it may seem. Although the national press was preoccupied with weightier issues, the *Rutland Mercury* found plenty of space for the Otherways Murder, as it was soon dubbed. The case was chronicled by its chief reporter, Donald Garvey, now retired. When I spoke to him at his home in Oakham recently, he told me why he still believed it had not been the simple matter implied at James Milner's trial.

'None of it ever made sense to me,' he said. 'That young fellow just wasn't the insanely jealous type. I'd met him at point-to-points and the like, along with his wife. They were as happy and relaxed a couple as you could wish to meet. I don't know about Cedric. He kept himself to himself. According to my police contacts, he was out cycling when the murder took place. But he'd got back by the time they arrived. Well, that was his story, and his brother's. He had no alibi, of course, but he didn't need one. I'm not saying he killed Mrs Milner and his brother took the blame, but when you look at what a cool, calculating schemer he turned out to be, well, it's possible, isn't it? If he doesn't like the idea, he can always come home and sue me for libel.'

Small chance of that, of course, so Garvey can rest easy in his libellous retirement. But something still nags at him. 'James Milner's confession to the police didn't include a word of explanation for his jealousy. I've seen it, so I know. Why not? Well, maybe because there was none to explain. It wasn't his only confession, you see. Not his last, anyway. That was written in the condemned cell at Leicester Gaol. I have the man's own word on that.'

Mr Garvey showed me a letter written to him by James Milner from prison on 7 November 1939, three days before his execution. 'I am aware of your continuing enquiries into my case,' it reads. 'I would ask you to desist from troubling those close to me and my late wife. I have spent some of my time here writing a complete and honest account of what occurred at Otherways last summer, for the benefit of the person most clearly entitled to receive it. If that person wishes to share its contents with the wider world, which I doubt, then so be it. If not, then so be it also. Please be so good as to content yourself with their judgement in the matter.'

Garvey was not content, of course. Nor is he to this day. Old-fashioned patriot that he is, he would very much like to pin something on Cedric Milner. But he is unlikely to be able to. Back in 1939, Daisy Temple, logical candidate for the role of 'person most clearly entitled', denied receiving any kind of confessional account from her brother-in-law. And today she refuses, politely but firmly, to say anything at all.

She still lives in the house she was born in, within easy reach of the churchyard at Hambleton where her sister lies buried. James Milner rests in a prison grave 20 miles away. Cedric Milner, meanwhile, moves in very different circles, teaching physics to Russian students at the University of Moscow. He presumably neither knows nor cares that the sunken garden at Otherways has vanished. It is in another country, his long-since abandoned past. He probably would not wish to revisit it even if he could. And he almost certainly would not wish to reveal what really took place there on the evening of 2 September 1939. Even, perhaps especially, if he knows.

I lay awake till well past midnight, thinking about what Fisher had written and what it implied. That, at least, was clear enough. He was suggesting that Cedric had murdered Ann and that James had taken the blame. But why should he have murdered her? And why should James have sacrificed himself to save him? As a theory, it was less satisfactory than the original conclusion. Anyway, it was a cheap shot, because Cedric was never going to answer the challenge. It had the merit of explaining why Daisy might have broken off their engagement. Maybe she suspected something. But she could just as easily have broken it off because she feared there was some justification for James's jealousy. I had no intention of trying to discover what her reasons had been. They were none of my business. If Daisy had secrets to keep, she was welcome to them. They didn't concern me. How could they?

I was never much of a dreamer, was I? Asleep or awake. You always said I was too logical. You chided me for my realism. And you couldn't credit how dreamless my memories of the night almost always were, whereas yours fairly teemed with surreal fantasies. You kept a diary of them for a while. You bought a special dictionary to interpret them. A waste of time and money, I said. Dreams are meaningless. That's the point of them. But I never believed that, even then. I just reckoned it was safer to tell myself it's what I believed. We spend a quarter of our lives asleep, our minds free to roam without restraint. Small wonder they roam where they're happiest. After your death, I dreamed of you constantly. It was wish fulfilment. Of course it was. At Otherways I began to dream of other things. But whether they were my darkest wishes or my worst fears, I didn't want to find out.

The dream I had that night, like those that followed, was set at Otherways. It was dark and I was walking round the moat, looking in through the brightly lit windows of empty rooms. Then, as I reached the drawing room,

59

a figure appeared inside. It was Lucy. She was dressed in black, in the clothes she'd worn at your funeral. But there was one difference. At her throat hung the sapphire pendant I gave you for your thirtieth birthday. She walked round the room, switching off the lights until only one remained: the standard lamp by the fireplace. She sat down in an armchair beneath it and looked towards me. Her face was in shadow. I couldn't see her expression. Then I noticed another figure in the room, standing close to the window and looking out. It was me. Not a reflection, but a separate, other self. And that me was smiling, though out in the garden, beyond the moat, I wasn't smiling. I was frightened. I grew more frightened still as my smiling self turned and walked away across the room towards the fireplace – and Lucy. His shadow, my shadow, fell across her. Everything was suddenly dark, nothing was visible. There was a scream.

The scream was mine; nothing more than a whimper in reality. I was wide awake, heart thumping and brain numbed by a kind of shameful fright. I felt stupid for a second, then relieved it had been nothing but a dream.

I was hot and horribly alert. Finding the glass beside the bed empty, I scrambled out and stumbled to the bathroom to refill it. On my way back, I walked over to the window, across which I'd only half drawn the curtains, and looked down into the garden as I drank the water.

To my surprise, there was lamplight spilling out from the windows of the drawing room beneath me. Matt couldn't still be up; it was gone two. Maybe he'd left a light on; several, to judge by the glare. It splashed out across the moat and the lawns beyond to the edge of the rhododendrons.

Something moved where the lawn and rhododendrons met, a figure slipping into the bushes at the borders of my vision. All I could see when I focused on the spot was a stirring of leaves and branches. Whatever it was, animal or human, it was gone – if it had ever been there at all. I was in no state to be sure of anything.

I lay on the bed, wondering if I should go down and check for intruders. But the house was fitted with a sophisticated alarm system. It didn't need checking. And gooning around the garden with a torch wouldn't achieve a lot. It had probably been a fox. As for the lights still being on in the drawing room, I put that down to forgetfulness on Matt's part. What else could it be? There was nothing wrong, I told myself, nothing at all. Eventually, I almost believed it. And, eventually, I slept. This time without dreaming.

Chapter Three

The memory of the dream was still with me next morning, vivid and undiminished. I tried to shrug it off, but it wouldn't let go, clinging to my thoughts, waiting to surprise me whenever I let down my guard. It would have helped to be able to discuss Fisher's article with Lucy. That might have taken my mind off the figure at the edge of the lawn and the figure of myself, moving of its own accord – troubling visions that refused to leave me. But it was no go where Lucy was concerned. It was the weekend, so Matt was with us for the day, and he showed no inclination to take himself off for a ride. It didn't look as if it was going to be easy to get Lucy on her own.

I went for a walk after breakfast, along the fishermen's track that ran round the peninsula. It was a grey morning, cool and moist, with a hint of rain. I should have found it refreshing, but the sunless solitude and the listless lap of the water in the creeks only depressed me. I so much wanted you to be walking beside me, or running ahead, laughing and beckoning. But it was becoming difficult now even to imagine what that would be like. You were slipping away so fast, so very fast.

I entered a spinney near the eastern tip of the peninsula, intending to take the quick way back along the lane into Hambleton as soon as I came to it. The path was narrow through the woods and muddy into the bargain. I was looking down, choosing my steps carefully, when I rounded a tree and nearly walked straight into a man on the path in front of me. He must have been standing there, waiting for something, otherwise I'd have heard his approach. I jumped back in surprise, but he didn't seem surprised at all.

It was Rainbird, Daisy's less-than-universally-popular lodger, kitted out in gumboots and a Barbour, with a pair of binoculars strung round his neck. He gave me a cautious smile.

'Mr Sheridan. Pleased to meet you.' The accent sounded as if he hailed from rather further north than Rutland. 'Daisy told me who you were and where you're staying. I wondered if I might bump into you on one of my lakeside forays. I didn't think it would be quite so literally.'

'Mr Rainbird, right?'

'Norman Rainbird, yes.' He put out a hand and I shook it. 'I'm quite a regular round these shores.'

'Birdwatching?'

'Principally. There's always plenty to see on the water. Or from it. I keep a little boat over at Edith Weston. You must come out in it one day.'

'Interesting idea.' I smiled as slightly as I could without actually insulting him. We'd only just met, but already I was sure I didn't want to be out in a small boat with him for company. 'Well, I must get back.'

'To Otherways? If you're walking that way, perhaps I could accompany you.'

'Why not?' I could hardly refuse.

We were soon out of the spinney and on the lane that traced the spine of the peninsula. I set a deliberately stiff pace, which Rainbird matched with some difficulty, panting along beside me like an overweight Labrador. 'Interesting house, Otherways,' he said, just when it had begun to seem we might walk in silence.

'You think so?'

'Fascinating, I'd say. Virtually unique. I'm something of an expert on architectural history.'

'Really?' It didn't seem at all likely.

'Yes. On a purely amateur basis, of course. Otherways is the only extant work of Emile Posnan.'

'So I believe.'

'You'd think it might have led to other commissions. Purely on grounds of eccentricity.'

'But it didn't.'

'On the contrary, it did. But Posnan refused them all. He closed down his practice and left the country.'

'For Portugal.' I saw Rainbird smile at that. It was a welcome sign to him, I suppose, that I too was interested in Emile Posnan, albeit against my better judgement. 'So Lucy said.'

'I didn't know she was so well informed. That being the case, I wonder if I could ask you a favour. I'd very much like to . . . visit the house.'

'Why?'

'To test my theory.'

'Which is?'

'That somewhere at Otherways is the answer to the riddle of Posnan's abandoned career.'

'Unlikely.'

'Its abandonment was unlikely. Wouldn't you agree?'

It was hard to disagree, but I felt obliged to. 'Maybe

he planned to continue practising as an architect in Portugal but something else cropped up. Things do.'

'Not in Emile Posnan's life. He lived alone in a succession of rented rooms in Lisbon, a recluse, drinking himself to death, though it took more than forty years to do it. A sort of very slow suicide.'

'He can't have been that much of a recluse.' I was thinking of the fact that, according to Fisher, Sir Clarence Milner had been inspired to buy Otherways by an encounter with Posnan in Lisbon. But suddenly I didn't want to reveal the extent of my curiosity on the point to Rainbird. I'm not sure why. Something in his darting looks and hesitant, high-pitched voice suggested that I'd regret revealing the smallest thing to him. 'What I mean is . . . you can't be sure.'

'Perhaps not. But still, I would be grateful if you'd ask Mrs Prior whether I could . . . take a look round.'

'I'm surprised you haven't asked her yourself before now.'

'I have.' We'd come to the entrance to the drive leading to Otherways and stopped there. The house was out of sight, thanks to the lie of the land, but Rainbird was looking towards it with a hopeful tilt of the head, as if he might catch sight of it if he craned his neck sufficiently. He'd have cut a pitiful figure if it hadn't been for the fact that I didn't quite swallow the act. There was something too calculating about it. And his enthusiasm for eccentric Edwardian architecture rang as true as a cracked bell. 'But I think I caught her at a bad time.'

'She has just lost her sister.'

'And you your wife. Yes. Daisy told me that much.' He offered no condolences. Strangely, I was grateful. It seemed oddly sensitive of him to understand how unwelcome such condolences would have been. Or maybe I was just the beneficiary of his complete *in*sensitivity. 'Actually, I think Mrs Prior may doubt the sincerity of my interest in architecture.' I reckoned he was right there. 'I had the same problem with the previous owner, Major Strathallan. But it was perhaps more understandable in his case.'

'Why?'

'Well, architecture and personal tragedy have a habit of colliding at Otherways, don't they? Major Strathallan had good cause to know that. Has good cause, I should say, remote in his Scottish fastness though he may be.'

'I don't follow.'

'Murder, Mr Sheridan. And treason.'

'You mean James and Cedric Milner.'

'Ah, you know about all that, do you?'

'It's no secret.'

'The facts aren't, no. But they arrange themselves oddly, nevertheless. I was reading a book about Cedric the spy only recently and a very odd arrangement emerged from that, I must say. It's a book about several spies, actually, of whom Cedric Milner is merely one. *Seven Faces of Treason*. You know it?'

'Can't say I do.'

'Not surprising. It's long out of print. I came across a copy at Goldmark's in Uppingham. An excellent bookshop. I can warmly recommend it. But look, if you're interested, I could lend you the book.'

'There's no need.'

'Least I can do. In return for you putting in a good word for me with Mrs Prior.'

'I didn't say I would.'

'True.' He winked at me. 'But I'll trust you to.' With that he turned and headed off along the lane, the heels of his gumboots scuffing the tarmac as he went. 'I'll drop the book in next time I'm passing,' he called back to me over his shoulder, waving cheerily. 'It'll be my pleasure.'

First Lucy, now Rainbird. Everyone was suddenly keen to satisfy my curiosity about the former inhabitants of Otherways. I'd have thought it suspicious if it hadn't been so difficult to see any harm in delving into the past.

At the house, another surprise was waiting. Nesta broke off from a round of vacuuming to tell me that Matt was in the garage, checking over his car in preparation for a long journey, and that Lucy was upstairs, packing with the same in mind. 'I was coming in this evening to cook for the three of you. Do you want a slap-up feed just for yourself?'

I said I'd probably go out for dinner and headed up to Matt and Lucy's bedroom, where Lucy was throwing toiletries into an overnight bag. She looked faintly harassed and more than faintly displeased.

'Sorry about this, Tony. Duty calls. Wifely duty, that is. Has Matt mentioned Dick Sindermann to you?'

'No. Who is he?'

'A possible backer for taking Pizza Prego to the States.'

'I didn't know Matt was considering such a move.'

'Neither did I.' She flung open the wardrobe and flicked through a choice of outfits. 'But why should I? Matt only needs me to look decorative over dinner while he prises the dollars out of Sindermann. The guy flew in from New York this morning and phoned to propose a powwow. Tonight, at Cliveden. He clearly does have dollars to spare. We'll be back tomorrow.'

'Well . . . have a nice time.'

'I won't.'

'About the magazine article—'

'I retrieved it while you were out. Let's talk about it when I get back. Monday, maybe.' When Matt was safely out of the way, she meant. 'I'm really sorry to be dashing off when you've only just arrived.'

'I'll cope.'

'I'd much rather stay here myself. Then you wouldn't have to cope.' She tossed the selected outfit onto the bed. 'Don't you sometimes long not to?'

'Is there a choice?'

'Oh yes.' She grew thoughtful, almost sombre. 'I'm sure there is.'

I found Matt in the garage, topping up the windscreen wash in his car. The rest of us would just take off with soft tyres and a low reservoir, but not Matt. He always was a walking safety manual. Stateside entrepreneur was a different matter, however.

'Is this a realistic possibility?' I asked him.

'That depends on Sindermann.'

'But as far as you're concerned?'

'Yes. Lucy's been complaining that we're in a mid-life rut. This might get us out of it. And stop her brooding. In fact—' He stopped and stepped back from the bonnet, frowning over something. Then he said, 'Well, we'll see.'

'Best of luck.' It was all I could manage to say. It didn't seem the right time to point out how unenthusiastic Lucy was about the idea. Maybe he already knew. Or maybe he didn't want to.

* * *

They left straight after lunch. By then Nesta was long gone. It meant, as I watched the car take off down the drive, that I was alone at Otherways, and would be for the next twenty-four hours. I walked round the moat, gazing up at the house as afternoon stillness reclaimed it in the sunshine that had broken through the clouds. All the things I could have done, and would have done, if you'd been with me lay heavy and redundant in my mind, coalescing into the leaden certainty that there was nothing I wanted to do without you.

But I could find something worth doing, if I looked hard enough. A leaf through *Seven Faces of Treason* held some appeal, even though I'd done my best to let Rainbird think it wouldn't. I washed the car and drove down to Uppingham, a few miles south of Oakham. It's a quiet little market town, strong on bookshops and tearooms. You'd have enjoyed wandering round. But all I did was search in vain for a book it seemed Rainbird had snaffled the last copy of. Not knowing the author's name didn't help, of course. I left empty-handed.

I'd only been back at Otherways for ten minutes or so when I heard a car draw up outside. Glancing out of the window, I saw Rainbird bundling out of his Morris Minor, clutching a book in his hand.

'I didn't think you'd be passing this way quite so soon,' I said, opening the door to him.

'To be honest, I wasn't.' He grinned broadly. 'I happened to overhear a telephone conversation earlier, quite by chance, between Daisy and Mrs Prior, indicating that you'd be alone here for the weekend.'

'Did you indeed?'

'Pure chance, as I say. But a happy one, don't you think? It occurred to me that you might . . . let me have a look inside . . . without troubling Mrs Prior at all.'

'I don't think I can do that.'

'Go on.' He winked and, with a swiftness that was surprising in so bulky a man, stepped past me into the passage. 'Just a glimpse.'

'Mr Rainbird,' I said sharply, wondering how to avoid physically throwing him out.

'Norman, please.' He plonked the book down on the telephone table. 'That all right there?'

'What? Yes, but look—'

'The Priors keen on watercolours, are they?' he asked, glancing at the paintings to the right and left as he strode towards the hall. 'Bit insipid for my taste. What about you, Tony?'

'Hold on.' I caught up with him at the foot of the stairs, gazing up appreciatively at the circular galleried landing. '*Norman*.'

'Yes?'

'This isn't my house,' I said levelly. 'I can't let you wander round without the owners' knowledge or consent.'

'No?'

'*No*.'

'Ah.' He stuck out his lower lip and looked crestfallen. 'Pity.'

'Maybe. But I'm sure you can appreciate my position.'

'Of course. Tricky. I do see that.'

'So—' The doorbell rang behind us, down the passage. I looked round. 'Who the hell . . .'

'Like Clapham Junction here this afternoon, isn't it?'

'I'll see you out while I answer that.'

'Righto.'

The doorbell rang again. Rainbird tagged along reluctantly as I went down the passage. I opened the door to a moon-faced bloke in a baseball cap and rumpled clothes. A taxi was parked in the drive behind him, its engine rumbling. 'Yes?'

'You ordered a taxi.'

'No I didn't.'

'This *is* Otherways?'

'Correct.'

'Then you ordered a taxi. To Peterborough train station.'

'Not me.'

'Four thirty.' He glanced at his watch. 'I'm bang on time.'

'There's been a mistake.'

'How d'you reckon that?'

'No idea.' Suddenly aware that I sensed no presence at my shoulder, I looked round. Rainbird was nowhere to be seen.

'Somebody phoned in, squire, with all the particulars. I didn't make it up.'

'I'm sure you didn't. Look, I'm sorry, but I didn't ask for a taxi and I don't want one.'

'Yeah, but—'

I slammed the door in his face and ran back into the hall. '*Norman!*' There was no answer. '*Norman!*' Still no answer. And no sign of him in the ground-floor rooms. I checked each of them in turn, as well as the kitchen, before heading up to the bedrooms.

And there he was, strolling casually round the landing to meet me as I reached the top of the stairs. 'Ah, Tony.'

'What the hell are you doing?'

'Nothing. You seemed busy. I just, well, went for it. He who dares wins, don't you know?' He gazed up at the conical ceiling and the plaster orb set in the centre at the very top. 'Poetry in stone.'

71

'Would you very much mind getting the hell out?'

'Sorry, I'm sure,' he said, looking hurt. 'I shan't stay where I'm not wanted.'

'I explained the situation to you clearly enough.'

'So you did.' He gave me a pseudo-apologetic smile. 'No harm done.'

'There'd better not be.'

'I don't quite know what you're suggesting.'

'I've just got rid of a taxi-driver who was convinced somebody here wanted to be taken to Peterborough.'

'A mistake?'

'Yes. But whose?'

'I wouldn't know. There's a house in Hambleton called Hathaways. Easy to mishear one for the other, I should think.' He ambled past me down the stairs, eyeing Matt's collection of *Spy* prints as he descended. 'They've fitted the place out nicely, I must say. These are a big improvement on Strathallan's stags' heads.'

'I thought you'd never seen inside before.'

'There were some photos in *Country Life* when the house was up for sale.' He paused at the foot of the stairs and nodded to himself. 'Didn't do it justice, though.' Then he looked round at me. 'Well, must be off.'

'Don't let me keep you.'

'Tell me what you think of the book,' he said, tapping its cover as he passed. He reached the front door and opened it, then turned and said, 'I'd be interested to know.'

After he'd driven away, I did a quick check of the house, wondering if I'd find any signs of drawers being opened or things moved. I didn't have Rainbird down as the light-fingered type, but nor could I accept that a glimpse of a Posnan interior was all he'd wanted. On the other hand, I couldn't bring myself to believe he'd ordered the taxi to distract me while he slaked his architectural curiosity. And I couldn't prove he had even if I did. It was all very odd. I felt wrong-footed and suspicious. But there was damn all to nail my suspicions to. Nothing looked out of place. Nothing seemed to have been disturbed. In the end I gave up and took a beer out into the garden, along with *Seven Faces of Treason*.

It was a faintly musty plain-covered hardback dating from 1975. And the author, as I should perhaps have guessed, was Martin Fisher. 'A freelance journalist specializing in intelligence matters,' according to the uninformative blurb. 'He is currently working on a full-scale history of MI5.'

Several of the seven faces of treason Fisher had chosen to study were predictable. Guy Burgess, Donald Maclean and Kim Philby virtually picked themselves. Anthony Blunt, of course, was yet to be unmasked back in 1975. George Blake made up an obvious quartet, followed by John Vassall and Alan Nunn May, two I'd certainly heard of but knew little about. And then there was Cedric Milner.

In the preface, Fisher explained that he was interested in the psychology of treason. By treason he meant the betrayal of one's country, and by one's country he meant the country where one was born and brought up. Hence his exclusion from the book of Klaus Fuchs, the German-born physicist who supplied the Soviet Union with information while working on the atom-bomb project at Los Alamos during the Second World War and who continued to do so when he was transferred to Harwell after the war. As a naturalized British citizen, Fuchs was technically guilty of treason. But, for Fisher's purposes, it didn't really count. He turned to Cedric Milner for the real thing.

His chapter on Milner began with the biographical information I'd already gleaned from his *Sunday Times Magazine* article, supplemented by photographs of a blond-haired square-jawed young man in cricket kit and hiking clothes. Cedric Milner at school and university was noted for academic brilliance, sporting exuberance and a liking for a good time. If he was a closet communist, it was a very deep closet. Fisher's view of him seemed to have changed since the *Sunday Times* piece. Although Cedric studied under Bernal, a noted Marxist, at Cambridge, he apparently wasn't active in the communist circles that eddied round Bernal, although he certainly socialized with those who were. It was a subtle distinction, and I wasn't sure where Fisher thought it led, other than to portray Cedric in an enigmatic light.

The Otherways murder certainly enhanced that effect. Fisher gave the facts of the case, such as they were, the same slant he had before, implying, without ever quite bringing himself to say he believed it, that Cedric was implicated in the murder of Ann Milner, if not actually responsible for it. He couldn't prove it and a motive was hard to come by, but perversely that rather suited Fisher. As the chapter entered post-Otherways territory, *terra incognita* as far as I was concerned, the outline of his Milner thesis began to emerge.

The autumn of 1939 was the making of Cedric Milner, where it could so easily have been the breaking of a less self-sufficient individual. His sister-in-law, with whom he had lived off and on for several years, was dead. *Her* sister, his fiancée, had broken off their engagement and

74

effectively ended their relationship. His brother had been hanged for murder. His family home, which he had inherited, stood empty, tainted by the recent memory of violent death. And the Second World War had begun.

Milner was halfway through the first term of his final year as an undergraduate at Cambridge when his brother went to the gallows. Outwardly, he seemed unaffected by the event, so much so that many of his contemporaries in the hermetically sealed world of university life were quite simply unaware of it. He threw himself into his studies and socialized less. This was scarcely unusual for a final-year student, but in Milner's case it may have been an excuse for engaging less with other people and so avoiding those unwelcome questions that some might have put to him about his role in the death of his sister-in-law.

Though withdrawn, Milner was not depressed. Fellow students at St John's College describe him as being as cheerful as ever, simply less conspicuous. 'He gave up sport,' says Clive Unwin. 'And one didn't see so much of him. But he was always in good humour. He never mentioned his brother to me. He never spoke about his family at all. But he never had done as I recall. Looking back, I can't think of anyone at Cambridge I spent so much time with yet knew so little about.'

Already, then, Milner had developed a habit of secrecy, whether because he had something to hide or because it was a feature of his personality. That secrecy has proved durable, making it as difficult to track his movements outside Cambridge as it is to guess the slant of his mind. Otherways was requisitioned for use as offices by the RAF early in 1940. From that moment on Milner was effectively rootless. He graduated with a first-class degree and was immediately recommended to the Ministry of Aircraft Production for their newest project: an investigation of the weapons potential of nuclear fission. Cambridge was one of the centres chosen for theoretical research into the subject. Most established physicists having been assigned to work on radar, Milner had found himself in the right place at the right time.

He remained in Cambridge, working on what was later code-named the Tube Alloys Project, for the next three years. During this period, his self-sufficiency and self-containment heightened. He lived alone in a flat near the railway station. Apart from occasional evenings out with fellow physicists, he apparently had no social life at all – no girlfriends, no regular companions. He often went to London at weekends, however, where he may or may not have pursued an exotic double life. There is simply no way to tell. Studying Milner's life is like eating a slice of Emmental cheese: bland, with lots of holes.

Nor is there the slightest flavour of communism. Milner's old Cambridge mentor, J. D. Bernal, frequented Guy Burgess's London flat, along with Blunt, Philby and Maclean. No doubt he would have been happy to introduce Milner to their pernicious circle, but there is no evidence he ever did. Milner steered adroitly clear of bad company. Or maybe he just covered his tracks more assiduously than most. Whatever he really thought or intended, he seems to have kept to himself.

There is nevertheless evidence that, on the quiet, he was a bit of a ladies' man. Cambridge was hardly the place for him to demonstrate that, but in November 1943, most of the Tube Alloys staff, Milner among them, were transported to the United States to help build the atom bomb. Milner was a member of the team assigned to a uranium-separation plant in Oak Ridge, Tennessee. Several of the female office staff there fell for his blond good looks and were taken up and put down with some frequency, according to colleagues. 'He enjoyed the company of women,' says Colin Selsey, who worked with him at Oak Ridge. 'But he ran a mile from anything serious. Sex, I assume, but never love. Personally, I found him easy to get on with but impossible to know. After a while, you began to notice how much better he was at asking questions about other people than answering them about himself.' It is uncannily similar to what Unwin said about him at Cambridge. Milner charmed, but never confided. He seems to have trusted no-one but himself.

One of Milner's colleagues at Oak Ridge was Klaus Fuchs, an even more self-effacing character than Milner himself. Fuchs had been feeding information to the Soviet Union since the start of his involvement in the atom-bomb project, and the two were to meet again at Harwell after the war. Meanwhile, in the summer of 1944, they went their separate ways: Fuchs to Los Alamos, Milner to Montreal, where he was to work on an Anglo-Canadian fission project kept separate from the Anglo-American effort. Progress at Los Alamos soon assumed historic proportions. The Montreal laboratory was, in that sense, a backwater. Milner had not been regarded as an essential member of the British team chosen for Los Alamos. Whether this was because of deficiencies in his work or conflict with superiors is unclear. 'He was sometimes too logical for his own good,' recalls Selsey. 'He was no sycophant, that's for sure, and he could easily rub people up the wrong way. He didn't care who they were. That wouldn't have mattered if his work had been vital, but there seemed to be a feeling that he wasn't quite pulling his weight.'

So, Milner went to Montreal under something of a cloud. He spent the rest of the war there and found himself working with a former colleague from the Cambridge Tube Alloys Project: Alan Nunn May. Nunn May, as we have seen, was already passing information to Soviet Intelligence. He and Milner became drinking companions in Montreal, according to other laboratory staff. They certainly saw more of each other than they ever had at Cambridge. There is nothing necessarily sinister in that. Though five years apart in age, they had shared interests and similar backgrounds, and they were both a long way from home. But this still constitutes a significant change in Milner's behaviour. Nunn May got suspiciously close to being a friend, the first real one Milner had had in years. And he happened to be a Russian spy. Whether Milner knew or guessed what he was really up to is, of course, impossible to establish. But the news of what had been achieved at Los Alamos must have been one of their recurrent topics of conversation. Nunn May later gave as his reason for passing samples of enriched uranium to his Soviet controllers in August 1945 the conviction that nuclear weaponry should not be exclusive to the United States. That was his solution to the moral dilemma confronting the first generation of nuclear physicists. What was Milner's?

At first it appeared to be to opt out. He returned to England in September 1945, took a teaching post at Bristol University and ceased to have any active involvement in nuclear research. Nunn May went to King's College, London. They saw little of each other during the few months of liberty left to Nunn May. Perhaps theirs really had been nothing more than a friendship of fellow exiles. In February 1946 Nunn May was arrested. Before his trial, Milner was questioned about their time together in Montreal. His lack of communist associations told in his favour and he was at no point officially under suspicion.

He told the police that he was 'appalled' by what Nunn May had done. Perhaps he was also appalled by the sentence meted out to him – ten years' penal servitude.

A few months later, Milner was offered a job, rather surprisingly in view of his albeit apparently innocent links with Nunn May, working under Klaus Fuchs in the theoretical physics division of the newly created Atomic Energy Research Establishment at Harwell in Berkshire. He accepted and was at once restored to the forefront of nuclear research. This could have peaceful applications, of course. Maybe Milner told himself he would be helping to develop a new, clean energy source for the future. The smog-ridden cities certainly needed one. And that was partly what Harwell was about.

But it was also about the Bomb. In July 1946, Congress passed the McMahon Bill, banning any traffic with other countries, Britain included, in information concerning atomic energy. That meant Britain had little choice but to go it alone. Early in 1947, Attlee took the decision to build an independent British nuclear deterrent. Fuchs' department at Harwell was set to work on it, in conditions of some secrecy. It was not until May 1948 that the Government made its decision publicly known. When Fuchs took a small team – Milner among them – to the Ministry of Defence Weapons Establishment at Fort Halstead, in Kent, to brief the ministry's head of weaponry research, William Penney, on progress at Harwell, they told no-one where they were going. Unless, of course, in Fuchs' case, it was his Soviet controllers.

Milner lived initially on site at Harwell, in one of the prefabricated bungalows erected for staff. It was an isolated location, given that most of them were married and too strapped for cash to buy a car. Milner did own a car, however, having inherited enough from his brother to afford a few luxuries. He soon moved to a rented cottage in Wantage and commuted from there. His comfortable financial situation, as a bachelor on a principal scientific officer's salary, is further illustrated by the fact that he made no move to sell Otherways when the RAF vacated it in 1947.

Milner's bachelor status also meant he was much in demand on Harwell's party circuit, and his way with women, first noted at Oak Ridge, resurfaces in the recollection of Emily Tucker, widow of Horace Tucker, personnel officer at Harwell. 'He gave you the glad eye in a cool take-it-or-leave-it way that some of the wives liked. He was good-looking and, yes, charming. Women liked him more than men, I think. I know Horace had to deal with several complaints about him from husbands who suspected he'd had his way with their wives. I dare say he had. But nothing was ever proved. Nothing formal came of any of it.'

Marital spats and sly adulteries apart, life proceeded placidly at Harwell until 23 September 1949, when the White House announced that it had 'evidence that within recent weeks an atomic explosion occurred in the USSR.' The Russians had the Bomb, and they had it so much earlier than anyone had expected that it seemed clear to many that they had been helped. The hunt for their helpers was on.

Just over four months later, on 2 February 1950, Klaus Fuchs was arrested on espionage charges. He had signed a full confession a few days previously. The Harwell community had to confront the fact that they had been harbouring a traitor in their midst. It was, for some, a traumatic realization. The deputy director, Herbert Skinner, was close to tears when he broke the news to a hastily convened staff meeting. Many felt betrayed, as well as shocked. Nobody seems to remember Milner's reaction.

Fuchs' undoing had been refinements in US Army code-breaking techniques, which had enabled them to start decoding messages sent from the Soviet Embassy and consulates in the United States to Moscow. Fuchs' name had cropped up in several of these. This was not revealed at the time, of course. If it had been, anyone with a good reason to fear their name might also have cropped up would have been running scared. They would have been distinctly uneasy, anyway. Where one goes, another may follow. And Klaus Fuchs was going to prison for fourteen years. It was not an appetizing prospect.

Henry Arnold, the security officer at Harwell, was hard hit by the Fuchs affair. It was a slight on his professional competence, as well as a personal betrayal. He was about to receive another blow, however. On 28 July 1950, with Fuchs five months into his prison sentence and the memory of his treachery still fresh in the minds of his former colleagues, Cedric Milner departed on a fortnight's leave. He let it be known that he was planning a walking holiday in the Black Forest. The following day, he drove onto a cross-Channel car ferry at Dover and left England, never to return. Ten days later, the Soviet news agency, TASS, announced his defection to the Soviet Union. It paid tribute to him as a vital contributor to the Soviet atom-bomb project. Fuchs had not been alone.

Since Milner was never tried or interrogated, and never volunteered any details of the 'contribution' that warranted TASS's fulsome words, it has never been known for certain what information he passed on, or when, or how. Inferential evidence can be found in the transcript of Fuchs' MI5 interrogation, in which Fuchs refers to questions from his Soviet controllers about technical matters he had not realized they had any knowledge of and which only somebody else on the scientific staff at Harwell *could* know of. Most crucially, Fuchs was asked in 1947 to gather information on the tritium bomb. Tritium was the key to the development of the hydrogen bomb, the so-called 'superbomb'. Fuchs was surprised, because he had told them nothing about it. Somebody else had.

That somebody was surely Cedric Milner. Within weeks of his arrival in the Soviet Union, he was assigned to the Arzamas-16 H-bomb plant, where he remained until the successful Soviet H-bomb test of 12 August 1953, which took place only nine months after the US H-bomb test at Eniwetok Atoll. His mission, however you define it, had been accomplished.

But here mystery intrudes. How did Milner know so much? His grasp of superbomb principles seems to have exceeded Fuchs', despite his junior status and lack of apparent day-to-day involvement in that area of work at Harwell. It was a mystery that troubled Henry Arnold, who began to fear there might be more than two rotten apples in the Harwell barrel. Perhaps he had been collaborating with an as-yet unidentified third traitor. The authorities seemed happy to forget about Milner. Since he had eluded them they did not propose to admit he was important. Hard on the heels of the Fuchs affair, it was an embarrassment they didn't need. They therefore did their best to imply that his real value to Soviet Intelligence was slight.

Arnold was having none of this. The Milner enigma worried him. He instructed his deputy, Duncan Strathallan, to conduct—

Turn over enough stones and sooner or later you'll find something. You used to say that about looking for the facts in a difficult case. So maybe you'd have been proud of me. Here I was, suddenly confronted by proof of what I'd already begun to suspect about Otherways. Everything really was connected with everything else. Rainbird already knew that, of course. It was the connection that drew him to the house, not its architectural foibles. It was a glimpse he'd had – and was determined I should have, too – of the invisible threads that strung themselves between the people who had lived there. I sensed this wasn't the only such thread. And I wondered if it was even the strangest, though it was certainly strange enough. I read on, seeking the answer I knew I wouldn't get.

Arnold was having none of this. The Milner enigma worried him. He instructed his deputy, Duncan Strathallan, to conduct a thorough inquiry into Milner's activities at Harwell and his life before arriving there. Strathallan recalls the inquiry as fascinating but frustrating.

'Understanding Milner was like trying to grasp a bar of soap you've dropped in the bath. Every time you think you've grasped hold, it slips through your fingers. There was plenty of tittle-tattle about him cuckolding a few husbands at Harwell, but nothing – not even a wee hint – about him working late or alone, or being seen in places he shouldn't have been, or always taking a bulging briefcase out through the gate: the sort of stuff you might expect to pick up after the event in a case like this. What's more, the man was either no Communist at all or the most crypto-kind you ever came across. Fuchs had been a party member in Germany before the war. Nunn May had all but gone round with a sandwich board denouncing capitalist imperialism. Man, it was there in their bones.

It took the brain power of MI5 to overlook it. But, as for Milner, there was nothing. He wasn't even pink, let alone red. That thing Churchill said about Russia – a riddle wrapped in a mystery inside an enigma – well, that was Milner to a T. And I never got past the enigma, let alone the mystery and the riddle.'

Strathallan's conclusion, much to Arnold's chagrin, was that Milner's motives were as unknowable as the damage he had done was unquantifiable. He did believe he had been working alone, though. That was one comfort. Arnold stopped looking for a third man. Shortly afterwards, in May 1951, Burgess and Maclean of the Foreign Office defected. 'That made our efforts at Harwell look like a sick joke,' says Strathallan. 'You spend your time stopping up a hole only to find you've been working in a colander all along.'

Pressed for his assessment of Milner, Strathallan says he thinks treachery rather than the purpose served by treachery was what appealed to him. 'You can see it in his sex life and in that business of his sister-in-law's murder. He was a traitor by nature. He enjoyed it. I take some consolation from doubting he'll have enjoyed his life in Russia, though. In the end, he was a traitor to himself.'

And how *important* a traitor was he? 'We'll never know,' says Strathallan. 'But considering how much sooner the Russians developed the H-bomb than the experts said they'd be able to, my feeling is . . . very important.'

Milner left Arzamas-16 in 1956 and took a teaching post at the University of Moscow, where he has remained ever since. He does not give interviews to, nor answer letters from, Western journalists. He is not known to associate with the likes of Philby and Blake. He is not, in any real sense, known at all. He has succeeded, more completely than any of the other subjects of this book, in concealing not only what he gave away but why he gave it away. He is the traitor's traitor, to be trusted with no secret – save his own.

I put the book down and looked across the lawn at the house. The sun had gone in again, behind stubborn midsummer clouds. It was colder than it had been, though dusk was still a long way off. The air was scarcely moving. Why had Strathallan bought the place? Why hadn't Fisher mentioned the fact in his chapter on Milner? Just how many secrets did Otherways hold? It looked, at that moment, in the mild grey light, as if it might hold an infinity of them, slowly revolving in its circles of stone.

I went indoors then, and made my way up to the second-floor room where Strathallan's junk had been stored. Junk it certainly looked for the most part: pots of paint and stiffened brushes; fishing rods and bait boxes; old raincoats and galoshes; gumboots and waders; battered suitcases and dented trunks; a rusting zed-bed; a fraying dog basket. I wondered where Lucy had found the hoarded copy of the *Sunday Times Magazine* among all this and tried a suitcase at random. It held the late Mrs Strathallan's old skirts and cardigans, to judge by their style. Another held several years' worth of something called *Army Quarterly*. It seemed odd, having kept such stuff, to leave it behind. He might as well have thrown it away. It was almost as if he couldn't bear to keep it near him but couldn't bear to be rid of it, either. Or maybe Otherways was where he thought it belonged.

I was interrupted by the telephone, and in a way I was grateful for the distraction. There was something indecent about rooting through a stranger's possessions, even if he had discarded them. Matt had it right there.

'Hello?'

'Norman here, Tony. Finished the Milner chapter?'

'I've only had the book a couple of hours.'

'Time enough, I'd say.'

'All right. I've read it.'

'Splendid. Bit of an eye-opener, isn't it?'

'In a sense, but—'

'Wonder if I could have it back. I'm in the Whipper-In at Oakham. Why don't you join me for a drink?'

He was at the farthest table from the bar, perusing a colour-illustrated handbook on British trees over an orange juice and the remains of a sandwich. I bought a drink and joined him, plonking *Seven Faces of Treason* down at his elbow.

'I thought you were more into birds than trees, Norman.'

'But where do birds roost, Tony? That's the point. Actually, I enjoy knowing more about the world around us than the average blinkered citizen. You could say I've devoted my retirement to it.'

'Retirement from what?'

'Does it matter? I've tried to forget. Retirement is both a euphemism and a misnomer, anyway. I was made redundant. But I've no intention of *being* redundant.'

'Well, I suppose being able to tell a rowan from a mountain ash is useful.'

'Very droll.' He sat forward in his chair and tapped the cover of *Seven Faces of Treason*. 'What are your thoughts on this?'

'One is that you already know the answer to the question it was bound to raise in my mind. Why did Strathallan buy Otherways?'

'An investment for when he left the service, I assume. Milner wrote to his solicitor from Moscow, instructing him to sell the place and to offer it first to his former colleagues at Harwell at a discounted price. Not so generous, really, when you consider that the proceeds could never legally be passed on to him.'

'But Strathallan went for it?'

'Yes. He'd recently married. Mrs Strathallan had private money, I believe. As to why, I suppose it must have seemed like a good deal. Didn't turn out that way, though.'

'Why not?'

'Tragedy and misfortune.' He smiled. 'They tend to hunt as a pair.' He paused to sip his orange juice. 'You haven't thanked me, by the way.'

'For the loan of the book? You were pretty insistent, as I recall.'

'That's not what I meant. You recently suffered a bereavement.'

'So I did.'

'I've never been married, so I can only speculate about what it's like to lose a beloved wife. I assume she was beloved?'

'Yes. She was.' And you were, Marina. Never doubt that, even though I may yet give you cause to.

'Well, I imagine it's difficult to think about anything or anyone else.'

'It is.'

'But you have, haven't you? Today, I mean. You've thought about Otherways.'

'True.' Something in the mystery of the place had

excited me, had given me a purpose. And Rainbird, damn him, had realized that.

'So, perhaps I've done more for you than any of your condoling friends.' He smiled again. 'Or perhaps you think I'm overstating the case.'

'What about Strathallan?' I was eager to change the subject. Rainbird's delusion of intimacy wasn't something I wanted to encourage in any way. '"Tragedy and misfortune," you said. Care to elaborate?'

'Not so fast, Tony. You must understand I had to go to great lengths to assemble the knowledge you seem to expect me to dispense with a free hand.'

'I suppose you've had the time.'

'We all have the same amount of time. The difference lies in how we use it.'

'And how have you used it?'

'In familiarizing myself with the history of Otherways and the people who've lived there.'

'Why . . . exactly?'

He shrugged. 'It presented itself as an obvious subject for study when I moved to the area.'

'Why did you move here?'

'That brings us back to birds. There are ospreys on Rutland Water, you know. It really is a fascinating habitat.'

'I'm beginning to realize that.'

'Quite so.' The smile came and went again. 'Now, largely thanks to my lengthy researches in the archives of the *Rutland Mercury*, I can tell you that Duncan and Jean Strathallan moved to Otherways when he left Harwell in 1952. He set himself up as a small-time sheep farmer, on land that's now underwater. Their daughter, Rosalind, was born at Otherways in 1955. Strathallan was a prominent protester against the coming of the reservoir, but had about as much success as Canute at holding back the water. In the midst of all that, one fine day in the summer of 1976, young Rosalind committed suicide.'

'Good God. How?'

'Paracetamol and whisky. Found dead in her car in a lay-by near Uppingham.'

'Do we know why?'

'We do not. She'd just finished a degree course at Leeds and was due to be married that autumn. Everyone seemed to think she was looking forward to the wedding and to moving to London with her husband-to-be. If she'd changed her mind about getting married, she would surely just have called it off. Suicide suggests altogether deeper trouble. But there was no mention of any at the inquest. The coroner called it an "unaccountable tragedy".'

'Otherways seems to attract them.'

'It does, doesn't it? That and coincidences. Such as the identity of Rosalind Strathallan's fiancé. He gave evidence at the inquest. You've already come across him, actually.' Rainbird's downward glance at the cover of *Seven Faces of Treason* was enough to tell me who he meant a fraction of a second before he spoke his name. 'Martin Fisher.'

Remember the aerial photograph of the area around Stanacombe you bought shortly after we moved in? The pattern of fields and lanes was there to be seen, but also visible were the shadows of other lapsed boundaries and forgotten ways from hundreds, maybe thousands, of years ago. I thought of that skeleton of history buried none too deep in the soil when Rainbird spilt the latest of his secrets about Otherways. How many more there were that even he had failed to glean I didn't know. But that there were more I didn't doubt.

'You'll admit I've been generous,' Rainbird said, grinning at me ingratiatingly as we emerged from the Whipper-In into the gathering dusk. 'And you'll agree one good turn deserves another, I'm sure.'

'What do you want?' I started walking smartly across the market place towards the car, which I'd parked immediately behind Rainbird's Morris Minor.

'I need a go-between.'

'Between you and who?'

'Strathallan. I'm afraid I rather rubbed the old fellow up the wrong way. To the extent that he wouldn't give me the time of day now.'

'But it's not the time of day you want from him.'

'No. It's James Milner's confession, penned in the condemned cell at Leicester Prison in November 1939.'

'What makes you think Strathallan has it?'

'Study of character and deductive reasoning. Plus his shifty reaction to my questions about it.'

'Daisy seems a more likely candidate.'

'Oh, I think it was addressed to her. But I think she passed it on to Strathallan after the death of his daughter.'

'Why?' We reached the cars and stopped. When I looked round at Rainbird, I found him smirking at me.

'I'll tell you why if you succeed in getting hold of the confession. If the confession doesn't tell you itself, that is.'

'I don't think I'll be racing up to Scotland with that as an incentive, Norman.'

'Oh, you will, believe me.'

'I don't even know where the man lives.'

'I do.' His smirk broadened.

'I still won't be going.'

'Just let me know when you change your mind.'

'I'm not going to change my mind.'

'Yes you are. You just need time. You can't leave it alone any more than I can. I recognize the signs.'

'I'm mildly curious, that's all.'

'That's all I was. At first.' He glanced at his watch. 'Well, must be off.' He climbed into his car and started the engine. 'I'll look forward to hearing from you.' Then he pulled away, waving goodbye to me as he vanished round the corner. Doubtless he wasn't in the least discouraged by the fact that I didn't wave back.

I drove back to Otherways, then walked down to the Finches Arms. I didn't like to admit as much to myself, but the prospect of spending the night alone at Otherways made me nervous. There was nothing I was specifically afraid of. It was just an empty house with an unfortunate history. But still I felt in need of some Dutch courage – and the deep sleep that several drinks seemed to promise.

The promise wasn't fulfilled. I stumbled back to the house through a moonlit night and went straight to bed, falling instantly asleep. But I didn't stay that way. Even saying that much confers a sense of order on what was much more bewildering than I can properly describe. I dreamed. Or did I? The most disturbing aspect of my Otherways dreams was their lack of unreality. Some part of your dreaming mind knows what's going on all the time, doesn't it? Some stubborn, rational monitor keeps it all in check. But not at Otherways. My dreams there dovetailed themselves into my waking thoughts. There was no straight dividing line between them.

I was woken by a noise and was conscious just too late to guess what it might have been. But I couldn't dispel the notion that it had been a human voice, somewhere in the house – a cry or a laugh. I hadn't been in any state to set the alarm. I lay still, my senses alert, ears cocked and heard it again. A moan, a murmur – something.

I rose and went out onto the landing, walking slowly and carefully. A milky splash of moonlight had cast giant shadows of the balusters on the wall adjacent to the stairhead. The rest of the landing was a gulf of blackness. Except for a yellow rectangle of light around the closed door of Matt and Lucy's bedroom. I moved towards it.

As I did so, there were sounds from within. I knew then what was happening in the room. And what I would see if I opened the door. But not *who* I would see. I reached for the handle, turned it and pushed.

They were on the bed, the sheets thrown aside, their naked flesh glowing in the golden lamplight. Lucy lay on her side with her back to me, one leg wrapped around the man's waist as he entered her with a moan, his hand tightening around her buttocks, his face hidden from me in front of her. Her neck arched and her head fell back, the hair falling away from her brow. Her lips parted and her eyes closed. She rolled over onto her back, the man sucking at her breast. Then he raised himself and pushed more deeply into her. She cried out and I cried out, too, as I saw his face for the first time, flushed and straining.

Then I was truly awake, standing where I'd been in the dream, in the doorway of Matt and Lucy's bedroom. It was in darkness. There was no-one there. There were no voices to be heard. There was nothing to be seen. I was alone. Lucy was a hundred miles away, not here, with me. I didn't want her. I couldn't. I mustn't. Nor she me. It was only a dream. Yet there I stood. Remembering. And imagining.

Chapter Four

The dawn was grey and breezy. The absence of any other sound magnified the wind into a keening presence in the eaves and chimneys of Otherways. Only in high summer do days begin this way, with the sun up before the human world has cranked itself into motion. It makes solitude almost tangible. You hear your own breathing, your heart beating, your clothes sliding across your skin.

I've never missed you more than that Sunday morning. It wasn't just the loss of your love. It was the fear of what I was becoming without you. And it was something worse, that I have to confess to you, that I need you to understand and forgive. It was the sick sliver of pleasure in not knowing what was going to happen, that day or in the days ahead. It was the wondering and the doubting, the wanting buried within the dreading.

I left the house and walked down the lane into Hambleton. I had no destination in mind, no purpose beyond a desire for motion. And I certainly didn't expect to see anybody up and about so early. But, as I passed the church, a movement among the graves caught my eye. A woman was threading her way slowly between

94

the headstones. She noticed me in the same instant that I noticed her. We stopped and looked at each other.

'Good morning,' I said. 'This is a surprise.'

'For me, too,' said Daisy, with a smile. 'I normally have the world to myself at this hour.'

'Is that how you like it?'

'Sometimes.'

She walked towards me, hurrying slightly, and blushing, I couldn't help thinking, as if I'd caught her out in some way. She'd been to see her sister's grave, I assumed. But why should she feel guilty about that?

'I find I sleep less and less as I grow older,' she said, stepping through the gate to join me in the lane. 'What's your excuse?' She frowned in annoyance at herself. 'I'm sorry. Why should I expect you to sleep well after what you've been through?'

'I don't do too badly. But last night . . . well, maybe sleeping alone in a large house didn't agree with me.'

'Otherways doesn't suit everybody. Some find the shape and feel of it . . . unsettling.'

'Did you?'

'When Ann lived there? No.' There was something strangely specific about her answer, almost as if her view of the house was different now.

'I don't, either.'

'No?' A shadow of scepticism flicked across her face.

'And Matt and Lucy seem very happy there.'

'You're right. They do. Of course, I've only known them since they moved here. I wouldn't be aware of any changes.'

'But I would.'

'So you would.' She stepped closer and leaned against

95

the churchyard wall, gazing back along the lane in the direction of Otherways. 'But I'm sure you'll tell me there haven't been any.'

I hesitated long enough for her to turn and look at me before I spoke. I tried to shrug off the significance of my hesitation, but it was palpably there, as clear to her, I didn't doubt, as it was to me. 'No changes,' I murmured.

'Lucy phoned me and mentioned you'd be alone. I'd have invited you to dinner, but unfortunately I was already committed to dining elsewhere.'

'It was a kind thought.'

'Lucy was to have sat for me this morning. Hence the phone call.'

'Right.'

'We rescheduled for Tuesday afternoon. Why don't you come along?'

'I'd be in the way.'

'I doubt it. You seemed interested in my work. The best way to understand is to watch.'

'Well, thanks, I'd enjoy that.'

'Good.'

'Perhaps you'd like to step back to Otherways with me. I could offer you some sort of breakfast.'

'I won't, thank you.' With a gentle, sad little smile, she moved past me, down the lane to where her car was parked beneath the spreading canopy of a horse chestnut tree, adding something as she went, which I just failed to catch.

'Sorry?' I called after her.

'Mmm?' She stopped and looked back at me, then smiled again. 'Talking to myself. Bad habit.' She raised a hand. 'Goodbye, Tony.' Then she climbed into the car and drove slowly away, the engine note audible in the vacant air long after she'd vanished round the bend towards Oakham.

I walked into the churchyard, heading for the part of it where I'd first seen Daisy. It took me five minutes or so of searching before I found her sister's grave. The headstone was small and plain, the vase empty. Daisy had brought her no flowers. There was nothing to show she'd been there at all. And nothing to reveal how Ann Milner had died. Unless it was the inscription beneath her name. It was in Greek, as good as the most cryptic of codes to the likes of me.

ANN GEORGIANA MILNER
1912–1939
πάντα χωρεῖ, οὐδὲν μένει

The solitude waiting for me at Otherways hung heavily on my mind. I drove into Oakham and breakfasted at the Whipper-In, then took off on a slow and aimless cross-country drive, south-east beyond Peterborough, into the solemn infinities of the Fens. I reached Ely, and sat for an hour or more in the cathedral close, watching the tourists and worshippers drifting in and out. I don't know what I was looking for. Something to snap me out of the weird centripetence of life at Otherways, I suppose. Nothing worked, though. Nothing could, without you. I had nowhere to go and no-one to be except myself. But who was I? What was left of me now that you were gone? I could hold on if I had to. But to what, Marina? That was the question I couldn't begin to answer. Hold on to *what*?

*   *   *

97

Matt and Lucy were already there when I got back to Otherways that afternoon. I was relieved to see their car in the drive, suddenly sensing in my pleasure at the prospect of seeing them again just how much of an ordeal the previous twenty-four hours had been.

They were in the drawing room, having tea, but Matt had done no more than say hello when the telephone rang and he hurried off to the library to take the call.

'Business,' said Lucy with feeling as she poured me some tea. 'Matt has a lot of rearranging to do between now and tomorrow morning.'

'Why? What's happening?'

'He's flying to New York with Dick Sindermann. They seemed to hit it off. Now the sky's suddenly the limit.'

'You sound unconvinced.'

'Uninvolved is nearer the mark. Matt's persuaded himself he's going into this for my sake as much as his. He seems to think I yearn to be a Manhattan socialite.'

'Not so?'

'What do you think I want to be, Tony?'

It was a disconcertingly direct question. I shrugged. 'I'm not sure this is the right time to . . . uproot yourself.'

'When is?' She glanced out of the window. 'Maybe this trip to New York will get it out of Matt's system. Whatever *it* is.'

'How long's he going for?'

'Undecided. Four or five days, I imagine. He suggested I go with him. But I prefer to stay here.'

'Not on my account, I hope.'

'Partly. And partly my own. I invited you up here so that we could help each other get over Marina, remember?'

98

'Maybe this is Matt's idea for helping you do just that.'

'Maybe so. He means well. He always does.'

'What did you make of Sindermann?'

'Nothing much. I didn't really pay him a lot of attention. I kept on thinking . . .' She looked at me, with a nervous sort of smile playing at the edges of her mouth. 'Of you, actually. Alone here. Without us.'

'I got by.'

'I even dreamed I was here. Last night.'

'Really?' I put my cup carefully back in its saucer and smoothed my hand over my knee to hide any hint of a tremor.

'It was . . . incredibly vivid.'

'Dreams can be.'

'Not mine. Not till we moved here, anyway. What about you?'

'How do you mean?'

'Have you dreamed of Marina a lot?'

'At first. Not so often lately.'

'What then?'

'Oh, nothing that made any sense.' I left my chair and walked over to the window, where I perched on the sill and looked back at her, sitting in the chair where I'd dreamed of seeing her. 'About the magazine article—'

'Leave it till Matt's gone, eh? We can talk about it as much as we like then.' She paused. 'That and anything else we want to.'

Matt spent most of the rest of the day on the telephone, rejigging his plans for the week ahead. During one of our brief exchanges, squeezed between urgent calls, he asked if I could drive him to Heathrow early the following morning. Joking that it was my only chance

99

of a decent conversation with him, I agreed. We were going to have to leave at dawn. The day, and the previous night, had left me drained and bone-weary. I went to bed early, counting on sheer fatigue to give me seven solid hours of sleep. But fatigue was never likely to be enough. I should have realized that. Another dream was awaiting its chance – the chance to show me that reality can seem to the unconscious mind like a dream within a dream, a distant memory of something that might be true and, then again, might not be.

Matt and I were sitting in the drawing room at Otherways, our chairs facing the open French windows, beyond which the heat-hazed garden dozed beneath a cloudless sky. The curtains billowed lazily in the warm breeze and, out on the lawn, Lucy lay sunbathing on a lounger, in swimsuit and sunglasses. I knew it was Lucy, though at that distance it could have been you, so close had your resemblance to each other become in my mind.

'Is she asleep, do you think?' I asked.

'Probably,' Matt replied.

'And dreaming?'

'Who can say?'

'I reckon she is.'

'Then you're probably right. You'd know the signs, after all.'

'There aren't any. But she always dreams. Didn't I ever tell you that?'

'No.'

'I've been dreaming a lot myself lately.'

'What about?'

'Always the same thing. It's weird. Almost as if . . . it's more of a memory than a dream. I'm here, at Otherways.

I mean, *we're* here, the three of us. Just like now. Except . . . different.'

'How different?'

'That's the weirdest part,' I replied. 'In the dream, she's your wife, not mine. I was *your* best man, not the other way round. I'm the old friend who comes to stay, not the one who bought this house for her and tried to make her happy here.'

'You're right.' Matt turned in his chair to look at me. 'That is weird.'

'It seems, in the dream, as if you and she have taken me in, to help me recover from some kind of . . . tragedy. I'm never sure what exactly. Or maybe I just don't remember. Like you do with dreams. Parts of them are always just out of reach.'

'How often do you have this dream?'

'Too often.'

'It worries you?'

'Its recurrence worries me. Why won't it go away, Matt? What's it trying to tell me?'

'Why should it be trying to tell you anything?'

'Because it keeps coming back.'

'Yes.' He gazed out through the French windows again, towards the distant figure on the lounger. 'It does, doesn't it?'

'You talk as if you knew all about it before I told you.'

'I did.'

'What?'

'I have the same dream.' He spoke in an undertone, almost a whisper. 'Every night.'

The following morning was dreamlike enough to take its place among the fantasies that were elbowing their way into my waking thoughts. Lucy was still in bed, her farewells to Matt said privately, if they'd been said at all. He and I breakfasted on black coffee in the kitchen, then we walked out into a dawn so still the whole world seemed to be holding its breath and climbed into the car.

We drove round Rutland Water in bleary-eyed silence, the lake stretching away behind us like some vast unknown estuary that had always been there and always would be. Then we headed east, across an empty tract of farmland, to the A1, and started south towards London and Heathrow Airport and the reassuring technological conveniences of the here and now.

'I never sleep well when I know I have to be up early,' Matt complained after several stifled yawns. 'What about you?'

'Not worried I'm going to nod off at the wheel, are you?'

'You look a bit washed out, that's all.'

'I slept all right.'

'Good. I'm sorry to drag you out at this unearthly hour, though.'

'It's no problem.'

'I'll only be gone a few days, whichever way things turn out. But even so, I'm glad you'll be at Otherways – to keep Lucy company.'

'I don't know why you're so worried about her, Matt. She seems fine to me . . . in the circumstances.'

'Too fine maybe. I don't feel she's grieved enough. Not that I know what enough would be. But I'd be reluctant to leave her alone just now, that's for sure.'

'I'll do my best to look after her.'

'I don't want Daisy monopolizing her company.'

'Why not?'

102

'Because seeing that woman makes it difficult for Lucy to drop the subject of the Milner murder, as I'd like her to. It can't be healthy, dwelling on what happened sixty years ago.'

'That room full of Strathallan's junk doesn't help, I suppose.'

'I can't see what that has to do with it. Strathallan never knew the Milners.'

'Didn't he?'

'No.' I sensed Matt frowning at me. 'Why should he have done?'

'No reason. I just . . . Well, you would like to be shot of the stuff, wouldn't you?'

'Of course. But the old bugger shows no sign of turning up to collect it.'

'Why don't you take the bull by the horns and send it to him?'

'I think I would, if I had his address.'

'He didn't leave it with you?'

'No. Afraid of complaints about the state he'd left the house in, I suppose.'

'Or about forgetting to mention the murder.'

'Maybe that, too.'

'Talking of which, I came across Ann Milner's grave down at the church.'

'Came across? Sure you didn't track it down, Tony? It's not getting to you as well, is it?'

'I found it by chance. Honest.'

'And now you want to tap my vestigial knowledge of Ancient Greek.'

'It's a thought. You've always boasted about your classical education.'

'You've always sent me up on account of it, you mean.'

'I just never saw its practical application.'

'Until now.'

'Are you going to tell me or not?'

'Heraclitus. Ephesian philosopher of the fifth century BC. It's one of his typically morbid epigrams. "Everything goes, nothing stays."'

'Morbid but true?'

'I'm not sure. The memories stay, don't they?'

'Oh yes. They do. But maybe that just makes it worse.'

'I'm sorry. I didn't mean to—'

'It's all right. I have no monopoly on grief. I only have to think of the tragedies meted out to former inhabitants of Otherways to realize that.'

'Hold on, Tony. One murder makes one tragedy, not a whole succession of them.'

'Sorry. I'm getting carried away.' He didn't know about Strathallan's daughter. That was suddenly obvious. How much more didn't he know about? How much more didn't he *want* to know about?

'I'd be grateful if you didn't talk like that to Lucy.'

'I'll be careful. Don't worry.'

'She's been saying some strange things lately.'

'Such as?'

'That buildings have memories, just like people do.'

'What does she mean by that?'

'I don't know. But, whatever it is, do your best to talk her out of it, would you? As a favour to me. She doesn't think I understand. Maybe she's right. As things are at the moment, I can't give her the time she needs. But you can.'

'I don't understand, either, Matt.'

'But you'll try to?'

'All right.' I glanced round at him. 'I'll try.'

104

Matt looked back and waved as he walked into the terminal building at Heathrow. Then he vanished into the maw of the revolving door and I drove away, thinking, without wanting to, of all the things that compose a lasting friendship: ease, humour, honesty, similarity, comradeship, the sort of love we call merely liking, and trust. We trusted each other implicitly and had done for nigh on twenty years. But maybe that trust had never been truly tested. Perhaps, in his way, Matt trusted me too much. And more, for sure, than I trusted myself.

I took the slow road back to Rutland, but still I felt unprepared for my arrival at Otherways. I parked on the southern shore of Rutland Water and gazed across the lake at the woods and fields of the peninsula. The morning slowly unwound itself. A few fishermen were already out, bobbing in their boats. The air was humid and expectant. Everything was waiting, watching, wondering. Nothing was decided.

'I was beginning to get worried about you,' said Lucy, with a smile of relief as I walked into the drawing room. She was sitting by the open French windows, sipping coffee, with the debris of the morning papers spread around her chair. She was wearing your coral-trimmed shirt and cream trousers, quite unself-consciously it seemed. She looked more genuinely relaxed than at any time since your death. She looked, to tell the truth, quite radiant. 'Did Matt get off OK?'

'No problems.'

'Want some coffee? There's plenty in the pot. Nesta made some fresh before she left. I brought another cup just in case.'

I poured myself some, drew up a chair and sat down opposite her. 'Anything in the papers?' I asked banally.

'They might as well be about another planet.'

'But who's on the other planet, Lucy? Them, or you and me?'

'Since you ask, I think it might be you and me.'

'What sort of place is it?'

'Strange. Unsettling.'

'That's what a lot of people say about this house.'

'A world unto itself, then. But it grows on you.'

'Matt's worried it might have grown on you more than it should.'

'He worries too much.'

'Because he loves you.'

'Sometimes love isn't enough.'

'It should always be enough.'

'Not between a man and a woman. There's something else. Something more.'

'I don't understand.'

'Yes you do.'

'No.' I stood up and walked out into the open air. 'I don't.'

'Don't be frightened, Tony.' She was suddenly standing at my shoulder, her hand resting lightly on my arm. 'Some things have to be.'

I took a few distancing steps out onto the bridge across the moat and leaned against the parapet, looking back at her. 'Marina's death,' I said, slowly and deliberatively, 'is a loss both of us have to learn to adjust to – to live with as best we can.'

'We can help each other.' There was nothing even remotely disingenuous in her gaze. She meant exactly what she said. But what she meant *by* it encompassed

106

my future as well as hers. 'We share the loss. We can share the healing.'

'It sounds so simple.'

'It is.'

'I don't think so.'

'You're lonely without her.'

'Of course.'

'So am I.'

'But you have Matt.'

'Not really.'

'What do you mean?'

She sighed, stepped closer and leaned against the parapet beside me. 'There's something you don't know about Matt and me,' she said in an undertone. 'He's impotent, you see. That is, he can't . . . hasn't . . . for a long time now.' She lowered her head. 'I don't know what the problem is. He won't try to find out. But it eats away at him. And at me. Worse than ever, since Marina died. I don't know why that should make it seem suddenly so unbearable, but it does.' She turned to me, tears brimming in her eyes. 'I can't go on like this, Tony.'

'I had no idea.' Instinctively, I put my arm around her. She sank against my shoulder. 'None at all.'

'Marina knew. I made her promise not to tell you.' I felt a stab of shock at that. We never had any secrets, you and I. Or so I'd supposed. And I didn't blame you for keeping this one. But still, it *was* a secret. 'I feel so sorry for Matt. And for myself. But I can't love him unconditionally. I need more than he can give.'

'Lucy.' She raised her head and looked at me, her eyes searching my face. 'We can't . . .'

'We can't not.' Then she kissed me. And I returned her kiss, the long denial of physical closeness swamping my doubts and scruples. Forbidden fruit is the sweetest, don't they say? With my first taste of it I knew they were right. Forbidden, yet faintly familiar. There was part of you in her. And I missed you so much. The rest was a dark longing that burst from its hiding place. My dream of two nights before flashed into my mind. It was going to happen. And I wanted it to. Everything else was futile resistance. 'Come upstairs,' Lucy urged, breaking away. 'Now. If we wait, we're lost.'

But we were lost either way. It was already too late to put our world back together. We were standing amidst its ruins. We didn't see them, but they were there. All around us. Waiting for us to notice. When we could notice anything again. Beyond each other.

'I'm sorry,' I said later, sitting on the edge of the bed, with Lucy lying against the pillows behind me, her hand on my hip, the noon sun warm on my thigh. 'That should never have happened.'

'We both wanted it to,' said Lucy, softly.

'What we want isn't all that counts.'

'Sometimes it has to be.'

I turned and looked at her, my eyes drifting across her body. 'You're beautiful.'

'Like Marina.'

'I'm not using you as a substitute for her.'

'I wouldn't care if you were. I'd understand, you know.' She took my hand and led it to her breast. 'You remember I said I dreamed I was here while I was with Matt at Cliveden?'

'Yes.' Her nipple stiffened beneath my palm.

'This is what I dreamed of. You and me. Like it just was. I mean, exactly like it was.' We'd both dreamed it.

We'd both seen it. And now we'd acted it out. 'It had to be.'

'Why?'

'I don't know. But it's true, isn't it? You sensed it as well.'

'Yes.' I looked straight into her eyes, sparkling with recent memories. 'I did.'

'There are no limits.'

'We can't go on.'

'We can't stop.'

'Matt is—' She pressed her fingers to my mouth, silencing me.

'Thousands of miles and hundreds of hours away. We have the present – and a small chunk of the future. Let's enjoy it.'

'What we're doing . . . is wrong.'

'But it's so good.' She reached down towards me as I leaned across her. 'Isn't it?'

And it was. God forgive me, it was.

Now you know. Maybe you're not so very surprised after all. Lucy was the closest I could be to you. There was a sort of logic to it. And a lot of passion. I hadn't realized just how much passion there was, waiting to be released, in me as well as her. You were gone. You were lost to me. There was nothing I did that betrayed you or our love. That was the past. This was the present. So I told myself, anyway. So I tried to believe. But even then I couldn't delude myself where Matt was concerned. Every moment I enjoyed with Lucy, every act I savoured, was a wrong I did him. We were all going to pay for what was happening. In our different ways.

* * *

'You haven't mentioned the magazine article,' Lucy said later, with a teasing smile. 'Has something taken your mind off it?'

'You could say so, yes.'

'Just as well. It's all ancient history, you know.'

'Not to Daisy, I imagine.'

'I never talk to her about it.'

'Do you think she has the confession James Milner wrote in prison?'

Lucy shrugged. 'I don't know.'

'Rainbird reckons Daisy gave it to Strathallan.'

'You shouldn't believe anything that man says. He's an obnoxious little shit. I keep telling Daisy to turf him out. God knows why she puts up with him.' She frowned. 'When did you and Rainbird have this heart-to-heart?'

'I met him by chance, in the Whipper-In at Oakham on Saturday night.' The lie was forgivable, wasn't it? I didn't know how she'd react to the discovery that he'd tricked his way into the house during her absence. 'He seemed remarkably well-informed.'

'What about?'

'The Milner family. And the Strathallans. Did you know Strathallan's daughter committed suicide?'

'Yes. Daisy mentioned it. But it's common knowledge.'

'How common?'

'Depends on who you ask.'

'Does Matt know?'

'I don't think so.'

'It doesn't seem to have been a lucky house.'

'It has been for me.' She grinned, then looked sombre. 'But it does hold a lot of secrets. Including Rosalind Strathallan's.' She paused, weighing something in her mind, judging, I suppose, how much trust went with our new-found intimacy. 'There was a diary. Hers. Of the last year of her life. It was on a shelf, concealed within the disused chimney breast in her room. The room you've been sleeping in. I found it when I redecorated. Her parents can't have known it was there. I showed it to Daisy. She realized whose it was and told me what had happened to her.'

'Does it explain why she killed herself?'

'Not exactly.'

'Does it explain anything?'

'You'll have to judge that for yourself.'

It was a Leeds University Guild of Students pocket diary for the 1975/76 academic year, small enough for Lucy to have concealed it, still wrapped in the plastic bag she'd found it in and sealed with a rubber band, in a drawer she was confident Matt would never go to. She left me to leaf through it while she took a bath.

There was a map of the Leeds University campus, then fifty pages listing term dates, departmental details and student societies – everything from change-ringing to transcendental meditation. The diary itself started in early September 1975 and ran to the end of August 1976. The entries, sometimes in green biro, sometimes blue, were in minute but perfectly legible script, more like printing than handwriting. They didn't start until late September, when term began, perhaps when Rosalind bought the diary. From there until December was terse, unremarkable stuff: the times of lectures and tutorials, social events, shopping lists, plus a suspicious number of appointments with somebody, or something, called HD, and several weekends crossed through beneath the name Martin – visits to or from Martin Fisher, presumably.

Term ended on 9 December and Rosalind went home. A train time was recorded – departure from Leeds, arrival at Peterborough – followed, in stark capitals, by 'OTHERWAYS'. Blank pages covered Christmas and New Year. Normal service resumed with her return to Leeds on 8 January. I hurried through the pages, seeking but failing to find anything of significance. Easter, however, wasn't the blank Christmas had been. Rosalind spent a week in Paris with Martin during the vacation and every day was crammed with a list of the sights they'd seen, plus potted reactions from Rosalind – 'dreamy', 'beautiful', 'magical', 'awesome', 'delightful'. It sounded as if it could hardly have gone better. Train and ferry times marked their return to England on 15 April, and the following day, Good Friday, struck a new and sinister note in the diary. 'They were waiting for me. Why oh why can't they leave me in peace?' Another entry, later in the weekend, was crossed out so fiercely that I couldn't make anything of it. Whatever kind of an Easter she'd had, it hadn't been a happy one.

Nor did the summer term start like its predecessors. The day after her return to Leeds, Rosalind wrote 'HORROR, HORROR' as her sole entry and, the day after that, 'They've followed me here.' Three days later, however, was her first HD appointment of the term. 'A shaft of light' she wrote in brackets after the time. She saw Martin the following weekend and 'Everything OK' seemed to sum up their reunion. The entries settled down after that, though there were many more deletions than in the earlier pages. She was using Tipp-Ex now to amend the record, though why, given that she was presumably keeping the diary for nobody's benefit but her own, I couldn't imagine.

June looked sane and carefree, with exams, followed by a round of parties, a couple of weekends in London with Martin and a graduation ceremony at the end of the month. July found her back at Otherways, however, and the tone changed instantly. 'So much worse than before,' written on 11 July, was typical of a string of entries. She seemed to have taken some sort of temporary job at a riding school, but references to that stopped abruptly after a couple of weeks. She saw a doctor, presumably her GP, twice in the following week, and started employing asterisks, sometimes one, sometimes two, occasionally three, as recurring symbols. She spent the weekend of 24/25 July in London, with Martin, and wrote, 'He doesn't understand. He can't imagine,' at the end of it. The next day she copied out the Heraclitus epigram, in Greek, from Ann Milner's gravestone and, beneath, wrote, 'No way out.' There was a run of blank days, then, on 5 August, in capitals, the entry 'THEY WON'T GET ME.'

But they had got her. That was the final entry. There was nothing else. She'd hidden the diary in her room and driven away to find the only escape she could contrive from whatever it was that refused to leave her in peace.

'What do you make of it?' asked Lucy, coming out of the bathroom to find me trawling through the pages for a second time.

'Hard to say. Something here, in this house, seems to have troubled her.'

'Maybe.'

'You have another theory?'

'I only know that Otherways seems warm and welcoming to me. Rosalind Strathallan's demon must have been the personal kind. Of course, it could have been the people, not the house, that troubled her.'

'Her parents, you mean?'

'Them or the journo, Fisher. They were due to be married, apparently.'

'It doesn't sound as if he was the problem.'

'Well, something was.' She plucked the diary from my hand, dropped it into a drawer and sat down on the bed beside me. 'But we're never going to find out what.'

'Probably not, no.'

'Perhaps we should concentrate on our own problems, then.'

'Or forget them.' I drew her closer.

'Yes,' she said, kissing me. 'We could always do that.'

Who was the leader and who was the led? I could blame Lucy for everything, if I wanted to. Or for nothing. The truth is as simple as it's shocking: we led each other. What we did, we did together. And the knowledge that everything we did was wrong, that it betrayed a friendship as well as a marriage, merely added a frenzy of guilt to our hours of secret pleasure. Nothing could stop us, once we'd begun. We confessed too many needs and desires to each other for the past to be retrievable. And, for the moment, we didn't care.

Cutting through the fog of carnality that filled my mind, however, was the strange capacity of my subconscious to conjure up dream images of still darker possibilities. On one occasion that night I started awake, convinced that Matt was standing over the bed, looking down at us. On another, I put my hand out to touch Lucy, only to find her stiff and cold and dead, her eyes staring, her mouth gaping. Then I woke, and this time, when I touched her, she was warm and alive.

I said nothing to Lucy about these experiences, or the other vivid dreams I'd had at Otherways. It wasn't just that I didn't want to worry her. I also didn't want to worry myself. She'd dreamed of us making love the same night as I had, two nights before we'd actually done so. Maybe we'd had the identical dream in the very same moment. But that was crazy. That just couldn't be.

I tried to write it all off as the work of my uneasy conscience, compounded by the strain of pretending to others that Lucy and I remained what we'd always been: friends brought together by marriage; not quite friends at all, in the truest sense. There were all kinds of domestic details that might have given us away where Nesta was concerned. How successful we were the next day at maintaining a front of normality for her benefit I wasn't sure. Lucy said there was nothing for her to notice, but I wasn't so confident. It seemed to me that Nesta could easily have detected the sexual charge between us. It was there, in the atmosphere of the house, in the air, like static electricity. Or maybe it was only there for Lucy and me. I don't know.

I accompanied Lucy to Maydew House that afternoon, against my better judgement, afraid that we'd somehow give ourselves away. Lucy assured me everything would be all right and, ostensibly, so it was. I sat watching as Daisy worked at the bust, too absorbed in her task, it seemed, to be aware of any change in the way we behaved towards each other. The bust was still disturbingly reminiscent of you. Lucy had always resembled you more closely than most sisters. I saw that now, so clearly that I could only wonder why I hadn't seen it before. I sat in silence for an hour, dodging Lucy's gaze as much as I could, while Daisy's long, nimble fingers pressed and prised at the clay, and dust-motes clouded in the sunlight that crept around the workshop walls. I realized quite clearly and unambiguously then that it wasn't your ghost I was chasing in Lucy. It was you renewed, and altered, too, moulded precisely to my liking, and my loving, as Lucy had implied she could be, willingly and freely. It was a sick and desperate thing. It should never have been. But looking at Lucy, sitting so patiently and placidly, waiting for me as well as Daisy, I knew it was what I'd anticipated at some level from the very moment she'd invited me to Otherways. And what she'd anticipated, too. The unimaginable had merely been the unacknowledged.

We were greedy for each other's company. We didn't want to share it with anyone else. Unconcerned now about how such things might look, Lucy told Nesta she needn't bother coming in for the rest of the week because we'd be out and about so much. We went nowhere, of course, although, in another sense, we went everywhere. I need you to understand that. For those few days at Otherways, we really were two lovers in a gilded cage. The door was open, but we had no intention of leaving.

The dreams diminished. Some echo of them remained, in a strange feeling that repeatedly came over me. It seemed to me that we weren't alone in the house, that there was somebody else close by, in another room, on the stairs, never heard or seen, but present. Sometimes I'd look up, expecting to see a figure in a doorway, or turn round, convinced there was a person standing just behind me. Always I was wrong. There was nobody there. Except Lucy and me.

We didn't talk about the Milners or the Strathallans or their sundry tragedies. Suddenly they'd become too much like ill omens for me to want to dwell on them. I had my own tragedy in the making now, anyway, blind though I was to the form it was already assuming.

'I'm not going to be able to give you up,' Lucy said to me after we'd made love in the cool lethargy of a still, grey dawn. It was the day of our projected trip to Newmarket with Daisy. The week was wearing on. Matt would be back soon. He was bound to be. Our small chunk of the future was nearly done.

'You have to give me up. *I* have to give *you* up.'

'Why?'

'Because Matt's your husband. He's also my best and oldest friend. This would destroy him.'

'He's stronger than you think.'

'Not strong enough.'

'Are you? Am I? How can we resist what's so obviously right?'

'But it isn't right. It's all wrong. You know that.'

'I know what I feel. And what you feel. We have to trust that. I don't really think we're going to be able to stop, do you? Not when it comes to it.'

'I—'

'Don't answer. Not now. I know what you think you ought to say. And I know what we'll do when the time comes. They aren't the same, believe me. Not the same at all.'

*   *   *

I remembered her words several times as the day unfolded. Daisy was with us for the greater part of it, so there could be no hint of intimacy between Lucy and me, no suggestion that any kind of crisis was looming. We were both pensive and distracted, though no more so than recent bereavement might account for. So I hoped, anyway. But I'd reckoned without Daisy's perspicacity. She chose a moment during the afternoon when Lucy wasn't with us to let me know she'd seen through us very clearly.

We'd gone down to watch the horses parade before one of the later races, leaving Lucy in the stand. 'Can you tell how they're going to run from just looking at them?' I asked, as the twitching thoroughbreds circled in front of us.

'Oh yes,' Daisy replied. 'Appearances aren't really as deceptive as some people like to think.'

'Perhaps it's your sculptor's eye.'

'Perhaps. Or just old age. One learns to recognize pretence when one sees it.'

I smiled. 'Are any of these pretending?'

'No. Only humans do that.'

'But we're talking about horses.'

'Are we?' She looked at me sharply. 'I rather thought we'd moved on to something else.'

'Had we?'

'You've recently lost your wife. Lucinda has lost her sister. Such experiences can lead to misjudgements: of what is right, of what will last, of what is truly . . . desirable.'

'I'm not sure I know what you mean, Daisy.'

'I'm sure you do. Lucinda isn't as strong as she supposes. Attribute *that* insight to my sculptor's eye, if you like. I see the frailty beneath the skin. Yours as well

118

as hers. You seem to me to be in the process of making a considerable mistake. Possibly the greatest mistake of your life.'

'But it is *my* life.'

'And is therefore none of my business?'

I shrugged. 'You said it.'

'Lucinda is my friend.'

'And would like to remain so, I'm sure.'

'Just think about what you're doing, Tony.' She paused. 'That's all I ask.'

Daisy said nothing in Lucy's presence that revealed her understanding of the situation. She was all bright-eyed levity as the meeting ended and we started back for Rutland. We stopped for a meal at a restaurant in Stamford on the way, and she went on behaving as if our conversation hadn't taken place. Such glances as we exchanged were on her part defiantly open, declaring to me, it seemed, that she withdrew nothing and resented nothing. The choice was ours to make. But she was determined to ensure that I appreciated there was a choice to make.

If I'd been in the slightest doubt about that, it didn't last much longer. When we got back to Otherways that night, after dropping Daisy at Maydew House, there was a message from Matt waiting for us on the answerphone.

'I'll be leaving tomorrow night. Flight BA174. It gets into Heathrow at seven o'clock Saturday morning. I'm hoping one of you – or both of you – will be there to meet me. Lots to tell you. Bye.'

'Lots to tell *us*,' said Lucy, as she switched off the machine. 'There's irony for you.'

'So soon,' I murmured numbly.

'What difference does it make? Whether sooner or later, we have to face it.'

'Face *him*, you mean. With this. With what we've become.'

'I'm not ashamed of it. Are you?'

'Not ashamed, no. Frightened, I suppose.'

'Of what he'll say?'

'No. Of what it'll do to him. Of what *we'll* do to him.'

'Do we have a choice?'

'Yes. Of course. We have to . . . think . . . about . . .' I stopped, hearing in my voice the echo of Daisy's words.

'I think we have to tell him the truth.' Lucy faced me, her eyes searching my face for confirmation, for reassurance – and for complicity. 'But if you can't bring yourself to, and if you won't let me . . .'

'Yes? What then?'

'We can go on in secret.' Her head fell. 'Somehow. I don't know. Without him realizing. We can find a way.'

'You'd be willing to do that?'

'I can't give you up. I told you. It's as simple as that.'

So now, here we were, where we were always bound to arrive, lured by passion and longing into the sordid beginnings of conspiracy. We could destroy him, or we could deceive him. There was no middle way.

'Do you love me, Tony?'

'How can I—'

'*Do you?*'

'I—' Breaking free of her gaze, I strode to the window and stared out at the dusk gathering moistly over the garden. I heard Lucy move in the room behind me. I sensed the whirl and confusion of her thoughts as well as mine.

'Well?'

'I need you. I want you. But . . .'

'Is that all?' She was at my shoulder now. 'Don't you understand? Yes, this will break Matt up. Of course it will. If he finds out. But he doesn't have to find out. There are ways and means. Trust me.'

'*He* trusts *us*. That's the problem, Lucy. There, in that inconvenient, stubborn little word. Trust. What do we do about that?'

'What do you suggest we do?'

'I suggest we stop. Now. Before it's too late.'

'*Stop?*'

'Take a step back. Think about what it means.'

'It means one of two things: either this is real and true and wonderful, or it's not. Either we give in to what we feel for each other, or what we feel, what *you* feel, is shown to be a lie.'

'It's never been that.'

'Then what is it – if you can walk away from it so easily?'

'I never said it would be easy.'

'But possible, right? Feasible. Survivable.'

'It has to be.'

'Not for me.' She pulled me round, forcing me to face her. 'For you, apparently. But not for me.'

'Maybe I should go away. Before Matt gets back. For a few days, anyway. While we both . . . think things through.'

'I don't need to think anything through.'

'But I do.'

'Yes. And your needs come first, don't they?'

'Of course not. I just—'

She hit me a stinging blow on the cheek and I staggered back, more in shock than pain. She aimed another blow and I raised my arm to fend her off. Her face crumpled and tears welled from her eyes. She pulled away. 'Bastard!' she cried. 'You fucking bastard.' Then she reeled to the door, sobbing as she went.

'Lucy!'

'Leave me alone.' She looked back at me from the doorway, her eyes red and brimming, her whole body quivering. 'Isn't that what you've been saying you want to do?' Then the door slammed and she was gone.

I forced myself to wait half an hour before knocking on her bedroom door. But there was no answer, not even when I called to her and pleaded with her to respond. Finally, I tried to open the door. But it was locked. I was excluded as well as rejected.

I went back downstairs and drank some Scotch, nursing the glass in my lap as I sat by the French windows, watching darkness close around the house. I'd known such a moment of lacerating misery was bound to follow as soon as Lucy and I had admitted our attraction to each other. It hadn't stopped me. But maybe, it bleakly occurred to me, Lucy *hadn't* known. If not, it was even worse for her than it was for me. Small wonder she thought I'd played her false. I'd betrayed her now, as well as Matt.

Eventually, around midnight, I crept upstairs and went to bed. In the morning, I told myself, things wouldn't seem so bad. We'd find some way out of this. We had to.

I must have fallen asleep quite quickly. I have no memory of lying awake at all. My next memory is of being roused, suddenly, by a movement in the room, and looking up to see a figure standing beside the bed. There was enough moonlight peeping between the curtains for me to make the figure out as a woman. She was naked, tall and slim, with dark hair falling over her shoulders, and she was trembling, not from the cold, for it felt stiflingly hot in the room, but from fear, it seemed, as she pointed and stared at me.

'Who are you?' she said in a quavering voice. 'What are you doing here?'

I tried to speak, but could only mumble. I reached for the bedside lamp, but my arm moved slowly, impeded by something, responding reluctantly to the urgings of my brain.

'You're real, aren't you?' she went on. 'I'm not imagining you.'

My fingers found the switch, but couldn't seem to move it, fumbling for a hold. I was gripped not just by alarm, but by sheer, unreasoning terror. I knew who she was. But I didn't want to believe it.

'Tell me who you are. I have to know. Why are you here?'

At last, the switch moved. There was a click. Electric light burst into the darkness.

And she was no longer there. I was awake, with the bedside lamp burning. I must have fallen asleep with it still on. The rest had merely been a dream. But the dream had seemed real enough to leave me bathed in sweat, bewildered by my susceptibility to the inventions of my subconscious.

I scrambled out of bed and blundered to the bathroom, tugging at the light cord as I pushed open the door, aware, as I did so, of unreasonable heat and humidity, and of the sound of water dripping into water. Then I saw the cause.

The bath was full, very nearly to the brim, with the hot tap dripping. I turned it off tightly, pulled the plug and watched the water drain away, asking myself whether there was any chance I could have run a bath and somehow forgotten doing so. But I was as certain as I could be of anything that I'd done no such thing. It was impossible. Yet there was the water swirling down the plughole. There were the streams of condensation on the mirror and the windows. There was the proof that somebody had, even if it wasn't me.

Sleep was out of the question after that. I bathed my face in cold water, threw on some clothes and went down to the kitchen. The night was just beginning to weaken outside, the sky paling as dawn made its first inroads. A few birds were already singing in the garden. I brewed some coffee and began seriously to wonder, as I sat at the table drinking it, whether I was losing my mind. Maybe, I reasoned, it was delayed shock, following your death: an unhinging of reason as well as emotion. If so, Lucy and I might be caught up in a mutual aberration that later, a few months down the road, we'd be happy to forget.

Lucy walked quietly into the room as I was sitting there. She was wearing a short towelling bathrobe and mules. Her hair was unbrushed, her eyes red-rimmed and hollow. She stopped and looked at me. A moment passed. Then she drew out a chair, the legs scraping on the floor, and sat down opposite me.

'Is that a bruise on your cheek?' she murmured.

'Could be,' I said, touching the place where she'd hit me and noticing for the first time how tender it was.

124

'I'm sorry.'

'I think I deserved it.'

'Not really. What you were saying . . .' She reached across the table, and I stretched out my hand to meet hers. 'Well, it had to be said, didn't it? We can't just . . . ignore everything.'

'And everyone?'

'Exactly.'

'Much as we'd like to.'

'I know I would.'

'Me, too. But . . . there are other people to consider.'

'I haven't slept much. What about you?'

'Not much. And not well.'

'Too many things to think about, I suppose.'

'Probably.'

'Well, I *have* thought. We've got to go into this with our eyes open, Tony. We've got to be fully committed, not just to each other, but to riding out however much anguish there's going to be along the way.'

'I agree.'

'So, maybe you were right. If you go away, for a few days, we'll know, won't we, whether we love each other enough . . . to make the rest of it bearable?'

'It seems that way to me.' It was only partly a lie. I was too unsure of myself, in that house, in her company, to judge what a breathing space might achieve. But that we needed one I didn't doubt.

'You will stay with me until tomorrow, won't you?'

I should have refused. I should have insisted on leaving that morning. It would have been kinder to both of us. But leaving was going to be a grim business. And I knew we still had one more day.

'Won't you?' she repeated. But by then she must have been able to read the answer in my face.

*　　*　　*

The knowledge that it was our last day together – at least for a while – tinged that Friday's pleasures with despair. The hours flashed by while we feasted on the things that would soon be denied us. I don't mean just sex. I mean lying side by side and watching the trees move in the breeze and the sunlight fade and flare between the clouds. And talking. We did a lot of that. But I'm not sure now what it was we talked about. It doesn't matter, anyway. You were our mutual confidante, Marina. We trusted you with our secrets. So, now you were gone, it was easy, in a way, to trust each other.

Some secrets we still kept back, of course. When I came as close as I dared to mentioning the strange things I'd seen at Otherways, I was aware that Lucy's candour was suddenly reined in. There were limits, I realized, to what she was ready to reveal to me. Perhaps, for both our sakes, there had to be.

'Have you ever experienced anything . . . ghostly at Otherways?' I asked, as we stood on the lawn, near the rhododendron bank, down which a path had once led to the sunken garden.

'No,' said Lucy, with a little frown of puzzlement that turned rapidly into a smile of amusement. 'Whatever makes you ask?'

'Something Matt said.'

'About ghosts?'

'Indirectly.'

'I don't know what he can have meant. There are no ghosts at Otherways. Perhaps there ought to be, in view of the things that have happened here. But I've seen nothing and sensed nothing. To me, the house seems . . .' She glanced towards it. 'Surprisingly peaceful.'

'I've had some strange dreams since arriving here.'

'How strange?'

'Stranger than any I've had before.'

She shrugged. 'I can't explain that.'

'You know you said you dreamed of us making love before we did?'

'Yes.'

'So did I.'

'Well, that I *can* explain.' She reached out and caressed my cheek, stroking the bruise across the cheekbone with her thumb. 'Your dream showed you what you most desired. And, as it happens, what I most desired too.' Her hand fell away. She looked at the house again. 'No ghosts, Tony. Just you and me. No nightmares. Just dreams. Maybe we're dreaming right now. If we are, I don't want to wake up.'

'Neither do I.'

'Then let's go on dreaming. For a little longer.' She began walking slowly back across the lawn, towards the bridge across the moat. And, after a moment's hesitation, I started after her.

Night came. If we slept at all, I don't remember it. But I remember the tears that filled her eyes as we lay together. And I remember the heavy foreboding that clamped itself around my mind one second after we'd as good as forced each other to a last despairing climax. The wrongness and the madness of what we'd allowed to happen between us was never clearer to me than in that long moment of unravelling limbs and slowing breath. There was no way forward and no way back. Waiting for us now there was only the cool grey finality of dawn.

*   *   *

'You won't be here when I get back with Matt?' Lucy asked as we stood by her car, both of us shivering in the misty chill of daybreak.

'No.'

'How shall I explain that to him?'

'Say a buyer's been found for Stanacombe and he's pressing for an early completion, so I've had to go down there to sort things out.'

'Is that where you'll be?'

'I'm not sure.'

'And how long will you be gone?'

'I'm not sure about that, either.'

'But you will be back, won't you?' There was a skittering anguish in her eyes, more than I had the power to dispel. Though I would have done, gladly, had I been able.

'Of course.'

'Promise?'

'I promise.'

Then she kissed and hugged me and, with a set little smile of false courage, she climbed into the car and drove away.

I could hear the roar of the engine as she accelerated down the lane towards Hambleton. It faded gradually into the pervading silence, until its distant note was finally extinguished. Then I was truly alone. I thought of that morning at Stanacombe, when you drove away for the last time. It had been the present once. Now it was the past. So, too, was this moment, a cusp between the altered states we call yesterday and tomorrow. I'd be back. Of course I would. But how and when and why – and what I'd find – lay still in wait for me. And for Lucy. The future was preparing its ambush. For both of us.

*　　*　　*

I'd already packed my bags and loaded them into my car. There was nothing left for me to do but drive away in Lucy's wake. I followed her route at first, round the northern shore of Rutland Water to Empingham. She'd be on the A1 by now, I reckoned, speeding south. I headed back round the southern shore, planning to stop at the lakeside car park near Edith Weston and consider my options. For the moment, I had absolutely no idea where I was going to go.

Before I'd reached Edith Weston, however, I noticed a car behind me in the rear-view mirror. It was a grey Morris Minor. It slowed as I slowed, accelerated as I accelerated. It was Rainbird. And he was following me.

He went on following, all the way to the car park. There wasn't another vehicle on the entire expanse of tarmac when we arrived. I stopped in the centre and watched him trace a wide arc round the white-lined bays that finally brought him to a halt right next to me, facing in the opposite direction. He wound down his window. Mine was already open.

'Good morning, Tony,' he said, giving me his scout-master's grin. 'Spot of insomnia?'

'What do you want, Norman?'

'It's more a question of what *you* want, isn't it? Something to do, perhaps. Somewhere to go.'

'I'm not running errands for you.'

'You'd be doing yourself a favour.'

'How do you make that out?'

'You're as eager to penetrate the secrets of that house as I am.' He pulled a piece of paper from his pocket. 'And this is your best chance of doing so.'

'Don't tell me. It's Strathallan's address.'

'Correct.'

'I'm not interested.'

Chapter Five

So I found myself on the A1 after all that day, heading north, not south. Rainbird had it about right, damn him to hell. I wanted answers to questions, and I had the best of all reasons to go in search of them. Whether I liked it or not, I was part of the mystery now. I'd left Otherways, but it hadn't left me. I'd seen things there, and done things there, I couldn't quite believe. But I couldn't deny them, either. I was running away, it's true – from Lucy, from Matt, from myself. But I was also running after something. I just didn't know what it was.

It was late afternoon when I crossed the Forth Road Bridge into Fife, early evening by the time I tracked down the address Rainbird had given me: Broomhaven, one of ten or a dozen large, bland modern bungalows in a cul-de-sac on the outskirts of a village a few miles inland from St Andrews. The houses themselves could have been in suburban Surrey. Only the distant view they commanded of St Andrews Bay, sparkling and benign in the mellow sunshine, testified to how far I'd travelled.

I spotted Strathallan even before I was certain which house was his. A short, straight-backed old man, with a full head of yellowy-white hair and a firm-jawed face, was mowing a lawn that didn't seem to need it in broad meticulous stripes. He was my man. I felt sure of it. And there was the neatly inscribed sign at the foot of the drive to confirm it: Broomhaven.

He throttled back the mower as I climbed out of the car and approached. 'Mr Strathallan?'

'Aye.' The mower engine cut out. Strathallan cocked his head and frowned enquiringly at me. He had to be pushing eighty, but he looked more like a fit sixty-five-year-old, a man unlikely to entertain notions of the kind I was eager to discuss.

'My name's Tony Sheridan. We've never met.'

'Nor have we. I've got a good memory for faces.'

'I'm a friend of Matt and Lucy Prior. The people who bought Otherways from you.'

'Is that so?'

'I've been staying with them recently.'

'At Otherways?'

'Yes.'

'You've come a long way, then.'

'I have.'

'To see me?'

'Yes.'

'Why might that be?'

'It's a little . . . difficult to explain. I was hoping . . . we might talk.'

'About what?'

'Some . . . strange experiences I've had there.'

The frown became more of a scowl. 'You've come to the wrong man, Mr Sheridan.'

'I don't think so.'

'I can't help you.' With that, he started the mower again and took off up the lawn at a measured tread.

I stood there, curbing my impatience, as he progressed up and down his clipped and shaved rectangle of weedless grass. Several minutes passed. He reached the end of the last swathe, stopped and turned off the mower. I walked across to join him.

'Still here?'

'It's too late to start back for Rutland.'

'Best find yourself some accommodation, then. There are several hotels in St Andrews.'

'You'd be doing me an enormous favour if you at least heard me out.'

'But I don't owe you a favour, small or large.'

'Maybe you owe the Priors one. For failing to mention the murder at Otherways.'

'*Caveat emptor*. They should know that.'

'I read Martin Fisher's article. In the magazine you left behind.'

'What magazine was that?'

'I read Fisher's book, as well. *Seven Faces of Treason*.'

'You've clearly been busy.'

'I also know about your daughter.'

'Leave her be.'

'I wish I could. The thing is, I think I may have seen her.'

He turned away slightly, leaning heavily on the handlebar of the mower. 'Rosalind's more than twenty years dead, man. What the hell do you mean by coming all the way up here to say a thing like that?'

'I can't believe you lived at Otherways for as long as you did without experiencing some of its . . . stranger qualities.'

'I didn't see any ghosts, if that's what you mean.'

'They may have been there, even if you didn't see them.'

133

'That's the kind of rubbish my wife used to—' He broke off with a snort. His knuckles were white where his hands clasped the mower. 'Will I never be free of it?' he growled.

'We can never be free of the past.'

'Nor the future, eh?' He seemed to look through and beyond me, smiling gently at some thought my words had planted in his mind. 'Well, we'll let that lie. I'll tell you this. Through all the years we lived at Otherways after Rosalind's death, she never appeared to us. Jean would have liked her to, God knows, but she never did. So, why to you, a total stranger?'

'I can't answer that. I may have been dreaming. I seemed to see somebody, in the room she slept in, where I've been sleeping myself. Of course, I've never even seen a photograph of your daughter, so how could I recognize her? But you must have a photograph.'

'And, no doubt, if I show it to you, you'll say that clinches it.'

'I'm not trying to make a fool of you, Mr Strathallan.'

'What are you trying to do?'

'Pin something down. For my benefit, not yours. I admit that.'

His eyebrows twitched in surprise. 'Well, you're candid. I'll say that for you.'

'Could I see a photograph of Rosalind?'

He thought for a moment, then he sighed. 'Very well. If you must. Come inside.'

The interior of Broomhaven was as immaculate as the exterior, though far too spartan to seem in any way homely. It was furnished smartly enough, but there wasn't a single picture on the walls, nor the merest hint of anything decorative. Strathallan had reverted to barrack-room order and cleanliness in his old age. He had no place left in his life for the detritus of former times, as the roomful of clutter at Otherways had testified. Even the promised photograph of his dead only child had to be fetched from a closed bureau drawer, loudly though the empty mantelpiece in the drawing room cried out for a framed snapshot or two.

'Here you are,' he said. 'It was taken at her graduation, a month or so before her death.'

'Yes.' I looked at it. 'I see.' And what I saw, beyond reasonable doubt, was the woman I'd dreamed of, standing by my bed at Otherways: a dream of a woman I'd never met.

'You look neither surprised nor disappointed.'

'Because I *am* neither.' I handed the photograph back. 'I believe it was your daughter I saw. But I don't expect you to believe it.'

'That's just as well.'

'Could I ask you . . . why you think she killed herself?'

'You could ask. But I couldn't answer. She had everything to look forward to. And we made sure she wanted for nothing. She was going to be married that autumn.'

'To Martin Fisher.'

'The very same.'

'Could he have been the reason?'

'No, no. Martin was a good lad.'

'But inquisitive about the past.'

Strathallan shrugged. 'It was his occupation. Still is, as far as I know.'

'Did he ever succeed in tracking down James Milner's confession?'

'I wouldn't know. He and Jean used to keep in touch. But, since Jean died . . . I haven't bothered.'

135

'Is it possible, do you think, that Rosalind's suicide and the Milner murder were somehow connected?'

'Utterly *impossible*, I'd have said.'

'She never . . . saw anything odd herself . . . at Otherways?'

'Certainly not.' His vehemence was too much. It was clear to me he was lying. I might have believed him, of course, but for the evidence of the diary. There I had the advantage of him. He didn't know the diary existed. 'She was a sensible, well-balanced girl.'

'Not altogether, surely.'

'What would you know?'

'Nothing. Obviously.'

'Aye. Aye, of course. I'm sorry.' He flapped a hand apologetically. 'It upsets me to talk about it, even now, after all these years. That's why I try not to. Not even to think about it. Such a waste. Such a criminal waste.' He walked off with the photograph, shaking his head dolefully. When he came back, he said, 'Will you have a drink?' He sounded as if he genuinely wanted me to accept. Perhaps none of his defensive strategies were quite proof against loneliness.

'All right. Thank you. I will.'

'Whisky?'

'Fine.'

He poured us both generous measures of an Islay malt, and we sat down in leather armchairs on either side of the gleamingly empty fireplace, the evening sunlight slanting between us.

'Why did you move here, Mr Strathallan?'

'I'm a local boy. I enjoy my golf. But only links golf is the genuine article. Those Midlands courses are effeminate creatures.'

'I wonder you didn't leave Rutland sooner, then.'

'I would have, but for Jean. She wanted to stay at Otherways, close to her memories of Rosalind. The girl was born there, after all. Jean felt leaving would be an admission that we had really lost her.'

'But you had.'

'Aye. So, when Jean died . . .' He shrugged and sipped his whisky. 'Who's been feeding you all this about the Milners, Mr Sheridan? I should like to know who I've to thank for your visit. Who I've to thank for passing on my address, come to that.'

'Lucy found the magazine amongst your stuff. You can hardly complain, since you left it there.'

'I suppose not.'

'For the rest, you can blame Norman Rainbird.'

Strathallan snorted in disgust. 'Rainbird? Good God. You can't rely on a word that man says. If he is a man, rather than some new species of amphibian that's crawled out of Rutland Water.'

'He can be disarmingly accurate about a lot of things.'

'Including my whereabouts, it seems. It makes my flesh creep to think he's keeping track of me. Why, in God's name?'

'You must know, surely.'

'The confession?'

'Yes. He believes James Milner sent it to Daisy Temple, by way of explanation, or expiation, for his murder of her sister, and that Daisy subsequently gave it to you.'

'Aye, aye. To help heal the wounds inflicted by Rosalind's suicide. I've heard all that. From Rainbird himself. God knows where he gets it from. It's all rubbish. Daisy Temple never gave me sight of such a document, far less the keeping of it.'

I had no sense now that Strathallan was lying. This

sounded like the unvarnished truth. 'Martin Fisher also seemed to believe Daisy was the recipient.'

'So he did. And so she may have been. But it's equally possible James Milner told that *Rutland Mercury* man, Garvey, that he'd written a confession simply to get him off his back. Alternatively, the recipient may have been Milner's brother, rather than his sister-in-law. Either way, the document would be conclusively out of reach. Poor Martin never cared to entertain that thought. He always wanted to believe the key to those two brothers' lives lay waiting somewhere for him to close his hand around it.'

'He seems to have abandoned the search since.'

'He abandoned it the day Rosalind died. That was the breaking of him, I should say. He took it hard. And that's to his credit, I suppose. Perhaps you don't know what it's like to lose the woman you love.'

'I do, as a matter of fact. My wife . . . died recently.'

'She did?' He looked at me more in amazement than sympathy.

'A cliff fall. Near our home, in Cornwall. I'm . . . trying to come to terms with it.'

'You'll not find that easy.' He rose and, without consulting me, topped up my glass. Then he topped up his own and sat down again. 'Have you considered that this could explain what you experienced at Otherways?'

'As a trauma-induced hallucination, you mean?'

'Aye. Something like that.'

'I'd be happy to. But for the fact that my hallucination turns out to be an uncanny likeness of somebody I've never met or seen – other than in the photograph you just showed me.'

'You can't be sure.'

'I feel sure.'

'It's not possible.'

'Everything is possible, isn't it?'

'No. I regret to have to tell you it isn't.'

'Didn't Rosalind ever once hint that something was wrong? That Otherways was . . . affecting her?'

'She did not.' He sipped his whisky and stared into the glass. Then he smiled, almost in spite of himself, and said, 'The truth is, Mr Sheridan, that *if* my daughter had started seeing – ghosts, shall we call them? – at Otherways, I'm the last person she'd have confided in.' He tapped his forehead. 'Too rigid a mind, do you see? Too many years of military conditioning. She'd have known better than to come to me.'

'Who would she have gone to, then? Your wife?'

'No, no. Jean was far too cowed by me to be any use in that regard. I see that now, clearly enough. And Rosalind saw it even then. Nor do I think she'd have cared to burden her fiancé with such stuff. They were still at the starry-eyed stage, you understand. A mite early for worrying psychological revelations.'

'Did she have a particularly close friend?'

'None so very close. Nor any who'd know Otherways at all well. Except . . .' He grimaced. 'There was Cristina.'

'Who was she?'

'Our au pair. Cristina . . . Pedreira, her name was. She lived with us that last year of Rosalind's life. We'd had others before, but none who'd been on Rosalind's wavelength the way Cristina seemed to be. After the funeral, she had the effrontery – and the heartlessness – to tell us we hadn't understood our daughter. That Rosalind had needed help and we hadn't supplied it.'

'Help with what?'

'God knows. She never said. Or if she did . . .' He drank

139

some more whisky. 'It was a grim time. I was angry as well as grieving. Angry at Rosalind for doing such a stupid, drastic thing. And at myself for not spotting the signs that she might. I was hardly in a receptive mood when that Portuguese bitch started—'

'Portuguese, did you say?'

'Aye. Cristina was Portuguese. The one before her was Finnish. The one before *her* was Greek. Oh, it was a regular United Nations.'

'But Cristina Pedreira was Portuguese. From Lisbon, perhaps?'

'Maybe. I can't recall.'

'Emile Posnan ended up in Lisbon.'

'What of it?'

'It's a coincidence, isn't it?'

'That's all it is, at best. We got her through the usual agency, man. There can't have been any . . .' He frowned. 'At least, I think that's how we got her. Jean handled all the arrangements. I don't . . . It's so long ago.'

'What's happened to her?'

'We sent her packing.'

'Back to Portugal?'

'Back to wherever the blue blazes she wanted to go. Out of our lives.'

'Do you wish you'd never bought Otherways?'

'Of course. It seemed a good deal at the time. It seemed about the only good thing to come out of the Milner case. Those security breaches at Harwell did my career no favours, I can tell you. But the Milners were bad luck, weren't they? I should never have had anything to do with them. Or their house.'

'Do you believe in luck?'

'It seems I have to. Otherways has obliged me to, you could say. Or the people who've lived there have.

140

Lived *and* died. I only hope the Priors have broken the trend.'

'You don't sound very confident.'

'How can I be? The record speaks for itself.'

'Is Cedric Milner still alive?'

'I've heard nothing to suggest he isn't. Eking out a miserable old age in some crumbling apartment block in Moscow is how I prefer to think of him. The collapse of the Soviet Union must have hit his sort hard, I'm glad to say.'

'Martin Fisher never seems to have got to grips with his reasons for selling out.'

'No more did I. The man was an enigma.'

'You really think the material he passed on was important?'

'It didn't come any more important. Not then. The Bomb, man. Death-dealing stuff. How could he give that away to a monster like Stalin?'

'Would you still like to ask him?'

'Oh yes. I still would.' A distant look came into his eyes. 'But I'm never going to get the chance.' I had the impression he was speaking of several chances, if not all the chances of his life, bundled into one. 'It's too late now.'

It was nearly dark when we finished talking. The whisky and the stream of his reminiscence had mellowed Strathallan. He offered me a bed for the night, which I gratefully accepted. I was tired after the long drive and the largely sleepless night that had gone before it. In the cell-like spare room I fell instantly and deeply asleep, beyond the reach of dreams, let alone those that had troubled me at Otherways. I felt safe under Strathallan's roof. Broomhaven was his kind of refuge:

141

plain, unadorned, untrammelled by associations with other people and other places. That night, it was my kind of refuge, too.

I slept late and rose to find myself alone in the house. Strathallan had gone out. I scouted around for some breakfast, and was sitting over the remains of it in the kitchen when he returned with a Sunday paper and the windblown look of someone who'd gone further than necessary to get it.

'You're up, then,' he said. 'I was beginning to wonder.'

'I haven't been getting enough sleep lately.'

'Why might that be?'

'Otherways hasn't proved restful.'

'We'll leave that subject alone, if you don't mind. Are you going back there today?'

'To be honest, I'm not sure where I'm going.'

'Try home. Wherever that is.'

'I had another possibility in mind.'

'What was that?'

'Martin Fisher.'

'You should leave it alone, man, you really should.' Strathallan shook his head at me, like a disappointed schoolmaster. 'As Martin should have done.'

'Would you know how to find him?'

'I used to. He may have moved on. More likely not. I spoke to him last year, to tell him Jean had died. He was still in the old place, then. A houseboat on the Thames. It used to give him Bohemian flair. Now I should think it just gives him bronchitis every winter. He takes phone calls at a nearby pub. Lives for the drink as well as in it, you might say. Blames me for introducing him to the hard stuff. But he only really took to it after Rosalind

142

died. Not a happy man, to be sure. *Samphire*, the boat's called. Moored at Chelsea.'

'I may look him up.'

'I wouldn't, if I were you.'

'Listen, there's something I've been meaning to tell you. About Rosalind.'

'What else can there be to say?'

'There was a diary, hidden in the chimney breast in her room. Lucy found it.'

'Rosalind's diary?'

'Yes.'

'Oh God.' He sank down in a chair. 'Oh dear God.'

'It's only a pocket affair. Just appointments and such. It runs from September 'seventy-five to August 'seventy-six. There's nothing sensational in it, nothing . . . revelatory.'

'Is that supposed to be a comfort?'

'I just thought you ought to know. If you contacted Lucy, I'm sure she'd be happy to send it to you.'

'I'm not sure I want to see it.'

'It's up to you. We all have to find the way that best suits us . . . to live with a thing like that.'

'So we do.'

'One thing I noticed, during her terms at Leeds, was a lot of appointments with somebody called H.D.'

'Means nothing to me.'

'I just wondered . . .'

'A tutor, maybe.'

'Maybe.'

'Or maybe not.' He looked at me soulfully. 'You'll have deduced already that I knew less about my daughter than I should have done, as a conscientious parent.'

'I'm not sure I—'

'Well, I would.' He rose, ambled across to the worktop,

143

checked the temperature of the teapot, then poured himself a cup and drank from it, leaning back against the sink as he gazed into the middle distance of his past. 'When Rosalind was a child, she used to have an imaginary playmate. Children often do, I'm told. I say playmate, but imaginary resident of the house would be more accurate. She called her Ann. We assumed she'd heard something about the Milners from other children at her school, but we could never prove that's where she'd got the name from. It could have been pure coincidence, of course. The name's common enough. It stopped when she went away to boarding school.'

'Just a phase, then.'

'Perhaps.' He drained his cup. 'Or perhaps she just stopped telling us about such things as she grew older. I lived at Otherways for more than forty years, Sheridan. I never heard or saw or felt anything . . . supernatural. But it wouldn't have surprised me so very much if I had. It's not what you'd call an entirely normal house, now, is it?'

'No. It isn't.'

'I wish, for Rosalind's sake, I'd realized a long time ago that it wasn't wise to live there. And, for her, not safe at all.'

'I've sensed nothing dangerous about the place.'

'I dare say not.' He turned away to rinse his cup. 'But if you'll take my advice, you won't wait until you do.'

The lure of the chase was too strong now. There wasn't the slightest chance I'd abandon the search for whatever amounted to the truth about Otherways. It had become a way of filling the void that your death had reduced most of my life to. And a way of postponing the reckoning where Lucy and Matt were concerned. *Everything goes, nothing stays*? I don't think so. There's always some trace, some clue left to be uncovered. Everything goes, yes. But a part of everything remains. Nothing is absolute, not even death.

London began south of Watford, in a haze across the sun and a horizon of lethargic suburbs. I'd driven for seven long hours, but felt more alert than I had any right to, sustained by nervous energy and a strange, almost indecent excitement at the prospect of tracking down Martin Fisher.

I didn't take the direct route from the end of the M1 to Chelsea. Instead, I followed the North Circular south-west, like we used to when returning home to Chiswick from the Midlands, all the way to our old house. I sat outside, looking at it. Nothing had changed outwardly. It was eerily imaginable that, if I walked up and rang the doorbell, you might answer the door. Or I might. Christ, it was a strange thought. It worried me that it had even formed in my mind.

I hadn't actually gone to Chiswick to act out a fantasy, though. I'd remembered the formidable stock of spirits at that wine merchant we sometimes used. I got there just as he was closing and found what I wanted, then I headed for Chelsea.

Samphire was even more dilapidated than Strathallan's description of its owner had led me to expect: a converted barge, in obvious need of painting, varnishing and caulking, sagging at its mooring alongside several much smarter craft near Battersea Bridge. I stepped gingerly aboard, got no answer to a shouted 'Hello' and ventured to an open hatchway.

It led down into a dark, sour-smelling cabin. The

145

sunlight outside was heavily filtered by grimy portholes and frayed curtains. What I could make out suggested the subfusc was a mercy. Old newspapers, foil takeaway cartons, empty bottles, discarded clothes and dirty crockery were a hazard at every step. The smell was a mixture of stale alcohol, unwashed flesh and stagnant river mud, in more or less equal quantities, plus a few other unidentifiable components.

A figure stirred on a bunk as I entered and rose on one elbow. 'Who the fuck's that?' he slurred, tugging back the nearest curtain for a look at me, then squinting painfully in the flood of light. Martin Fisher he had to be: a man in his late forties, with a thinning mop of grey hair, several days' growth of beard and the watery, ill-focused gaze of the confirmed alcoholic. He was wearing a grubby T-shirt, jeans and socks. He made it into a sitting position, rubbed his eyes and stared blearily at me. 'Did you hear me?'

'I'm Tony Sheridan.'

'Never heard of you.'

'That's right. You haven't.'

'What do you want?'

'You *are* Martin Fisher?'

'So they tell me.'

'I brought you a present.' I stood the bottle I'd bought in Chiswick on the empty corner of the table nearest him.

He leaned forward and peered at the label. 'Fuck me,' he muttered. 'Lagavulin. Just what the doctor ordered.' Then he frowned at me. 'How did you know this was my favourite?'

'I guessed.'

'Who are you?'

'I'm a fan.'

146

'What?'

'I've read some of your stuff.'

'Must be a fucking historian, then.'

'Kind of. *Seven Faces of Treason*, Fisher. Remember?'

'Where'd you pick that up? Car-boot sale?'

'I'm interested in the Milner case.'

'Which Milner case?'

'Both of them: the murder and the treason.'

'What for?'

'Some friends of mine live at Otherways.'

'Somebody has to.'

'Strange things happen there.'

'Yeah.' He lifted the bottle off the table and traced the lettering embossed on it with his finger, like a blind man reading a sacred text in braille. 'Too true they do.'

'Do you still write?'

'Cheques. When I can't avoid it. Fuck all else. See a glass anywhere?'

'Not a clean one.'

'It should be clean for Lagavulin. Try that cupboard.' He pointed unsteadily at a small cupboard behind me. I opened the door. Inside, on a shelf, stood a set of six crystal tumblers. They were dusty, but otherwise clean enough. I took one out and offered it to him. He nodded his approval, opened the bottle and poured a surprisingly modest tot for himself. 'Thanks,' he murmured. Then he took one restrained sip and sat there with his eyes closed, savouring the flavour. 'Fucking perfection, you know? The finest medicine known to man.'

'I got the idea from Duncan Strathallan.'

'You've been to see him?'

'Yes.' I pulled the only chair in the cabin out from beneath the table and sat down.

'Why?' He took another sip of the whisky, then set

the glass down on the table. His hand was steadier now, his words less slurred. 'Otherways, Fife, Chelsea. You an explorer as well as a historian?'

'A bit of both. I need to understand what's gone on in that house.'

'Madness. That's what's gone on. It's in the stone.' He sipped some more whisky, then turned to pull back another curtain, adjusting slowly, it seemed, to the fact that it was still light outside. 'And it's cost a few lives, hasn't it? More than a few.'

'How do you make that out?'

'The Milners. The Strathallans. Your friends.'

'My friends are fine.'

'No they're not. You wouldn't be here if they were. If *you* were, come to that.'

'Strathallan reckons his daughter's suicide was too much for you to take. Is he right?'

'Look around you. What do you think?'

'I'd say he has a point.'

'Yeah. So would I. But it's not a simple case of the grieving lover declining into the pitiful drunkard. I know. I've monitored the process, you could say. I loved Rosalind. But I could have got over her. Of course I could. That's not what did for me.'

'What did, then?'

'I lost it.' He sighed. 'The confidence. The touch. Call it what you like. The certainty that I could get a grip on the truth. The belief that I could see what was really going on. I didn't see a fucking thing. She fell apart in front of me. And the first I knew about it was when she was lying there at my feet. In pieces. In fucking pieces. She tried to tell me. But all I thought I heard was hysterical blather about bad dreams and strange visions. The spark went out in me when she died. She

148

was the only person who ever trusted me. And what good was I to her? A byline on the front page of the paper lying beside her on the seat of the car in that lay-by where they found her. That was me. Just a name. Ink on paper. Nothing else.'

'It's more than twenty years ago.'

'Yeah. And nearly sixty since James Milner murdered his wife. But what difference does that make if you can't move on?'

'And you can't?'

'There have been lots of times when I thought I could. But I was kidding myself. Now I've stopped kidding myself.'

'You never found James Milner's confession?'

'No.'

'Nor what made Cedric Milner tick?'

'That neither. I went to Moscow, you know, looking for the confession and the secret of brother Cedric's soul, a year or so after Rosalind died. I was trying to get back on the rails.'

'What happened?'

'Before I could smoke out Cedric, I got leaned on by the KGB. That's like being leaned on by an elephant. You either move or get crushed. They didn't want anyone bothering him. I never even found out where he was living. I got one fleeting glimpse of him, walking down a corridor in the physics department at the university. A tall, grey-haired man, moving fast. That and a few bruises were all I had to show for the trip. I'd stopped being lucky. No surprise, really. I suppose I'd used up all my luck with Rosalind. She was seventeen when I first met her. Magically beautiful. And something else, which made her look older. Something in her eyes. Something . . . otherworldly. I should have known then what would happen. But you don't, do you? You never do.'

'Strathallan mentioned an au pair. Cristina Pedreira.'

'Did he?' He drained the glass and poured another tot. 'Trust good old Dunc to call that bitch to mind.'

'You disliked her?'

'Dislike's a watery word for it. She filled Rosalind's head with all kinds of crap.'

'What kinds, specifically?'

'She did her best to push Rosalind over the edge,' he went on, ignoring my question and drinking more quickly as he spoke. Cristina Pedreira was clearly a sensitive subject. 'You know why? Because I turned her down. Just for that. She couldn't have me, so she made sure I couldn't have Rosalind. What a piece of work, eh? What a fucking piece of work.' His head rolled. His eyes closed for a moment, as if he was in pain. Then he clunked the glass down on the table and stared at me, holding himself steady with visible effort. 'I never told Dunc the worst of it. Not then. Not since. I'm not sure how he'd take it. But now, with Jean gone, well, I'm not sure I really care. Anyway, it doesn't actually arise as a question, does it? He isn't going to walk in here any time soon. The undertakers will have to come to scrape my leftovers off this bunk before Major Duncan Strathallan pays me a call.'

'What *was* the worst of it?'

'The worst? Oh yeah. Well, a bottle of Lagavulin buys that, I suppose. The day before she died, Rosalind phoned me, from a call box. That was weird in itself. She didn't make any sense. It was crazy stuff. She said she knew Cristina and I were having an affair. She said she'd seen me in Cristina's room at Otherways, when I was supposed to be in London. When I *was* in London,

150

as a matter of simple fact. What she was saying wasn't just untrue, it was impossible.'

'Surely you could have proved that to her?'

'Maybe. If I'd got the chance. I wasn't going to get anywhere over the phone, though. It was midweek and I couldn't get up to Rutland till the weekend. And she refused point-blank to come down to London. There was nothing I could do till I saw her. But I never did see her. She was dead before the weekend. And you know what the last thing she said to me was, her very last words before she slammed the phone down? "I saw you screwing Cristina." Nice, eh? A sweet thing to remember her by. A really touching sentiment.'

'How do you explain it?'

'There's only one way. Cristina told her it was happening. And Rosalind imagined it was true.'

'What did Cristina say?'

'Nothing. I couldn't accuse her openly. I had no way of countering any lies she invented. Dunc and Jean were so desperate to find a reason for Rosalind's suicide they'd have swallowed the story whole. When I managed to get the bitch on her own, she just denied everything. Even giving me the come-on in the first place. She just brazened it out. Then, while I was still getting my head straight, she left. Fucked off back to Portugal. There was some row with Dunc and Jean about her influence on Rosalind. They sent her on her way. She was probably pleased to go. There was nothing to stay for, was there? Not with Rosalind dead and me plotting a gruesome revenge, for all she knew.'

'Were you?'

'Sort of. I wheedled her address in Lisbon out of Jean and went looking for her a few months later. If I'd found her . . . well, I might be in a Portuguese gaol now, serving a life sentence for murder, rather than sitting here, in my very own prison hulk.'

'Why couldn't you find her?'

'She'd moved, without leaving a forwarding address. Vamoosed to Brazil with a new boyfriend, according to a neighbour.'

'What did you do?'

'What do you think I did? Flew to Rio and scoured the city, block by block? She was gone. Her sort don't leave a trail. I gave up.' He sighed. 'Story of my life, really.'

'Did you follow up the Posnan connection while you were there?'

'What connection?'

'He lived in Lisbon. Like Cristina Pedreira.'

'So what?'

'It's a thought-provoking coincidence, wouldn't you say?'

'No. Coincidences happen all the time. That's almost too paltry to count as one, anyway.'

'Can you be sure?'

'Her little bit of shit-stirring was personal. Between her and me. Nothing to do with Emile fucking Posnan.'

'Isn't everything at Otherways something to do with him?'

'It's getting to you, Sheridan.' He frowned at me, apparently in genuine pity. 'It's getting to you bad.'

'Do you know how the Strathallans came to employ Cristina Pedreira? The old man couldn't seem to remember.'

'Some agency or other?' He shrugged. 'Your guess is as good as mine.'

'What if it wasn't through an agency? What if she approached them direct, specifically in order to inveigle her way into the household?'

152

'You're more paranoid than I am.' He reached for the glass and took a gulp from it. 'You want to watch that.'

'But if it was true . . .'

'Yeah? What if it was?'

'It would change everything, wouldn't it?'

'Well, why don't you go and ask her?'

'Go where?'

'Lisbon.' He leaned slowly back against the panelling on the far side of the bunk. 'I still read the papers, even though nobody pays me to write for them. It's a habit. Another one I can't seem to kick. One of the Sundays had a splash on Lisbon a few months back. Recommended restaurants and the like. Where to go for the tastiest fish and the gloomiest fado. One of the places they wrote up was the Cristina. Eponymously named, apparently, after its charming proprietress, famed for her Brazilian specialities.'

'Cristina Pedreira.'

'Not a question. There was a photograph of her out front to clinch it. Horribly unchanged by the passage of time. Still looking good. And successful to boot. Doesn't it make you sick? Still, success has one disadvantage. It means you're conspicuous.'

'Tempted to go there and have it out with her?'

'Not for a single moment. But you seem to be, Sheridan. Yeah.' He smiled crookedly at me. 'I'd say you were very tempted.'

'Who was H.D.?' I fired the question at him aggressively, keen to deflect his sarcasm.

'What?'

'Somebody Rosalind saw a lot of at Leeds University. Initials H.D.'

'How would you know who she saw at Leeds?'

'Strathallan mentioned it.'

'He's never mentioned it to me. Anyway, I went up there enough weekends to meet all her friends. There weren't many. And those there were didn't hide behind initials.'

'Another man, maybe. Hence the anonymity.'

'Nice line in humour you have, Sheridan.' He scowled. 'Must endear you to a lot of people.'

'Maybe you've just forgotten. Alcohol does that, I believe.'

'Fuck you.'

'Like I told you, Fisher, I read your stuff. Sharp, incisive, pacy. Sad it all comes down to this in the end.' His self-pity had riled me and now I was deliberately trying to provoke him into some kind, any kind, of reaction. 'Like the dregs of a wine bottle: sour and messy.'

'You bastard.' He launched himself at me on the fuzzy memory of a lost machismo, but the edge of the table got in his way long before I did, and his lunge ended in a stumbling fall. The bottle of Lagavulin went with him, hitting the floor hard enough to smash, but contriving to remain intact. The whisky splashed out as it rolled away, and Fisher, lying crumpled in the opposite corner of the cabin, watched it in horror, even as he grabbed at his knee with a grimace of pain. 'Jesus,' he exclaimed through gritted teeth. 'Jesus Christ.'

I retrieved the bottle before it emptied itself and put it back on the table, then turned towards Fisher. 'Want a hand up?'

'Fuck off.' He made an effort to sit up, abandoned it, either because his knee or his brain wasn't up to it, and slumped back into the corner, panting and glaring at me.

'I'm only trying to do what you should have tried to

do a long time ago,' I said, crouching down beside him. 'Run the secrets of that house to earth.'

'You won't succeed. I know, because I *did* try. Like you say. A long time ago.'

'There are things that don't make sense.'

'Yeah. The world's full of them.'

'Why did Posnan abandon architecture?'

'Nobody knows.'

'But he lived as a virtual recluse in Lisbon, didn't he?'

'So they say.'

'Then how did Clarence Milner come to meet him?'

'The story was that Posnan got invited to an embassy do for ex-pats. Maybe he ran into some clerk in a bar. He spent a lot of time in bars, so we're told. Anyhow, he went there, sounded off to Milner about Otherways and . . . bingo.'

'When did Posnan die?'

'Sometime in the Fifties, I think.'

'Is Cristina Pedreira old enough to remember him?'

'Wouldn't have thought so. She was about the same age as Rosalind when I knew her.'

'Who did James Milner send his confession to?'

'It has to be either his brother or his sister-in-law. Take your pick. But blood's thicker than water, so Cedric's my bet.'

'You implied in the *Sunday Times* piece that Daisy was favourite.'

'I was trying to put pressure on her. Nothing happened. She's a tough nut to crack.'

'What did Garvey think?'

'That Cedric murdered Ann and James covered up for him.'

'Is Garvey still alive?'

'No. Died about ten years ago. Jean sent me his obit from the *Mercury*.'

'Do you go along with his theory?'

'It's as good as the next one. If I wasn't – what was it you called me? Sour and messy? – I might take another shot at old Cedric, now the KGB aren't cotton-wooling him. But what would be the point? Nobody cares, Sheridan. Nobody's interested.'

'I'm interested.'

'Why?'

'There are reasons, believe me.'

'Better make sure they're good ones.'

'I'm already sure of that.'

'So was I.'

I stood up and looked down at him. He managed a rueful smile, aware of how squalidly pointless his life had become. But that awareness could always be drunk away. He seemed to take comfort from knowing that. And from knowing I knew it, too.

'Are you going after the Pedreira bitch?'

'Possibly. Want me to take a message?'

'No.'

'Or let you know how it goes?'

'No.' He winced and closed his eyes. 'I don't want to know how anything goes, Sheridan. That's my message. I'm just surprised you haven't got it yet.'

'I have,' I said, turning away, towards the stairs and the fresh evening air waiting outside. 'Loud and clear.'

I should have waited till Monday and made all kinds of checks. I should have stepped back and thought carefully about what I was doing. But I didn't want to wait or think. I wanted to trust my instincts. As you always said I should. 'Be more impulsive, Tony. Make

156

things happen. Don't just let them happen.' Your words, Marina. Remember them? I do. I did. Good advice, I reckoned, even at the time, when I pretended to believe otherwise.

So, I didn't wait. Till Monday, or for anything. Directory Enquiries gave me the number for the Restaurante Cristina in Lisbon, and the man who picked up the phone there spoke excellent English.

'Senhora Pedreira is not here this evening. She will be back tomorrow.'

'Fine. I'll call again.' In person, I didn't add.

I drove straight out to Heathrow, checked into one of the hotels strung along the A4 and booked a morning flight to Lisbon.

Chapter Six

Lisbon was steamily hot and sweatily busy. I wish I could tell you about the architectural glories and the cultural delights, but the city was just a jumble of obstacles which stood between me and the discoveries I hoped would at last expose the truth about Otherways.

I took a taxi from the airport, straight to the Cristina. It was in the Lapa district of the city and, according to the driver, was a *de prestigio* establishment, catering for well-heeled businessmen and diplomats from the many embassies in the area. We passed several of them as we rumbled up, down and around the narrow cobbled switchback streets west of the city centre. Eventually, I was deposited outside a cream-fronted building, whose awnings bore the name Cristina in curlicued script. It was near the crest of one of the steeper streets, commanding a dazzling view of the Tagus in one direction and a hazy reach of the suburbs in the other.

Lunch was in full swing. The taxi-driver seemed to be right about the clientele: predominantly male, dark-suited and cosily confidential. Maybe things were different in the evening. The interior was cool, panelled in mellow wood. There were lots of big gilt-framed mirrors and masses of flowers, their fragrance drifting in and out of the aromas of cooking and cigar smoke. I stood at the bar, toying with a drink and a menu, and watched a woman move unhurriedly between the tables, smiling and greeting valued customers as she went. I heard her name used enough times to clinch her identity and went on watching.

She wasn't slim and you couldn't call her beautiful. Her face was sharp-featured, almost rapacious when she wasn't smiling. Her hair was shoulder-length, sleek black, threaded with silvery grey. She used her hands a lot, touching, patting, gesturing. Her fingers were long and supple. She was wearing a powder-pink suit, with a very short skirt and a jacket cut to reveal a glimpse of black bra. It might sound like mutton dressed as lamb, but she had a poise about her, a knowingness that created an altogether different impression.

By the time they found me a table, most of the lunch parties were winding down. Senhora Pedreira was saying her farewells to favoured patrons. The waiters were beginning to relax. I sat waiting, knowing the moment would come.

It was just a sidelong smile and a faint nod when it did. I wasn't a regular and didn't warrant any special attention, just a courteous acknowledgement and a sparkle of fleeting eye contact as she walked past my table.

'Senhora Pedreira,' I said quietly.

I'd tried to keep my tone neutral, but she seemed to detect something odd in it straightaway. She stopped and looked at me, with a slight eyebrow twitch of curiosity.

'Could I speak to you?'

'*Certamente.* You are English?'

'Yes.'

'I hope you are being well looked after.'

'Everything's fine.'

'How can I help you?'

'My name's Tony Sheridan. I've come a long way to meet you.'

'I am flattered.' She didn't look it. She was in fact just beginning to look suspicious.

'It's about Otherways.'

'Otherways?' Now the suspicion had turned to caution.

'And Emile Posnan.'

'A long way, you say? A long time also.'

'Won't you join me?' I indicated the spare chair at my table. 'For a moment.'

'It can only be a moment.' She sat down, crossed her legs and looked enquiringly at me. The directness of her gaze challenged now, where before it had charmed. 'I am a busy woman.'

'So I see.'

'What exactly do you want, Mr Sheridan?'

'Information. Any information that can begin to make sense of what goes on in that house.'

'That house?'

'Otherways. Come on, Cristina. Can I call you Cristina? Strathallan does. To him, you're still the uppity au pair who got too friendly with his daughter, not the sophisticated restaurateur who gets write-ups in the weekend press.'

'You seem to know quite a lot.'

'But not enough. That's why I'm here.'

The waiter approached with the fish I'd ordered. Cristina waited while he served it, then spoke to him in Portuguese. She seemed to be asking for coffee and a cigarette. When he'd gone, she said, 'What is your connection with Otherways . . . Tony?'

'Friends of mine live there.'

'You are here . . . on their behalf?'

'In a sense. Mostly on my own behalf.'

'Why?'

'I think you might have some answers.'

'To what?'

'Questions. Starting with why Rosalind Strathallan killed herself.'

'It is more than twenty years. An old tragedy better to forget, I think.'

'If only that were possible.'

'Why is it not?'

'I've seen her.'

'Who?'

'Rosalind.'

She said nothing. Only a quick little lick of the lips betrayed any reaction at all. Her coffee and cigarette arrived. She looked at me, frowning in concentration as the cigarette was lit. She took a long, stalling draw on it.

'You heard what I said?'

'Rosalind is dead.'

'I know.'

'You saw her ghost?'

'If that's what you want to call it. In her old room. At Otherways. Strathallan showed me a photograph. I've no doubt it was her.'

'You live at Otherways?'

'I've been staying there. With my friends.'

'Who are they?'

'Matt and Lucy Prior.'

'The Strathallans have left?'

161

'Duncan Strathallan has. Jean died there, last year.'

'Why have you come to me?'

'Strathallan seems to think you were an unhealthy influence on Rosalind. Likewise Martin Fisher.'

'They would.'

'But are they right?'

'I tried to understand. They liked not to understand. That is all.'

'A diary of Rosalind's has come to light. For the last year of her life. She writes about "they" as some kind of shorthand for whatever was tormenting her. Any idea who "they" were?'

'Some.'

'Care to share it?'

'Rosalind was my friend. She trusted me. I do not break a trust. Except for a very good reason. You have not given me that reason, Tony.'

'I can only tell you I have to find out what's behind the strange things that have happened at Otherways. To me. And to other people.'

'A ghost at Otherways is maybe not so strange.'

'There have been other things. Weird, vivid dreams. Unexplained events. Uncharacteristic . . . behaviour.'

'Your behaviour?'

'To some extent. But look' – I was eager to block that particular road before we went down it – 'to give a concrete example, what about a bath that fills itself? In the bathroom attached to Rosalind's old bedroom.'

'The room you have been sleeping in?'

'Yes. I found the bath filled with warm water. In the middle of the night.'

She paused and sipped her coffee. 'Perhaps you should stay with different friends.'

'I need your help, Cristina,' I said in sudden exaspera-

162

tion. 'I can't force you to give it. I can only ask. That's what I'm doing.'

'What makes you so sure I *can* help?'

'A hunch. Based on your affinity with Rosalind and your connection with Emile Posnan.'

'What connection?'

'This city. Where he died and you were born. Around the same time, I believe.'

'It is a big city. Many people die and many are born in it.'

'I don't believe it's a coincidence.'

'I did not say it was.'

At last, she'd admitted something, albeit obliquely. I looked at her as openly as I could, spreading my hands to indicate that I could say no more. Either she would tell me what she knew, or she wouldn't.

'I need to think.'

'I can wait.'

The wait amounted to several minutes, while she finished her coffee and cigarette. She leaned forward to grind out the butt in the ashtray, sat back again and finally said, 'Come back at six o'clock. It will be quiet then. Ring the bell on the side door. I live above.'

'All right.'

'In the meantime, I want you to visit a house in the Bairro Alto. Rua do Bispo, number ten.'

'Why?'

'Emile Posnan died there, in a rented room on the third floor, in 1959.'

'You do know about him, then?'

'Go see it.' She smiled. 'And I will expect you at six.'

I took a taxi down to modern-hotel land: a traffic-choked drag north from the centre, called Avenida da Liberdade. After booking into the first one with a vacancy, I got the concierge to mark Rua do Bispo on a map for me and set off straightaway.

The city was an oven by now, with several unsavoury ingredients cooking in the enveloping heat. I rode a funicular up to the heights of the Bairro Alto district and followed the map through a tangle of narrow streets to 10 Rua do Bispo, the end house in a crumbling eighteenth-century terrace. The terrace had apparently had at least one more house in it once, because the side wall of number 10 was supported by massive wooden props, planted in a shelving patch of wasteland.

I gazed up at the façade of peeling stucco and rotting wood, and wondered which of the third-floor windows had been Emile Posnan's vantage point on the world. There was a bank of bell-pushes at the top of the steps, with most of the nameplates either blank or indecipherable. I tried one at random, waited for someone to answer, then tried another.

The door was opened by a small, weary-looking old woman in a stained dress. When I said I was looking for somebody in a flat on the third floor, she clearly didn't understand, so I pointed and mimed as best I could. She shook her head violently and repeated one word emphatically. 'Ninguém. Ninguém.' She was still repeating it when I dodged past her and started up the stairs.

Her meaning became fairly obvious when I reached the first-floor landing and looked on up. The higher floors were empty and derelict, a dusty spiral of stripped walls and splintered floorboards. I retreated, telegraphing a futile apology to her as I went.

I stopped on the doorstep and turned back to ask,

just for the hell of it, 'Do you remember Emile Posnan?'
But she shook her head in an all-purpose denial. If she
did remember him, she wasn't about to admit it.

It was all very different back at the Restaurante Cristina
at six o'clock – quiet, shuttered, elegantly subdued. The
side door had a polished lion's-head knocker and a
state-of-the-art entry phone. Cristina released the lock,
apparently without checking it was me. Maybe there
was a camera concealed in the door. Or maybe she just
trusted my promptness.

She was waiting, holding the door of her flat open,
when I reached the top of the stairs. She'd changed into
jeans and a striped shirt and had tied her hair back. She
could almost have been a different person, so dramatic
was the contrast with her lunchtime outfit. There
seemed to be an amused acknowledgement of this in
her gaze as she greeted me.

'How was Rua do Bispo?'

'There were a lot of vacancies at number ten.'

'For a long time now.'

'How do you know he lived there?'

'Always the questions.'

'Am I going to get any answers?'

'Come in.'

I walked past her, down a short passage and into a
large drawing room, richly furnished in dark wood
and exotically patterned fabrics. Curtains hung like
sashes across the tall windows. Air conditioning, which
must have cost a fortune in such an old house, had
the temperature pegged comfortably back. There were
rugs and urns and mysterious *objets* in abundance, but
still the room didn't seem cluttered. Over the fireplace
hung a huge antique map of the Amazon. And in the

alcove beside the chimney breast, something instantly familiar, even at a distance.

'It is what you think,' said Cristina.

I stepped closer. It was a framed architect's sketch of a house, with the floor plans reproduced below, headed, in the architect's spidery script, 'Residence for B. H. Oates, Esq: Otherways, nr Hambleton, Rutland. E. F. Posnan, Archt.' There it was, in Posnan's mind's eye, exactly as it now appeared when viewed from halfway up the drive, complete with the trees he'd planted, depicted in the state of full-crowned maturity they'd only attained since.

'An artist,' said Cristina from close behind me. 'Like all good architects.'

'Where did you get it?'

'Come and see.'

She led me back out into the passage and along to the room at its far end. It was dimly lit by one small window and had been used for storage. An iron bedstead and a vast old mantelpiece were propped against one wall. Cardboard boxes tied shut with string, several big leather-strapped suitcases and a dozen or so pots of paint took up most of the floor space. In the centre of the room, however, as if recently dragged into prominence from a corner, stood a large wooden trunk with the initials E. F. P. stencilled above the keyhole.

'My mother cooked and cleaned for Posnan, as her mother did before her,' Cristina continued. 'He was helpless as a baby, she used to say. She often took me with her to the flat on Rua do Bispo when I was a child. It was a smarter place then. Not much smarter, but some. I enjoyed going there, because Posnan was good with children. He could tell stories and make things out of string and cardboard which would keep me busy

166

for hours. He was a small, thin man, with bright eyes and shiny black hair. He used to cock his head when he smiled at me. It made him look like a bird. He had a squeaky voice and never got angry, even when I laughed at him. He smelled of alcohol. My mother told me it was hair oil, but I realized later what it really was. I can still see him light a cigarette, if I close my eyes. He held the burning match at arm's length and slowly brought it closer, until it reached the cigarette. Like he was trying to touch his nose with a blindfold on. Such a strange man.'

'How did you come by the trunk?'

'He gave it to my mother when he found out he was dying. Lung cancer, it was. He had no friends or relatives, he said, and was afraid the landlord would burn the contents.' She stepped round me and opened the lid. 'He told my mother his papers had to be saved for historical reasons. My mother waited for a historian to call round for them until the day she died also.'

The trunk was about three-quarters filled, with bundles of pages covered in Posnan's distinctive script and larger sheets of paper bearing floor plans, elevations and artistic impressions of buildings he'd apparently designed. I unfolded one and looked at it. It was for a large private house, bizarrely raked down at one side, with a long, sloping roof, pepper-pot turrets at every corner and a strange, swooping external staircase.

'You look surprised, Tony.'

'I thought Otherways was Posnan's only completed piece of work.'

'It was.'

'Then . . . what's this?' I dropped the plan back into the trunk. 'And all these others?'

'The houses he dreamed of building.'

167

'But . . .' I looked at several other sheets. More houses, large and small, in contrasting settings – leafy lowland, rugged highland. Some were almost conventional, others wildly experimental. 'There must be hundreds here.'

'There are.'

'And all of them . . . just fantasies?'

'He wrote to himself about them.'

'What?'

'There are letters.' She pointed to a stack of pages. Flicking through them, I saw they were letters written in Posnan's hand, apparently from an address in London – 8 Piedmont Place, WC2. But they all dated from his self-imposed exile in Lisbon, mostly the Twenties and Thirties. 'Dear Emile,' they began, before detailing the progress of various commissions. 'I am well on with Dr Armitage's villa, and only poor materials can prevent me from fulfilling our ambitions for it,' the top one read, typically. The rest were in similar vein, as far as I could see. They were signed Fenby. 'His middle name,' said Cristina, over my shoulder. 'Emile Fenby Posnan.'

'And the London address?'

'Where he practised before coming here. It was destroyed by a German bomb in 1940.'

'No envelopes, of course. No London postmarks.'

'These letters went nowhere, Tony.'

'Except round and round in his head.'

'Except there.'

'It's crazy.'

'He was crazy.'

'What was it all for?'

'He was an architect.' She shrugged. 'He went on being one.'

'But why not a real one?'

'I think Otherways frightened him.'

'What do you mean?'

'I think he realized he had built something more than he intended.'

'You're talking in riddles.' I closed the trunk and stood up. 'And I've had about enough of riddles.'

'*Ma sorte*. Otherways *is* a riddle.'

'Why did you go there?'

'Because I read what the strange man who looked like a bird left in his trunk. It fascinated me. When I found out that Otherways was a real house, solid and standing, with real people living in it, I wanted to see it, to live in it, too, if I could. I went to England in the summer of 1975. I told my mother I planned to find work and improve my English. One of the first places I went, of course, was Rutland, to see Otherways. It was just like the drawing: amazing. I met the Strathallans' au pair, Ulla, in the pub at Hambleton. She told me she was soon leaving. She took me back to the house and introduced me to Mrs Strathallan. I persuaded her to take me on as Ulla's replacement. It seemed to me a chance too good to miss. Ulla told me she would be glad to leave. She said the house upset her. I did not understand her. I thought she was talking nonsense. Later, I was not so sure.'

'What changed your mind?'

'Rosalind changed it.'

'How?'

'Come back into the drawing room. You want coffee? Tea?'

'Nothing.'

'I will have a glass of wine, maybe. Will you join me?'

'All right,' I agreed, impatiently.

We reached the drawing room, and I stood looking at the sketch of Otherways while she fetched a bottle and some glasses. Emile Posnan had lived up to his reputation – eccentric, recluse, dreamer, drunkard – and had died in accordance with it. What he'd bequeathed to his cook-cum-cleaner was a paper mountain of schizoid fantasies: so many houses in the air. There was nothing concrete, nothing actual. Except at Otherways. There he'd achieved something permanent, something, at least, that would outlive him. And then he'd recoiled from it. But why? How could an architect be frightened by a building?

'Thanks,' I said, as Cristina handed me my wine.

'Tell me why Otherways is so important to you,' she said, sitting down in an armchair and looking up at me quizzically over the rim of her glass.

'I thought that's what *you* were going to tell *me*.'

'You have to make me want to tell you first.'

'Oh, come on.' I clunked my glass down irritably on the mantelpiece, and looked at it in dismay as the stem snapped clean off to leave me holding the severed bowl. 'Damn.'

'Clumsy.' She jumped up and took it from me. 'And angry, too.'

'Do you blame me? I've had Strathallan and Fisher leading me in circles. Now you.'

'What did they say about me?'

'Nothing you'd want to hear.'

'I can guess. Major Strathallan resented me because I understood his daughter better than he did. And Martin Fisher . . .'

'Yes?'

'Hated me for making him want me.'

170

'Not very nice of you, was it, to make a play for Rosalind's fiancé?'

'I made no play. It was just . . . a thing that could have been.' She looked away. 'I'll get you another glass.' From the kitchen she called back to me, 'You have been staying at Otherways with your friends?'

'Yes.'

'How long?'

'Long enough to have some very strange experiences.'

'Tell me about them.' She returned with the glass, handed it to me and sat down again. 'Tell me all about them.'

I sipped my wine and tried to be calm, to see things from her point of view. I was demanding honesty and candour from her, but had so far given her no good or compelling reason to supply them. She'd told me what had taken her to Otherways and it was only fair to ask me to do the same. I smiled at my own unreasonableness, and she smiled back.

'Why don't you sit down?'

'All right.' I took the armchair facing hers. 'My wife died recently, in a cliff fall near our home in Cornwall. Lucy's her sister. Matt's an old friend, as well as my brother-in-law. They invited me up to Otherways to help me get over it. Since then . . .' Once I'd begun, it was easy to recount the things that had happened. It was almost a relief to describe them to someone who seemed willing to believe bad dreams and weird sensations could amount to something more than grief and nervous exhaustion. I didn't tell her the whole story, of course. I said nothing about my relationship with Lucy. Shorn of that element, my account sounded overwrought and faintly hysterical, even to me. There just wasn't enough in it to prompt my tireless pursuit of answers. Hence, I suppose, the hint of scepticism in Cristina's gaze. She didn't seem to doubt that what I said was genuine, but she wasn't taken in by it, either. A distance was kept on both sides, a caution maintained. Each of us was still adhering to our own hidden agendas.

Cristina lit a cigarette when I'd finished, prowled around thoughtfully for a moment, then sat down again and said, 'I will tell you what I can, Tony. I will tell you what I think. You will either believe me or not. It will be your choice. I will not try to convince you. This is how it seemed to me. This is how it still seems. If you don't like it, don't blame me. If it worries you – as it may – don't try to argue me out of it. You asked for answers. I'll give them to you. Then the questions are over. And we part. Agreed?'

I shrugged. 'Agreed.'

'Good. Rosalind and me, we were not really . . . *simpatica*. We could never have been good friends. But there was no-one else for her to turn to when she was at Otherways. Her university friends were far away. Her parents didn't want to admit anything could be wrong with their darling daughter. And Martin Fisher, I suppose, just hoped marrying her and getting her away from that house would solve all her problems. He might even have been right. But his method was wrong. Pretend it's not there and it'll go away. That just made it worse for Rosalind. If she'd told him what was happening to her, he'd say she was imagining it all. So, she told me instead. She had to tell someone. I was her last resort.'

'And what did she tell you?'

'That she had strange dreams. Very vivid, very real. Sometimes when she was awake, too. Sometimes when

172

she wasn't sure if she was awake or asleep. She saw things and heard things. She saw people moving and heard them talking. People who weren't there.'

'Ghosts?'

'She never said they were ghosts. Prints, she called them. Traces of people who'd lived at Otherways: Basil Oates, the Milners, other people she could not identify. She thought they might be people who would come to live there later, in the future. Or it could be the present now, if you were one of the people she saw.'

'What?'

'You saw her. You told me you did. And she spoke to you, didn't she? She told me she did that. Tried to communicate with them. But they never spoke back. Did you?'

'I couldn't . . . seem to.'

'They wouldn't leave her alone, these people from the past and the future. They wouldn't stop coming to her. And the things she saw were getting worse, she told me. She was afraid she was beginning to enter their minds, or they were entering hers. She started going to some kind of psychotherapist at the university in Leeds. Maybe this H.D. you mentioned. She never said his name. He was no use, anyway. He told her they were delusions. The usual Freudian nonsense.'

'Perhaps they *were* delusions.'

'I don't think so. I think that house, Otherways, has a . . . resonance . . . that some people pick up and some people do not.'

'Which are you?'

'I had strange dreams there, Tony, like you did. Some of those dreams were as real as sitting here in this room with you. I remember, early one morning, I looked out of the window of my bedroom and saw a man sitting on a shooting-stick on the grass verge halfway up the drive. He had a sketch pad propped on his knee and he was drawing in it. It was Posnan, I swear it, years and years younger than I had ever known him. He was drawing the house, before it was there. Maybe he was drawing that picture on the wall.' She pointed to it, and her eyes drifted out of focus. 'The first time I saw that picture, when I pulled it out of the trunk and held it up to the light, I sensed something. I can't tell you what. But I sensed it again that morning. Posnan was there. While I watched him, he stopped drawing, cocked his head and looked up at my window, as if he could see me looking down. When I ran out to the front of the house, he was no longer there. But he *had been* there. It was a meeting, an intersection, like you and Rosalind.'

'So, you believe she genuinely saw these things, these people?'

'Oh yes. Don't you? She was born at Otherways. She lived there. She died there. It was part of her. So were the other people who lived and died there. She couldn't escape them. She could leave, of course, and at first that was enough. But eventually they followed her, wherever she went. She described it as a weight pressing down on her, slowly increasing all the time, a weight that one day would crush her. Do you doubt it?'

'I think I have to.'

'No. You have to believe it. She admitted to me she had thought of suicide as a way out. She said she had planned to cut her wrists in the bath. The same bath you saw full of water when you had not filled it.'

'But it *was* full. That was no—'

'Delusion? No. It wasn't, was it? No sort of delusion at all. James Milner saw things that convinced him his

174

wife was committing adultery with his brother. What did he really see? The future, without him? What would happen, what could have happened, between them if he wasn't there? Don't you understand, Tony? Alternatives. Possibilities. They *are* the future. Nothing happened between me and Martin. But it could have done. What Rosalind saw . . . could have happened. It was real to her. It was true, in the way that all the things she saw were true, in the way that all the things James Milner saw were true. Martin thinks I put the idea in her head to hurt him. But the idea did not come from me. It came from the house that Emile Posnan built.'

'Why did Rosalind kill herself?'

'Because she believed the two people she trusted most were going to betray her. And maybe because killing herself seemed the only way to stop us betraying her. Or maybe because, in the end, the pressure became too much. Suicide changes the future, doesn't it? It is our only . . . veto . . . on what other people have planned for us.'

I sat there, looking at Cristina and wondering if she could possibly be right. My own experiences tended to support her theory, though I was in no position to reveal the most compelling example of their doing so. In the realm of the rational and reasonable, such ideas had no place. But I'd been drifting out of that realm ever since your death. Maybe Lucy had been, too, ever since moving to Otherways. I rose and walked across to Posnan's sketch of the house to take a closer look. It was a brilliantly accurate depiction of how the house would appear. Even before the first trench was dug, he'd seen the whole thing in his mind's eye: the strangeness that was also the aptness of its design; the elusiveness of its appeal, which was superficially aesthetic yet essentially ethereal. Maybe he'd seen a whole lot more than that, too.

'If I was you, Tony, I would persuade my friends to leave that house.'

'Easier said than done.'

'I would do it, *apesar disso*.'

'And if they wouldn't listen?'

'Find a way to make them.' She stood up and joined me by the picture. 'For your sake, as well as theirs.'

I walked to the Bairro Alto after leaving the Cristina, and sat drinking in a bar not far from Rua do Bispo, wondering if it had been one of Posnan's watering holes. It was old and dark and dowdy. It had probably looked much the same fifty years ago. He could have stood at the counter where I stood, his foot propped on the rail, staring at himself in the mirror behind the bottle-laden shelves, signalling to the barman with a cock of his head whenever he wanted a refill, watching life slew and slop around him, listening vaguely to the chatter of the other customers while, in his mind, buildings shaped themselves to his fanciful designs. I imagined him taking a letter out of his pocket, and reading it as he stood there – a letter from one version of himself to another. Emile Fenby Posnan, lapsed architect and lost soul, in hiding from his past and in flight from his future.

'You realize, don't you,' I'd said to Cristina as she was showing me out, 'that this can't possibly be true?'

'*Naturalmente*,' she'd replied. 'It can't, can it?'

'Yet you believe it.'

'Yes. And so do you.'

176

I still wasn't sure what to say when I rang Lucy the following morning. I'd booked an afternoon flight back to London, with no clear idea what I'd do when I got there. But I had to try to explain myself to her. That much I *was* sure of.

It was Nesta who answered. And she had a surprise for me. 'Lucy's not here, Tony. She's had to go down to Bournemouth. Her mother's ill. She's staying in a hotel. Do you want the number?'

This was something I hadn't anticipated. When I tried the hotel I fully expected her to be out, probably at the nursing home. But no, she was in her room. And she had another surprise for me.

'Mother's fine. Well, as fine as she'll ever be. The truth is I just had to get away. I haven't enjoyed deceiving Matt, you know. You can't imagine how difficult it's been. Thank God you rang. Where are you now?'

'It doesn't matter. I just . . . wanted to see you.'

'Same here. Christ, Tony, I've been through hell these past few days, wondering how I was going to go on making Matt think everything was all right, wondering if you were ever going to—' She broke off. 'It's such a relief to hear your voice, you know that?'

'I'm in Lisbon. I had to get away . . . to think.'

'When are you coming back?'

'This afternoon.'

'Why not join me down here?'

It was what I wanted to do so much. Suddenly, the way out seemed clear. Lucy and I could be free of all the half-suspected dangers that Otherways seemed to hold if we simply walked away from it, together. The house would be sold as part of the divorce settlement. We'd all be rid of it, even Matt. And though the next few weeks and months would put each one of us through an emotional mincer, that was surely preferable to dragging out the lies and evasions till some ghastly moment of discovery that couldn't, in all probability, be so very far off, whatever we did.

'Say you'll come, darling. Please.'

Chapter Seven

I remember you once said that Lucy's most endearing, yet sometimes most infuriating, characteristic was her single-mindedness. She could never be mildly enthusiastic, never slightly annoyed. For her, there were no halfway houses. Perhaps it should have been no surprise that, when Lucy said she loved me, as she did many times that night in her hotel room in Bournemouth, she meant she adored me, she would do anything to keep me, she was mine, body and soul, unconditionally, undeniably.

I wish it had all been as simple for me. Because Lucy was so like you in so many ways, there was an ease between us, a familiarity that made it seem, at times, as if we'd been lovers for years. But that was also the fault-line of doubt that ran through my feelings for her. Her love for Matt had withered to a mere wish not to hurt him if she could avoid it. Mine for you was as strong as ever. She loved me instead of him. I loved her to fill a void in my heart, as a substitute for you. It wasn't the same. Our loves weren't equal.

For the moment, though, that changed nothing. Lucy simply wasn't capable of sustaining a pretence for Matt's benefit, as her flight to Bournemouth demonstrated. I didn't want her to, anyway. We either ended it or declared it openly and faced the consequences. And that night proved we weren't about to end it. The sex was important, of course, especially for Lucy, after several years of sexless marriage. But the real appeal of it was the intimate involvement with another human being, which we'd both come to miss for different reasons. We're all more vulnerable than we like to think. The truth is, Marina, I just wasn't any good at being lonely. I always used to say, 'Where would I be without you?' I wish to God I'd never found out.

Next morning, we walked out onto the pier, coated up against the drizzle that had cleared the beach of bathers. Lucy didn't seem to think we needed to plan the immediate future. In her scheme of things, love provided for all. I thought differently. Some of my reasons for doing so were tangled up with Otherways and my ever more bewildering discoveries about its former occupants. I'd been unable to explain them properly to Lucy; I was scarcely able to explain them to myself. But the most immediate and compelling reason was my certainty on one point: we couldn't go on deceiving Matt.

'We must tell him,' said Lucy, with stark simplicity. 'The sooner the better.'

'And what then? You'll move out of Otherways and join me at Stanacombe?'

'If that's what you want.'

'Perhaps we should go abroad. At least for a while.'

'You choose, Tony. I honestly don't care. As long as we're together.'

'First things first, then. How do we break it to Matt?'

'We just tell him the truth.'

'*We?*'

'We'll both have to explain ourselves to him eventually. Wouldn't it be better to get it over and done with?'

'Yes. But I don't want him to think I'm hiding behind you. We've been friends for so long I can't help feeling I should . . . tell him to his face.'

'Man to man?'

'Something like that.' If there was a way of letting Matt down gently, I had to find it. And I knew I wouldn't find it if we confronted him together: then there'd be only anger and recriminations.

'You want to see him alone?'

'I think it might be best.'

'When?'

I glanced out to sea. 'Straightaway. If I left now . . .'

'You could be waiting for him when he gets home.'

'Yes.'

'He might be late. He's been working long hours since he got back from New York.'

'Christ, the New York trip.' I slapped my forehead. 'I'd forgotten all about that.'

Lucy smiled. 'So had I.'

'What's happening? Is he going ahead with this expansion?'

'Probably. He told me all about it. But it seemed so irrelevant. I didn't take much of it in.'

'It could help. Give him something to concentrate on.' Or somewhere to go, I thought to myself. Matt in the States, throwing himself into franchising out a new chain of *Pizza Prego*, meeting new people, making new friends. Who knew what might come of it? A viable future for him, as well as us, was all I asked. And there on the pier, with Lucy beside me and a shaft of sunlight breaking through the clouds away to the west, it didn't seem too much to hope for.

I reached Otherways late that afternoon. The weather was different in Rutland, a stiff breeze chasing clouds across a clearing sky. The sun came and went, switching brightness and shadow across the lake and the surrounding hills. There was no-one at the house. I sensed that as I approached along the drive. I'd beaten Matt to it. Posnan's creation stood deserted in its mellow fold of lawn and moat and trees.

I let myself in with Lucy's key, fumbled with the alarm until it eventually fell silent, then walked slowly along to the hall and gazed upwards, letting my eye follow the sinuous circuit of balustrading round the stairs and landings. With all the doors and windows closed, the absence of noise was profound. The tick of various clocks in different rooms was clear and audible, the hum of the heating system surprisingly loud. Nothing else made a sound, except my own footfalls as I moved from room to room. The house was empty, yet ready, like the stage in a darkened theatre, prepared for whatever was about to happen.

It was nearly six o'clock. It might be an hour or more before Matt got home. With Lucy in Bournemouth, there was nothing for him to hurry back for. He had no reason to expect that anyone, least of all me, would be waiting for him. I went into the drawing room and opened the French windows, reckoning it would ensure I heard his car when he arrived. Then I poured myself a large Scotch and sat down. The light went on changing in the garden as I gazed out across the moat, so fast it could almost have been a time-lapse film I was watching – hours compressed into minutes, rather than minutes stretched into hours. Outside, the world sped by. Within, Otherways held its breath. We waited, the house and I, for one possibility to become the future.

The longer I sat there, the more I thought about Matt and what he meant to me. I remembered our student days at Durham: the drunken sprees; the felltop walks; the long, late-night talks. I'd known then that he'd stick like no other friend I'd ever made or ever would make. I hadn't expected us to end up married to each other's sister-in-law, but, once we were, it somehow seemed highly appropriate. In many ways we felt more like brothers. It seemed how it ought to be.

That was over now. With your death, the threads that held our cosy quartet together had broken. The relationships had skewed and toppled. Everything was out of kilter. Everything was wrong. And that was why I sat there, waiting to bring down one last part of the whole around our heads. In the end, I didn't hear the car. I must have been too absorbed in my thoughts to register the sound. The turning of the key in the lock was what snapped my attention back to the here and now. I jumped up and hurried out into the hall.

Matt was muttering to himself as he came in and closed the door behind him. Then he saw me standing there, smiling uncertainly. 'Tony,' he said, grinning broadly. 'I could hardly believe my eyes when I saw your car in the drive. How long have you been here?'

'An hour or so.' Glancing at the clock, I saw it was nearer twice that.

'I didn't know you had a key.'

'Lucy gave me hers.'

'You've seen Lucy?'

'In Bournemouth. This morning.'

'You went down there? Is her mother in a bad way? If I'd thought it was serious—'

'She's OK.'

'Really?'

'Really.'

'Then why's Lucy staying on?'

'Because that's not why she went down there.'

He dropped his briefcase and frowned at me. 'What do you mean?'

'Come into the drawing room. I have . . . something to tell you.'

'All right.' He followed me in. 'You've really got me guessing, Tony.'

I helped myself to another Scotch. 'Want one?'

'Wouldn't say no.'

I poured him a large tot, added a little water and handed him the glass.

'We can drink to the success of Pizza Prego in the States.'

'I doubt you'll want to drink with me to anything when you hear what I have to say.'

'It can't be that bad.'

'Yes it can.'

The frown that had lingered on his face deepened. 'What the hell are you talking about?'

'Lucy.' I forced myself to look straight at him. 'And me.'

'Pardon?'

'I'm sorry, Matt. Really I am.'

'About what?'

'We're in love with each other.'

'You . . . and Lucy?'

184

'Yes.'

'You're joking.' His half-formed smile was more plead-ing than disbelieving. 'Aren't you?'

'I wish I was.'

'*You . . . and Lucy?*' he repeated, as if the meaning of the words was only now beginning to dawn on him. 'That . . . can't be true.'

'But it is.'

'No. No, that's crazy.'

'Maybe. But it's true.'

'This is absurd. You're saying that you and Lucy . . . you and my wife . . .'

'There's no easy way to explain it. We didn't plan it. We didn't want it. It just . . . happened.'

'What happened?'

'I'm trying to tell you. We've fallen in love.'

'*Fallen in love?* I don't believe you. You can't have.'

'For God's sake, Matt, listen to me. This is the worst thing I've ever had to say to you – to anyone. While you were in New York, Lucy and I . . .' I stared at him, hoping he wouldn't force me to spell it out. 'Realized we needed each other.'

'You slept with her?' At last, he believed me. There was fear and horror and revulsion in his face. And suddenly I wished to God I could restore his disbelief. 'I never would have dreamed . . . in a million years . . .'

'Neither would I.'

'You're my friend. My best, oldest, most trusted friend.' He seemed to weigh each word as he spoke. We were where friendship couldn't hold, in a squirm-ing shameful place of too much knowledge and too few certainties. 'Christ almighty.' He sat down slowly in the armchair, on the very edge of the cushion, his brow creasing. He put the glass on the floor and held his hands to his lips. Then he looked up at me and I appreciated for the first time just how foul and unforgivable what I'd done to him was. For Lucy to have an affair was bad enough, but to have it with me was worse than bad. It was an over-turning of everything. 'How could you?' he murmured.

'I'm not sure. I . . .'

'How could you? After all this time? After so many years?' He seemed genuinely at a loss to understand. 'Then to come here, while she hides in Bournemouth, and calmly announce . . .' He stood up so suddenly I thought he was going to rush at me. Instead, he strode across the room and out through the door.

'Matt!'

He didn't respond. I hurried after him. He was heading for the kitchen. As I followed him down the stairs and through the door, I saw him pluck a piece of paper from the little message board near the fridge. Then he grabbed at the telephone and began punching in numbers.

'Who are you phoning?'

He ignored me, and I had my answer soon enough anyway. 'Mrs Prior, please,' he said to the hotel receptionist. 'She's a guest . . . What? . . . I'm her husband . . . Yes . . . Thank you.'

'She wanted to come with me, Matt. I insisted on coming alone. This isn't going to get us anywhere. Ring off and let's talk this through.'

But he went on ignoring me. Then Lucy picked up the phone in her room, no doubt hoping it was me calling. 'Lucy? It's me . . . Yes . . . He's here now . . . Oh yes, he's told me . . . How do you think? . . . Tell me this isn't true, Lucy. Tell me this isn't happening . . . What? . . . Is that all you can say? . . . I love you

186

and I *thought* you loved me . . . *What?* . . . Because of that? . . . Oh no, that's just too . . .' His voice fractured. His whole face crumpled. He pressed his free hand to his brow and squeezed his eyes shut, as if to ward off tears. A sob escaped him. Then a choking cry of pain. He slammed the phone down and turned towards me. 'How long?' he said thickly. 'How long has this been going on?'

'I told you. It began while you were in New York.'

'I don't think so. I think it's been going on much longer than that.'

'It hasn't.'

'Since before Marina died, I reckon.'

'Come on, Matt. You're not thinking straight. That's ridiculous and you know it.'

'Yes.' His gaze narrowed. 'That explains everything. Now I understand. It all fits together. It was you, wasn't it? All along.'

'This isn't helping.'

'Handy for you, Marina dying. Really convenient. A chance for you to trade in one sister for another.'

'It wasn't like that. You know it wasn't.'

'Give her a helping hand over that cliff, did you?'

For a moment, I couldn't speak. I hadn't expected anything like this. He was angry, as he had every right to be. But he was virtually accusing me of murder – *your* murder. And he had no right to do that.

'You think you've been very clever, don't you, Tony, you and Lucy? My God, how could I have been so blind?'

'It began last week. That's the truth.'

'No. That's a lie. A blatant lie.'

'I came here today because neither of us could bear to go on deceiving you. You're upset. Of course you are.

187

We've hurt you. We didn't want to, but we have. Don't make it worse by—'

'Shoving your lies back down your throat?' His eyes were wide and bloodshot and staring. He didn't believe a word I was saying. 'Lucky for you I can't prove anything, isn't it?'

'You're not making any sense.'

'Yes I am. You just don't like what you're hearing.'

'I don't know what you're talking about.'

'I wish I could believe that.'

'You can.'

'Can I?' He broke off. His anger seemed marginally diminished. He was still suspicious, but no longer certain of some imagined conspiracy. 'It's just possible, I suppose, *just possible*.' And then it twisted again in his mind. 'She's set you up, too, hasn't she? She's lied to you as well as me. She's lied to everyone.'

'You have to stop this, Matt.'

'No. It's you who have to stop, Tony. You have to stop believing in her.'

'I love her.'

'She's got you exactly where she wants you. She's sucked you in. And now she's going to spit you out.'

'You don't know what you're saying. You've got everything out of proportion.'

'I know exactly what I'm saying. Don't trust her, Tony. Don't believe a word she says.'

'I'm not going to listen to any more of this madness.' I turned towards the door. 'We'll talk again tomorrow. When you're calmer.'

'Tomorrow?' he called after me as I went up the stairs. I was trembling with anger of my own now, as well as guilt, which only made the anger worse. 'Maybe I won't be here tomorrow.'

188

But he would be. I was sure of that. He had nowhere else to go. And it wouldn't take long for him to begin to see reason and to regret his outburst. I was sure of that, too. We were old friends, after all. I knew him nearly as well as I knew myself.

'Listen to me while you still can,' he shouted.

But the best thing to do was clear to me in that moment. And listening wasn't it. I crossed the hall and made for the front door. Before I reached it, the telephone started ringing. It was still ringing as I slammed the door shut behind me and strode towards the car.

I didn't get further than the end of the drive before remorse kicked in. I pulled over, wound down the window and breathed in the cool evening air. What the hell was I doing? How could I have so badly mishandled the situation? Matt was in a state of shock. He wasn't responsible for what he'd said. He didn't mean any of it. He wasn't really accusing me or Lucy of anything, other than what I'd already confessed to him. I should have expected him to lash out in all directions. I should have made allowances. What I shouldn't have done was lose my temper and turn my back on him.

I don't know how long I sat there, trying to decide whether I should go back to the house or not. There was a danger that if I did it might make things worse. But I only had to think of the state I'd left Matt in to realize the risk was probably worth taking. In the end, there didn't seem anything for it but to go back.

I started the engine, and was about to pull out into the lane to turn round when I saw Matt's car in my wing mirror, speeding towards me along the drive. He roared past, braked late and took the bend into the lane virtually on two wheels. Instinctively, I went after him.

He'd turned left, which led to the eastern tip of the peninsula, a mile ahead, with only fields and spinneys between. There were gates across the lane before you got there, to prevent people driving down to the water's edge. Matt was on a fast run to a dead end. I put my foot down, but he was still pulling away. Then he was out of sight, round the next bend.

As I rounded it myself, I saw him ahead and the gates beyond. I suppose it was then that I realized what he was doing. He hit the gates like a battering ram, aiming at the weakest point, where they were padlocked together. They crashed open, the car bucking and slewing with the impact. Then he was through, skidding the rear tyres as he fought for control and, gaining it, pressed the accelerator to the floor.

I steered through the wreckage of the gates and crested the last rise before the lake. The water was a grey wind-whipped mass, into which the lane plunged abruptly at the edge of the spinney where I'd met Rainbird. Once it had led across the fields to Normanton. I could see the church on the other side, dead ahead. Now it led nowhere. It was a drowned way.

Matt picked up speed as he descended the slope towards the lake. A pontoon for fishermen stretched out into it from the end of the lane. The pontoon was too narrow for the car, but Matt was going so fast when he reached it that momentum carried him out halfway along it, on the offside wheels, before he sheered off and careered into the water, the engine's roar ending in a hissing gurgle as the bow wave swallowed him.

I kept going as fast as I dared, then jammed on the brakes and came to a halt just short of the water's edge. Matt's car was out of sight now, air belching up from below the surface to mark the spot, ten yards or so beyond the end of the pontoon, where it had sunk. I leaped from my car, ran out along the pontoon and dived towards the churning bubbles.

The cold shock of the water hit me an instant after it closed over my head. It was darker and quieter than it seemed possible to be so close to the surface and my hands touched the roof of the car before I even saw it. As I pulled myself round towards the driver's door, I noticed that the windows were open. Matt had wanted no life-saving pocket of air. He'd wanted to end it quickly. But this also meant I could reach him without a struggle. I glimpsed him, slumped and belted at the wheel, but he didn't seem to be aware of me. He didn't seem to be aware of anything. His eyes were closed and his mouth was open. He was drowning in front of me. I stretched in through the window to reach the seatbelt release.

Suddenly, his eyes opened. He stared at me. Then he grabbed my arm and pulled me into the car. I tried to cling to the door pillar, but he was too strong for me. My hand slipped and I rolled across the steering wheel. For a long, muffled second, his face was close to mine. He tried to say something. Bubbles streamed from his mouth. I struggled to turn round, but his grip on me tightened. My breath was failing, my lungs straining. I reached towards the passenger door with my free hand, hoping to pull myself loose and escape that way. But my fingers touched solid glass. The windows on that side were closed. I grabbed the passenger headrest and tried to gain some kind of purchase. But it was too late. I couldn't hold my breath a second longer. I opened my mouth.

*   *   *

And screamed. I was sitting in the drawing room at Otherways. It was real and true and solid. The evening light was clear and crystalline. The air was cool, almost fragrant as I sucked it in in soothing lungfuls. I looked at the clock. It wasn't yet seven. And Matt hadn't yet come home. I'd been dreaming, that was all. Just a dream. Nothing more.

But nothing less, either. And nothing like any dream I'd ever had before, even in that house. Every word, every action, every detail: inscribed on my mind more sharply than any memory, acute and unforgettable. It didn't feel like a dream. I didn't even feel as if I'd been asleep. How could I have slept anyway? I'd been anxious and apprehensive, my thoughts ranging over the past and future in search of—

I looked at the clock again. Not yet seven. It had been close to eight when Matt walked through the door. In my dream. If it was a dream. An hour from now. Part of the future. Imagined, or already experienced. It wasn't possible. It simply couldn't be. So I'd have said, at another time, in another place. It was madness. A fantasy. And I could prove it easily enough. I had only to wait till Matt returned. Whenever he happened to. And then—

But I wasn't going to wait. I had to change the rules. I couldn't tell him there. Not tonight. Not after what I'd seen and heard. The anguish I'd glimpsed on his face was part of me now. Maybe it was all of me, my own creation, the bad dream of a worse conscience. But I couldn't stay to find out. That was the only thing I knew for certain. I couldn't stay.

I left in sudden, blinding panic – fear like I've never felt before. But it ebbed fast, draining out of me as I drove away down the drive. I slowed and stopped, forcing myself to think hard and rationally. Then I started again, turning left, towards the lake shore, down the nowhere road.

The gates were across the lane, fastened and intact. I left the car there and walked on down to the dead watery end. There was nothing. The pontoon was empty, the vista of lake and sky plain and unremarkable. Waves stirred by the breeze lapped placidly at the tarmac. I stood staring at the spot where I'd seen the bubbles rise from Matt's submerged car. So vivid, so actual. But not real. Not yet.

Time passed. I couldn't have said how much. Then I walked back to the car and started driving along the lane towards Hambleton, passing the entrance to Otherways without a sideways glance. I wasn't sure where I was going or what I was going to do.

As I slowed for the bend near Hambleton Church, Matt's car came the other way round it. There he was, face expressionless, eyes trained ahead. Then he was past me and gone. He could have looked across and seen me. A single glance would have done it. But he didn't.

I pulled in by the church and watched his car in the rear-view mirror, shrinking in the glass as it accelerated out of the village towards Otherways. Then I looked at the clock on the dashboard. It was seven minutes to eight.

I made it to Oakham and booked into the Whipper-In for the night. As soon as I got to my room, I picked up the telephone, noticing with a strange, disconnected curiosity the tremor in my hand as I held the receiver.

I'd intended to call Lucy, but before I got halfway through the number I stopped and slowly put the phone back down. There was nothing I could say to her that wouldn't sound either crazy or weak-willed. Later, I could call and say Matt hadn't shown up and I'd decided to hold off till morning. But not yet. It was too early. I went down to the bar and ordered a drink.

I was waiting for the barman to pour it, when I felt something brush my elbow, and realized Norman Rainbird was standing next to me.

'Good evening, Tony.' He grinned at me. 'What a happy coincidence. Though not a pure one. I saw your car outside.'

'What do you want?'

'That's very civil. I'll have an orange juice. With just a little tonic.' The barman nodded in acknowledgement and I couldn't be bothered to correct him. 'I'm surprised to see you here, I must say.'

'Why?'

'Because I thought you'd be in touch as soon as you returned from Scotland. Unless you just have returned, of course, and were wondering how to contact me. I realize phoning Maydew House isn't always feasible. I really should have given you my mobile number, but I do so resent the exorbitant tariff, even when someone else is paying.'

The last thing I needed was a dose of Rainbird's double-edged patter. The quickest way to be rid of him that came to mind was to make it clear I had nothing to tell him. But somehow I doubted he'd believe me. 'I drew a blank with Strathallan. The whole trip was a waste of time.'

'What kept you, then? You've been gone four days.'

'I had to go down to London.'

'And what did that turn up?'

'Nothing.'

'Why don't you favour me with the chapter and verse? You don't really look like someone who's turned up nothing. More than you bargained for would be my bet.'

'Then you'd lose.'

'On the contrary. I always win my bets. Now' – he lowered his voice – 'why don't we adjourn to a corner table and flesh out the details of your little voyage of discovery?'

'I'm fine here.'

'Trust me. There are a few points I want to run over with you that require a degree of . . . privacy.'

In the end, it didn't seem worth arguing. We moved to the same table I'd found him sitting at the first time we'd met there. It had an invisible RESERVED FOR RAIN-BIRD sign on it.

Since James Milner's missing confession had ostensibly been what Rainbird wanted to lay his hands on, I stuck to the facts about that and went no further. Two fruitless meetings at opposite ends of the country – with Strathallan and Fisher – were as much as I offered him. Lisbon, and Cristina Pedreira, I kept to myself. Rainbird looked far from satisfied. But satisfying him wasn't any kind of priority for me. I needed time and solitude in which to try to make sense of what had happened to me at Otherways that evening. Rainbird was just grit in my shoe. Hard to dislodge, maybe, but no worse than that.

'I'm a disappointed man,' he announced when I'd finished.

'I said you would be.'

'Not because you found out so little, you understand,

but because you think I'm gullible enough to believe it's all you did find out.'

'Are you questioning my honesty, Norman?'

'No. Questioning implies doubt. I have none. You simply aren't playing fair with me.'

'Is that so?' I was too weary and distracted to rise to the bait. I was glad, in a way, that he'd come out and said he distrusted me. That made it easy to end our tête-à-tête. 'Well, there's no more to be said, then, is there?'

I'd got halfway out of my chair when he said, 'Sit down,' so softly yet insistently that I found myself obeying. His gaze was cold and steely now, his grin a cicatrice of abandoned geniality. 'What you lack, Tony, is an incentive. As it happens, I'm in a position to supply one. When you've heard what it is, I think you'll agree you could wish for none better.'

'I doubt it.'

'Bear with me, please. Mrs Prior is away from home at present, I believe.'

'So?'

'Has there been a falling out with Mr Prior?'

'No. There hasn't. And, even if there had, it wouldn't be any of your business.'

'I take a keen interest in the vitality of our national institutions, of which marriage is one. It always distresses me when I hear that any such union is threatened, perhaps the more so because I have never had the good fortune to experience the love and companionship of—'

'Why don't you just come to the point?'

'Very well.' He dropped into his *sotto voce* mode. 'You and Mrs Prior are engaged in an adulterous relationship.'

'What?'

'You heard. And it is a fact known to us both, so your incredulity, or rather your poor attempt at it, is unnecessary.'

'Now hold on—'

'To the following strand of logic, Tony. It will serve you well in the days and weeks ahead – the days and weeks of our close collaboration.' He allowed himself the briefest pause for effect. 'I took the opportunity you somewhat carelessly afforded me of the run of Otherways the weekend before last to secrete listening devices in the principal rooms. One must keep abreast of the latest technology. In the realm of covert surveillance, it seems to know no limits. The recorded material is very high definition. Explicitly so, you might say. Hence my clear understanding of how matters stand between you and Mrs Prior.'

He was wrong about my incredulity. It wasn't faked. I genuinely couldn't believe what I was hearing. Just grit in my shoe? The shoe, it seemed, was on the other foot. And I was underneath it. What was worse, in the half-full bar of the Whipper-In, I couldn't even raise my voice in protest. Rainbird had my full attention. Whether I wanted to give it or not.

'I have faith in you, Tony. You either have James Milner's confession or you have a very good chance of obtaining it. A better one than me, for certain. Now you have a compelling motive as well. I'm doing you a favour in that sense. The greyhound will not run without the hare. So, here is the hare, jugged. Or, in this case, taped. Matthew Prior is your best and oldest friend. You have said so yourself. I have *heard* you say so. Do you want him to hear as well? Not just that, of course, but other, less congenial, material. It could hardly be pleasant for a husband to listen to his wife being brought to orgasm by his best and oldest friend. What she wants, how she wants it, where she wants it. Mrs Prior really does believe in speaking her mind, doesn't she? And what a mind. I can't deny I felt quite envious when I—'

'*Shut up.*' I couldn't stay silent any longer. I didn't care if my shouted interruption caught the attention of others in the bar. 'Just shut your filthy mouth.'

'I don't believe I've uttered a profane word, Tony,' said Rainbird, mildly. 'I've simply laid the facts before you and added my perfectly reasonable interpretation of them. But, since the ins and outs of the situation, so to speak, appear to distress you, let us come to the crux of the matter. I will give you one week to deliver James Milner's confession to me – the original, mind, a copy will not be acceptable – failing which I shall furnish Mr Prior with a tape, comprising what we might call the edited highlights of life at Otherways during his trip to New York.'

'I have no way of finding Milner's confession,' I said, through gritted teeth. '*If* it still exists, his brother probably has it.'

'An interesting theory. Perhaps a bucket-shop flight to Moscow is in order. Do remember to take a bath plug with you.'

'I'm not going to Moscow, or anywhere else, on your say-so.'

'Am I to take that as an outright rejection of my proposal?'

'You can take it as an outright refusal to be blackmailed.'

'Shouldn't you at least think about it?'

'Maybe I don't need to.' I summoned what I judged to be a confident smile. 'Maybe I don't care what you do.'

'Your recorded agonizings over Mr Prior's reaction

to news of your relationship with his wife hardly support that hypothesis. Even if you do intend to tell him the truth, the tape will still be an unnecessary twist of the knife, one you should be anxious to spare him. He's a loving, indeed uxorious, husband. And he's also your friend. Just what is this savage disillusionment going to do to him, Tony? That's what you have to ask yourself.'

I *had* asked myself. To make matters worse, I knew the answer: it was going to destroy him. I'd seen it happen, with my own eyes, at Otherways that very evening. 'For God's sake, Norman, be reasonable. I can't do what you ask.'

'You can try. And you can hope proof of a sterling, if unavailing, effort on your part will persuade me to be charitable. I wouldn't bank on it, though. Delivery of the confession within a week is your only certain course of salvation.'

Was it? In the unlikely event of my coming up with the goods, what was the betting he'd impose some additional demand? It seemed awfully like odds on to me. 'Why do you want the confession so badly, Norman?'

'Find it and you might also find the answer to that question.'

'You're just as well equipped as I am to hunt it down.'

'*Au contraire*. You have become an insider at Otherways. You have the ear of all the players in this drama. Doors that are closed to me will open for you. Likewise, hearts and minds. No, no. The job's made for you, Tony. I'm backing you to make a success of it.'

'You're crazy.'

'I've often thought that of people I've worked for. I

199

was nonetheless obliged to do their bidding, just as you're obliged to do mine.'

'Am I really?'

'I think so, unless you're more ruthless than I suppose.' He was right there, damn him to hell. This was something I couldn't walk away from. 'Oh, I nearly forgot.' He took a piece of paper out of his pocket, scribbled something on it and slid it across the table towards me. 'My mobile phone number. You may need to contact me urgently. Feel free to do so as soon as you make any progress. Or even if you simply need some tactical advice. If I don't hear from you in the interim, I'll expect to see you next week.' He drained his glass. 'Same time, same place?'

It was nearly dark when Rainbird left. I walked round the tomb-still streets of Oakham, trying to think my way out of the trap he'd caught me in. I was tired, but my mind couldn't rest. There was no escape. Reason it how I pleased, I had no answer to his ultimatum, except to comply with it. Yet I had no realistic hope of finding the confession and hardly any that Rainbird would let me off the hook even if I did. That left only one course of action open to me: tell Matt the truth, nurse him through the shock of it, stall Rainbird as long as possible and pray Matt was over the worst if and when he got to hear the tape. In my mind, I'd already told him the truth, with consequences too awful to contemplate. But they couldn't be worse than those that would follow if I let Rainbird enlighten him. Nor could I delay without telling Lucy about the tape, the existence of which she'd justifiably blame me for, unless I explained that some sort of dream had convinced me it was too dangerous to go ahead

200

with our original plan, which would probably have her doubting my sanity, also justifiably.

It would have been easy enough to doubt it myself. But precognition, if that was what the dream represented, gave me one precious advantage to cling to. I already knew some of the mistakes I was likely to make. I didn't propose to make them again. Next time round was going to be different.

'Hello.'

'Matt, this is Tony.'

'Tony. Are you at home? I've phoned a couple of times but got no answer.'

'I've been away.'

'Really? I thought you left because you had a buyer for Stanacombe.'

'No buyer.'

'Lucy must have misunderstood, then. I'd ask her, but she's in Bournemouth at the moment. Her mother's none too well.'

'Her mother's fine.'

'Sorry?'

'Look, can we meet? Tonight?'

'Meet? Where are you?'

'Oakham.'

'Well, why don't you just come on here? You could have done that anyway. There was no need to phone.'

'I don't want to meet at Otherways.'

'Why the hell not?'

'Too complicated to explain. Can you be at the railway station here in Oakham half an hour from now?'

'The railway station? Haven't you got your car?'

'I've got it. But that's not the point.' The point, had I tried to explain it, would have sounded crazy to him.

I needed to get him, and me, away from Otherways and Rutland Water. I needed us to meet on neutral, un-haunted ground. 'Can you be there, Matt? It really is very important.'

The last train from Oakham in either direction had already left when I got to the station. The ticket office was closed and the platforms were empty. I stood on the footbridge over the level crossing, gazing down at the silent rails glistening in the lamplight, listening to a dog barking somewhere in the night, the noise drowned out at intervals by cars rumbling over the crossing. Then I saw a figure walking slowly along the southbound platform towards me. I raised my hand, and Matt raised his in acknowledgement.

'Was my journey really necessary?' he asked, with a smile, as he reached the top of the steps.

'I'm afraid so.'

'You sound serious.'

'I am.'

'Recognize the signal box?' He nodded towards it.

'How do you mean?'

'Hornby based their trackside model on the Oakham box. I had one on my model railway as a boy. Didn't you have a Hornby set?'

'No. I didn't.'

'I always said you had a deprived upbringing.'

'I wish it was true. Maybe I could use it as an excuse.'

'An excuse for what?'

'The way I've behaved.'

'What's wrong with the way you've behaved?'

'Everything.'

'What the hell are you talking about?' He spoke ironically now. His tone was entirely different. But my blood ran cold at the echo of his words in my memory of the dream I'd had at Otherways. I'd switched the venue, I'd changed the time, but I couldn't alter everything. What I had to tell him remained the same.

'Lucy,' I said, numbly obedient to the logic of his question. 'And me.'

'Pardon?'

'I'm sorry, Matt. Really I am.' I turned to look at him, my mind racing to reconstruct and simultaneously deconstruct the conversation we'd already had. 'Lucy and I . . . are in love with each other.'

'You . . . and Lucy?'

'Yes.'

'You're joking.'

'I wish I was.'

'*You . . . and Lucy?*' he repeated, just as he had before, *exactly* as he had before. 'That can't be true.'

'But it is.'

'No. No, that's crazy.'

'Yes. Crazy *and* true.'

'This is absurd. You're saying that you and Lucy . . . you and my wife . . .'

'There's no easy way to explain it. We didn't plan it. We didn't want it.' These, it seemed, were still the best words I could find. 'It just . . . happened.'

'What happened?'

'We fell in love.'

'*Fell in love?* I don't believe you. You can't have done.'

'For God's sake, Matt, listen to me.' I put my hands on his shoulders, forcing us to face each other, literally clinging to our friendship to ward off what I feared would follow. No weasel words this time, I told myself; tell him straight. 'While you were in New York, Lucy and I slept together.'

203

'What?'

'We realized we loved each other. It's as terrible as that. And you never would have dreamed it in a million years, would you?'

He jerked my arms away, stumbled back, steadied himself against the parapet and stared at me. I could hear him breathing, fast and shallow. 'You're my friend. My best, oldest, most trusted friend.' He turned away, raising a hand to his face. 'Christ almighty.' Then came the murmured afterthought, as I knew it would. 'How could you?'

'I don't know. But—'

'*How could you?*' he almost screamed. 'After all this time? After so many years?' It didn't matter how often he asked the question, I would never have an answer. Nor would he. 'A buyer for Stanacombe popping out of the woodwork. Lucy's mother falling ill. None of that was true, was it?'

'Look—'

'Then you come up here, while she hides in Bournemouth, and calmly announce . . .' He swung on his heel, the plan to phone Lucy forming in his mind around the faint hope that she'd say everything was really all right and that I didn't know what I was talking about. It was the moment I'd waited for. It was my chance to make a difference.

'*Stop!*' I flung myself at him, pinning him against the parapet. Our faces were inches apart. In his eyes I could read all the fear and horror and revulsion I knew I somehow had to hold in check. 'Listen to me, Matt. Please. Lucy wanted to come with me. I insisted on coming alone. But I was wrong. We have to face this together. You, me *and* Lucy. We have to deal with it. You can't phone her now. It's too late. The hotel switchboard

204

won't put you through to her room at this hour. Besides, how can you talk to her about something like this over the phone? Drive down to Bournemouth. That's the answer. We'll go together. Travel through the night.'

'We're not going anywhere together.'

'We have to. I won't let this destroy everything.'

'Pity you didn't think of that sooner.'

'Yes. It is. But I'm thinking of it now, Matt. I'm thinking of *you*. Believe me.'

'Why should I?'

'Because I've told you the truth, even though I hated doing it.'

'Have you? Did it really begin while I was in New York?' Why did he doubt it? There had to be a reason. And for both our sakes I had to find out what it was. 'I don't think so, Tony.' He pushed me away, but stood where he was. The sequence of events, as I thought I knew them, teetered on some invisible brink in the darkness between us. 'I think it's been going on much longer than that.'

'It hasn't.'

'Since before Marina died.'

'Think I gave her a helping hand over that cliff, do you?'

'Maybe. It would explain—'

'*I loved Marina. I worshipped her.*' I was shouting now, letting him hear and understand that this crazy suspicion of his had no basis. 'Maybe losing her is what made me capable of betraying our friendship, Matt. It could well be. Lucy's so like her in so many ways. But to suggest—' I lowered my voice. 'It began last week. That's the absolute truth.'

'Is it?' His anger ebbed, as I'd seen it ebb before. 'It's just possible, I suppose, *just possible*.' And, as I waited, a new suspicion took hold of him, as I knew it would. 'She's set you up, too, hasn't she? She's lied to you as well as me. She's lied to everyone.'

'What has she lied about?' We were there, at the question I sensed everything else turned on.

'You don't know, do you? You really don't know.'

'Tell me.'

'She's got you exactly where she wants you.'

'Where's that, Matt?'

'Don't you understand?'

'No. Explain it to me.'

'She's planned this. Every step of the way.'

'Planned what?'

'Stealing you from Marina.'

'That doesn't make any sense and you know it. None of this would have happened but for Marina's death. Lucy couldn't have planned that.'

'Couldn't she?'

'Of course not. For God's sake, what are you suggesting?'

'What do you think?'

And there, in the silence that suddenly overwhelmed us, I had my answer.

A man trailing a dog on a lead walked slowly over the crossing below, glancing up at us as he went, the chain links of the lead tinkling softly. The night was windless now, moonless and still, a blank stretching to infinity on every side.

'That's crazy,' I murmured.

'Like you said. Crazy *and* true.'

'No. Just crazy. Otherways does strange things to people, Matt. You've imagined this.'

'If only.'

'Lucy was at home, at Otherways, when Marina died.'

206

'No. She wasn't. Which of us answered the phone when you rang with the news?'

'Well . . . you did, I think.' My memory of that evening was patchy at best. All I could be sure of was that I'd spoken to both of them at some point. 'But . . .'

'She got back later and phoned you then.'

'Right. So she did. Even so—'

'She and Daisy had gone to Worcester races.'

'Well, there you are, then. She was in Worcester. With Daisy.'

'That's what I thought. That's what she said. But a round trip to Worcester's about a hundred and fifty miles. I checked the mileage she'd done in her car. She clocked up over five hundred that day.'

'*Five hundred?*'

'Yes. About as far as—'

'Stanacombe.'

He nodded. 'And back.'

'There must be some mistake.'

'No mistake. I'd been thinking for some time that their horse-racing jaunts might be cover for something else. Befriending someone like Daisy just isn't Lucy's style.'

I couldn't follow him there. Their friendship had seemed natural and genuine to me. The question I was already asking myself wasn't whether what he was suggesting could be true – clearly it couldn't – but how he could bring himself to believe it might be. Maybe it wasn't so much a case of bringing himself as being brought. It wouldn't have taken a lot for him to start suspecting that Lucy was looking elsewhere for the sexual satisfaction he could no longer supply. Paranoid inquisitiveness about her activities could have made her cagey and evasive. To back that up, there was his insistence that I keep a close eye on her while he was in New York. From fear of being lied to it's a short step to the real thing. And in that frame of mind anything becomes conceivable. He couldn't have detected the discrepancy in mileage without checking it regularly, if not obsessively. Yet obsessive was the last thing I'd have said he was. But all that had changed. At Otherways.

'The trip counter was right for Worcester,' he went on. 'She'd thought of that. It was only the total on the clock that gave her away.'

'Are you sure? You could have miscalculated.'

'No. The extra miles were there. Figures can't lie.'

He was right. They couldn't. But what story had they really told? He'd been looking for evidence to justify his suspicions and he'd found it. But to me it sounded awfully like a search that was bound to yield something. He'd passed the point where suspicion becomes self-fulfilling.

'You don't believe me, do you?'

'I'm saying there has to be an innocent explanation.'

'Don't you think I'd like there to be?'

'It's easy enough to find out if there is. Ask Daisy.'

'She'd say they went to Worcester.'

'You think she's lying, too?'

'She has to be. Otherwise Lucy wouldn't have involved her. An alibi has to stand up, doesn't it? Lucy didn't get home until gone ten that night. She said she and Daisy had stopped for dinner on the way. Well, she couldn't risk saying that if Daisy was likely to contradict her, could she?'

'Why would Daisy cover up for her?'

'I don't know. It's something to do with Otherways. You're right about that place. It does do strange things to people. Lucy hasn't been the same since we moved here. Maybe I haven't been, either.' He rubbed his eyes with the heels of his thumbs and I realized he'd been crying, probably for some time. I just hadn't noticed. 'Daisy and that house go back a long way together. The Milner murder isn't the half of it. There have been other tragedies there. Strathallan's daughter killed herself.' So, he knew about Rosalind, which must have made Lucy's attempt to keep it from him look like one of a host of deceptions. 'It's deeper and darker than you think, Tony. And Daisy Temple's somewhere at the heart of it.'

'Come on, Matt. That can't be.'

'You mean you can't bring yourself to see it. Lucy's blinded you to what's going on.'

'No. She hasn't.'

'It's not really her fault. None of this would have happened if we hadn't bought that bloody house. That's what's done for us. It's why I went for Sindermann's proposition in such a big way: to get Lucy away from here.' The tears were glistening on his cheeks. His voice had thickened and slurred. 'But she won't be coming with me to New York now, will she? You've seen to that.'

'For God's sake, Matt. What are you saying? You can't really think Lucy killed Marina.'

'Can't I?'

'They were sisters. And best friends. All their lives.'

'Yes. That's right. Best friends. Like I thought you and I were.'

'We are. Look, this . . . this is madness.'

'That's what you think, is it?'

'What else *can* I think?'

'Nothing, I suppose. If you're in love with her. Because you can't be in love with your wife's murderer, can you? Not unless—' He broke off, clamping his mouth shut, as if he dare not say what he was thinking. And instantly I knew what it was. I'd broken the pattern, only to create a new and far worse version of it.

'Nobody murdered anyone, Matt. Be reasonable.'

'Reasonable?' His voice cracked as he raised it. 'I'll bet you'd like me to be. That would suit you very well, wouldn't it? Both of you.'

'It's you I'm concerned about, not us.'

'No cause to be, is there? Not now you know I can't prove a bloody thing. That's what this was all about, wasn't it? Making sure I didn't have any clinching evidence. Well, congratulations, Tony. You're in the clear. And don't worry, I'll make things very easy for you. I won't stand in your way.'

'What do you mean by that?'

'Why should you care?' He turned suddenly and started walking towards the steps. I followed and put a hand on his shoulder. He shrugged it away and turned back to face me. *'Leave me alone,'* he shouted. 'You've got what you wanted. So has Lucy. I don't have to stand here and listen to you explaining why it's all really for the best.'

'I never said that.'

'But you would have, if I'd let you. It's what you think, isn't it? It's what'll let you sell people a this-thing-was-bigger-than-both-of-us story, while hoping anyone I tell the truth to writes me off as a nutter. That's your strategy. And it'll probably work. Except for the last bit. I'll see to that.'

'Matt—'

He struck out so suddenly I was on the floor before I realized he'd hit me. I think it took him by surprise as much as it did me. I was aware of a burning pain around my left eyebrow, and of Matt staring down at me, his right fist slowly relaxing into an open hand, until it formed a strange, inadvertent gesture of farewell. Then he whirled round and started running towards the steps.

'Matt!' I called after him. But he didn't stop. I scrambled up in time to see him reach the foot of the steps and run on, over the crossing and up the road, towards the station forecourt, where he must have parked his car. Slowed more by the shock of being hit than the blow itself, I went after him.

The dream was as real in my mind as the present. I saw the narrow dipping lane beyond Hambleton. I saw Matt's car surging out onto the pontoon and tipping into the water. And I saw his face, submerged and staring, bubbles streaming from his mouth. I'd changed nothing, absolutely nothing. I'd only made the end more certain.

There was never a chance I'd overhaul him on foot. He'd already started his car when I reached the forecourt. He reversed it round in a skid, then accelerated straight at me. I flung myself out of his path and watched as he roared back towards the level crossing, then swung left, heading for the high street and the Stamford road. I ran to my own car, stalled once, then took off in pursuit. All I could think of now was finding a way, any way, to stop him before he reached the far end of the peninsula.

But maybe I didn't have to do anything. A police car was laid up in the market place. I saw it pull out ahead of me as Matt flashed past, doing about twice the speed limit. Its light and siren came on. I kept pace, hoping they only had eyes for the car in front.

Matt certainly gave them plenty to keep their eyes on. As far as I could judge by the speed of the police car and the parallax of headlamps and rear lights, he wasn't slowing down. He went straight over a roundabout, forcing another car to brake hard, then swerved left onto the Stamford road and put his foot down. The police went after him, siren wailing, blue light flashing. And I followed.

We were touching eighty as we left the town behind. It had to end soon, I told myself. Matt would slow down any minute and pull in, realizing he couldn't lose them and that he'd only make things worse if he tried. Or would he? What was in his mind? Did he really mean to go all the way? Surely he couldn't hope to. Not now.

Half a mile out of Oakham was the Hambleton turning, a sharp right off the Stamford road. The police wouldn't be expecting him to take it. I flashed my lights at them and signalled right, in a desperate bid to warn them, but I had no way of knowing if they'd even noticed. In the next few moments, it ceased to matter. Matt gave no signal. I wondered if he meant to drive on by, as the police must have assumed he would. I could see the headlights of an oncoming vehicle ahead, with smaller safety lights at roof level, the sort you get on articulated lorries. Matt must have been able to see them, too, dangerously close, dazzlingly bright. His brake lights flared. He was going to stop. He had to. 'Thank God,' I said to myself.

But he didn't stop. The braking was only enough to take the turn at a skid, and the skid was enough to slew him into the path of the lorry. I heard the deep blare of its horn and a squeal of brakes. There was a fraction of a second of total silence, then an immense splintering thud.

Chapter Eight

When I heard the crash, I remember thinking, Please God, don't let him die. I suppose the prayer was as much for me as for Matt. I'd engineered some kind of second chance for both of us and I'd thrown it away. Now I wanted a third chance more desperately than I'd ever wanted anything. But even second chances are rare. I was asking for the impossible. When I pulled in at the side of the road and ran ahead to where the collision had ended in a tangle of crushed metal and shattered glass, all I could see of Matt's car was a distorted shape beneath the cab of the lorry. It scarcely looked like a car at all. Anyone inside had to be dead. It simply wasn't survivable. I stopped for a moment and stared at the flattened lump of metal, from which glass smashed to powder was falling slowly and irregularly, like snow from the branches of an overladen tree. It wasn't quite real, yet I knew it was true. This was where our friendship came to its close, bleeding out, cold and slow, into the lengthening night.

But chances, first, second *or* third, are always double-edged. They can go one way or the other, irrespective of what you want, or fear, or even deserve. They owe you no favours, but they bear you no grudges. They lie where they fall. Nine times out of ten, maybe ninety-nine out of a hundred, the crash would have been fatal. But that night was the one time, maybe the only time. That night, Matt didn't die.

He was lucky. He was very lucky. The air-bag had inflated between him and the windscreen. And one of the two policemen in the patrol car was able to staunch the worst of his bleeding, while the other one summoned an ambulance and a fire crew with cutting equipment. All this while I was still standing and staring. Matt was trapped in his seat, unconscious but still breathing, with blood from minor cuts bathing his face, while the blood from some more serious wound was already dripping out of the car into the trails of petrol and water seeping from the fractured tank and radiator.

The lorry driver was unhurt, but disorientated by shock. He kept talking to me, in a stream of disbelieving reruns of what had happened, while I watched the policeman working on Matt. Then the other policeman was at me with questions. Did I know the victim and his next of kin? Had he been drinking? Had there been an argument? I tried to explain, but the look on his face suggested I wasn't making a lot of sense. I probably sounded about as coherent to him as the lorry driver did to me, and for the same reason: shock had reduced me to a stumbling, slow-witted shadow of myself.

I stayed that way throughout the hour it took them to cut Matt free and load him into an ambulance. Paramedics, doctors and firemen milled around the car, working calmly and efficiently, while I stood a little way off, my mind clinging to the fierce wish that Matt should survive, and the belief that every moment he didn't die made it likelier that he'd live. At some point it started raining. I remember the fine mist of it blurring the lights around the wreckage and glistening on the yellow reflective coats and the petrol-slicked tarmac. I remember watching its slow steady fall out of the darkness above and around me. I remember it better than anything else that happened that night. I don't know why.

The police, evidently realizing I was in no fit state to drive myself, took me to the hospital in Leicester. By the time I arrived, Matt was in the operating theatre. The tight-lipped answers I got to questions made me gradually understand that I was probably wrong about his chances improving all the time. It was very much touch and go.

I phoned Lucy's hotel, only to be told she'd left. The police had apparently already contacted her. Presumably, I'd given them the number, then forgotten doing so. A sympathetic nurse assured me such confusion was entirely normal in the circumstances, found me an empty room to sit in and brought me a cup of tea. The surgery was likely to be protracted as well as unpredictable, according to somebody in a white coat who looked in on me. Did I know when Mrs Prior would be arriving? I did not. Nor much else, come to that.

It was at least a three-hour drive from Bournemouth, and something like that long must therefore have passed when Lucy arrived, though in the state I was in, time had become bewilderingly elastic. The crash seemed both an age and a few minutes ago. I could still feel the rain on my face, blurring my first sight of him, slumped in the crumpled wreckage of his car.

Lucy was hollow-eyed and trembling faintly. She

looked to be having as much difficulty as me in adjusting to what had happened. We hugged as we would have done in former times, as friends, as brother- and sister-in-law. It was as if shock had catapulted us back into the relationship we'd had before we became lovers. Or maybe neither of us could quite face the responsibility we shared *as* lovers for Matt's close encounter with self-destruction.

'The doctors talked about severe chest and pelvic injuries,' she said. 'Do you know any more?'

'They've already told you more than they've told me. But the injuries have to be severe. When I saw the crash, I thought he was dead for certain.'

'How did it happen?'

'He was driving like a madman. The lorry hit him as he tried to turn in front of it onto the Hambleton road.'

'I don't understand. Matt's a careful driver. Highway Code stuff. Infuriatingly correct.'

'I'd just told him about us.'

'But why was he on the road? You were going to wait for him at home.'

'I decided . . . neutral ground . . . would be better. We met in Oakham.'

'Why? He was bound to be upset. Letting him drive away was surely—'

'Risky. Yes. So it seems.'

'You didn't—' She looked at me doubtfully for a moment. 'I mean . . .'

'Mean what?'

'Nothing.' She shook her head, but the thought remained, unspoken and unrefuted. Maybe I'd set it up. That's what had crossed her mind as a distinct possibility. Maybe I'd planned for this to happen.

'Did they say what his chances are?'

'Fifty:fifty.'

'No better than that?'

'They'll know more when he's out of surgery. But I keep wondering what they mean by "severe". Just how bad is it?'

'Bad. But not fatal.'

'Not yet.'

'We just have to wait. And hope.'

'I hope he lives, Tony. I hope he makes a full recovery. I don't want him to die.'

'Of course you don't.'

'But I don't want this to change anything. Between us, I mean.' She reached out and stroked my face. I winced as her fingers touched the bruise above my eye. 'What's happened here?'

'Not sure. I think I hit the door frame as I scrambled out of my car just after the crash.'

'Nothing *has* changed, has it?' She looked at me imploringly, willing me to say what she wanted to hear. 'Has it, my love?'

'Not a thing.'

'You seem so . . . distant.'

'This has knocked me sideways, Lucy. You, too. But it'll pass. Matt will live. It'll be all right.'

'And we'll be together?'

'Yes.' We hugged again. I looked over her shoulder at the blank beige waiting-room wall. I'd said it. But I didn't quite believe it. It wasn't just Matt's life hanging in the balance. It was all our futures, complicated by the present, compromised by the past. It wasn't a question of what Lucy wanted or what I wanted, it was a question of what would actually happen. And I had no idea of the answer. 'We'll find a way,' I murmured. 'I promise.'

217

An hour or so later, the surgeon came to see us. He looked every bit as tired as us, but in his case it was just professional fatigue. What he gave us was a dispassionate assessment of his patient's condition. There was nothing riding on it for him.

'We've done as much as we can for the present. He'll be in intensive care for some time and he'll look pretty alarming, but I think we've been able to stabilize him. He's unconscious and may well stay that way for some days. The trauma's been considerable. But, in the circumstances, he's doing very well. There's no sign of brain damage. We've had to remove his spleen, but that should have no adverse long-term consequences. One of his lungs was punctured, but we've repaired that and done all the other patching up. He's not out of the woods yet. Problems can flare up unexpectedly in cases like this. Shake a complicated mechanism like the body as badly as his has been shaken and all sorts of connections can work loose. But . . . I'm guardedly optimistic.'

We went in to see him. He was hooked up to a forest of drips and tubes and was surrounded by ECGs and EEGs and God knows what else, monitoring his vital signs. He'd been fitted with a ventilator to assist his breathing. Purely as a precautionary measure, we were told. He was in no pain. And he was alive. Somehow, against the odds and in spite of my worst fears, he was alive.

We sat in the hospital canteen afterwards, drinking coffee and staring into the middle distance, saying little but thinking a lot. Lucy left me at some point to phone Matt's brother. She'd already been in touch with him apparently, and he'd undertaken to break the news to his parents. The ripples of the event kept on radiating out across the hitherto placid pond of Matt's existence.

When Lucy came back, she said she'd also phoned Nesta; and Daisy. Instantly, I was reminded of Rainbird and his devious attempt at blackmail. I hadn't the heart to tell Lucy about it just yet, but suddenly I saw it in a new light, as something squalid and insignificant that I now had the means to deal with, even though those means had been delivered to me in the last way I would have wished.

'Daisy asked if I wanted to stay with her,' Lucy said distractedly. 'It was a kind thought, I suppose.'

'I think you should take her up on it.'

'Why?'

'Otherways is . . . well, a big place to be alone in.'

'Won't you be there with me?'

'I'm not sure that would be right, just at the moment. We need time to . . . sort ourselves out.'

'Otherways is my home, Tony. Why should I leave it?'

'I can't explain. But, as a favour to me, Lucy, would you? Just for a while. I'll stay at the Whipper-In. I won't be far away.'

'All right.' She seemed too tired to argue, weary to the depth of her soul. 'Have it your way. Daisy's way, too. She said much the same as you about Otherways. I don't know why you both have it in for the place.'

'We just don't want you to be on your own at a time like this.'

'I don't have to be on my own, do I?'

'I did ask it as a favour.' I looked appealingly at her. 'A few days, Lucy. That's all.'

'It better had be. As far as I'm concerned, a few days

under the same roof as Norman Rainbird is a few days too many.'

'Don't worry about Rainbird.' The plan that had been forming in my mind was solidifying now into a definite intention. 'I'll deal with him.'

Lucy was too preoccupied with Matt's condition to analyse my remarks about Rainbird or indeed to mount more than a token challenge to the plans Daisy and I had inadvertently colluded to make for her. The intensive-care staff made it clear that Matt's progress, if sustained, would be slow and uneven. He was unlikely to be aware of his surroundings for some time. He would probably experience some memory loss as well, especially relating to the period immediately before the crash. In other words, he might easily not remember our encounter at Oakham railway station at all. In a very real sense, the third chance I'd prayed for had been granted. But only if he went on making progress. Given the severity of his injuries, that was by no means guaranteed. Reading between the lines of what the doctors told us, I detected a hedging of bets; it could still go either way. I'm not sure Lucy appreciated that. The shock of the accident had thrown up a screen between her and the world's harsher realities. She'd become unnaturally timid and compliant. But her concern for Matt was unfeigned. None of the nurses could have doubted that she loved him. I couldn't doubt it myself. It made me question our feelings for each other. Was it the real thing, or a passing infatuation? We were two desperate people clinging together. And now we were more desperate than ever.

*   *   *

Telling Lucy the police had insisted I remove my car from the roadside at the scene of the accident without delay, I left her at the hospital and caught an early morning train to Oakham. It took me back to last night's meeting place with Matt. The place looked and felt different in daylight: bland, peopled, perfunctory. A bridge, a crossing, a part of a town. As at those fatal crash sites where grieving relatives have left a bunch of flowers, nothing of what had happened there had been preserved. Like Matt's memory, the scene had been wiped. All my wasted words and hopes had been rubbed away.

I took a quick shower at the Whipper-In, then ordered a taxi and travelled out to the Hambleton turning on the Stamford road. There was a deep, muddy gouge in the right-hand verge, but Matt's car had been removed. Converging skid marks showed where it had collided with the lorry. Somebody, presumably the police, had spray-painted a series of arrows around the marks, their dispassionate record of the geometry of the event, photographed for possible later use in a prosecution, or an inquest.

I reached Maydew House half an hour later. Rainbird's car was on the drive. It seemed I wouldn't have to look far for him. But first I wanted Daisy to understand why I was looking for him.

I found her in the workshop, sipping at a mug of coffee and staring soulfully at the unfinished bust of Lucy. 'She'll look different next time she sits for me,' she said, so unsurprised by my arrival that she simply included me in her train of thoughts. 'An experience like this leaves its mark. If I'd known you before your wife died, I expect I'd be able to see the change that wrought in you.'

'Matt isn't dead.'

'No, thank God. But it was a close call, I gather.'

'Very. And it might yet go against him.'

'Really?' She sighed. 'Lucinda didn't tell me it was *that* close.'

'I'm not sure she realizes it is. She's not taking everything in at the moment.'

'She did sound slightly confused, it's true. That's why I suggested she might like to stay here for a few days. She'll spend most of her time at the hospital, I suppose, at least for a while. But I thought, between visits, it might help to . . .'

'Not be at Otherways.'

Daisy raised one eyebrow as she looked at me, in the faintest of signals that she understood what I meant. 'Well, I can only offer.'

'She's changed her mind. She asked me to tell you.'

'Good.' The eyebrow was raised again. 'I'm a little surprised, I must say. Her attachment to Otherways is so strong.'

'Unnaturally strong.'

'I wouldn't go that far.'

'I would.'

Daisy put her mug down, carefully draped a sheet over the bust and joined me in the doorway. 'Lucinda said you witnessed the crash.'

'Yes. I met Matt in Oakham last night and told him about Lucy and me.'

'Ah. I see.'

'I didn't handle it as well as I should have. He took off in his car like a bat out of hell. I went after him. I was afraid, well, that . . . he meant to do himself harm.'

'You're not suggesting—'

'No. It was an accident, right enough. But the way

222

he was driving made a crash of some kind more or less certain.'

'And you feel responsible?'

'I should have stopped him. Somehow.'

'I'm sure you tried.'

'Not hard enough.'

'You weren't to know how he'd react. And he had to be told. Sooner or later.'

'Before he heard it from another source?'

'That's not what I meant.'

'No? Well, it was a factor, even so. That's one of the reasons I'm here, actually. Your lodger, Daisy. Mr Rainbird.'

She frowned. 'What about him?'

'I think you should consider giving him notice.'

Her frown deepened. 'Why?'

Rainbird responded promptly and jovially when we knocked on the door of his room. 'Come in, do.' It was almost as if he'd been expecting us.

The room hardly looked as if he'd been living in it for six months or more. The furnishings and decorations were clearly Daisy's. Rainbird's possessions, whatever they amounted to, were out of sight. It was as if he was making an overnight stop rather than a prolonged stay. He was sitting in an armchair by the window, reading a well-thumbed paperback. When he put it down on the table beside the chair, I saw it was *Tristram Shandy*. You tried it once and gave up, I remember. I never tried it at all. But Rainbird was two thirds of the way through.

'A deputation, no less,' he said, looking up as we entered. 'What can I do for you?'

'Matt Prior was seriously injured in a car accident last night,' I said.

'Oh dear. Not the smash on the A606 near Oakham? It was on the local news.' He wafted an explanatory hand towards a transistor radio on the bedside cabinet. 'It sounded bad.'

'It was.'

'Well, I'm sorry to hear it.'

'Its only blessing is that it puts your blackmail attempt into proper perspective.'

'My . . . what?'

'Tony's told me all about it,' put in Daisy.

'Has he really?'

'You don't deny it?'

'It depends what you mean by "deny".'

'You admit threatening Tony with illicit tape recordings of private conversations?'

'I admit discussing such tape recordings with Tony at the Whipper-In last night, a few short hours before Mr Prior's . . . accident.' He beamed at us, as if he'd perfectly refuted any suggestion of impropriety on his part.

'This is inexcusable and intolerable,' said Daisy. 'You've behaved outrageously.'

'I have?'

'I want you out of this house. Today.'

'Don't think I'm being unreasonable, dear lady, but I've paid my rent up to the end of this month.'

'Then I'll repay it. You either leave or we call the police.'

'You're bluffing.' He looked from one to the other of us. 'Somewhat unconvincingly, I must say.'

'Try us,' I said, looking him in the eye.

'Well, I certainly have no wish to stay where I'm not wanted.' He shrugged. 'Perhaps it *is* time to move on.'

'I want the tapes, Norman. And I want to know where the bugs are.'

'I can't help you there, I'm afraid.'

'I'm not asking. I'm telling you. Hand them over.'

'If I could, I would.' He spread his hands and smiled. 'There *are* no tapes, Tony. No bugs, either. No concealed listening devices of any kind.'

'What the hell do you mean?'

'I made it up. It was a ruse. A litmus test for my theory concerning you and Mrs Prior. I entirely lack the technical expertise to use or deploy such equipment, even supposing I knew where to obtain it. No, no. It had no basis in fact. Why should it have?' His smile broadened. 'When I could obtain such gratifying results simply by . . . exercising my imagination.'

'*You're lying.*' Angered by the thought that he *wasn't* lying, I launched myself across the room and hauled him out of his chair. 'And I mean to—'

One moment he was staring at me, goggle-eyed, a limp weight sagging in my hands, the next he'd somehow slipped from my grasp, grabbed me by the wrists and whirled me round as effortlessly as a child spinning a top. And then I was bent across the table beside his chair, my face pressed against the cover of *Tristram Shandy*, my right arm doubled up behind my back, pain searing through my shoulder. 'You mean to what, Tony?' Rainbird mildly enquired as he ratcheted up the pressure on my arm. 'I'd so like to know.'

'*Let him go!*' cried Daisy. '*Let him go at once.*'

'By all means.' Suddenly, I was released. Rainbird stepped away from me and I eased my arm back to my side. 'Your wish is my command.'

'Are you all right, Tony?' Daisy looked at me anxiously as she helped me up.

'It's OK,' I panted. 'I'm fine.'

'Of course he's fine,' said Rainbird, smiling blithely at

us, and displaying not the least hint of breathlessness. 'There was never any possibility he wouldn't be. I was merely defending myself. Tony was in . . . expert hands, so to speak.'

'Get out of my house,' said Daisy, speaking slowly and coldly, but with alarm bubbling audibly behind her self-control. 'This minute.'

'It will take me rather longer than a minute to pack, seasoned traveller though I am. But pack I will. And be gone within the hour, without further ado. Nor a moment's quibbling about the unexpired portion of my rent. Can I say fairer? I think not.' He dropped to his knees beside the bed, pulled a suitcase out from underneath it, stood it upright and released the catches. Then, holding the case shut, he turned and grinned at us. 'Until then, I should appreciate some privacy.' The grin dropped away and was replaced by a steely glare. 'Get out of my room. Both of you. This minute.'

Daisy asked me to stay until Rainbird had left. I think she was unnerved by the sudden switch in his character. He was certainly physically stronger and more agile than I'd given him credit for. I felt unnerved myself, as well as foolish. Rainbird the oleaginous schemer was one thing; Rainbird the man of action quite another.

'I'd always thought him a harmless eccentric,' she said, as we sat in the drawing room, drinking coffee in an atmosphere of fragile calm. 'I had no idea, you must believe me, that he was capable of anything like this.'

'He's after something at Otherways. It's the house that really interests him. I expect that's why he chose to lodge with you in the first place.'

'He's never mentioned Otherways to me.'

'Probably because he was afraid you'd send him packing if he did.'

'Why should I have done that?'

'Because the house holds a lot of secrets. And quite a few of those secrets involve you.' I looked at her frankly. 'Cards on the table, Daisy. Lucy warned me off the subject, but too much has happened for me to mince around it any longer. If I believed in ghosts I'd call Otherways a haunted house.'

'But you don't believe in them.'

'I'm not sure. What about you?'

'I've never seen a ghost, Tony. At Otherways, or anywhere else.'

'When did you last set foot in that house?'

'I've not been there for a long time.'

'How long?'

'Many years.'

'But how many? Precisely.'

'It was the day of Ann's funeral.'

'That long?'

'Yes.' She looked towards the bust of her sister, standing in the window, filtered sunlight moving across its green-veined marble features in time to the gentle movement of a curtain behind it. 'Precisely that long.'

'It's only a few miles away. You knew the Strathallans. You're Lucy's friend. How have you avoided going there?'

'It's not the how you're interested in, Tony. It's the why.'

'True enough.'

'Memories are the problem, not ghosts. Memories of Cedric as well as Ann.'

'When did you last see him?'

'The spring of 1947. He visited Otherways shortly

after the RAF vacated it and he called here to see me. It was a somewhat strained encounter. I sensed there would never be another. And there never was.'

'Why did you break off your engagement?'

'We could hardly *not* break it off, given that Cedric's brother had murdered my sister. But that is a superficial answer, of course. Our love would have endured had it been strong enough. Clearly, it wasn't.'

'You know some people have suggested Cedric witnessed the murder – may even have *been* the murderer?'

'By "some people" you mean the late Donald Garvey. I'm well aware of the story he put about. It's complete nonsense. Cedric was out cycling at the time. He got home to find Ann dead and James waiting calmly for the police to arrive.'

'So, you never doubted his version of events?'

'I did not.'

'Nor his brother's?'

'No. I'd seen enough of James and Ann that summer to know something was wrong between them. Ann told me James seemed to be suspicious of her, but she couldn't understand why. There were no grounds for it, Tony. Ann wasn't having an affair with Cedric. She wouldn't have been able to conceal that from me.'

'But James convinced himself she was.'

'Yes.'

'There must have been a reason.'

'Indeed there must. But I have no idea what it was. He refused to see me or Cedric after his arrest. And he said nothing in court. All we have is his barrister's statement at his trial. And that didn't give a reason.'

'We might have more, if the confession Rainbird's so anxious to lay his hands on really exists.'

'Quite so. *If*.'

'Do you think it does?'

'I honestly don't know. My only advantage over everyone else where that's concerned is that I know for a fact I don't have it and have never seen it.'

'But Cedric?'

'It might have been sent to him. He might have decided to keep it from me. If it was ever written in the first place. Assuming all of that, which is a good deal, well, Cedric's silence suggests he didn't want it to see the light of day. In which case, he probably destroyed it. Hunt as high or low as he likes, Mr Rainbird isn't going to find it. And nor—' She broke off as footsteps sounded on the stairs. 'Ah. Talk of the Devil.'

We watched through the window as Rainbird clumped out onto the drive, a suitcase in either hand and a briefcase wedged under one arm. He loaded them into the boot of his car, then walked back into the house, without so much as a glance in our direction.

'I'll be glad to see the back of him,' said Daisy, as his heavy tread receded up the stairs. 'I should have asked him to leave months ago, when I realized Lucinda found his presence here worrying.'

'Why didn't you?'

'He gave me no specific cause. Clean, tidy, quiet, and a prompt payer. The model lodger, in some ways.'

'But not in others.'

'No. Not in others.'

'Where did he come from?'

'London. He supplied a reference from a landlady in . . . Brentford, I think it was.'

'What do you know about his background?'

'Nothing really. He's always been so vague.'

'A man of mystery.'

229

'If you like. But most mysteries merely conceal a hollow core.'

'Not in this case.'

'You may be right.'

'What's he really after? That's the question. He said, if I found the confession, I'd find out why he wanted it.'

'He was teasing you. Since he's never seen the confession, it follows he can't promise it will tell you anything.'

'It was more than a tease. I had the impression . . . he meant it.'

A door slammed above us. We listened as Rainbird descended the stairs. He paused in the hallway. We heard him tap the barometer and tut-tut at the reading. Then he knocked at the drawing room door and came in.

'Your keys, Miss Temple.' He dropped them on a console table beside the bronze bust of a bald middle-aged man. 'You have my word I hold no duplicates. But you could always have the locks changed, if you thought it necessary.'

'Goodbye, Mr Rainbird,' said Daisy, with studied neutrality.

'Goodbye, dear lady.' He smiled at her, then looked across at me, his smile curling out and up into a smirk of satisfaction. 'I'll be in touch, Tony. Never fear.'

I planned to return to the hospital as soon as Rainbird had gone. But there was a question I'd yet to put to Daisy. Her answer, whatever it turned out to be, was important, more important than just about anything else.

'People who live at Otherways imagine things, Daisy. You could say they see things. There's a pattern to the lives they lead there. Some of them – the susceptible ones – fall under its spell. James Milner. Rosalind Strathallan. And Matt Prior.'

'Come, come.'

'When we met last night, he said some strange things. They made me realize he was harbouring certain . . . unaccountable suspicions about Lucy.'

'About her and you?'

'No. Something else. Something . . . worse.'

'What could be worse?'

'He seemed to think she'd lied to him about where she was . . . the day Marina died.'

I was looking straight at her as I finished the sentence, alert for any hint of discomposure in her face. There was none. Her expression was as placid, or as well sculpted, as that of her sister, preserved in marble on the other side of the room.

'Lucy was with you, I gather.'

'That's right.'

'You went to the races?'

'Yes. At Worcester. I remember it well. We had such a nice day. Then, the following morning, I heard the terrible news . . . about your wife.'

'You were together all day?'

'Yes. We were.'

'And you didn't go anywhere else, apart from Worcester?'

'No. Well, we stopped for dinner on the way back. Near Warwick. But that was all. What are you getting at?'

'Matt reckoned there were too many miles on the clock in Lucy's car for a round trip to Worcester.'

'That's absurd. I can assure you we went there and back and nowhere else.'

'I believe you.'

'So I should hope.'

'But that means Matt imagined the discrepancy, doesn't it?'

'Yes. I suppose it does.'

'A discrepancy he was expecting to find. Otherwise he wouldn't have been looking for it.'

'Why would he have been looking for it?'

'You tell me.'

'I can't.'

'No. Exactly.'

'Exactly what?' She frowned at me. 'I don't understand.'

'The house, Daisy. It's got to him the way it got to your brother-in-law. Something there seeps into the mind and distorts it. Something there . . . is dangerous.'

She shook her head. 'I . . . I can't believe that.'

'Neither can I.' I paused. 'But I can't disbelieve it, either.' I stood up and moved towards the door. 'Not any more.'

One thing was settled between Daisy and me before I left. Neither of us would breathe a word to Lucy about Matt's manifestly unfounded suspicions. This was no time to burden her with such stuff. Maybe there never would be a time.

As for Rainbird, we agreed she'd probably be too pleased he was gone to query the circumstances. I couldn't shrug them off so easily, though. Maybe he'd conned me about listening devices, maybe not. If he had, his guesswork had been uncannily good. If he hadn't, his denial that there were any in place was the real con. I needed to know which, badly. And that was when I remembered how grateful a former client had been for my headhunting of an electronic security expert to render their City HQ leak-proof. I had a favour to call in.

Lucy was at Matt's bedside when I reached the hospital. There'd been no change in his condition. He remained unconscious: drained, dripped and ventilated. Lucy herself was beginning to look ill with fatigue. The ICU ward sister advised her to go home and get some rest; it was going to be a long haul. I tried to talk her into following the sister's advice over a canteen lunch, which she ate even less of than I did.

'I want to be there when he wakes up,' she countered. 'To make him understand I still care about him.'

'If you go on like this, you'll be in the next bed by the time that happens. Why don't I drive you to Maydew House? You can get a few hours' sleep and come back here this evening.'

'I don't want to go there. Not with Rainbird hanging about.'

'He won't be. He's moved out.'

'When did that happen?'

'This morning. A snap decision, apparently. Just like the man.'

'Rainbird's moved out?' She didn't seem to have the energy to make much of it. 'He's gone?'

'Perhaps flown's the more appropriate word to use about him.'

She thought for a moment, utterly failing to notice the joke, then said, 'All right.'

'You'll go?'

'Everyone seems to think I should.'

'I'm sure it's—'

'Megan was here earlier.'

'Sorry?'

'Megan Blackwell, Matt's PA. She was terribly upset. She's always been devoted to him, you know. Well, Matt inspires devotion, doesn't he? Except in those closest to him.'

'Listen, Lucy, I—'

'Why did this have to happen? I keep asking myself. *Why?*'

'It didn't have to.'

'That's worse, then, isn't it?'

'What do you mean?'

'Well, if it didn't have to, it shouldn't have, should it?'

A silence fell. There was no answer to Lucy's question. 'I'd better phone Daisy and tell her we're coming,' I said, pushing back my chair with a squeal of rubber on lino. 'I won't be long.'

When I got back to the table a few minutes later, Lucy had pushed her plate to one side and was holding a pocket diary in her hand, studying the entries intently. I wondered for a crazy moment if it was Rosalind Strathallan's, since I'd never known Lucy to use one, but, as I sat down, I recognized the handwriting as Matt's. And then I noticed the bloodstains on the cover and the edges of the pages.

'They seemed very concerned to give this to me,' she said listlessly. 'God knows why.'

'Protocol, I suppose.'

'There's hardly anything in it. Megan kept his business diary. Just . . . odd jottings.' She held it open and pushed it across the table. 'Funny entry for today, though.'

I looked down at it. *Lois Carmichael*, Matt had written. *Ram Jam*, 6. 'What does it mean?'

'The Ram Jam's a pub on the Great North Road, near Stretton. Looks like he was planning to meet Lois Carmichael there this evening.'

'And who's she?'

'I don't know. Nor does Megan. No idea at all. Strange, really. There's no phone number, either, so I can't even tell her she's going to have a wasted journey.'

'Perhaps someone should be there to explain.'

'Could you go?'

'Sure.' It was stranger than Lucy seemed to appreciate. Matt's smooth, orderly, predictable existence didn't really have room for appointments with people his wife, his best friend and his personal assistant had never so much as heard of. 'No problem.'

We got to Maydew House around mid-afternoon. Daisy had already made a room up for Lucy, who obediently took a couple of the sleeping pills the hospital had given her and went off to bed. She'd said something during the journey about needing clean clothes and I'd volunteered to fetch some from Otherways. I said I'd call in there on the way to or from the Ram Jam. What I omitted to mention was that I had another reason for going to Otherways. Like Matt, I had an appointment no-one else knew about.

The train from London pulled into Peterborough dead on time, just after five o'clock. Among the very last people to leave the platform, displaying his usual economy of effort, was Lester Kidmore, cutting edge security specialist. I knew he was earning a lot more money than when I'd first met him, but he still looked as if he bought his clothes at Oxfam. Nor had life in the square mile led him to do anything about his hair, which was as wild and woolly as ever.

'Good of you to come at such short notice, Lester.'

'Nothing's too much trouble for you, Mr Sheridan. What have you got for me?'

One of Lester's greatest assets is his tunnel vision. He concentrates on what he's asked to do to the exclusion of all else. That probably explains his dress sense. It probably also explains why he passed no comment whatever on Otherways' architectural oddities and failed to ask what had taken me so far from London.

His company robbed the house of much of the eeriness I'd undoubtedly have detected if I'd arrived alone. The sensation of being watched would almost certainly have crept up on me. As it was, I was able to keep it at bay and concentrate on the matter in hand: not was I being watched, but was I being listened to?

'You want me to do every room, Mr Sheridan?'

'I need a thorough check.'

'Then I'd best get on.' He snapped open his case. 'It'll take a while.'

'How long?'

'A couple of hours, at least.'

'That's OK. I have to meet someone at six.' I glanced at the clock: I was going to be a few minutes late, at least, and could only hope Lois Carmichael was the patient type. 'I'll leave you to it.'

It was nearly quarter past six when I walked into the Ram Jam Inn. Food looked to be its strength and at that stage of the evening business was slack. Apart from the barmaid, there was only one woman in the place: lithely built, in her late twenties or early thirties, with short-cropped dark hair and wide teak-brown eyes which swivelled towards me as I approached the bar. She was sitting on a stool at one end, dressed in trainers, leggings and some sort of ski jacket, unzipped over a scoop-necked T-shirt. There was a bottle of Budweiser – the genuine Czech article – in front of her, and no sign of a glass. She didn't exactly leap to mind as Matt's normal line in drinking companions.

'Lois Carmichael?'

She arched a faintly surprised eyebrow. 'That's me.'

'I'm Tony Sheridan. A friend of Matt Prior's.'

'Yeah?'

'You're here to meet him, I believe.'

'That's right. The man himself, not a friend of his.' She softened slightly. 'No offence, but he was more anxious than me to meet up. The least he could do is—'

'He's in hospital. He was involved in a car crash last night.'

'Sorry to hear that.' She sounded more disappointed than sorry. 'How is he?'

'Out of it at the moment. In intensive care at Leicester Royal Infirmary.'

She winced. 'Sounds bad.'

'It is. His wife's very upset, naturally. I'm doing my best to help. You see, none of us had ever heard of you before. But since your name was in his diary – Ram Jam, six o'clock this evening, no phone number – I thought . . .'

'You'd find out what it was about.'

'Something like that.'

'Wish I could tell you. But that's what the meeting was for, actually. For him to tell me what it was about.'

'I don't understand.'

'You didn't know he was interested in my work?'

'What is your work?'

237

'I'm an astronomer. I lecture at Hull University.'

'Really?'

'Yeah,' she said tartly. '*Really*.'

'Sorry. I didn't mean—'

'Why don't we go and sit down?' She nodded towards a table. 'It'll help you get over the shock.'

'I'm not shocked. Look—'

'OK.' She smiled. 'Relax. But *shall* we sit down?'

'Why not?'

She set off, carrying her Budweiser. I bought myself a drink and followed. By the time I caught up, she'd lit a cigarette. She offered the pack to me and, to my surprise, I found myself taking one.

'Matt's never shown the slightest interest in astronomy,' I said, savouring my first draw on the cigarette. It tasted better than the drink. There are natural nonsmokers, who insist on smoking, you used to say, and then there are the natural smokers who refuse to. You always reckoned I was one of the latter. 'That's all I meant.'

'Forget it. Fact is, astronomy's not really what it's about. I stray way beyond the telescope. Too far, according to my colleagues.'

'Into what?'

'Parascience, I suppose you'd say. Well, hunting ghosts is more interesting than logging stars, that's for sure.'

'And do you . . . hunt ghosts?'

'Not often. Usually I just talk about it. And write about it.' She shrugged. 'That's academics for you.'

'These talks . . . and writings . . . are how you met Matt?'

'Yeah. I gave a guest lecture at Leicester University towards the end of last term. Evening event, open to the general public. "The Psychomorphology of Paranormal Phenomena". Catchy title, don't you reckon?'

'What does it mean?'

'Cutting a long story short? It means I believe there's a scientifically explicable structure to what we think of as paranormal phenomena: clairvoyance, clairaudience, precognition, retrocognition, ghosts, doppelgängers, déjà vu, hauntings – the whole bag of tricks. Only they're not tricks, in my opinion. At least, not all of them. They're evidence of a modified level of reality. We—' She stopped and frowned at me. 'Do you want me to go on? I've seen that glazed look in too many lecture theatres to miss it across this table. A lecturing fee kind of obliges me to press on. But there's no fee here, so would you rather I skipped it?'

'I'm listening.' I sat up straight. 'OK?'

'You'd better be. Anyway, your friend *was* listening. No question about that. He was with me every step of the way.'

'The way to where?'

'I'll keep it simple. When we look at a star – any star – we're seeing the past, often the very remote past, because of the time it takes the light from that star to reach us. We don't think that's strange or paranormal. We understand it. We accept it. But, if we saw the publican who ran this place two hundred years ago walk out from behind the bar smoking a clay pipe, we'd say he was a ghost. Yet his image, his voice, even the smell of his tobacco, is here, around us, electromagnetically recorded as sensory information within the world-line web.'

'The *what*?'

'The world-line web. The mesh of intersections of every living thing's presence in space and time. Think

239

of our friend the long-dead publican as a radio signal from some weak and distant transmitter, blotted out by the much stronger signals of the here and now. Almost always blotted out, anyway. But sometimes, in certain places, *for* certain people, a resonance is set up that enables the signal to break through the interference. Then . . . we see a ghost.'

'From the past?'

'Well, that's generally where ghosts are supposed to come from.'

'Not the future?'

'Are you trying to be funny?'

'No. Not in the least.'

'Only you could be quoting your friend, word for word. He asked me about that at the end of the lecture. Within the psychomorphology I was positing, what theoretical obstacle prevented information reaching us from a transmitter out there in the future rather than back there in the past?'

'What was your answer?'

'That the future, being almost infinitely variable from our point of view, has much less chance of establishing the necessary degree of resonance.'

'Much less, but not none at all?'

'That's right. Not none at all. Not quite.'

'Did that satisfy him?'

'Apparently not. He phoned me on Monday and asked if we could meet. Said he had something I ought to see, bearing on our discussion in Leicester. Something he'd value my opinion of.'

'What was it?'

'He wasn't specific. I came here to find out.'

'A long journey, with so little to go on.'

'You get a feeling about some people.'

'A resonance?'

'Yeah. A resonance. I sensed your friend had something. So I came.'

'In search of evidence to support your theory.'

'Well, with more evidence I could run to a lecture tour of the States instead of the East Midlands. You bet I'd go in search of it.'

'Sorry you had a wasted journey.'

'So am I. How bad is he?'

'About as bad as you can get without being dead.'

'I hope he pulls through. Not just for my sake. I mean, I hardly know him, but . . .'

'Understood.'

'You have no idea what he had for me?'

'None at all.' That wasn't true, of course. Otherways was what he had for her. But something she ought to see? He couldn't simply have meant the house. Why not meet there if that was so? No, no. This was something he meant to take with him to the Ram Jam. Something he'd discovered. Something Lois Carmichael could be looking at right now, but wasn't. 'And I'm afraid we may never know.'

She set off back to Hull with nothing to show for her journey. I hadn't even mentioned Otherways to her, or Emile Posnan, or the Milners, or the Strathallans, or my own weird experiences there. I'm not sure why. I suppose I just wasn't ready to trust her with all of that. And I couldn't be certain Matt meant to trust her with it, either. My perceptions of him were blurring and changing. He wasn't the genially untroubled soul I'd been happy to believe. He was a lonely man in need of help. I'd given him less than none. Maybe he'd seen Lois Carmichael as a potential ally. Someone who'd believe him. Someone who'd believe *in* him. But how was he going to convince her? What was he going to show her? What had he found?

Lester was still hard at it when I reached Otherways. But his progress report suggested Rainbird really had been flying a kite. 'The ground-floor rooms are clean as a vicar's joke book, Mr Sheridan. I'll be finished upstairs soon. So far, you're totally bugless.'

I went into Matt's study and phoned Daisy. There'd been no news. Lucy was having a bath. I said I'd join them within the hour. Then I headed upstairs to pack some clothes for Lucy.

Hearing me on the landing, Lester popped his head out of the bedroom he was working in and said, 'I should have mentioned, Mr Sheridan, that the clean bill of health downstairs comes with a small proviso.'

'What is it?'

'One of the desk drawers in the study is locked. If you hold the only key, it's a non-issue, since it's obviously not been tampered with, but—'

'Locked?'

'Yes. You know. Key turns, engaging bolt.' He grinned. 'We call that locked.'

Of course. A locked drawer. In Matt's desk. He wasn't the secretive type. But then, maybe he hadn't needed to be – until now. 'Can you open it?'

'I should have a skeleton that'll do the trick. Haven't you got the key?'

'No.' It would be with Matt's possessions at the hospital, or with Lucy at Maydew House. Not that it mattered where it was. I had no intention of going to look for it. 'Too complicated to explain, Lester. I just need that drawer opening. Right now.'

*   *   *

There was only one thing in the drawer: a large, bulky buff envelope, torn open at one end. Matt's name and address were scrawled on it in rain-smudged black handwriting. It had been sent to him through the mail, postmarked Sussex Coast, 22 June, which meant it must have reached him only a day or so before I came to stay.

I pulled out the contents: a sheaf of photocopied pages, on which the rulings of the original paper showed through faintly between lines of copperplate handwriting that clearly didn't belong to the person who'd addressed the envelope. The top of the first page told me at once who they *did* belong to. And he was nearly sixty years dead. *Leicester Prison, 7 November 1939*. It was James Milner's confession.

Chapter Nine

There was a car I didn't recognize parked on the drive at Maydew House when I arrived. I suppose I should have guessed who it belonged to. Matt's brother – you remember Jeremy – had arrived with his parents, following a visit to the hospital. Lucy, still drowsy from the sleeping pills, was trying to explain how the accident had happened, but Mr and Mrs Prior seemed too dazed by shock at the state they'd found their son in to comprehend very much at all. Jeremy was more analytical, as you'd expect. He knew from the police that I'd witnessed the crash, and was in the middle of expressing his puzzlement over why Matt and I should have been travelling towards Otherways in separate cars at the same time when I walked in.

It was a problem I should have foreseen. I couldn't face them with the truth, but I'd failed to agree a cover story with Lucy. Fortunately, Jeremy's doubts hadn't yet organized themselves into anything specific. Thinking on my feet as fast as I could, I said I'd seen Matt driving dangerously fast through Oakham and had followed out of concern for his safety. I couldn't remember whether this clashed with my statement to the police, but I was confident Jeremy wouldn't know. It went nowhere towards explaining *why* level-headed cautious old Matt should have been driving like Jehu, but it got me off the hook, at least temporarily.

The person I really wanted to speak to, in order to pose some questions of my own, was Daisy. But getting her to myself with four other people in the house was no easy matter, especially with Lucy shooting pleading looks at me across the room that implied she badly needed me to stay put. Eventually, when Daisy went to rustle up some supper for everyone, I excused myself on the grounds of needing to fetch something from the car, which happened to be true. I returned to the house by the back door and surprised Daisy in the kitchen.

'We have to talk,' I said, signalling with my finger that we also needed to keep our voices down.

'About that?' she asked, nodding at the envelope tucked under my arm.

'Yes.'

'What is it?'

'James Milner's confession.'

'Impossible.'

'But true. I found it at Otherways. It's a photocopy, not the original. Somebody sent it to Matt through the post – anonymously.'

'Why?'

'I don't know.'

'Are you sure it's genuine?'

'As sure as I can be. As sure as I think you'll be, when you've read it. Unless, of course . . .'

'Unless what?'

'You've already read it. Have you, Daisy?'

'I told you this morning that I didn't even know for sure if it really existed.'

'Yes. So you did. But—' I told myself to stop. Daisy

245

deserved the benefit of the doubt, at least until she'd read the confession. And she did look genuinely thunderstruck. I put the envelope down on the dresser next to her. 'Lucy mustn't know. Nor must Matt's family, especially not logic-chopping Jeremy. This stays between us. OK?'

'As you wish.'

'Read it tonight. Then meet me tomorrow morning, in Oakham. Tell Lucy you need to do some shopping. Whatever.'

'All right. But I can't promise. You can see how things are.'

'We have to discuss this, Daisy. As soon as possible. I'll see you by the pump at nine o'clock.'

'Is it really so urgent? I mean, it's nearly sixty years since—'

'Read it. Then I think you'll realize that it really *is* urgent.'

'Are you trying to frighten me?'

'No. But I think what James Milner wrote may frighten you.' I paused and looked straight at her. 'It did me.'

It was true. James Milner's last recorded thoughts, penned in the condemned cell three days before his execution for the murder of his wife, were part of me now. They weren't going to go away. And nor was the fear they were grounded in.

When I drove back to Oakham two hours later, through the midnight-black countryside, I thought of Milner, lying in the shadow-barred darkness of Leicester Prison, staring into the void he was soon to be consumed by. I thought of Daisy, too, opening the envelope I'd left with her and scanning the topmost page of his long-ago

246

message. The years fell away then. Even death dissolved. Only the words remained.

Leicester Prison,
7th November 1939.

Confession is good for the soul, so they say. The judge who condemned me enjoined God to have mercy upon mine. The chaplain who ministers to me here assures me that he will, if I am genuinely repentant. Poor fellow. He did look so crestfallen when I said to him this morning, 'Perhaps I don't want his mercy. Perhaps what I really want is his wrath.'

I loved Ann. I still do. More than ever, now she is no longer here to be loved. Yet I murdered her. I killed the thing I loved most in all the world. How is that possible? How can that be? Jealousy and rage do not suffice. Ann's death, and mine, cannot be dismissed as a stage tragedy. I *was* jealous. I *was* angry. I must have been, in that moment when I clapped the gun to her head and pulled the trigger. But now, when I recall the scene, it still seems, as it has ever since, as if I am recalling a bad dream, a nightmare, a sleeping vision of impossible actions. I could not have done it. Yet I did.

How to account for it? It is so hard, so very hard. But I will try. Dr Johnson said that a man's mind is concentrated most wonderfully by the knowledge that he is to be hanged in a fortnight. I have only three days. It should not be a difficult thing. Why, then, do I find that it is? Why do I prefer to lie on my bed and think of Ann in happier times than to chronicle the steps I took along the road that led me to destroy her?

Let us begin, since we must. Let me not die with this story untold. Let the warning stand.

I was in the Michaelmas term of my second year at Oxford when my father bought Otherways. He collected me one Indian summer weekend near the end of his leave and we motored up to Rutland to see the house. He had already told me about his encounter with the architect at an embassy reception in Lisbon. I had paid his account of it scant heed, having the pressing concerns of a typically sybaritic Oxford undergraduate to distract me from my father's plans for his retirement. He had left Mama in London. Ced was busily engaged in his studies at Harrow. The excursion was unusual in that it threw my father and me together for a whole weekend, with nobody else for company. We put up at the George in Stamford.

Papa had told me to expect something unusual in Otherways. Superciliously, I had resolved to be unimpressed by what I felt sure would be a so-so Midlands hunting box. It was, of course, anything but that. There was no disguising the effect it had on me as we walked round it. I was bowled over, as my father had been and as he must have known I would be. The rooms were empty. The late Mr Oates's belongings had been removed, leaving only dirty marks where the furniture had stood. The house should therefore have looked shabby and uncared for. Instead there was instant beguilement. Otherways stripped bare is Otherways revealed in all its dangerous allurement.

Posnan's design is intoxicatingly simple. It touches something primal in the soul. There is that word again. The chaplain would be pleased to know that I am thinking of it. But in the reason and in the recollection I fear he would detect what I am now sure formed even then, that first day, a small but glittering part of my attraction to the house. It was a sickness, almost a lust. It was temptation. And we fell, my father and I, in our different ways.

Papa said Posnan had told him at the reception, 'I have built a house you would be suited to. I see you living there, I really do.' Those words of Posnan's recur to me often. 'A house you would be suited to.' Not, as one might more commonly say, 'A house that would suit you.' And 'I see you living there.' It bears a double meaning, does it not, especially for those of us who *have* lived there? Papa never discovered how Posnan came to be at the reception in the first place. His name did not appear on the guest list. He was a recluse, we were told. He was the unlikeliest of gatecrashers. Yet there he was. Perhaps he felt he had to be. Perhaps he felt he had no choice, or that we had no choice, about becoming part of the history of the house he had built.

I met Ann for the first time that day, too. It was pure chance. She was riding past as we nosed out of the drive from Otherways. Her horse was alarmed by the car engine, but she soon had him under control. She was a graceful rider and I was struck by her beauty. Who could not be? We exchanged a few polite words, nothing more. I never for a moment imagined that I had met the person whom I would one day marry. Nor, I had her word on it later, did she. But so it was. First Otherways, then Ann. In the course of an unportentous hour, it was done.

Hindsight is a valueless commodity, yet one cannot but be haunted by it. My father was so very pleased with himself for acquiring Otherways. I was delighted that he had. Ann was carefree and radiant. The world was a kind and flattering place in which to be young and privileged. Seven years have passed since then, that is all; a mere seven years. The people I shared the day with are dead, one of them at my hand. The world is changed, changed utterly. Yet Otherways still stands, ready to charm another as readily and easily as it charmed me.

At first, its charm really was all there was to be noticed. Only my mother seemed other than enchanted by the house. She and Papa moved into it the following summer, and it thereupon became my home as well as theirs. I lived there only during the vacations, of course, and subsequently, after I had followed Papa into the diplomatic service, when I was granted home leave. It was never my home from month to month. Perhaps that is why its less charming qualities revealed themselves to me, in so far as they ever did, with excruciating slowness. One found oneself, as it were, stealthily invested by a well-camouflaged enemy, only becoming aware of the fact when one was utterly surrounded.

I blamed the contrast of a quiet provincial life with the glamorous whirl of ambassadorial entertaining for the low spirits into which Mama sank after the move to Otherways. So did Papa, though for him the contrast came as a vast relief. Mama disagreed. 'It is this house,' she more than once complained. 'It oppresses me.' Her English was never perfect. We thought she meant it depressed her. Now I think she had it right all along.

Dr Temple attended Mama during her illness. It began abruptly, within a year of the move, and dragged its sorry way through most of another year before she died. The good doctor could not drive. He visited most of his patients by pony and trap. Ann could drive, however, and often conveyed him to the homes of his farther-flung patients. So it was that our acquaintance was renewed. We met at point-to-points, as well, and rode to hounds together. Soon we would take drives around the countryside in Papa's Delahaye. From hesitant beginnings, our courtship blossomed. It was a happy counterpoint to my mother's doleful decline.

One of the last things Mama said to me was also one

of the first intimations I had that Otherways was not a wholly benign environment. 'There is evil in this house, James,' she said, gripping my arm ferociously as she spoke. 'I have seen it.' I attributed the remark to the delirium which often accompanied her fevers, though she was not feverish at the time.

Ann and I were married a few months later. Many at the wedding said how sorry they were that my mother had not lived to see the day. I did not demur. But Mama had conspicuously failed to express any enthusiasm for the match, though she must have realized that we were sincerely in love. It is strange. She was never mean-spirited. It is hard for me to doubt now that she had serious reservations about our future. 'There is evil in this house. I have seen it.' Just what had she seen?

For my own part, the future then seemed an inviting, indeed exciting, prospect. I had my way to make in the diplomatic service and a loving wife to support me. She insisted on going with me when I was posted to Moscow, though I had grave doubts about how she would cope with the privations of life there. For that matter, I had some about how I would cope.

The embassy was large enough to house most of the diplomatic staff and the few wives foolhardy enough to accompany them, as well as a dubious band of servants and hangers-on. It was an externally ornate but internally dilapidated building, with a potentially lethal heating system. Edible food was in short supply and the details of day-to-day living were both dismal and debilitating. It was not the kind of existence I wanted Ann to have to endure, bravely and uncomplainingly though she did.

We came home sooner than we had anticipated, because of my father's death. It was a stroke, while he was alone in the house, as he mostly had been of late. Suddenly, I was the master of Otherways and Ann was the mistress. It was a transformation in our circumstances and it came much sooner than I would ever have predicted. But I was still just a humble third secretary with duties to return to. It was agreed between us that Ann should remain at Otherways, at least for a while. Frankly, I feared for her health in Moscow. She would have Ced's company during the holidays, and her family was near by. She and Daisy were always very close. I had no wish to uproot her at irregular intervals to face an existence that was at best tedious and at worst downright dangerous. Stalin's excesses were multiplying by the day. The first of the show trials had begun in my absence. There was no telling what might happen next. It had also been suggested that I should do a stint at the consulate in Leningrad, where dysentery and typhus were rife. All in all, I was mightily relieved when Ann agreed to stay at home in Rutland.

My hope, shared by Ann, was that I would soon be posted to a pleasanter capital, where we could be together, lead a civilized life and start a family. Unfortunately, my fluency in Russian was so rare a talent in the diplomatic service as to minimize my chances of such a transfer. Lord Chilston said I should be flattered by how indispensable he found me, and so I was, to an extent. But I was also frustrated, and ultimately depressed.

My jealousy began there, I suppose, in the knowledge that Ann, Ced and Daisy were sharing a comfortable, congenial existence at Otherways, which I could only sample in sparing doses between long stretches of Soviet austerity. When I went home, Ann would tell me of all the things they had done together – without me – and I began to wonder, back in Moscow, how many more things there might be that she did *not* tell me of.

Occasionally, during home leaves, I would have strange

dreams, in which Ann was not my wife and I was a stranger to her and Ced, or at best a friend, but neither husband nor brother. I heard whispered conversations in adjoining rooms, which I seemed to recognize as the two of them, but would find the room empty when I went into it. Either I had imagined it, or they had somehow eluded me. I did not know what to make of such experiences, but they would not leave my mind. They grew rather, expanding into fantasies I did not always recognize as such.

Ced's visit to Moscow during his Easter vacation last year gave me an opportunity to set my mind at rest by questioning him closely about life at Otherways without me. His answers should have reassured me. They revealed nothing suspicious. But that merely convinced me of the subtlety of the deception being practised upon me. Likewise, I should have taken comfort from the announcement this spring of his engagement to Daisy. Instead, I grew more suspicious still.

My state of mind soon began to affect my work. Nervous strain was not uncommon among the staff in Moscow; it was an occupational hazard. Spectating at the show trials, as I did, acquainted me with the bizarrerie of human behaviour. Guilt and innocence seemed not to be easily definable concepts. Doubt was everywhere, within and around me. I suffered some kind of nervous collapse shortly after returning to Moscow in May. The embassy doctor diagnosed complete mental and physical exhaustion. An extended period of sick leave was granted and I was shipped home.

There, at first, I felt better. Ann was worried about me. Her attentiveness consoled me. All was well, I told myself. There was nothing to fear, nothing to suspect. I would soon be my old self.

Then Ced came home from Cambridge for the summer

253

and, little by little, as my strength returned, so did my doubts, reinforced, as before, by strange dreams and disquieting misapprehensions: glimpses of Ann and Ced strolling together in the garden, apparently hand in hand; snatches of whispered endearments carried bewilderingly to my ear on fickle breezes and wavering draughts. A summer of rest and recuperation changed into a prolonged agony of mind.

There came a point when my dreaming and waking hours merged. I would see or hear something, only to realize later from the comments of others that I had dreamed it. Or I would dream that I saw or heard something, only to realize by the same retrospective process that it had actually occurred.

During a Sunday tennis party, when we rigged up a net on the lawn and entertained a dozen or so people – friends of Daisy's and some college chums of Ced's – to tea, I met one of the company, as I supposed, in the house. She said her name was Rosalind. But, when I mentioned her to the others, they were clearly bemused. There was no-one there called Rosalind.

On another occasion, I woke from an afternoon doze and saw something very strange through the bedroom window: a body of water, blue and glistening in the sunlight, filling a space between Otherways and Whitwell, where I should have been able to see cattle grazing the meadows along the banks of the Gwash – indeed, where I had seen them only an hour before. My first thought was that there had been some kind of flood, that Burley Fishponds had somehow overflowed. But there was too much water for any such event, far too much. I ran downstairs, expecting to find . . . I know not what, but not the calm that actually prevailed. When I ran into the garden and looked again the water was gone, the Gwash was meandering its placid way through gentle pastures; I was mistaken.

Ann was aware that all was not well with me. Ced must also have been. Nothing was said, nothing laid bare between us. But in their eyes I could see pity and concern, or scorn and complicity, if I chose to read it that way, which often I could not help but do.

One night, towards the end of August, I had my most disturbing dream yet. In it I was indeed married to Ann, but utterly persuaded by irrefutable evidence that she and Ced were having an affair behind my back. I say it was a dream, for it was, but it seemed real at the time, wholly and horribly real. I had entered the house late in the afternoon, unannounced and undetected, and spied on them through Ced's half-open bedroom door, making love; my wife and my brother, in passionate coition. Appalled and enraged, I had retreated outdoors and lain in wait for them. Only Ann emerged, however. There was no sign of Ced. Ann went down to the sunken garden and sat in the gazebo. I followed and watched her sitting there, smiling to herself as she recalled what had just happened. Then I took the revolver from my pocket, walked up to her and—

I swear I thought she was dead, that I had actually shot her, when I woke from that dream and found her sleeping peacefully beside me. There had been nothing to distinguish the dreamed experience from the genuine action, nothing at all. Only the fact that she was alive proved I had not done it.

That was only a couple of days before my appointment in London with the ministry doctor, who was required to decide whether I was fit to resume work. I travelled to London on Friday 1st September and saw him that afternoon. He asked me a good many questions. I answered them as reticently as I could, fearing that a recital of my apparent delusions would deter him from giving me a clean bill of health, which I was anxious to obtain, an early return to Moscow seeming to represent, at that point, my only hope of salvation. Alas, my evasiveness told against me. The doctor said I should remain at home for at least another month.

I stayed overnight at the Hotel Russell. I telephoned Ann and told her I would take in some cricket at Lord's before returning the next day by an evening train. It was agreed that she or Ced would drive into Oakham and collect me off the ten o'clock train. I prevaricated when she asked how my medical examination had gone and said that I would explain when I got home.

The truth is that I had no intention of going to Lord's. My mind was a ferment. I was the deceitful one now, paying them back, as part of me sincerely believed, for deceiving me.

I suppose London must have been awash with war talk. It is a testament to my distracted condition that I was more or less unaware of it. I caught an early afternoon train from St Pancras, got off at Manton rather than Oakham, and walked to Otherways from there. It was a still, tranquil evening, I remember. I felt strangely calm myself, calmer than I had in months.

I entered the house stealthily, expecting to find . . . something that would damn them, I suppose. But there was nothing. There was no sign of either of them. I looked into Ced's bedroom, as I had in the dream. It was empty. He was not there. Nor was Ann. The bed was unmade, though. It had recently been slept in. The sheets were still warm beneath the covers.

Something snapped inside me as I spread my hand across those warm sheets. It was as if I were living the dream anew. I fetched the revolver from the safe, loaded it and walked into the garden. If Ann was sitting in the gazebo, it would be, I seemed to know, a confirmation of all my worst fears. If not—

But she *was* sitting in the gazebo. I saw her there as I approached. It had to be true, then. She had betrayed me. I did not call out, nor did she see me approaching. I walked straight up to her. And then I made the dreamed action real.

For hours thereafter, even subsequent to my arrest and removal to Oakham police station, I believed that at any moment I would come to myself and realize that it had merely been another dream. Eventually, in the small hours of the following morning, I realized that it really had happened: I had killed Ann; I had murdered her.

I did not want to excuse what I had done, or attempt to mitigate the awfulness of it. I was guilty and admitted as much from the first. I had condemned myself long before the judge donned his black cap in court.

I have not set foot in Otherways since the evening of Saturday 2nd September. Nor, since then, have I dreamed in the way that I dreamed there; nor yet been assailed by the irrational and the unnatural to the extent that I was beneath its circular roof. I am free of all that, just as I am bound by the consequences of what I was driven to do there.

'What have you done?' asked Ced, in horror, when he returned to the house that evening and found me waiting for the police to arrive. 'What have you done?' There was no answer, beyond the deed itself. Too much had ended to be encompassed in words. Even the many words I have written now fail to circumscribe it. It is a circle without a circumference. It is a razed plane.

My father once made some enquiries about the mysterious Mr Posnan. I paid them little attention at the time. I think of the meagre information he gleaned more and more as I sit here and wait for the end I have already made to become a legal fact. It says much or little, according to your taste.

Basil Oates was a near neighbour, it appears, of Posnan's father, in Hertfordshire – somewhere near St Albans, I seem to recall. The elder Posnan was an amateur bee-keeper, the younger already then some kind of architectural student, seldom seen at home. He had constructed a bee-house for his father – a circular structure, designed to resemble a summer house but actually intended to hold a dozen or more hives, to which the bees gained access through flight holes beneath the windows, while old Mr Posnan inspected and harvested them from within. There was some suggestion that it was the elegance of this building that prompted Oates to choose the younger Posnan as his architect when he decided to set himself up as a Rutland squire.

At some point during the construction of Otherways, the elder Posnan was attacked by a swarm of bees while working in the beehouse and stung to death. The beehouse itself was later demolished. That is all my father discovered. Whether it explains why Emile Posnan abandoned architecture and fled to Lisbon is no clearer to me than it was to Papa. It lingers in my mind, however, and will not readily leave it. Emile Posnan had a great gift. Presumably, he still does. But he does not exercise it. Why is that? What has deflected him? I do not know. Or do I? Am I, perhaps, the reason? Or am I a victim of the reason? If so, I am not alone. But in this company there is no comfort.

It was a delusion. I understand that now, with dreadful

clarity. Ann did not deceive me. But something did, something that resides at Otherways, whether it is occupied or not: a madness of bees and humans; a circular despair. It is there. It will be there for as long as that house stands. It should not be. In all logic, it cannot be. Yet it is. I am the proof of that. I do not expect to be believed. Except by those who experience it for themselves. And not necessarily even by them, for it is surely easier not to believe it. Perhaps one needs to be forced to, as I have been. Then there is no choice. And only one escape.

James Clarence Milner

I phoned the hospital before leaving the Whipper-In next morning. There was no change in Matt's condition. He was said to be 'holding his own'. I imagined Jeremy and his parents would already be there; they were staying at a hotel in the centre of Leicester. It was undeniably convenient for hospital visiting, odd though it must have seemed to them that Lucy couldn't, or wouldn't, offer to put them up at Otherways. Whether Lucy was at the hospital with them was less certain; she'd looked very tired the night before. Either way, I was relying on Daisy to have engineered a solitary departure from Maydew House. Once she'd read her long-dead brother-in-law's confessional, I didn't doubt that she'd want to see me – alone.

It was still a few minutes short of nine o'clock when I crossed the market place. The rendezvous I'd specified, the town pump, was a small roofed structure, sheltered by trees, at the corner of the street, where it swung left towards the post office and Oakham School. A queue

259

had formed outside the post office, waiting for opening time. But there was nobody on the other side of the road, by the pump.

As I approached, a figure detached itself from the queue and moved off at a smartish pace away from me. It was Daisy. She was carrying the envelope in her hand. You might have thought she'd suddenly changed her mind about posting a letter. She glanced back at me, but didn't stop or slow down. She was heading for the school end of the market place, where a footpath led out past All Saints' Church. By the time she reached it, I'd caught up.

'I felt rather conspicuous back there,' she said as I drew alongside her.

'You didn't look it.'

'Good.'

'Are we going somewhere in particular?'

'No. But we can talk as we walk. Won't that appear more natural?'

'If you say so.' How things appeared seemed supremely unimportant to me. Daisy's anxiety on the point was a puzzle, but I didn't spare it much thought. 'You read it?'

'Of course.' We stepped through a gateway into the churchyard. 'I've done little else since you left last night *but* read.' She raised the envelope in front of her and sighed. 'Over and over again.'

'You agree it's authentic, then?'

'Yes.' We started along the path that circumnavigated the church, the long way round to the gate on the other side of the churchyard. 'James wrote it, no question.'

'You recognize his handwriting?'

'No. But the details . . . Only he *could* have written it.

260

No-one else called Cedric Ced. And the tennis party, when he met the non-existent guest . . .' She gave another sigh. 'I was there.'

'So it's all true?'

'I'd forgotten her name, you know.' She shook her head. 'All those years, without making the connection.' My question had apparently been disregarded. Perhaps questions weren't really necessary. 'Rosalind, of course. It had to be.'

'If this . . . confession . . . had come to light at the time, he might have had his sentence commuted.'

'On what grounds? Insanity? Diminished responsibility? He wouldn't have wanted that.'

'Because he was determined to pay with his life for what he'd done?'

'Cedric would have understood.' Again my question had been ignored. 'He wouldn't have intervened.'

'Not then, anyway.'

'What do you mean?' The meaning behind my remark hadn't escaped her.

'You know what I mean.'

'Do I?' We were leaving the churchyard now. Daisy frowned at me as she turned into the street, not, I sensed, because she didn't understand my remark, but because it somehow disappointed her.

'Why was the confession sent to Matt, Daisy?'

'Why do you think?'

'Somebody thought he should be warned of the dangers of living at Otherways.'

'That certainly seems the only plausible explanation.' Her head fell. She knew what was coming next. 'I agree.'

'Who?'

'You asked just now if I recognized James's

handwriting, and I said no. That was true. I don't remember it well enough to say.'

'But the name and address on the envelope?'

'That writing I do recognize.'

'It's Cedric's, isn't it?'

She made me wait for an answer until we'd crossed the road and turned down Dean's Lane, a narrow, curving street leading west. Then, almost in a whisper, she said, 'Yes. It's Cedric's.'

'Not dead.'

'No.'

'Nor in Russia.'

'No.'

'But here. In England. Alive and well.'

'Alive, certainly.'

'Living on the Sussex coast.'

'Perhaps.'

'Come *on*, Daisy.' She stopped and looked round at me, roused from her reverie by my exasperation. 'I've worked it out.'

'You have?'

'It wasn't difficult. The extra miles on the clock in Lucy's car? Matt didn't imagine them. You didn't stop at Worcester. You didn't even go to Worcester.'

'Where did we go, Tony? You sound as if you think you know.'

'The Sussex coast.'

'To see Cedric?'

'Well? Didn't you?'

'No. Not as such.'

'Then why don't you tell me what you did do – as such?'

'All right.' She glanced past me. There was a nervous edge to her expression and I wasn't the reason. Not the

262

whole of it, anyway. I glanced round myself, but the street behind us was empty. 'Let's go this way.'

She crossed to the other side, nodding towards the next turning on the right. It looked as if she meant to circle back to the church.

'Cedric contacted me several months ago. It was a telephone call, completely out of the blue. We hadn't spoken in all the years he'd been away. It was a shock, as you can imagine. Doubly so when he explained he was back in England and was anxious to meet me.'

'Why did he want to meet?'

'Because we're both old and don't have many years left to us. Because there is so much . . . unresolved . . . between us.'

'So you agreed to meet him?'

'No. I did not. Some things are better unresolved. Cedric committed treason, Tony. He betrayed his country. He betrayed me. It may be an old-fashioned attitude, but I'm afraid that, as far as I'm concerned, certain actions are unforgivable. I would have preferred him not to have contacted me at all. It would have been easier for both of us. But there it was. Thanks to that phone call, I knew. I couldn't unknow it.'

'What did you do?'

'I told him I needed time to think. Then I wrote to him, explaining the hopelessness of what he'd proposed, that it was far too late for any kind of reconciliation, or expiation – if that was what he was looking for. The letter required no answer. I wanted none. But he wrote back, saying there were factors I didn't understand. By then, apparently, he'd been busy researching the history of Otherways, subsequent to his selling it to Major Strathallan, I mean. About that, too, he said there were things I needed to know. He said he'd returned to set

263

certain matters right and hoped I'd agree to help him do so.'

'But you wanted none of it.'

'There's a reproachful edge to your voice which I don't deserve. I owe Cedric nothing. I made my peace with the past a long time ago. That he's been unable to is hardly surprising in view of what *his* past comprises.' We were heading back towards the church now. It lay straight ahead of us, along the street. 'I'd hardened myself to forget him. I didn't care to be reminded. Therefore I refused to be reminded. I believe I had every right to.'

'Yet in the end you *did* meet him, didn't you?'

'As I said, not as such. I ignored his letter, but another followed. Then another. Eventually, I confided in Lucinda. She agreed to meet him face to face and explain that all I required of him was a resumption of the long silence he should never have broken.'

'That was hard.'

'But not unjust, I think.'

'So only Lucy went to see him. You *did* go to the races.'

'No. I accompanied her all the way. But I waited in the car while she went in to see him.'

'What answer did she come back with?'

'The only answer he could give. Lucinda told him, you see, that if he continued to bother me, I would inform the authorities of his return to England.' She briefly let me catch her eye, and she could not disguise her shame at this. 'That *was* hard, wasn't it, Tony?'

'Yes. I think it was. But who am I to say?'

'Someone who's had the benefit, as I now have, of one of the "settings right" he alluded to. But remember this. Others beside me could expose Cedric. His insistence on delving into the past seemed to me positively to invite discovery. And discovery is a threat to me as well as him. The newspapers would have a field day. "Old spy comes home to die." What about the old spy's former fiancée? I'd be fair game, wouldn't I? Especially if the authorities pressed charges. Besides, there was Rainbird to worry about.'

'What's he got to do with this?'

'I don't know. Nothing, in all probability.' We'd arrived at the road we'd crossed a few minutes earlier, on leaving the church. But Daisy turned north now, away from its soaring spire. 'I wasn't certain of that, though. It had occurred to me that Cedric might be what Rainbird was looking for, that Cedric was his reason for lodging with me in the first place.'

'That can't—' I broke off. What I'd been about to dismiss as an absurdity wreathed itself in sudden and disturbing plausibility. 'Why would Rainbird be after Cedric?'

'I'm not saying he is. I'm just—' She shook her head. 'Lucinda always encouraged me to get rid of him. But I was reluctant to see him gone, because with him under my roof I always felt . . .' She smiled faintly. 'I always felt I could keep watch on him, even if the price I had to pay was that *he* could keep watch on *me*. Norman Rainbird is a mystery. Yet the mystery that really troubles me is not *who* he is, but *what* he is. I sent him packing. But you could hardly say he's out of our lives, could you?'

'Do you have any reason to suppose he was aware of your contact with Cedric?'

'None. But if he *was* aware, I wouldn't expect him to reveal it.'

'Has Cedric left you alone since your trip to Sussex?'

'Yes. But there's something you don't know. When we went to see him . . . it wasn't Sussex. He may have moved there since. Or the postmark may have been a deliberate blind. I don't know.'

'Not Sussex?'

'No.'

'Where, then?'

There was a park on our right now. Daisy crossed the road and started along a diagonal path leading across it. A bandstand stood in the centre. There were a few dog-walkers about and one old man on a bench, reading a newspaper. The dominant sound was of late-rush-hour traffic on the bypass to north and east of us. The sunlight was turning milky. A breeze was getting up. I remember all this so clearly – the trivial details of a humdrum locale – because of what Daisy said next. The shock of hearing her words branded our surroundings on my memory.

'We went to Devon.'

'You went—'

'Yes. Devon. I'd sworn Lucinda to secrecy. And she's honoured her promise never to tell another living soul. But I see that you *must* be told. Cedric was – and may still be, for all I know – living in Torquay. How far is that from your home?'

'Fifty or sixty miles. An hour's drive, if you pushed it.'

'Not far enough for comfort, then.'

'What do you mean?'

'You told me Matthew suspected Lucinda had lied to him about where she was the day her sister died. Now you know she *did* lie.'

'At your request.'

'Yes. At my request. And I lied, too. Just yesterday, to you.'

'But you're not lying now.'

'No. The confession – the fact that Cedric sent it to Matthew – leaves me no choice but to face you with the truth.'

'And that's what you've done.'

'Yes. But the truth runs to one more thing.'

She walked ahead, up the short flight of steps onto the bandstand, then she turned and looked down at me from the platform.

'We drove to Torquay. We visited Cedric. Then we left.'

'And drove back here?'

'No. That is, Lucinda put me on the train at Newton Abbot. We travelled back separately.'

'Why?'

'She said there was something she had to do. Alone.'

'What?'

'She didn't tell me. She said there was no need for me to know. After all she'd done for me, I didn't feel I had any right to press her on the point. Nor have I pressed her since.'

'What time train did you catch?'

'I can't recall exactly. Half-past two. A quarter to three. Something like that. It got into Birmingham about six o'clock.'

'And Lucy?'

'She didn't wait to see me off. She seemed to be in a hurry, as if . . .' She spread her hands helplessly. 'I don't know.'

'You don't *know*?'

'No. Perhaps because I don't want to. But you, Tony . . .' She shook her head at me, almost pityingly. 'You *have* to know. Don't you?'

Chapter Ten

It was just a macabre coincidence. That's what I kept telling myself. And coincidences happen. You used to say people made too much of them. You know the sort of thing: go on holiday to Fiji and meet somebody you went to school with staying in the same hotel. It's a random event, nothing more. The odds probably aren't even that remote.

But the odds didn't matter. Nor did any amount of reasoning. Lucy had been fifty miles away while you were driving home to do some gardening. Just fifty miles. And nobody except Lucy knew where she'd been going or why. It was a mystery, a blank I could fill with whatever my mind conjured up. Why did you leave Stanacombe that afternoon? Why did you go to Morwenstow? A surprise visit from your sister was a plausible answer. I didn't want it to be, but it was.

'What will you do?' Daisy had asked before we parted.

'I'm not sure,' I'd replied. 'I need to think. I need to . . . I don't know.'

'Are you going to try and find Cedric?'

'Yes.' She'd guessed my next move even before I'd acknowledged it to myself. 'I suppose I am.'

'Because of the confession?'

'It's all I have to go on. *He's* all I have to go on. If there's an answer, he's the only person who's likely to know what it is.'

'What should I tell Lucinda?'

'Nothing. Tell her nothing.'

I left Oakham that morning and started south, following the route Daisy and Lucy must have used that other morning all those weeks before, when you were still alive and our world still revolved on its comfortable axis: cross-country into Warwickshire, down the Fosse Way through the Cotswolds, then the motorway to Devon. Torquay was my destination, just as it had been theirs. But I had no appointment with Cedric Milner, or William Hall – the alias Daisy had told me he was going by – and no strong expectation that he'd still be living at the address she'd given me.

Yet I had to try. There was nothing else I could do, not least because nothing was itself no kind of option. I couldn't confront Lucy with what was, in all logic, a crazy suspicion. But I couldn't wish away the suspicion, either. Cedric had sent his dead brother's confession to Matt as some form of warning. That much I was sure of. But what, or who, was he warning him against? There had to be a way to find out.

Cedric had been living in a boarding house too far inland to count as seaside, even in a seaside town. Hatchmead was about the smartest house in a short and otherwise shabby terrace near the boundary between Victorian Torquay and post-war little-box land. It didn't look like the kind of place anyone stayed for long. About that I turned out to be wrong. Not because William

269

Hall was still in residence. He wasn't, according to the landlady, a garishly dressed woman with a smoker's cough and a face to match. 'Been gone, oh, it must be a couple of months.' And without, unsurprisingly, leaving a forwarding address. 'I don't bother asking, dear.' But Hatchmead wasn't quite a dead end. 'You could ask Wisdom. He's been here so long he's nearly a member of the family. He was the only one to get two words out of Mr Hall.'

I never got round to asking whether Wisdom was a Christian name, surname or nickname. The man himself wasn't in, anyway. But you were likelier to see an iceberg floating across Torbay, apparently, than fail to find him on his favourite bar-end stool come opening time at the Top Hat, the second closest pub to Hatchmead. (He'd fallen out with the landlord of the closest.) I killed an hour out at a headland car park above the bay (no icebergs), then drove back in search of him.

The Top Hat was a small street-corner local, possessed of some secret appeal that meant it was three-quarters full within ten minutes of opening. Nobody had beaten Wisdom to his regular berth, however. There he was, propped against a quart bottle of whisky, weighed down by a pint of pennies, drinking Mackeson and poring over a jumbo crossword puzzle that filled half the page of a newspaper he'd folded open in front of him. I didn't question his identity for a second. He was somewhere, if not anywhere, between sixty and eighty, dressed in a threadbare old suit, fraying shirt and grubby-knotted tie. He was almost completely bald, with a face as grey as his few remaining tufts of hair and a strange half-smiling expression that managed to mix timidity with obstinate pride.

270

'Mr Wisdom?' I ventured after squeezing into a narrow space at the bar beside him and buying a drink.

'Just Wisdom,' he replied in a reedy voice, letting his glasses slip down his nose so that he could give me a darting glance of his water-rat eyes.

'Your landlady said I might find you here.'

'Did she?' He grimaced. 'It's the wrong day of the week for a Lottery win. So, it can't be good news.'

'Sorry about that.'

'Bet you're not, Mr . . .'

'Sheridan. Tony Sheridan. Actually, it's really a former fellow tenant of yours I'm looking for. William Hall.'

'Is that right?'

'You know him?'

'He used to live at Hatchmead. I still do.'

'Why did he leave?'

'A better question is why I stay. Vi Thursby's not the motherly sort, let me tell you.'

'She said you and he . . . got on.'

'Chatting to her's not worth the secondary smoking. You can't rely on a word she coughs out.'

'But did you . . . get on with him?'

'We might have passed the time of day.'

'Here?'

'He's not a drinking man.'

'"He's not." Present tense. Sounds like you still know him.'

'I never said that.'

'You don't seem to be saying much at all.'

'You catch on fast.'

'Look.' I pulled the envelope holding James Milner's confession out of my coat pocket. 'I'm trying to contact Mr Hall on an urgent matter.'

'Life and death?'

'You could say that.'

'I just did.'

'This is his writing. Recognize it?'

Wisdom stared down at Matt's name and address. 'You said your name was Sheridan, not Prior.'

'Matt Prior is a friend of mine. He's ill.'

'What kind of ill?'

'Car accident. He's in hospital.'

'Accidents.' Wisdom wrinkled his nose thoughtfully. 'Nasty things.'

'Yes. They are.'

'Sheridan.' He nodded. His brow furrowed. 'Don't I remember that name? In the paper, a couple of months back. Accidental death. A cliff fall, wasn't it?'

'You have a good memory, Wisdom.'

'For some things. You weren't related to that Sheridan, were you?'

'My wife.'

'Sorry.' A tilt of his head seemed to be a signal that his sorrow was genuine.

'Thanks.'

'I lost my wife quite a few years ago. Still wear the ring, though.' He pushed his wedding ring proud of the finger with his thumb and frowned at it, then looked up at me. 'You, too, I see.'

'Yes.'

'Mrs Sheridan wear a ring, did she?'

'Of course.'

'I thought it might have gone out of fashion.'

'No. Look, I—'

'Which finger?'

'What?'

'Which finger did she wear it on?'

I stared at him, more puzzled than I was exasperated.

It was a bizarre question. People wear their wedding ring on their ring finger. He knew that. Of course he did. Everybody knows that. But it wasn't true of you, was it, Marina? Not after you broke your ring finger a few years ago. The break left you with an enlarged knuckle, so you had to wear the ring on your middle finger. A trivial fact known to few. And it shouldn't have been known to this man at all. But, if it wasn't, why was he asking? And if it was, the same question applied.

'Which finger?' he gently prompted.

'Middle.'

'Is that so?'

'Yes. Why did you ask?'

'Curiosity.'

'Nothing more?'

'What more could there be?'

'I don't know.'

'Neither do I. And I don't know that there's anything I can tell you about Bill Hall, either. Not a forthcoming man, our Bill. Not one to tell you his life story at second or third acquaintance. Or a hundred and third, come to that.'

'I'm anxious to contact him.'

'You said.' There was that little tilt of the head again, the one he seemed to reserve for his more sincere remarks. *Message received and understood*, it somehow implied. Or was I kidding myself? I couldn't be sure. There was either more to Wisdom than met the eye – or less. But no amount of interrogation was going to clinch the matter, one way or the other. 'If I see him, I'll be sure to tell him.'

'Do you expect to see him?'

'No. I've not clapped eyes on him since he moved out of Hatchmead. I've no idea where he is. Torquay, or Timbuktu, or Tobermory. Your guess is as good as mine.'

'I doubt it is.'

'Well, some people are better guessers than others, it's true. I keep in trim.' He nodded down at the newspaper. 'You have to at my age.'

'And what's your guess?'

'That unlikely things do happen.' He swallowed some Mackeson. 'Not often, but not never.'

As soon as I left the Top Hat, doubt started to undermine my frail confidence in Wisdom as a conduit for communication with Cedric Milner. He might be no more than a lonely old man, eager to grab the merest hint of intrigue. Running verbal rings round me had to be more exciting than solving last week's crossword.

I didn't really believe that, of course. But I was tired, my mind numbed by too many questions. The only people I could trust absolutely were out of reach. And the people I wanted to trust instead were compromised by discoveries I'd have preferred not to make. Yet, as Daisy had said, once you know something, you can't unknow it. Driving across Dartmoor that evening, my thoughts refused to leave the subject alone. Had Lucy come this way after dropping Daisy at Newton Abbot? Had she planned what she meant to do?

Beyond Okehampton, in the empty stretches of northwest Devon, fingers of declining sunlight stretched themselves across the landscape, casting shadows of trees and hedges and a solitary speeding car beside and behind me. I didn't know what I was running from any more than I knew what I was running towards. But everything was open to question now. Everything was tinged with doubt.

When I entered Stanacombe, only the must of desertion and neglect was waiting for me. There was nothing else. Our life there, our life together, was suddenly and tangibly past. This was the moment, I realized, when the future should have arrived. This was when and how I was supposed to begin forgetting you. But I couldn't forget a past I was still rewriting. Why had Wisdom asked about your ring? How could he have known?

And then there was the guilt I'd spent so long talking myself out of. Wisdom had noticed I still wore a ring. But I couldn't help remembering lying with Lucy, your sister, in the bed she shared with Matt, my friend, and all the time – every time – *our* ring had been on my finger. You were dead. I couldn't betray you. Yet I could betray myself.

I rang the hospital and was told there'd been no change in Matt's condition. I thought of Lucy and the anxiety she was enduring on his account, compounded now by my unexplained absence. Then I thought of the day of your death. One figure at the top of Henna Cliff – or two? There was a single true version of events. But in my mind all the possibilities – the mad, the sad and the downright unthinkable – swirled together until I couldn't focus on what was probable or conceivable any more, until everything was as unlikely as everything else.

I'd given Wisdom our number, so I resisted the strong temptation to unplug the phone. Lucy didn't call, as I'd feared she might. What she was thinking I couldn't imagine. Perhaps the Priors weren't leaving her much time to think about anything. Or perhaps Stanacombe was the last place she'd have expected me to be.

Nobody else called, either. There was no reason why

they should. The idea of Cedric Milner contacting me, or even knowing I wanted him to, began to seem more and more absurd. I made up the bed and lay there, too cold and weary to sleep, staring into the utter blankness of the night until it filled my mind.

Early next morning I drove into Bude to buy a few basic foodstuffs: milk, butter, bread, cheese. I wasn't sure why I was stocking up, even to this basic level. I had no intention of staying at Stanacombe for long. But then I had no real intentions of any kind. I must have been on autopilot, I suppose, functioning according to your domestic rules. Except that you'd have gone to the grocer and the baker in Holsworthy, not Bude's very own soulless superstore.

It was in the car park, as I was leaving, that I recognized the policeman who'd been waiting for me at Stanacombe to tell me you were dead. He was off duty, dressed casually, unravelling himself from a car which looked too small for him. A woman was with him, and a child she was busy strapping into a pushchair. It was the Saturday morning supermarket run for him and his family. On an impulse, I walked across and said hello.

At first he couldn't remember how we'd met. Why should he have done? It hadn't been memorable for him. It was what he did for a living. Eventually, he did remember. 'How are you getting on, then?' he asked with wary amiability.

'I'm not sure,' I replied, with total accuracy. 'Could I ask you about a couple of things?'

Denying himself the start of a tour of the shopping aisles didn't seem to be a huge sacrifice. He told his wife to go ahead and he'd catch up. 'What sort of things?' he asked.

'There never was any doubt about . . . the outcome of the inquest, was there?'

'Why should there be?'

'Well, I've sometimes wondered if . . . it could have been more complicated than we thought.'

'Complicated?'

'I mean, how can we be sure it was an accident?'

'The coroner was satisfied.'

'But you'd have . . . checked other possibilities, wouldn't you?'

'You seemed adamant, as I recall, Mr Sheridan, that your wife wasn't the suicidal type.'

'I didn't mean suicide.'

'What *are* you suggesting, then?'

'In situations like this, how do you rule out . . . foul play?'

'There were no indications of anything like that.'

'But what indications would there be? I mean, if my wife was taken by surprise, while she was near the edge of the cliff, there wouldn't be any signs of a struggle, would there? And there were no witnesses to her fall. Nobody can say for certain what happened.'

'No.' He frowned. 'They can't.'

'So, there has to be some doubt. Doesn't there?'

'Not as far as we're concerned, Mr Sheridan. It was just a tragic accident. The case is closed. Unless . . .' He shrugged.

'Unless what?'

'You can give my superiors in CID a good reason to reopen it.' He looked me in the eye. 'Can you?'

'No.' I shook my head. 'Not really.'

I drove back to Stanacombe and drank some coffee, standing in the kitchen and looking out at the garden

277

you'd had all sorts of plans for. It was overgrown now, the grass lank, the shrubs straggling. Nature was making short work of our aspirations for the future.

It was a fine morning, though clouds were bunching out to the west and there was a keen edge to the breeze. I put on my boots and walked out across the fields to the cliff path. The spring flowers were gone now, reabsorbed within the greenery of the hedges. But the sea didn't change. It was as blue and limitless as it must have appeared to you that afternoon, lit from the west rather than the east, the shadows reaching inland behind you, not out into the surf, as they did for me.

I turned north, towards Duckpool and the cliffs beyond. Morwenstow was where I was going. Morwenstow and Henna Cliff, where I could sit on the bench by the stile and remember the times when you'd sat beside me.

I got there an hour later, scrambling up the rocky path from the bridge across the stream below the cliff. I'd only passed a couple of walkers on the way. It was still too early for most of them. That's why I thought I'd have the cliff top to myself. But, as I approached the stile, I saw there was a figure sitting on the bench: a white-haired man, smoking a cigarette. He was dressed in tweed, with a yellow woollen scarf knotted round his neck.

He looked round and up at me as I mounted the stile. His face was lined and bearded, his beard merely grey where his hair was snowy, a schoolboyish quiff of it wafting across his forehead in the breeze. Our eyes met. His were a rheumy blue, like two small mirrors of the ocean. There was a faint tremor in his hand, where he

278

held the cigarette. He drew on it, still looking at me as I climbed down onto his side of the stile.

'Good morning,' I said.

'Good morning,' he responded. The words came slowly, gravelly and unaccented. 'Come far?'

'No. I live just to the south.'

'Whereabouts?'

'A house called Stanacombe. D'you know it?'

'I'm a stranger here,' he said, his tone somehow implying this wasn't an answer to my question.

'On holiday?'

'No. I'm here to meet someone.'

'Up *here*?'

'Yes.'

'Strange place for a rendezvous.'

'Not if you like to be able to see people coming.' He glanced around at the empty fields and the blank sea-filled horizon. 'But I don't exactly have an appointment.'

'No?'

'This was just a guess on my part. Somewhere I thought he might turn up. Somewhere that has . . . associations for him.'

'Is he expecting you?'

'Expecting. Or hoping.'

I looked straight at him. 'My name's Tony Sheridan.'

'I know.'

'Yes. I thought you probably did.'

'Why don't you join me?'

I walked across to the bench and sat down beside him. He offered me a cigarette. I took one and he lit it for me. The taste was pungent and unfamiliar. I coughed.

'Russian,' he said expressionlessly.

'In a Benson and Hedges pack?'

'A precaution. It *doesn't* pay to advertise.'

'Hence William Hall, rather than Cedric Milner.'

'Who put you on to me?'

'Daisy.'

He nodded. 'Technically, a breach of our understanding.'

'I left her little choice.'

'Because of my communication with your friend?'

'Among other things.'

'I gather he's ill.'

'Severely injured in a car crash.'

'Accidental?'

'Yes.'

'Sure of that?'

'Absolutely.'

'Only it can be difficult. To be absolutely sure of such things.'

'Why did you send him your brother's confession?'

'Why do you think?'

'As a warning of some kind.'

'If that's what you think, you must be aware that there's something to warn him about.'

'Otherways.'

'It did for James. And for Ann. Since returning, I've discovered there have gone on being victims. There's no need for the Priors to be added to the list.'

'You could have explained that to Matt face to face.'

'Not without breaking my word to Daisy.'

'The penalty for which could have been exposure for what you are: a spy, a traitor, a wanted criminal.'

'Do I look like any of those things, Mr Sheridan?' He watched the smoke he'd just breathed out drift away into the air. 'I'm just a harmless old man.'

'Like Wisdom.'

'Not quite like Wisdom.'

'Why did you leave Hatchmead?'

'Because I'd been there long enough.'

'Where did you go?'

'You don't need to know.'

'What *do* I need to know?'

'That Otherways is dangerous for those who live there, or are close to those who live there. When I first read James's confession, I thought the effect the house seemed to have had on him must have been self-induced. But since I came back here—'

'Why did you come back?'

'Because I'm an Englishman. This is where I was born and this is where I'll die.'

'But conceived in Russia.'

He gave a wintry little smile. 'And by the same token to be buried there? I don't think so.'

'How long have you been back?'

'Long enough to become familiar with the recent history of Otherways.'

'And that's convinced you your brother didn't imagine its baleful influence?'

'I once surveyed the place, you know. To satisfy my intellectual curiosity about Posnan's design. About the mathematics of it, I mean. It always seemed to me that there was something odd going on with the ratios of curvature.'

'And was there?'

'Not exactly. That was the oddest part of it. I could never assemble a consistent set of figures. Every time I double-checked . . . they changed.'

'That's not possible.'

'It shouldn't be, certainly.'

'What did you expect Matt to do after you'd sent him the confession?'

'I *hoped* he would leave Otherways. For his sake – and for his wife's.'

'You've met Lucy, I believe.'

'She acted as Daisy's messenger.'

'How would you describe her state of mind on the day she came to see you?'

'Calm. Decisive. Detached.'

'Did she say where she was going afterwards?'

'No. She volunteered nothing.'

'Nobody knows, you see. She had a car. But she put Daisy on the train at Newton Abbot.'

'Daisy was with her?' He looked round at me, eyes wide with surprise. 'In Torquay?'

'Apparently.'

'I didn't know that.' He looked away again and made a slow sweeping gesture with his free hand. 'If I had . . .'

'I wondered if it was something . . . in Lucy's demeanour . . . that prompted you to write to Matt. That . . . plus the coincidence of my wife's death, of course.'

'It *was* quite a coincidence.' He was staring at me intently now. 'And coincidences can be worrying.'

'Hold on. Are you saying . . .' Another link forged itself in my mind. 'You knew Marina was Lucy's sister?'

'Of course. It explains why Mrs Prior used such a distant solicitor for the purchase of Otherways.'

I gaped at him, literally dumbstruck. You'd handled the conveyancing for Matt and Lucy when they bought Otherways, just as you had for all their previous houses. Naturally. What of it? What in God's name was Cedric getting at?

'I wanted to find out who the current owner was, so I asked the estate agent who'd handled the sale. They referred me to the owner's solicitor – your wife. That's why I went to her. I thought the link with Otherways might make her more—'

'You went to her? To Marina?'

'Yes.' He gazed at me calmly. 'As of earlier this year, I became a client of hers.'

'*What?*'

'As I say, I chose her because the Priors were also her clients. I judged that would make things easier . . . in the long run. Besides, who else could I choose? It was better than sticking a pin in the Law Society handbook.'

'That's how you knew which finger she wore her wedding ring on.'

He nodded. 'Correct. I notice things, you see. It can be useful.'

'But I don't understand. Why did you need a solicitor?'

'I wanted to test the water, see whether the sky really would fall in if I admitted who I was. I hoped the authorities would agree to turn a blind eye. Naïve of me, I dare say.'

'They turned you down?'

'Not exactly. As far as I know, your wife hadn't done more than make a few tentative enquiries when she died.'

'She knew who you were?'

'Necessarily.'

'And what you'd done?'

'In outline terms.'

'And that you'd once lived in the house Lucy and Matt had just bought?'

'Yes. Confidentially, of course. I trusted her to keep the information to herself. Even the enquiries she made on my behalf were . . . in principle only.'

'Marina *was* trustworthy.' Perhaps too trustworthy is what I was thinking. Lucy had trusted you with the secret of Matt's impotence and Cedric with the secret of his identity. You hadn't breathed a word to me on either score. You'd been the ideal sister and the model solicitor. You never told me a lie. You never would have done. If I'd asked, you'd have answered truthfully. But I hadn't known the questions. And now I was learning the answers the hard way. 'What have you done since she died?'

'Lain low.'

'Why not find another solicitor?'

'Because the first one met with a fatal accident.'

'You thought . . . No, no. That's ridiculous. No-one's after you, Cedric.' Weren't they? What had Daisy said about Rainbird? *It had occurred to me that Cedric might be what Rainbird was looking for.* 'You said Marina had made enquiries in principle only.'

'So she had.'

'Then how could anyone have known?'

'Somebody could have told them.'

'Who?'

'Daisy. Or Mrs Prior.'

'That's crazy. Why should they?'

'I don't know. Maybe precautions have been taken, pressure been brought to bear. I could have been . . . pre-empted.'

'No you couldn't. For God's sake, why would anyone kill Marina to get at you? Why not just—'

'Kill me instead?'

'Yes. If you like.'

'Good question.' He looked out to sea. 'A final warning, perhaps. Don't make waves.'

'What is there for you to make waves *about*?'

284

'Safer for you not to know, Tony. Can I call you Tony? I carry a . . . dark secret with me, wherever I go. I burden no-one else with it. I certainly didn't inflict it on your wife. But . . . if it was thought I had . . .' He shook his head and drew deep on his cigarette. 'She *was* my solicitor.'

'But who knew that?'

'Another good question. With an answer you'll care for even less.'

'Well?'

'Lucy Prior.' He turned towards me, letting me see by the set of his eyes that he was in earnest. 'She told me so that day, when we met in Torquay. "Withdraw your business from my sister's practice." Those were her exact words.'

'How could she have known?'

'I didn't ask. She didn't allow me the luxury of asking very much at all, as a matter of fact. The terms she put to me for her and Daisy's silence about my return to England were strictly nonnegotiable. I was to leave, as quickly and quietly as—'

'Hang on. You were to leave? As in leave the country?'

'That's what she told me. And that's what I told her I'd do.'

'But Daisy said she only wanted you to stop bothering her.'

We looked at each other for several long moments as the wind stirred the grass that clung to the edge of the cliff a few yards from where we sat. Then Cedric said, 'It seems Mrs Prior applied some conditions of her own.'

'Why would she do that?'

'You tell me.'

But I couldn't. Nothing made sense any more. You'd been this man's solicitor, a fact known to Lucy, apparently, but not to me. You wouldn't have broken a professional confidence, though. You simply wouldn't, would you? Why should Lucy have been so anxious to be rid of him, anyway? And why had you come to Morwenstow that afternoon? To meet her? Was that it, Marina? Was that really it?

'I didn't honour our bargain, of course,' Cedric went on. 'I didn't go back to Russia. I'm never going back there. At my age, retreats aren't worth the effort. Besides, your wife's death cancelled the agreement as far as I was concerned.'

'Why?'

'I got her into it, and I should have been able to get her out. I failed her. But even so . . .' He lowered his head. 'They needn't have killed her.'

'Who are "they"?'

'That's what it comes down to, doesn't it? Who. And why, of course. I came to see you because, whatever I owe your wife – and that's a lot – I owe you, in a sense, as well. You were entitled to know as much as I've told you, for her sake. I can't tell you everything, though. It wouldn't be fair. And it wouldn't be wise.'

'You believe Marina was murdered?'

'I do.'

'So do I.' He looked at me sharply as I spoke, as if noting and acknowledging what those few words meant. I'd stopped trying to reason my way out of the unthinkable. The sooner I knew the worst – all of it – the better. 'Who's responsible, Cedric? Who did it?'

'I'm not sure.'

'But I have to be.'

'Of course.'

'Are you going to help me?'

'Oh, I expect so.' He smiled ruefully. 'I don't suppose I'd have come here otherwise.'

286

Cedric had left his car by the farm, just above Morwenstow Church, so we set off in that direction, along the side of the coomb. The church and the rectory beside it stood bowered in trees ahead of us. Sheep were grazing the sloping field between. The scene was tranquil, heavy with summer's ease. But I felt anxious and fretful, unsure what was happening, uncertain, in the truest sense, of where we were going.

'Those dishes on the horizon,' said Cedric between gulps of air – the walk was testing him. 'What are they?' He was pointing to the CSO's aerials, which had struck me as weird and otherworldly when I'd first seen them, only for me to cease even noticing them within a few weeks of moving into Stanacombe.

'Composite Signals Organization Station,' I replied.

'Ministry of Defence?'

'Don't think so. Why? Hard to kick the habit, is it?'

'Very funny, Tony. Really. Very funny.'

'Why did you do it? I'd like to know. Honestly. So would Duncan Strathallan.'

'You spoke to him?'

'Yes. And what he said stuck in my mind. Stalin was crazed, evil. How could you justify giving a man like that the means to turn London into another Hiroshima? Even if you are, or were, a sincere communist, how could—'

'Balance of terror.'

'What?'

'The only time the Bomb was dropped was when only one side had it. You said so yourself: Hiroshima. But not Shanghai. What stopped Truman ordering a nuclear strike against China after the fall of Seoul in

287

January 'fifty-one? The knowledge that Stalin might retaliate in Europe. That's what.'

'So, you were just a broker for world peace.'

'If you like.'

'In that case, I'm surprised you don't welcome the chance of a trial. You could end up with a Nobel Prize instead of a prison sentence.'

Cedric pulled up. He was breathing heavily now and suddenly looked frail and old. He leaned on my arm and smiled, or winced. It was hard to tell the difference. 'There'll be no trial.' He coughed. 'Damn tobacco. And age. Damn them both. I feel quite young, if I sit still and do nothing. Then . . .' His voice trailed off.

'You could have done that in Moscow.'

'And died there. I know. Then, some time soon, you could have read my obituary in the *Daily Telegraph*. A few tart little Cold War paragraphs. They've probably been on file since Brezhnev's day. Well, they wouldn't have told you much. Certainly not the truth.'

'What is the truth?'

'Something you don't need to know. And something we don't have time for, anyway. You want to know who killed Marina.'

'Yes.'

'And why.'

'Yes.'

'Then we have to start with her sister. We have to find out what she did that day. Do you know her well enough to say if she's lying or not?'

'Yes.'

'Then I suggest we put her to the test.'

'This isn't a good time.'

'For any of us, I dare say.' He started walking again. 'But it's the only time we've got.'

288

*　　*　　*

We laid our plans, such as they were, between there and the car park serving the tearoom at the farm. Several cars were sharing the space, though none of the occupants were anywhere to be seen. Either drinking tea or walking the coast path, I assumed. The oldest and most rust-pocked vehicle in view was Cedric's, licensed to Wisdom, I gathered, though seldom driven by him. We'd agreed to leave it at Stanacombe and drive north in my car.

Cedric said nothing during his short spell at the wheel. It seemed as if he needed all his concentration to cope with the narrow lanes. We spent only as long at Stana-combe as I needed to pack my bag, then switched cars and started off again, heading for Stratton and the A3072. I reckoned on joining the motorway beyond Tiverton and making as good a time as I could back to Rutland. I reckoned on many things, I suppose. But Cedric, well, maybe he reckoned better. Because he was the one of us who wasn't surprised by what happened next.

A red saloon car started tailgating me a few minutes after we left Stanacombe. I was doing about 45, which was pushing it, but they wanted to go faster. Local youths out for a Saturday morning spin? The car looked too smart for that, and I couldn't make out the driver in the mirror. There was too much reflection on the windscreen from sunlight filtering confusingly through the trees.

'They followed us from Morwenstow,' Cedric calmly announced.

'What?'

'You need to be observant in my profession.'

'You're wrong. Nobody's following us. Except in the literal sense.'

289

'No. *You're* wrong. They're following.' He pointed at the rear-view mirror. 'They've been on your tail since you left Rutland, waiting for me to show myself.'

'Rubbish.'

'I wish it were. Sadly, it's the only possible conclusion. They must have singled you out as the one person I'd be willing to show myself *for*. Patient and cunning, as ever.' He shook his head. 'I should have guessed.'

The lane broadened and straightened slightly ahead. I slowed, daring the red saloon to overtake and so disprove Cedric's theory. To my relief, it did just that, surging past in a burst of acceleration. 'See?'

'I see.'

'Just joyriders.' The car vanished round the next bend. 'You're getting paranoid.'

'I really should have guessed,' he repeated. 'Maybe I did.'

'For God's sake, Cedric. There's nothing to worry about.'

'If you let them stop us, we're finished.'

'What are you talking about?'

'Our lives. What's left of them. Yours and mine.'

'You're mad.' As I spoke, we rounded the bend. And there was the red saloon, slewed across the lane dead ahead. The driver, a burly figure in dark clothes, was walking towards us, signalling for us to halt. Another man was moving on the far side of the car. He was holding something in his hand that looked awfully like a gun.

'If you stop,' Cedric said softly, 'we're dead.'

I glanced round at him, then at the car ahead and the man moving slowly to meet us. Part of me wanted badly, so very badly, to believe this wasn't happening. But it was.

290

I slowed fractionally, then instinct kicked in and I pressed the accelerator to the floor. You'd always said we should change to a smaller car after leaving London, one better suited to the West Country lanes. This was the moment I was glad we'd never got round to doing anything about it.

I aimed for the bonnet of the other car, hoping the impact would push it clear of the hedge and let us through. The driver leaped out of our path and the other man ran for cover. We hit nose to wing in a jolting yowl of metal and headlamp glass. We rolled to the right, but kept going ahead. There was a screech, then a bump, as first the hedge, then the wall within it, bounced us off, and we were through, lurching back into the centre of the lane. For a second the swerve was too much for me, then I regained control, or perhaps the car did it for me. I risked a glance in the mirror and saw the two men piling back into their car. One of them was holding something to his ear – a phone, maybe.

'If you know any back routes, take them now,' said Cedric. 'Your local gen is about our only advantage.'

'What the hell is going on, Cedric?'

'Damage limitation, in the official jargon. And we're the damage.'

'This doesn't make any sense.'

'Oh, it does. Believe me, it does.'

'Who were those people?'

'Civil servants, I imagine. Of the licensed-to-kill variety.'

'That can't be.'

'But it is. And crashing past their roadblock isn't the end of it. I'm where they want me now, Tony. Out in the open. And I'm sorry to say . . .' He looked round at me. 'You're out there with me.'

Chapter Eleven

The incident in the lane near Stanacombe had lasted less than thirty seconds from start to finish. Yet it had changed everything. Until then, I'd been able to keep an open mind about Cedric's claim that you'd been killed to get at him. I'd told him I believed it, but that wasn't really true. How could I believe something so outlandish? Well, I could now. And I did.

Cedric was right about my familiarity with the area giving us an edge. A diversion through Poughill and Bude, then a winding switchback across the Ottery valley towards Launceston, kept us clear of our pursuers. Cedric reckoned they'd guess the motorway was our destination and have somebody lying in wait for us if they failed to catch up *en route*. Yet it was only the car that made us readily identifiable. It might be slower to go by other means, but it might also be safer. Hence Cedric's plan: drive to Plymouth and catch a train. I went along with the idea because crowds suddenly seemed to offer a meagre kind of protection. Protection from what exactly was a moot point. Cedric wouldn't say and I had only a glimpse of the hard-faced driver of the red saloon to go on.

'This is crazy, Cedric.'

'I never said it wasn't.'

'Why should anyone be out to kill you?'

'You'd do better to concentrate on how they found me.'

'By following me.'

'Yes. But who knew you were worth following?'

'Daisy?'

'Exactly. And she gave you just the incentive you needed, didn't she, by dropping that bombshell about Lucy Prior?'

'I don't understand where Lucy fits into this.'

'Maybe she doesn't, Tony. Don't you see? Who told her Marina was my solicitor? And whose word do we have for it that she drove back from Torquay alone?'

'You're saying Daisy set me up?'

'Maybe. Maybe she was told to. By whoever Marina contacted on my behalf.'

'Why would Daisy do that?'

'My brother murdered her sister. And I betrayed her country. They could be reasons enough. Besides, I don't suppose she thought . . . extreme sanctions . . . would be brought to bear.'

'Why are they being brought to bear, Cedric? You have to tell me.'

'No. What I have to do is a deal. To get you, and me as well with any luck, off the hook.'

'And how can you accomplish that?'

'By meeting someone who has influence in the right quarters.'

'You know such a person?'

'I do.'

'Then why the hell didn't you contact them months ago? Why use Marina at all?'

'Because that way I could avoid the central issue and so could they. I was trying to offer them a painless solution to the problem.'

'But they rejected it?'

'Conclusively.'

'If Daisy's on their side, whichever side that is, why did they let you slip through the net the first time? Why not simply send the police round to Hatchmead to arrest you?'

'Because arresting me is the last thing they have in mind. And because they were still willing then to let me go quietly. For old times' sake, I suppose. I was owed that much, apparently.'

'Owed for what?'

'We come back to the same old question. I'm not going to tell you, Tony. They killed Marina because they thought I'd told her. And I don't think you could successfully pretend not to know once you did. So, cling to your ignorance. It may save your life.'

'Or it may not. You're going to have to tell me eventually.'

He thought about that for a moment, then gave a reluctant little nod. 'You're probably right. But eventually's not yet.'

A summer Saturday meant lots of traffic in Plymouth. But delay was strangely reassuring. The red saloon hadn't reappeared in the rear-view mirror and it didn't seem feasible to suppose that anyone could have calculated the indirect route we were taking. There were crowds of holidaymakers at the station and they had a similar effect to the traffic congestion. I began to relax, or at least feel marginally less anxious. Cedric's state of mind was hard to read. I suppose he'd spent so long

294

concealing his true emotions that it had become more of a habit than a technique.

'I think we're in the clear,' he grudgingly admitted, 'but I can't be sure.'

'Let's try and look on the bright side. Assume we are. Do we just get on the next train to the Midlands?'

'No. I have to make a phone call first.'

'I ought to make one myself. To the hospital. Check how Matt's doing.'

'That's too risky. They may have anticipated you'd do that. If they traced it here, they'd know we'd taken the train.'

'How come your call's worth the risk, then?'

'Because it's one they won't have anticipated.'

'To your mystery man.'

'Exactly. So, if there is any risk, it has to be taken. While I do that, buy us a couple of tickets for the next train to London.'

'London?'

'Safety in numbers, Tony. That makes London as safe a place as we'll find. Oh, and you'd better pay in cash.'

'I'm not sure I've got enough.'

'Allow me.' He took out his wallet and handed me a wad of twenties. 'Just as well I never use plastic, isn't it?'

The mystery man turned out not to be in. What we were going to do if he'd gone to Tuscany for a month didn't bear contemplation. Not, at least, until Cedric had tried again later. We boarded the next train to London, due into Paddington at three o'clock. There was nothing to do till then but sit where we could find a space amidst the families and elderly couples making their way home after a West Country holiday. I bought a drink to steady my nerves, then another, but they didn't have any noticeable effect.

'I get the impression', said Cedric, shortly after we'd left Exeter, 'that Lucy Prior's guilt or innocence matters a great deal to you, Tony.'

'Of course it does. She's my sister-in-law.'

'Did you seriously suspect her of . . .' He lowered his voice and smiled thinly at the abstruseness he felt obliged to resort to, despite the raised voices all around. 'Sororicide?'

'I did for a while.' I smiled myself then. This was one small relief: if an official conspiracy to silence Cedric Milner really existed, Lucy was exonerated.

'Why?' His voice was soft, no more than a verbal nudge.

'Circumstances . . . made it seem possible.'

'Really?'

'Yes. Really.'

'Then you must have . . . imputed a motive.'

I had, of course. But I couldn't tell him what it was. It was too shameful to admit. 'Blame Otherways. You know the tricks that place can play.'

'Only too well.'

'Did it ever play any on you?'

'Oh yes. I wasn't immune, though clearly nothing like as susceptible as James. I was already a boarder at Harrow when we moved there, so I always spent as much or more time elsewhere – Harrow, then Cambridge. The surveying experiment was my first real insight into the peculiarities of the house. I did that the summer before I went up to Cambridge. I just couldn't get the measurements right. There was always a . . . marginal inconsistency. I blamed my tools. Then I blamed myself. Then I gave up. The house beat me, I suppose you could say. Or maybe it showed me its secret without my being able to grasp what it was.'

'Do you grasp it now?'

'Put it this way. There's more to it than limestone and mortar. If I had to guess why you became suspicious of your sister-in-law, I think I'd guess right. But I have the advantage of experience. Ann and I, during the months we spent alone at Otherways, while James was watching the show trials in Moscow . . .'

'You had an affair?'

'No. But we came close. So very close. And history repeats itself, doesn't it?' He looked at me quizzically. 'Especially at Otherways.'

'Not any more,' I said briskly, trying to brush off his implication before he could force me to acknowledge it. 'I've persuaded Lucy to move in with Daisy while Matt's in hospital. That could be a long time. So, for the present, the house stands empty.'

'Empty. But always waiting.' His gaze lost its focus. 'Maybe that's why I came back.'

At some point – blame the drink or the motion of the train – I fell asleep. When I woke, Cedric wasn't there. I wasn't worried at first – he'd gone out several times before for a smoke. But when his absence had stretched to half a pack's worth, I became really concerned. For some stupid reason the idea came to me that we'd stopped without my waking and he'd got off. We were running alongside the Kennet and Avon Canal, which put us somewhere between Pewsey and Reading, but I couldn't remember if we'd been due to call at Westbury. It didn't make any sense, of course, unless he'd decided I'd be safer without him. That *was* possible.

I got up and made towards the front of the train,

wondering where he could be if he *hadn't* got off. I reached the buffet with no sign of him and pressed on into the first-class carriages. Going to the very front seemed pointless, but nevertheless I went.

And there he was, standing calmly in the vestibule beyond the last carriage, smoking one of his Russian cigarettes. He was clinging to the handrail, as if it was the only thing holding him up, and he looked pale and haggard, a cough growling deep in his throat as he drew on the cigarette.

'Sweet dreams?' he asked, with an ironic cock of the eyebrow.

'None that I can remember.'

'I believe they're the best kind.'

'Are you all right? You look like death.'

'You can't have seen much death if you think that. I'm tired, Tony. Tired and old. Simple as that. Far too old for all this cloak and dagger. It's got to stop.'

'Can it be stopped?'

'Perhaps. I came up here to use that.' He pointed to the payphone in the cubicle behind us. 'I've just come off it.'

'Well?'

'Heraclitus has agreed to meet us.'

'*Who?*'

'An old code name. Conferred by me. A pompous choice, I dare say. Designed to demonstrate that physicists can also be classicists.'

'Heraclitus was the source of the inscription on Ann's gravestone.'

'So he was. "All things pass, nothing remains." My suggestion, as it happens. Daisy was still prepared to listen to me then. Not any more. But Heraclitus, he'll listen. For what it's worth.' He frowned and raised his hand, the smoke from the cigarette wavering in the draught from the window. 'Sorry. That's the fatigue talking. It *is* worth a try. Really. It's the only thing we *can* try, as a matter of plain and simple fact.'

'When do we meet him?'

'Tomorrow. At six.'

'Why wait so long?'

'He has a fair way to come. More than forty years is quite a journey. I suppose that's why I suggested a venue we both know.' I knew then, without doubt or elaboration, the venue he'd chosen. 'Well,' he added with a shrug, 'you did say it was standing empty.'

He bought a couple of miniatures of Glenfiddich on the way back through the buffet and polished them off as the train sped on towards London. It made his cough worse, but it also put some colour back in his cheeks, and some optimism into his soul.

'You never took to the vodka, then?' I asked, as he stared out at the trackside scene.

'You only drink a mother's milk if she *is* your mother,' he replied, without diverting his gaze.

'Isn't Russia yours, at least by adoption?'

'I'm an Englishman.'

'But also a communist.'

'Did I say I was?'

'I realize they're thin on the ground in Russia these days, but even so . . .'

'I was never a party member where it matters: in my heart.'

'Then why defect?'

'There came a point when I had no choice. If I'd stayed, I'd have been thrown to the wolves. Little did I

299

know they'd still be waiting for me all these years later, out there in the forest.'

'How long did you spy for the Russians?'

'Three and a half years.'

'Did you really give them the H-bomb?'

'A helping hand towards it, certainly. My services hadn't been required at Los Alamos. I was in Montreal at the time of the Trinity test. It's not the sort of thing you expect to get a second chance of witnessing. But I did, of course. At Semipalatinsk, in August 'fifty-three. There was devastation such as you cannot conceive. Ground zero means just that: nothing. It isn't destruction, it's . . . erasure.'

'Were you proud of what you'd helped to achieve?'

'I was satisfied that I'd done my job.'

'For which you were amply rewarded, no doubt.'

'Not particularly, since you ask. Defectors have their uses, but nobody exactly admires them.'

'Strathallan thought you enjoyed the act of treachery itself. He reckoned that was a stronger motive for you than politics.'

Now Cedric did look round at me. 'He said that?'

'To a journalist called Martin Fisher. It's quoted in a book about you, among others. *Seven Faces of Treason*. Fisher went to Moscow to interview you, back in the Seventies. But the KGB saw him off.'

'That's what they were there for.'

'Do you regret nothing, Cedric?'

'Oh, a very great deal.'

'But selling secrets to Stalin isn't one of those regrets, is it?'

'I didn't sell. I gave.'

'Either way.'

'It makes a difference.'

'It's still treason. It's still betraying your country.'

'Is it?'

'Of course. You know that. You sleep with the knowledge, I imagine, every night of your life.'

Cedric leaned back in his seat and closed his eyes. 'Are you much of a churchgoer, Tony?'

'No.'

'Thought not. Me neither. But I absorbed a fair amount of Christian teaching as a boy. Didn't have much choice about it.'

'So?'

'Judas always worried me. I never could understand him. The arch-traitor of all time. Thirty pieces of silver and the Field of Blood. A byword for treachery over two millennia. That's quite an obituary, don't you think? But why? Why did anyone need to betray Jesus? He wasn't exactly inconspicuous. The high priests wouldn't have had any trouble picking him out in a crowd of a hundred, let alone a huddle of twelve. Why did they need Judas at all?'

'I don't know.'

Cedric opened his eyes and looked intently at me. 'It was to fulfil Old Testament prophecy. The Messiah had to be betrayed, otherwise he might not be the Messiah. Somebody had to do it. And he had to do it sincerely, in the full knowledge of what his reward had been prophesied to be. "Let his habitation be desolate, and let no man dwell therein: and his bishoprick let another take." That's one Bible passage I *do* remember.'

'What are you getting at?'

'The heart of treachery, not the face of treason. There's a difference.'

'And the difference is why Heraclitus has agreed to meet us?'

301

'Me, actually. Not us. He doesn't know about you. But he's due a surprise, so you can be it.'

'You haven't answered my question.'

'No. But I expect it will be answered.' He looked back out through the window. 'Tomorrow.'

But tomorrow was still half a day and a night away. Until then we had to lie low – and wait. When the train reached Paddington, we set off on foot in search of the sort of hotel that respects privacy if not fire regulations. There were quite a few of them between the station and Hyde Park. We chose the cheap and cheerless Allerline House in Sussex Gardens, booked in, then walked down to the park and wandered vaguely in the direction of the Serpentine.

There was the usual assortment of joggers, dog-walkers, frisbee-throwers and solitaries. The sun was shining and childrens' voices could be heard from the lakeside ahead of us. It was a bland and unexceptional scene: a London park in summer, safe, shadowless, unhaunted. But the world is what you carry with you, not what surrounds you. Our safety was provisional. And our ghosts were only keeping their distance.

'What did you expect Matt to do with James's confession?' I asked, as much to break the silence that had fallen between us since leaving the hotel as to glean an insight into Cedric's thought processes.

'I had no expectation. I just wanted him to understand what sort of a house he was living in.'

'Did you think he'd take it seriously?'

'If he's already experienced some of Otherways' stranger qualities, he was bound to.'

'He was actually planning to show it to a scientist at Hull University – an astronomer, called Lois

Carmichael. She's a sort of ghosthunter. I think he wanted independent confirmation that those . . . stranger qualities . . . really exist.'

'That suggests he *had* experienced them.'

'Yes. So it does. But he never said so. He never confided in Lucy. Or me.'

'Perhaps he didn't trust you.'

'That's what worries me.'

'What's lost can be won back.'

'Can it?'

'I hope so.' He paused to light a cigarette and recover his breath. 'You'd better hope so, too.'

A short walk in Hyde Park was enough to tire Cedric out. The quickness of his brain and the keenness of his eye had made me forget how old he was. We had to rest on a bench halfway before we could even make it back to Allerline House.

'I think I'll take a nap,' he announced when I saw him into his room, a twin in every shabby detail of my own room further down the passage. 'It's been quite a day.' A coughing bout interrupted his progress to the bed. He sank onto it with palpable relief.

'Perhaps you should cut down on the smoking,' I said, as he tossed his half-empty pack of cigarettes onto the bedside cabinet.

'If cancer's going to get me, it won't be because of the cigarettes.' He slowly lay back against the pillow and gazed up at the peeling plaster on the ceiling. 'When we did the thermonuclear test in November 'fifty-five, I remember feeling the heat of the blast on my face. It was like standing in front of an open furnace. Yet it was freezing weather and we were seventy kilometres from ground zero. That was a *real* health risk.'

'To the whole world.'

'Yes, yes.' His voice was slurred now and dreamily indistinct. 'I know what you think.' For a moment, I thought he'd fallen asleep. But no, his mind was still ranging over the past. 'There was a celebratory banquet at Nedelin's house after that test. Scientists and generals rubbing shoulders. I still had hopes then. I'd . . . accomplished what I'd set out to do . . . and genuinely believed . . . there'd be a way . . .'

He said nothing else. When his breathing had lapsed into the slow, heavy pattern of sleep, I slipped out, closing the door gently behind me.

Cedric needed to rest, but nothing could be further from my own thoughts. Now we were in London, a phone call to check on Matt didn't seem very risky to me. Partly to appease Cedric, however, should he find out, I put a precautionary half-mile between me and the hotel before dropping into a pub in Marylebone to load the change from buying a drink into their payphone.

The phone was mounted on the wall at the head of the stairs leading down to the loos. Had it been in the bar, I probably wouldn't have been able to hear what the hospital switchboard operator said to me. The pub was crammed with people far gone along the road to ensuring this was a Saturday night they wouldn't remember. I literally crossed my fingers when the operator put me through to Matt's ward, praying this wouldn't turn out to be a Saturday night *I* wanted to forget.

'Good news, Mr Sheridan,' said the ward sister. 'Mr Prior's recovered consciousness.'

'That's great.'

'He's still drowsy, of course, and in a certain amount of pain, but—'

'He's going to be all right.'

'Well, obviously there's—'

'But he *is*, isn't he? That's what it amounts to.'

'Let's just say we're very pleased with his progress.'

'OK.' She could probably have heard me grinning in Leicester. 'Let's just say that.'

'He's been asking about you, actually.'

'He has?'

'Can I tell him you'll be in to see him?'

'Sure.' I crushed myself against the wall to make way for somebody going down to the loo. He hesitated at the top of the stairs, forcing me to stay where I was. I had a view across the bar now. As I glanced towards the doorway on the far side, my eyes met those of a burly figure in dark clothes. His gaze was stern and unflinching. He wasn't smiling. And we both recognized each other.

'Mr Sheridan?'

At that moment, I felt a sharp pain in my right thigh. I turned towards the man at the top of the stairs and realized he was looking at me, intently but expressionlessly. I tried to speak, but a wave of nausea and weakness swept over me. My vision suddenly blurred. I began to fall, hearing the phone strike the wall behind me as if it were the echo of a sound in the far distance. Then it, and everything else, was gone.

My mind freewheeled for a long time. Not that time had any meaning in the cocoon of oblivion I was somehow wrapped in. It was unconsciousness, but not unawareness, a dreamless and euphoric suspension in a place where nothing mattered at all. It felt like infinity. I think I thought it was probably death.

Then glimpses of reality began breaking in. Voices and

faces, movement and sensation. Pain gouged through to wherever I was hiding. Recollection followed and, with it, confusion. Where was I? What had happened to me? I saw a window, beyond which a bird flew across a blue sky and sunlight glinted on glass. I saw a tubular metal bar, with my own disembodied hand resting on it. I closed my eyes.

When I opened them, the window was black. Night had fallen. I was in a bed, a hospital bed, propped up in a room on my own, brightly lit, with an open doorway to my right. A nurse walked in and smiled at me and checked a drip attached to my arm.

'What's happened to me?' I mumbled.

'I'll fetch the doctor,' she said, with a gentle smile.

Whether the doctor came straightaway, or an hour later, I had no way of telling. He was a small balding man with a clipped moustache and a faintly fretful expression. His name was Bose, according to the badge on the lapel of his coat.

'What's happened to me?' I repeated.

'I was hoping you could tell us, Mr Sheridan. The cocktail of drugs in your system is an exotic one. Amphetamine-based, clearly, but that *is* only the base. Was this some kind of . . . experiment?'

'What?'

'Do you remember collapsing?'

'A pub . . . in Marylebone.'

'That's right. You very nearly fell down a steep flight of stairs, apparently.'

'What . . . time is it?'

'Gone eleven. You've been out for nearly six hours.'

'And where . . .'

'St Mary's Hospital, Paddington.'

'This . . .' I raised the arm to which the drip was attached.

'A glucose-saline solution. We'll take you off that now you're conscious. Not knowing what you took, it's all—'

'I didn't take anything.'

Dr Bose smiled. 'Analysis of your blood suggests otherwise.'

'I don't understand.'

'A pity. There's a policeman outside who's hoping you can help *him* understand. Do you feel well enough to answer his questions?'

'What if I don't?'

'He'll wait.'

'He won't go away?'

'I don't think so.'

'Perhaps that's just as well.' The truth was that I wanted answers every bit as much as the policeman was likely to. 'Send him in.'

I'd somehow expected a uniformed bobby. Instead, he was a plain-clothes detective, tall and broadly built, with crew-cut hair and a nose that had clearly been broken at least once. He looked more like an East End villain than a policeman, but the resemblance ended at his voice, which was soft and neutral, but somehow far from reassuring. He introduced himself as Detective Sergeant Harmison and drew up a bedside chair.

'Good of you to see me, Mr Sheridan,' he said, without seeming to mean it.

'What's going on, Sergeant? Was I attacked?'

'Are you claiming to have been, sir?'

'Somebody injected me with something, I think. At that pub.'

'The Orb and Sceptre.'

'I don't remember the name.'

'It's where you collapsed.'

'Right. Well, there, then.'

'You were alone, sir. No-one saw you with anyone.'

'Possibly not, but—'

'What brought you to London, sir?'

'Is that relevant?'

'To my inquiries, yes, sir.'

'And they're into . . . what, exactly?'

'You booked into the Allerline House Hotel in Sussex Gardens this afternoon in the company of a Mr Hall. Is that correct?'

'Yes. But how did—'

'You had your room key in your pocket. The name and address of the hotel was on the fob.'

That couldn't be right. I had a distinct memory of dropping my key off at reception on the way out. But how reliable *was* my memory?

'When did you last see Mr Hall?'

'About . . . five o'clock.'

'How was he?'

'He was fine.' But he wasn't any longer. Somehow I knew that's what Harmison was going to say next. 'Has something happened to him?'

'I'm afraid so, sir. Mr Hall's dead.'

'Dead?'

'Found in his room at Allerline House earlier this evening. The door had been left ajar by . . .' He raised one eyebrow quizzically. 'Somebody.'

'He's *dead*?'

'Yes, sir.'

'But . . .' Cedric was gone. All those years of waiting for his chance to come home had only led to this: a stranger's death in a cheap hotel. 'How? How did he die?'

'That's why I'm here, sir.' Harmison leaned forward enquiringly in his chair. 'I'm hoping you'll be able to tell me.'

Chapter Twelve

My brain seemed to fluctuate between hyperactivity and extreme lethargy. After Harmison had left, sooner than he'd wished to, thanks to Dr Bose, I lay where I was, alternately numbed by the rush of events and galvanized into a torrent of deductions. Harmison would be back in the morning. I had his word. He might tell me the full story then. I didn't, of course, have his word for that, because he'd assured me he already had told me all he knew.

William Hall – I volunteered his supposed Christian name – had been found dead in his room at Allerline House shortly after seven o'clock. Some sort of drugs overdose appeared to be the cause; the results of the post-mortem were currently awaited. There were signs of 'a struggle of some kind'. The room was 'disordered'. The occupant of the room next door reported hearing 'a commotion' sometime between five and six. Meanwhile, I'd been hospitalized following 'a drugs-related collapse', and the 'connection' between me and William Hall had been made. Nobody at the Orb and Sceptre had seen anyone near me at the time of my collapse. Nobody at Allerline House had seen me leaving the hotel. Could I 'shed any light' on what had happened?

The true answer was yes *and* no. Cedric had been murdered, presumably by the same pair of toughs who'd failed to waylay us near Stanacombe that morning, but who had succeeded in pumping a disabling mix of doubtless illegal drugs into me at the Orb and Sceptre that evening. But why? And how? More to the point, why was I still alive? And what was I intended to do next? Fending off Harmison for one night had been relatively easy, but it was only a postponement of the reckoning. What they'd really found in Cedric's room – what had been placed there for them to find – I had no idea. A used syringe? A cache of drugs? Proof of William Hall's true identity? I simply hadn't a clue. Except my certainty that Harmison was holding out on me. Perhaps I'd already incriminated myself. Perhaps I'd said just what I'd been expected to say.

William Hall was a stranger to me. We'd met on the train from Plymouth, fallen into each other's company and looked for a hotel together after reaching Paddington. I knew nothing about him, absolutely nothing. Nor about the drugs in my system. I'd been attacked and I was reporting the offence. William Hall had been fine when I'd last seen him. His death was a mystery to me, a total mystery. That was my story – the only story I could safely tell.

Harmison didn't believe me. I was sure of that. The desultory attention he paid to my admittedly vague description of the two men in the pub clinched it for me. He thought William Hall's blood would be found to contain a fatally stronger dose of the same drug punch that had knocked me out. What he had me down as wasn't clear – murderer, drug addict, pervert – but innocent wasn't it. He proposed to question me again in the morning, subject to Bose's say-so. Soon my version of events, such as it was, would be on the record. And in due course I'd be held to account for it.

The nurse detached the drip and gave me a sleeping pill, which I made a show of swallowing, only to slip it under the mattress when she'd gone. I felt drained and bewildered enough to sleep without any help, but I was afraid of waking up next morning to find Harmison looming over the bed with a warrant for my arrest. I had to think. I had to find a way out of this.

Cedric was dead. But Heraclitus might not know that. He might yet keep his appointment with us at Otherways. That was my only chance of learning the truth and persuading whoever had set the dogs on us to call them off. It was too late for Cedric, but I could at least hope it wasn't too late for me.

So, I had to get to Otherways. And I had to set off before morning. One wobbly walk to the loo had shown I was in no fit state to leave the hospital. But, fit or not, I had to. An attempt to discharge myself would probably bring a squad car speeding to the door. A clandestine departure hardly seemed any likelier to succeed. In the end, though, I had to try it.

The fact that I'd been allocated a room on my own was suspicious in itself. Was it to prevent me talking to other patients? Or was I considered a potential threat to them? Either way, solitude gave me the only advantage I was likely to get. My clothes had been hung in the closet. I could put them on without being seen and hope to slip out of the ward when everyone else was asleep.

I fell into a shallow slumber, anxiety keeping full unconsciousness at bay and probably ensuring the rest did me little good. At two o'clock I made my move.

Dressing took more out of me than I'd expected. Part

of me wanted to give up there and then, so groggy did I feel. But the other part – the thinking part – knew I had no choice. I sat on the bed, waited till my breathing and heartbeat returned to normal, then went to the door and peered out.

The ward was in virtual darkness. A pool of subdued light beyond marked the nursing station, presently unoccupied. The exit was to the right of it. I walked softly and slowly along between the beds, unnoticed as far as I could tell, paused in the doorway long enough to be fairly sure no-one was about, then took a brisk turn into the passage and headed past the loos to the stairs. There was a lift on the landing, but some instinct made me take the long way down.

And a long way down it certainly was – three flights at a shuffling pace. My head ached and so did every joint. I felt as if I had flu without the fever. I wasn't so much making a run for it as a stagger.

There was a receptionist on duty in the dimly lit lobby at the bottom of the stairs. I could see her round the corner as I reached the last step. The main exit – double doors and a cool hint of night air – lay just beyond her. I gave myself a minute to stop panting, then set off.

She was drinking what smelled like soup and reading a paperback. She looked up as I passed, the light from her lamp glinting on her glasses. But she didn't speak. She was probably grateful I didn't want anything.

Outside was as dark and silent as a London night gets. I remembered St Mary's as a maze of old and new buildings, not far east of Paddington station, and I reckoned the station was my best bet. There might be a taxi to be had there. Where I wanted to be taken was another matter. I couldn't risk going back to Allerline House for the rest of my stuff, but it was still a long time before I could hope to catch a train north, probably longer than ever because it was Sunday.

The street was damp and deserted, the kerbs lined with parked cars. I turned left. I was at the back of the building, so the station had to be in that direction. I went under a footbridge linking one wing of the hospital with another. I walked slowly, conserving what energy I had. I began to think my plan, such as it was, really could work.

Suddenly, my path was blocked by the nearside door of a parked car swinging wide open in front of me. In the same moment I heard another door opening and the sound of running footsteps behind me. I turned just as a tall dark figure closed in on me. I was thrust back against the car and held there, my brain reacting so sluggishly to events that it was almost as if I was observing them rather than experiencing them at first hand. There were two men, one either side of me. I tried to push them off, but they'd have been far too strong for me, even if I hadn't been as rubber-limbed as I was. I was bundled into the back seat of the car. One of them followed me in. The other raced round to the off side and jumped in beside me. Then the car accelerated away. The driver glanced back at me. He was the man I'd seen in the lane near Stanacombe, and later in the pub. His face was set and expressionless.

'Thought you needed a lift,' said one of the others, with a sneering little smile. There was a crazy gleam in his eyes, caught in the amber downwash of the street lamps as we flashed past them. 'No need to thank us.'

'You don't look too well,' said the third man, calmer, graver, somehow stiller than his companions. 'Been overdoing it, I expect.'

'What do you want?' I gritted out.

'To find a Picasso in my attic,' said the mad one. 'Let's leave our wants out of this, shall we?'

'And concentrate, instead,' said the other, 'on your dealings with the late William Hall.'

'Go to hell.'

It was a pointlessly defiant thing to say. The mad one's grip on me tightened. Suddenly I saw a glint of dark metal between us. The next strobe of lamplight showed me a gun in his hand, the barrel a few inches from my chest. 'We're authorized to kill you, Sheridan. You ought to understand just how easy that means it would be. Very easy. You know?'

'What was William Hall's real name?' the calm one calmly enquired.

'That was his real name.'

The barrel pressed against my head. 'Want to reconsider?'

'Cedric Milner.'

'Good boy.' The gun moved away from me.

'Cedric Milner, the traitor,' said the calm one.

'Yes.'

'A friend of yours?'

'Not exactly.'

'A confidant?'

'Sort of.'

'He told you things.'

'A few.'

'Did they include why he betrayed his country?'

'No.'

'We think they did.'

'You're wrong.'

'If we are, that's your bad luck.'

He nodded, and suddenly the gun was back, prodding at my temple.

'Why did he betray his country?'

'I don't know.'

'You're going to die, Sheridan, here, now, tonight, if you don't tell us.'

'How can I tell you what I don't know?'

'That's your problem.'

'For God's—'

They didn't kill me. What they did do I'm not exactly sure. It must have been another shot of drugs. I have a recollection of being moved, roughly lifted and put down again. I saw their faces, gazing down at me. I remember the motion of the car as well, jolting and swaying so much I slid across the seat, and a rumbling noise – distant, yet oddly familiar. What sequence they came in, what they amounted to, I didn't know and, in a strange kind of way, didn't care. I had no control over anything, no responsibility, no crushing sense of guilt or failure. I was out of everything.

When I next became aware of my surroundings, it was morning, a cool, clear, summer Sunday morning. I was lying half up against a transmission box, on a patch of waste ground near some railway lines, in the giant shadow of a graffiti-smothered flyover support. Birds were singing, undaunted by the periodic rumble of traffic on the flyover above me.

My head was aching, throbbing with the slightest movement. The glare of the sun, still low in the sky, made my eyes water and my head pound all the more. My neck felt as if it was broken, and darts of pain shot up my back as I pushed myself into a sitting position. That was all I could do for several minutes, while I struggled to patch my thoughts together, which seemed to be as easy as putting a scrambled egg back into its shell.

I was alive. That was about all I was sure of. But why? What was the point of threatening to kill me if they weren't going to do it? Why pick me up in the first place if they were just going to put me down again, safe even if not very well?

I hauled myself upright and leaned against the transmission box, trying to get my bearings. It was just after six o'clock, according to my watch. There were tube tracks beside the main line in front of me. I could see a station in the distance, too far off to make out more than the Underground symbol on its pole. The flyover could easily be the A40, though, in which case they might not have taken me very far at all – Royal Oak, Westbourne Park, somewhere like that.

I began limping in the direction of the tube station, reasoning as best I could along the way. What had saved me? It could only be my inability to answer the question about Cedric's defection, even with a gun pressed to my head. They must have believed me. They must have been convinced I didn't know the truth. Which meant the truth couldn't be what anyone thought. It had to be worse – far worse.

Maybe this was my final warning, my last chance to get out of the whole mad business. But that didn't quite make sense. There was my supposed part in Cedric's death to complicate matters. A suspect who goes AWOL is much easier to explain than one who gets a bullet through the brain. I couldn't walk away from it. I wasn't going to be allowed to. Heraclitus was still my only chance. I had to be at Otherways when he arrived, and then I had to find a way to make him help me.

*   *   *

317

I bought a bar of chocolate from a machine at the station and forced myself to eat it, then I lay full length on a bench and waited for the first eastbound train. I had no idea when the east coast expresses started running from King's Cross on a Sunday, but they all called at Peterborough, and I had the whole day to get where I was going. If anyone was determined to stop me, it wasn't likely to prove difficult. But I was too tired to worry much about that. I meant to take this just as far as I could.

And then? I didn't know. You'd have felt sorry for me, Marina. God knows what I looked like, slumped on that bench in rumpled clothes, with a bad night's worth of tears and stains, unshaven, unwashed, battered and bruised. I was close to the end of my tether. It had stretched further than either of us might have expected, but it wasn't going to stretch much further.

My weary mind turned to you, to the memories it held of our shared past. The life we'd had together seemed so joyously simple, set against everything that had followed. Why couldn't it just have continued? Why couldn't the hell I'd been through since your death be the dream, and the fantasy of seeing you again the reality?

For a moment, maybe for several while I lay there, I almost believed it could. When the rumble of the approaching train dragged me out of my reverie, I thought I was waking from a doze in the armchair at Stanacombe, hearing your car drive in off the lane. Then the brazen light and bludgeoning noise were all around me. I lost you again, as I had so many times, sensed you slipping away from me. You were gone. And a chunk of me was gone with you. The rest – the remainder, the leftover man – lurched up from the bench and made for the opening doors of the train.

I cleaned myself up as best I could at King's Cross, had a breakfast of sorts on the train and probably looked relatively normal by the time I reached Peterborough. I booked into a hotel halfway between the station and the cathedral, had a bath and a second breakfast, then slept for four bizarrely untroubled hours. By three o'clock I was on my way back to the station, planning to catch the next train to Oakham. And there didn't seem anything to stop me.

Until a car that was somehow familiar pulled in ahead of me, its hazard lights flashing. I stopped and whirled round, fearing I'd see one of them closing in on me from behind. But there was nobody there. Then I heard a voice calling my name.

'Tony!'

And at once I remembered whose car it was.

'Do you want a lift, Tony? I'm probably going your way.'

Nesta Worthington lived in Oakham, but she had a daughter in Peterborough. She was on her way back home after Sunday lunch. Her presence in the city made good and simple sense, unlike mine.

'I came up by train,' I explained, accurately enough, as we headed west along the A47. 'I was just killing time. You know what connections are like on the railways these days – non-existent.'

'What's happened to your car?'

'Just wouldn't start. Dead. But when I heard Matt was on the mend, I decided I couldn't wait for a garage to give it the once-over.'

'It's good news about Matt, isn't it? Lucy phoned me last night. It was obvious a load had been taken off her mind.'

'It's a load off all our minds.'

'Are you going into the hospital this afternoon?' Already there was an inflexion in her voice, if not of suspicion, then of disquiet. If Leicester was my destination, why had I gone via Peterborough? 'I could drive you there.'

'I, er, have to stop off in Oakham first.'

'That wouldn't be a problem. I could wait. I'd like to see Matt myself.'

'You go ahead. I really—'

'Have no intention of going there?' She glanced sharply round at me. 'Lucy asked me if I'd heard from you. Odd, wouldn't you say? I had the impression she was clutching at straws. I mean, why would I have heard from you when she hadn't?'

'I can't imagine.'

Nesta didn't believe that. I reckoned she'd heard or seen enough to know what had gone on between Lucy and me. That didn't equip her to understand what was happening now, but she didn't know that. My behaviour probably looked like a straightforward case of guilt to her.

'I like Matt. And Lucy.'

'So do I.'

'Since you came to stay at Otherways, things haven't worked out well for them.'

'My fault, do you think?'

'I'm not saying that.'

'But you're wondering it.'

'Yes. I suppose I am.'

'If only it was so simple.'

320

'What do you mean?'

'What I mean, Nesta, is that you don't know what's at stake here. And you're better off not knowing. Better by far.'

The rest of the journey passed in a tense and grudging silence. We headed up past Stamford on the A1, then turned off on the Oakham road and soon caught our first sight of Rutland Water, benign and shimmering in the afternoon sun. It was the warmest and stillest part of the day. Yachts and pleasure craft were out on the lake. Sunday cyclists were thickly bunched on the track around its perimeter. It all looked placid and pretty and oh so permanent.

But, as we started up Barnsdale Hill and I gazed across at the Hambleton peninsula, I remembered James Milner's dream of just this scene. What couldn't be and what was were threaded into the past as well as the future.

Suddenly I noticed the circular roof of Otherways, a smudge of honey-brown slate, almost lost from view amidst the dense green patch of surrounding elm and oak. What had Cedric said about Henna Cliff as a place to meet? Ideal, 'if you like to be able to see people coming'. The creation of the reservoir had done that to Otherways, had given it a larger outer moat, a perpetual warning of approach. If Oates had bought land lower in the valley, Posnan's house would no longer stand. But that could never have happened. Wherever high water had been decreed to be, Otherways would have been higher still.

I had Nesta drop me at the market place in Oakham. It wasn't exactly an amiable parting, but antagonizing her had been a price worth paying to ensure she didn't know where I was going or why. I phoned for a taxi from the Whipper-In and was in Hambleton twenty minutes later.

I paid off the taxi in the car park of the Finches Arms. Seeing the pub was open, I bought a beer and sat with it at one of the tables facing the church. I had more than an hour to spare till my, or rather Cedric's, appointment at Otherways. There was no hurry. There was indeed every reason not to hurry. The less time I spent at Otherways the better. I'd be far more nervous there, and more vulnerable, than I was in the garden of the Finches Arms. I finished my beer and followed it with a whisky. Then I set off.

There was still ample time to reach the house by six o'clock. And I was still reluctant to arrive there. I walked round to the church and went in through the gate, intending, for no particular reason, to take a look at Ann Milner's grave.

I was most of the way to it along the path when I pulled up sharply. There, kneeling beside her sister's grave, was Daisy. She had her back turned to me. Her head was level with the top of the stone. That and the greyish tweed coat she was wearing had camouflaged her so effectively that I'd got within a few yards of her without realizing she was there.

I stood where I was, wondering if she'd heard me approaching and, if so, whether she'd turn round. In the churchyard hush my accentuated hearing suddenly caught the slightest of sounds. Daisy was crying. There was a faint sob. I saw the moist track of a tear round her left cheekbone, which was as much of her face as I could see. Then she stretched forward and began dropping long-stemmed cut flowers, one by one, into the vase beneath the headstone. Even I could identify those flowers. They were a strange choice, given how many were growing wild all around us. And yet it wasn't so strange, since she shared their name.

I had a lot to say to Daisy. I had a lie to nail and an accusation to level. But this wasn't the time, and her sister's graveside wasn't the place. I turned slowly on my heel and retreated down the path.

At the gate I glanced back. There was no sign of her, just as there hadn't been when I entered. It looked as if I'd come and gone without her being aware of my presence. And that was how I wanted it. For the moment.

The quickest route to Otherways was straight along the lane. I preferred to take the footpath out of the village and across the fields, to the fishermen's track round the peninsula, then follow that for a while before cutting back across the fields to the house. As I was crossing the last field, before the stile onto the track, I had the momentary impression there was somebody close behind me. But when I spun round . . . nothing. My narrow escape at the church must have spooked me. Or maybe it was my proximity to Otherways. There wasn't far to go now. Or long to wait. What there was to know I'd soon know.

I carried on to the stile and paused there in the shade of a tree. I checked my watch and wiped the sweat from my face. It seemed hotter than it had been earlier, as if the sun was strengthening, not weakening, as it should have been at this faltering point of the late afternoon. I'd have gladly smoked a cigarette, but I'd bought none along the way. I was all out of delaying tactics. I clambered over the stile and pressed on along the track.

I'd never approached Otherways by this route before. It made me realize how carefully Posnan must have chosen the site. It stood above its surroundings, yet concealed by them, a topographical chance Posnan had eagerly seized. Time and the maturing of the trees he'd planted had enhanced the effect. The house was there, detectable before it was visible, and seemed always to have been there. But, like the lake, that was an illusion. It was easy, in fact, to imagine that the lake was part of Posnan's architectural sleight of hand. Had he somehow foreseen its construction? Had he anticipated which contour it would follow?

Impossible, of course, but it was easy to believe as I crossed the last field before the wall marking the boundary of Otherways. I clambered over it and hurried through the trees encircling the garden. The sun was behind me, shafting through the branches above to fall in random splashes of gold on the curving flank of the house. The drawing-room windows lay ahead, and I could see straight into the room. There was the chair where I'd sat waiting for Matt at around this time four evenings before. It was empty now. As was the house. But not for much longer.

As I started across the lawn, I saw a vehicle approaching along the drive. It was a dark-blue Volvo estate. I hesitated, then went on. There was nothing to be gained by caution.

The Volvo drew to a halt in front of the house just as I reached the edge of the drive. The sole occupant of the car was a tubby middle-aged man, with centre-parted greased black hair, dressed in an office suit. He pushed open the door with his foot, heaved himself out in a flash of giant scarlet braces and squinted at me over half-moon horn-rimmed spectacles. I met his gaze and held it as I slowly rounded the bonnet. Then he smiled and spoke.

'Mr Prior about?'

I stopped and frowned at him. 'Are you here to meet Mr Hall?'

'No. Mr Prior.'

'And you are?'

'Frank Bissell.' He flourished a business card. 'Bissell, Unsworth and Hegg.'

'Who?'

'Bissell, Unsworth and Hegg. Estate agents.' His smile frayed into irritability. 'Look, coming here on a Sunday afternoon has caused me no little domestic friction, but Mr Prior insisted it was the only time he could manage, so—'

'You have an appointment with him?'

'Certainly. I'm sorry if I'm a few minutes late, but—'

'No, I'm sorry, Mr Bissell. You obviously haven't heard. I'm a friend of the family. Mr Prior's in hospital. He was involved in a car accident.'

'Oh God.' Bissell winced. 'Bad?'

'Serious, certainly. He's going to be out of action for quite a while.'

'Damn.'

'Quite.'

'Sorry. I mean, I'm sorry to hear it. All this' – he gestured vaguely at the house – 'will be on the back burner, then.'

'All what?'

'The sale.'

'The sale of the house?'

'Of course.' He looked at me as if I were being

325

deliberately obtuse. 'That's what I came here to discuss with Mr Prior.'

'Yes.' I nodded, yielding to the logic of the discovery. Matt had wanted out of Otherways. And who could blame him? 'Of course.'

'Is Mrs Prior about?'

'No.'

'Pity.'

Bissell wouldn't have thought it was much of a pity, of course, had he realized that Lucy was totally unaware of Matt's decision to sell, though not, I ruefully admitted to myself, of what had led him to that decision.

'Well, I wish Mr Prior a speedy recovery.'

'So do I.'

'You'll tell him I called?'

'I'll tell him.'

'And Mrs Prior? I mean, should she wish to proceed while Mr Prior's still . . . *hors de combat*. Perhaps you could pass on my card.' He handed it to me. 'Awfully grateful.'

A thought came to me as I took it. 'Did your firm handle the sale *to* the Priors, Mr Bissell?'

'We did, as a matter of fact.' So, Frank Bissell was probably the man who'd given Cedric your name. He was, in his way, someone with a lot to answer for. 'Bit of a surprise, really.'

'What was?'

'Mr Prior's call. I mean, it's a tad soon to be moving on. Especially when I had the impression they'd fallen in love with the place.'

'That's the trouble with love. You can fall out as well as in.'

'Yes.' Bissell eyed me uncertainly. 'Well, I'd better get back to the love of my own life. Do excuse me.'

I watched Bissell's car vanish along the drive, then I took Lucy's keys from my pocket and crossed the moat. I paused at the foot of the steps leading to the front door of the house and looked at my watch. It was eight minutes to six. I took a deep breath, mounted the steps, slid the mortice into the keyhole and turned it.

But it wouldn't turn. I strained at it for a second, then realized what was wrong. It wasn't locked. I'd locked it when Lester and I had left on Thursday night. I could remember him standing next to me as I'd done so, my mind teeming with the contents of James Milner's confession, while Lester wittered on about the statistical evidence for global warming. Lock it I definitely had.

But it wasn't locked any more. Which meant that either somebody had been and gone in the meantime, leaving the door on the latch, or somebody had been, but hadn't gone.

I opened the door with the Yale, stepped into the passage and closed it behind me. The alarm stayed silent. It was operated by the third key on Lucy's ring, and I'd certainly set it. But it had been turned off – or disabled. It looked intact, but I was no expert. I dropped the keys into my pocket and walked slowly along to the hall.

Nothing stirred. The house always did exclude external noise with astonishing efficiency. I'd wondered if Posnan had incorporated some form of sound-proofing in the design. It wouldn't have surprised me.

'Hello!' I shouted, determined not to be cowed. My voice echoed up into the conical roof and I stared after it. Nothing moved on the landings. 'Is anyone here?'

Several seconds passed. Then I heard three clinking notes, like a spoon being tapped against a glass, as if to quieten an audience in readiness for a speech. The noise seemed to come up from the kitchen. I strode to the stairs and headed down them.

The kitchen door was ajar. I pushed at it with my foot. As it swung open, I saw a man sitting at the table in the centre of the room. In his left hand he was holding a glass tumbler, with what looked like whisky in it; in his right, a gun.

'Strathallan,' I gasped. 'You're . . . Heraclitus?'

'In a manner of speaking,' he replied. 'But in no manner of speaking are you Cedric Milner.' He trained the gun on me. 'Where is he?'

Chapter Thirteen

Strathallan resembled an elderly gent about to perform as guest of honour at a village fête in his pale-blue trousers, navy-blue crested blazer, white shirt and cravat – an urbane and elegant throwback to a bygone era. The gun was old, too. It could easily have been a wartime model. But it looked in excellent repair. And Strathallan's grip on it was as steady as a rock.

'You're not going to shoot me,' I said. 'Are you?'

'I'm not at all sure. *Where* is Cedric?'

'He's dead.'

There wasn't so much as a flicker of a reaction from him. 'How?'

'It's a longish story. I'll tell it better if you put that gun down.'

'Did you come alone?'

'What do you think?'

'I think you meant to.'

'There you are, then.'

'But I'm not sure. So, until I am, the gun stays pointed. Start talking, Mr Sheridan. I'll tell you when to stop.'

I told him the story more or less straight, from the dead end I'd reached in Lisbon, via the chance discovery of James Milner's confession, to my meeting

329

with Cedric, and the dead end that had also led to. Strathallan listened impassively, not even tempted, it seemed, to interrupt. Nor did he have to call a halt, as he'd said he would. The conclusion of my account was obvious and inevitable. It was where we were. It had always been there.

When I'd finished, he lowered the gun and slipped it into the drawer beneath the table. Then he signalled to the chair opposite him, inviting me to sit down. The tension had eased between us, but nothing in his expression or the tone of his voice had altered. A bottle of Lagavulin and two glasses stood on the table. The empty one must have been intended for Cedric. Strathallan poured some out for me as I sat down, the sunlight from the window to our left sparkling on the crystal of the tumbler.

'I'm sorry to bring you bad news,' I said, swallowing some of the whisky and feeling instantly grateful for its warming effect. It had been a hot afternoon in the world beyond Otherways, but none of that heat seemed to have penetrated the walls of the house. 'If you think it *is* bad news, that is.'

'Cedric was a fool to come back,' said Strathallan, a hint of feeling seeping into his voice at last. 'He knew the risks he was running.'

'But you came here to meet him.'

'I did.'

'So you must have backed him to get this far.'

'Not really. But he had a chance. I had to do him the favour of assuming that chance would be enough.'

'Why?'

'Because, in the timeworn phrase, it really was the least I owed him.' He sighed. 'You asked me if I was sorry to hear of his death. The answer is that I should be

330

relieved. In my official capacity, I should toast the solution of a problem and the neutralization of a threat.'

'What is your official capacity?'

'I can't say.'

'Why not? If the problem's solved—'

'Let it stay solved.'

'Was Cedric a traitor?'

'Of course.'

'But is that your official opinion, or the truth?'

'It's both. If you define truth as that which is and ever will be universally believed.'

'And what about the *absolute* truth?'

'You'd not want to burden yourself with that.'

'It's not just Cedric's death we're talking about, it's my wife's.'

'Aye. I know.' He sipped some whisky and rolled it around his mouth before swallowing. Then he sat back in his chair and frowned at me. 'It's a hard business.'

'I have a right to—'

'Understand if not to know?' His mouth curled slightly, in the beginnings of a smile. 'Well, well, perhaps that's accurate enough. The first thing you need to understand is that I have more to lose than you.'

'How do you figure that out?'

'You surely don't suppose being able to keep this appointment was some kind of lucky break on your part. By your own account, your pursuers had you at their mercy twice: at the pub in Marylebone and when they picked you up leaving the hospital. Why do you think they let you go?'

'Why do *you* think?'

'It's obvious, man. To smoke me out. They knew Cedric would contact Heraclitus if he was in a tight enough corner. And they knew Heraclitus would respond. But they didn't know who Heraclitus was. They couldn't afford to give Cedric an inch. But they could give you a mile of rope, and follow it straight to me, before looping it round my neck.'

'Nobody followed me.'

'They'd have done a poor job of it if you thought otherwise. Take my word for it, though. They followed.'

'No. I'm telling you—'

'I'm afraid Major Strathallan is correct,' came a voice from behind me.

I jumped up from my chair and swung round. The door was wide open. Through it strode Rainbird, transformed by a lightweight suit and polo-neck shirt into a bewilderingly metropolitan version of himself. Behind him was the grim-faced man who'd driven the car I was bundled into in Paddington. He stopped in the doorway, as if to guard it. But Rainbird ambled into the room and propped himself against the Aga. He folded his arms across his chest and treated us both to a rubbery smile.

'Sorry to interrupt,' he said. 'You must have been so engrossed in your conversation that you didn't hear the bell. Hope you don't mind us letting ourselves in.'

I felt anger surge through me before I had a chance to analyse it. 'You bastard,' I shouted, launching myself towards him. But I didn't cover more than a yard before the man in the doorway moved to intercept. And a second later I was back in my chair, arms pinned behind me.

'Thank you, Walker,' said Rainbird. 'Tony's just a little overexcited. Further restraint's unnecessary, I feel sure.' Walker's grip slackened, but still I was held, effectively enough. 'Isn't that right, Tony?'

'I expect so,' I reluctantly agreed.

'Good.' Walker released me and moved back to the door. 'Now, Major,' Rainbird continued, 'I don't want to seem high-handed, but certain colleagues of mine are eager to meet you and talk over old times, if you know what I mean. So, would it be possible to get straight off? We've a car waiting for you.'

'Why not?' Strathallan hesitated for a second. I wondered if he meant to make a grab for the gun. His gaze seemed to flicker down towards the drawer. But no, in the end, he merely drained his glass and rose slowly from the chair. 'I wouldn't want to keep them waiting.'

'Not when they've already waited so long. Quite.' Rainbird glanced across at me. 'Tony and I will stay here and have a little chat of our own about matters of mutual interest.' Then he looked back at Strathallan. 'It's been an education, Major, it really has. Not a surprise, though, I must admit. I had my eye on you from the first. Others may have been deceived by your show of bitterness towards Cedric Milner, but I always suspected you were just too bitter to be true.'

'How very perspicacious of you,' said Strathallan, as he buttoned his blazer and shot his cuffs. 'It must be satisfying to be able to tell the decoy ducks from the dead ones with such accuracy.'

'It is, I have to confess. But we must press on. At any rate, you must. Walker will escort you.'

'Where are you taking him?' I put in.

'A comfortably appointed Chilterns retreat,' said Rainbird. 'He'll be well looked after and he'll come to no harm, I assure you.'

'Aye,' said Strathallan. 'I'm sure the service will be very attentive.' He squared his shoulders, nodded a perfunctory farewell to me, then strode from the room, Walker falling in beside him.

'What the hell's going on?' I glared at Rainbird. 'What gives you the right to do any of this?'

'Parliament, I rather think,' he blithely replied. 'I should be able to quote the relevant statutory instrument word for word, but I seldom need to, so I fear I'm a little rusty.'

'Why didn't you just arrest Cedric?'

'Because he was no ordinary traitor. In fact' – he raised one hand, as if to say that the subtleties of the situation weren't his fault – 'the reality is, Tony, that you've seen and heard enough to be convinced Cedric Milner wasn't at all the devious Marxist spy depicted by friend Fisher in his book. As to what he really was, I ought to leave you in the dark. But I suspect that would only encourage you to delve further, which might oblige us to . . . well, cut you off in your prime, so to speak. Believe it or not, I would personally regret such an outcome.'

'I *don't* believe it.'

'No. Of course not. The truth is often hard to accept, the truth about Cedric Milner being a case in point.'

'And what is the truth?'

'Are you quite sure you want to know?'

'Just tell me.'

'Very well.' Rainbird pushed himself away from the Aga and moved across to the dresser beneath the window. He stretched his arms until his elbows clicked, then leaned on the dresser, gazing up at the window as he spoke. 'Cedric Milner passed technical information on the design and construction of nuclear weaponry to the Soviet Union . . . on behalf of the British government.'

'What did you say?' For a moment I genuinely believed I must have misheard.

334

'On behalf of the British government,' Rainbird repeated.

'That can't be.'

'I did warn you that the truth isn't always easy to accommodate within one's preconceptions. What I'm telling you is totally accurate, and totally unverifiable. Cedric is dead. His contact, the person who instructed him on what to pass on and acted as a conduit for supplying much of that information to him, code name Heraclitus, is being taken in for questioning. The issue of proof does not arise. Cedric's code name, incidentally, was Columbus – Latin for pigeon: the messenger bird. But a pigeon may also be a dupe, a half-willing victim of deceit. This pigeon was never intended to fly home to its loft.'

'Are you saying Cedric was some kind of double agent?'

'Not exactly. The material he supplied was genuine. And valuable. It appreciably advanced the Soviet H-bomb programme. It's hard to say by how much. The Soviets were making great strides for themselves. And a real traitor – Fuchs – was giving them a helping hand, unbeknown to Cedric's sponsors. But he certainly made a difference. As he was intended to.'

'Intended by whom?'

'I told you. HM government. The political powers that be. Our elected masters. The decision came from the top. And by the top . . . I mean precisely that.'

'The Cabinet?'

'Good God, no. A sensitive matter like this wouldn't have been discussed with anything like that many people. But naming names is essentially a speculative exercise until the good major unburdens his conscience and, more to the point, his memory. A political decision was taken. That is all we know for certain. SIS – the intelligence service – was not involved. And small wonder. This was, after all, officially sanctioned treason. But it remained *un*official, of course. Secret. Unrecorded. Deniable. That was the vital point. Such a project could never be allowed to become known within the intelligence community, let alone the community at large. It was a reversal of every tenet of publicly declared policy. It was heresy as well as treason. It was aiding and abetting the enemy. And yet, of course,' he smiled, 'it had its rationale.'

'Which was?'

'A seductive one, viewed in a certain light. Within a year of dropping two atom bombs on Japan, the United States made it clear, by passing the McMahon Bill and deadlocking the Combined Policy Committee, the Anglo-American advisory body on the question, that it had no intention of sharing the secrets of its nuclear weaponry research, present or future, with anyone, whether they'd been wartime allies or not. The Nunn May case had given them the excuse they needed. The British weren't to be trusted. Attlee's response was to order the development of an independent British nuclear deterrent. The strategy was obvious and inevitable. But it risked antagonizing the Soviet Union, who weren't thought to have the technical know-how to build their own bomb, and who already resented the Americans' tendency to throw their weight around on account of the bomb to end all bombs nestling permanently in their hip pockets. You have to understand that Britain's hard-up-uncle relationship with the US was still in the evolutionary stage then. As was the carve-up of the globe between the American and Soviet blocs. Everyone was feeling their way. The future was in flux. Stabilizing it meant creating a balance of power. And balance required parity. A British bomb was only likely to make the Soviets feel more inferior and more resentful, running the risk that they'd be so keen to show the Americans they couldn't be intimidated that a confrontation between the two would get out of hand, with Britain caught in the middle. Hence the other highly secret element in the new strategy. Britain would enable the Soviets to catch up and gain parity by feeding the necessary technical information to them. But the Soviets weren't to know where it was really coming from. No-one was. A traitor was required; a loyal traitor.'

'A Judas,' I murmured.

'Judas?' Rainbird nodded. 'Yes, I suppose so, in a sense. And look what happened to him.'

'So that's what Cedric was.'

'Yes. Why he was chosen we don't know. How he was talked into doing it is unclear. What he was promised – if anything – we can only guess. Major Strathallan may be able to shed some light on those issues, as well as on a good many others. Milner's Russian mother may be the key to it. One theory, at the time, was that a cousin of hers, who fetched up at the Russian Embassy in London after the war as a cultural attaché, was Milner's contact. There's no real evidence for that, but it fits the facts – those few that are known, at any rate. The Fuchs case threw a spanner in the works, you see. It brought the bloodhounds to Harwell and more or less guaranteed Milner's exposure in the long run. Strathallan couldn't cover his tracks indefinitely, nor could the truth be revealed if he were caught. He had to go. Well, Arzamas-16 was preferable to Wormwood Scrubs, no question about that. So, he went. As to whether he was encouraged to believe he could ever return . . .' Rainbird shrugged. 'The truth *was* revealed, of course. To SIS if not to the public. The change of government in October 'fifty-one led to the discovery of the project's existence. But it had been wrapped in so many precautions that Heraclitus remained anonymous. His controller had died a few months previously and no-one else knew who he was. It didn't really matter. Milner could safely be demonized and forgotten about. He didn't turn out to be the only traitor, after all. He was one of several. The irony is that they'd probably have done Milner's job for him, had he but known. His sacrifice wasn't strictly necessary, but it was real enough – and potential dynamite to Anglo-American relations. Can you imagine the effect its disclosure would have, even today? I don't like to, let me tell you. It just doesn't bear thinking about.'

'No need to think about it now, is there? You've made sure Cedric can never tell his story.'

'It had to be done. An old man with nothing to lose and God knows how many ways of actually proving his claims. As soon as it became known he'd left Russia, the alarm bells began ringing. He had to be found. And he had to be stopped. Hereabouts was the obvious place to lie in wait for him: as close to a home as he had. Maybe that's why Strathallan bought this house. We approached Miss Temple and found her sympathetic. Of course, we did nothing to disabuse her of the notion that he was a cold-hearted traitor. She agreed to co-operate with us in the event of his contacting her. I think her suspicion that he'd never told her all he knew about her sister's murder may have stiffened her resolve. I was on hand to deal with the situation as, when and if it developed. Spywatching rather than birdwatching, insofar as there's a difference. Both require a hide, some camouflage and plenty of patience.'

'Well, you got what you were waiting for. Cedric contacted Daisy, as you'd guessed he would. Why didn't you pick him up then?'

Rainbird sighed. 'My superiors became over-ambitious. A besetting fault of theirs. They wanted Heraclitus as well as Columbus: the fancier as well as the pigeon. We tried to string him along. The theory was that Daisy's ultimatum would drive him to Heraclitus as his only remaining ally. But it was too long a shot in my view. And it was beginning to involve too many people. The approach his solicitor made to the Home Office was a particularly worrying development. We didn't even know he *had* a solicitor.'

'His solicitor was my wife, Norman. You seem to forget that.'

'I'm well aware of what she was to you. To us, she was a problem. And we already had quite enough of those.'

'Of course.' The dismissive tone in his voice finally crystallized the anger that hadn't left me throughout his supercilious analysis of Cedric Milner's tragedy. But it was anger I had control of now. I rose casually from my chair and strolled round to the other side of the table, trailing my hand across the top, between Strathallan's emptied glass and the bottle of Lagavulin. 'How very inconvenient for you.'

'I make no complaint.' Rainbird was still staring up at the window, apparently unaware of my progress towards the drawer – and certainly unaware of what the drawer contained. 'Problems are what I'm paid to solve.'

'You seem to be good at that.' I slid the drawer open as I spoke, masking the sound with my words. 'Really very good.'

'Kind of you to say so.'

'And in this case the solution' – I grasped the gun and lifted it out – 'was murder.'

'Murder?' He turned round with a look of puzzlement on his face, which intensified into open-mouthed astonishment when he saw what I was holding.

'Yes.' I pointed the gun at him, steadying my wrist with my other hand, my forefinger curling round the trigger. 'That's exactly right.'

'I murdered no-one.'

'It doesn't matter to me whether you actually did it, Norman, or one of your goons did. Walker, perhaps. Or one of those headcases he goes around with. You'll answer for it anyway. I reckon that's fair.'

'You're making a big mistake, Tony.'

'Am I?'

'We had nothing to do with your wife's death.'

'Pull the other one.'

'I assure you, we weren't involved.' He spoke softly and calmly. He wasn't frightened. Or, if he was, he was too well-trained to show it. 'It would have made no sense for us to move against her at that time. Consider the effect her death actually had. It alerted Milner to the vulnerability of his position and drove him underground. One minute we knew where he was, the next he was gone. Do you think we wanted that? Of course not. It put us back to square one, if not off the board altogether. It obliged me to devote a considerable amount of time and effort to luring him back into the light, courtesy of your good self. From our point of view, your wife's death was a disaster.'

If only he hadn't made so much sense I'd have pulled the trigger there and then. I still wanted to. I wanted a target for the grief and rage memories of your death

340

still evoked. And there he was, in front of me, a prime target if ever there was one. But was he the *right* target? I had only a single chance – one shot at the truth. But the truth was like a pattern in a kaleidoscope, swirling and changing before me. Somewhere, beyond and behind the shifting scene of different people's versions of the same events, lay the answer. But killing Rainbird wasn't the way to find it.

'Put the gun down, Tony,' he said, moving slowly and cautiously towards me as he spoke. 'I didn't throw your wife off that cliff, and I didn't order anyone to. It was nothing to do with me or mine. You know that. You'd like me to be responsible, but you don't really believe I am. And I'm sure you don't believe the satisfaction of putting a bullet through my brain is worth twenty years in prison. It would be at least that, by the way. The judiciary come down hard on those who murder public servants. Too close to home, I suppose.' He stopped when he was within an inch or so of the barrel and held out one hand in gentle invitation. 'Do put it down, there's a good fellow. Better still,' he cradled his hand beneath mine, 'let me put it down for you. These old weapons can be treacherous things.'

There was nothing I could say that wouldn't amount to an admission of defeat and no doubt he could read that in my eyes anyway. I was breathing hard and my hands were shaking. God, what a stupid, pointless, bloody mess it all seemed. When Rainbird prised my fingers from the handle, I was grateful – and sickened by knowing that I was grateful.

'Thank you', he said, 'for not making a fool of both of us.' He uncocked the gun and peered curiously at it. 'Major Strathallan's, I assume. A virtual antique, yet pre- served in full working order. One would expect nothing

341

less.' Then he opened the chambers and gave an appreciative whistle. I looked down and saw that they were empty. 'Well, well. Would you believe it? I shouldn't care to play poker with the major, I must say.'

'You knew it wasn't loaded.'

'No. I thought it probably was, as a matter of fact. But I never thought you'd fire. You're just not the type. And believe me, there *is* a type. Besides, you despise me, but you don't hate me. There's all the difference in the world.'

'You've been very clever, haven't you, Norman?'

'I've been as resourceful as I needed to be.'

'Did Daisy know how you meant to deal with Cedric?'

'Her reaction when I told her what had happened to him suggests not. Actually, I think she knew, all along. She wanted some kind of revenge and we offered to supply it. But, now that it's come to pass, she recognizes the malice that drove her. An ugly trait, malice, especially in an old woman. And, as an artist, Daisy has a horror of ugliness.'

'Did you really have to kill him?'

'We had no choice. He could have ended his days quietly in Moscow, but instead he insisted on a grand exit. He knew what coming back here meant. The legal negotiations were just for show. He was well aware of how impossible compromise was. Spies and defectors are occupational hazards – embarrassing but tolerable. Cedric Milner, on the other hand, represented a threat to the ideological order. The British government donating the bomb to Stalin because it reckoned Uncle Sam was getting too big for his cowboy boots? If you think that's a tale we could ever allow to be told, Tony, you're more naïve than I supposed.'

'So the best kind of patriot is to be remembered as the worst kind of traitor?'

'He must have known that would be his epitaph when he agreed to take the job. Maybe the tragedy that engulfed his family helped, by rendering him a free agent. It meant there was no-one to feel personally betrayed by his apparent defection.'

'Except Daisy.'

'Except Daisy, yes.' Rainbird pursed his lips. 'His nemesis. As he was hers.'

'You haven't told her the truth, have you?'

'Certainly not.' He looked at me as if the idea was absurd. 'This kind of information is strictly embargoed.'

'Why tell me, then?'

He grinned. 'Let's call it a special concession. In acknowledgement of your invaluable contribution.'

I struck out at him in a reflex that showed how close to the surface my anger remained. But he grabbed my arm before it was more than half-raised and held it in a powerful grip. Then I relaxed and he lowered it slowly to my side.

'I'm offering you a very good deal, Tony. I'm being more generous than I either need or ought to be. You know the truth now. I'd advise you to keep it to yourself. Nobody would believe it, and there isn't a shred of proof, so you'd simply make yourself look ridiculous by bruiting it abroad. Worse still, you might attract the hostile attention of some of my colleagues, who wouldn't be anything like as accommodating as me. I trust you catch my drift.'

'I catch it well enough.'

'Good. Now, as to the police, getting them off your back is part of the package. Give them a call, make out a statement in which there's no reference whatsoever to

343

the subject we've been discussing, and I can guarantee you'll hear no more of the matter, bar a brief and painless appearance at an inquest into the death of William Hall some months hence.'

'All right.'

'You agree?'

'I said *all right*.'

'So you did.' He clicked his tongue. 'Though I have the impression you're far from that state.'

'Is that another of the problems you feel obliged to solve, Norman?'

'Outwith my area of expertise, I'm afraid.'

'I thought it probably was.'

'Quite.' He gave another grin – the kind he never seemed to run short of. 'Well, perhaps I ought to be on my way.'

He looked around the room, as if making sure he wasn't about to leave something behind. Then he nodded in evident satisfaction, dropped the gun into his pocket and walked past me to the door. I didn't turn round to watch him go. His footsteps stopped after a few yards. I knew he was standing in the doorway, studying me, waiting for something. But I made no move.

'I think it's very wise of you,' he said after a few seconds. 'Not asking me, I mean.' Now I did turn to look at him. 'If you did, I'd feel obliged to give you an honest answer. And I'm not sure you really want that.'

'I don't know what you're talking about.' But I did know. I knew exactly.

'Of course not. I quite understand.' He winked at me. 'Goodbye, Tony. I won't be in touch. Never fear.'

Chapter Fourteen

I sat there for a long time – an hour, an hour and a half maybe. The light shafting through the window changed in angle and intensity. The evening advanced. I drank several large, slow glasses of Lagavulin. I watched the tremor in my hands fade into a numbed steadiness. Otherways' enveloping version of silence held me fast. There was nothing to do. There was nowhere to go. I'd stopped running. Now I could only wait. Something would happen. Someone would come. They had to. And when they did, I'd know what I had to do.

I wish I could turn the clock back, Marina. I wish I could rewind the past to that last afternoon of your life. I could change it, you see. I could make it right. You wouldn't have to die. And I wouldn't have to wonder any more. I'd know. The doubt would be over and the grief would be averted. Neither ghost would follow me. I'd be free. And so would you.

But the past isn't like that. The way it was – known or unknown – is the way it will always be. And this telling of it to you is the closest it will let me get. I can alter nothing. I can only try to understand. And hope you do, too.

*   *   *

One question filled my thoughts as I sat there: the question Rainbird had said I was wise not to ask him. He'd convinced me MI5, or whatever branch of the security services he represented, had played no part in your death. I was left where I'd started, confronting the mystery of Lucy's movements after leaving Torquay that afternoon. And that was the question. Had Daisy lied about returning to Rutland separately? Rainbird might have instructed her to, reasoning correctly that sowing suspicion of Lucy in my mind would make me determined to track down Cedric, something I stood a much better chance of doing than anyone else, on account of his connection with you. Alternatively, of course, there might have been no need for Daisy to lie. Her account of the homeward journey might have been nothing less than the truth.

If so, it couldn't be the whole truth, though. For that I needed to establish where Lucy had gone after dropping Daisy at Newton Abbot. *Where and why.* One question simply bred another. And one person's word could never be the whole answer. But it was all I was going to get. If I asked at all.

That was the final choice I confronted: the choice Rainbird had warned me about. Knowledge could be worse than doubt, the truth more painful than any half-admitted fear. What sort of a future Lucy and Matt and I had to look forward to turned on my decision. And I had no idea which way it was likely to go.

'Tony?'

I heard Lucy's voice from the hall, echoing down the stairs. I wondered for a second if I was dreaming, but the sensation was far more like waking from a dream, my brain dragging my reactions and calculations into the here and now. I looked up at the clock on the kitchen wall. It was a few minutes to eight and there was a granular hint of twilight in the room.

'Tony?'

She came through the door, stopped and looked at me. She was wearing jeans and a dark sweater. Her face was drawn, her eyes hollow.

'Why didn't you answer when I called?'

'I . . . I'm sorry, I . . .'

'Isn't it great about Matt?' She smiled, but there was a nervous edge to her expression, as if she was uncertain what her delight at Matt's recovery meant for us.

'Of course. I—'

She ran forward and hugged me as I rose from the chair. In that moment, it was possible to believe I'd dreamed what had happened between us, that we were simply sharing the relief we felt that her husband, my best friend, wasn't going to die. Then she kissed me and the moment passed. She was seeking to reassure me, and herself, that we could go on together, that there really could be a way ahead for all of us. But there was no reassurance to be had.

We drew apart awkwardly. Lucy collided with a corner of the table. I stood where I was, staring at her, too drained to disguise my confusion. I could sense it in her, too: the refusal to admit it had all gone wrong, the fear that she'd misread the signs mirrored by the fear that she'd read them all too well.

'Why didn't you come to the hospital with Nesta?' she asked, her voice cracking as she spoke. 'Matt would have liked to see you.'

'I had . . . other commitments.'

'What other commitments?'

'It's too complicated to explain.'

'Nesta told me she bumped into you in Peterborough. What were you doing there?'

'Do we have to account to each other for our movements, Lucy? Is that what it's come to?' It had, of course. That's exactly what it had come to.

'It was a natural enough question.' She looked hurt, as she had every right to be. She hadn't expected this.

'How did you know I was here?'

'Where else could you be?'

'Anywhere.'

'But you're not, are you? You *are* here.'

'Yes. And I can't explain that either.'

'What's the matter, Tony?' She took a step towards me, frowning as she did so. 'What's wrong with you?'

'A lot's happened to me in the past couple of days. Too much for me to pretend that everything's OK, or that it ever will be again.'

'I don't understand.'

'I wish I didn't.'

'Why don't you come to the hospital with me now? There's still time for a visit. You'll feel better for seeing Matt. He really is doing well.'

'I don't think so.'

'He doesn't remember, you know.'

'What?'

'He has no memory of the hours before the crash. None at all. It's been wiped away.'

'But not wiped clean.'

'You're not making sense.'

'Oh yes I am.'

'Listen to me, Tony.' She took another step closer and put her hand on my shoulder. It was a tentative kind of caress. I could have raised my hand to meet hers.

She certainly wanted me to. But I didn't. Neither did I shrink away, though. It was still possible for us to draw back from the brink. 'Matt doesn't know about you and me. But we know how he's likely to react if he finds out.'

'If?'

'His loss of memory gives us a second chance. We can put it right. We can make sure he comes through. You and me, too. We can . . . shape a future for the three of us.'

'What sort of future?'

'I don't know. I only know we have to try.' Her hand moved to my cheek. As she stroked it, I saw tears brimming in her eyes. 'Please. For me. I love you, Tony.'

'And Matt?'

'I love him, too. Just like you do.'

Her fragility was never more obvious than in that moment. There was so much of your openness in her, your lack of guile, but so little of your strength. Whatever lies she might have told, she believed them now. To take them from her, to force her to face the truth, would be like tearing the wings off a butterfly. The only future we could have required the lies to remain as they were – intact, unchallenged, never to be questioned.

'Come with me now. Please. You'll be glad you did.'

'Will I?'

'Oh yes. I promise.'

She meant it. And for that fragment of the present that seemed like the future, I believed her. It really could be all right. There was a way to *make* it all right. And we could find it. We only had to believe it was possible and it would be.

She moved her hand to my mouth, tracing the line of

my lips with her forefinger. Then she smiled, cautiously but genuinely. 'Trust me,' she said softly. 'That's all I'm asking you to do. It's not too much, is it?'

It should have been. In so many ways, it was. But I couldn't find the courage to break her, and me, there and then, in cold blood. 'No,' I said, shaking my head. 'I suppose not.'

She glanced down at the table, noticing the bottle and the two glasses for the first time. Then her eyes moved back to mine. She wasn't going to ask who the second glass had been for. She wasn't going to ask anything. Nor, now, could I. She'd bought my silence with her own. A pact had been concluded.

'Are you sure it's not too late to go to the hospital?'

'They won't mind. And Matt certainly won't. We don't have to stay long.'

'No. Of course not.'

'Let's go, then, shall we? If you're ready.'

'I'm ready.'

Lucy kissed me, then turned and hurried out. I followed, watching her climb the stairs ahead of me, moving faster than I seemed able to. Everything was moving too fast now. And none of it seemed to be in my control.

As we crossed the hall, there was a flicker – a shadow of something stirring – above me in the stairwell. I stopped and looked up. There was nothing there. The landing was empty. It had been a trick of the failing light, or of my tiring brain. Yet I couldn't dismiss the fleeting certainty that it had been more than that.

'What's wrong?' Lucy had stopped halfway along the passage towards the front door and was staring back at me.

'Nothing. I thought I . . .' I shrugged. 'I was mistaken.'

'There's no-one else here, is there?' The second glass on the kitchen table had prompted the question. But what suspicion it had planted in her mind I couldn't tell.

'No. No-one else.' I hurried to catch up with her. 'Honest.'

'It's just that you're not the only one to have done a disappearing act.'

'Who else?'

'Daisy. She went out before I left for the hospital this morning and hasn't been back since.'

'Are you sure?'

'I've phoned several times. She hasn't answered, and she hasn't phoned back. If I hadn't had so much else on my mind, I'd have been quite worried about her.'

'There's probably no need.' I could have told her about seeing Daisy in the churchyard, but that would have meant telling her a lot of other things I didn't dare to. 'Why not give her another call now?'

'No. Let's press on.' She led the way to the door and opened it. 'As you say, there's probably—'

She broke off with a gasp. Looking past her, I could see Daisy standing next to Lucy's car in front of the house. She was gazing up at us, as if she'd been waiting for us to appear and had known it wouldn't be long before we did.

'Daisy,' Lucy called, recovering her composure almost as quickly as she'd lost it. 'What are you doing here?'

'Nothing,' Daisy replied in a murmur. 'Nothing at all.' She looked old and weary, her hair whiter than I'd have said it was, her eyes a greyer shade of blue than I remembered.

'Where's your car?' Lucy asked, starting down the

351

steps while I closed the door behind us. As it clunked shut, I heard the telephone ring, stirring a memory I couldn't quite place.

'I left it in Hambleton,' said Daisy.

'You walked from there?' Lucy queried.

'I was in no hurry.'

'But there might have been nobody here.'

'There was bound to be.' She looked up and beyond us as we approached, following the curve of the house with her eyes. Out here, beyond the moat, the telephone was inaudible. But it was easy to believe I could still hear it ringing. 'There always is.'

'Where have you been all day?'

'There's no need for you to know.' The words were an echo of what she'd told me Lucy had said when she'd asked her why they had to travel back separately from Devon. Whether the echo was deliberate I couldn't tell, far less whether it was intended for Lucy's benefit or mine. 'Good evening, Tony,' she added, with a sudden glance in my direction.

'What's this all about?' Lucy asked, looking from Daisy to me and back again.

I shrugged. And Daisy gave the faintest of smiles. 'I don't know,' she said. 'I don't know anything any more.'

'We were going to the hospital,' said Lucy. 'To see Matt.'

'Don't let me stop you.'

'But we can't just leave you here.'

'You can, my dear, I assure you.'

'No, no. We'll drive you home first.'

'There's no need.'

'I think there is. You don't look well.'

'I've never been better.'

352

'Come on, Daisy. Get in.' Lucy opened the passenger door for her. 'Don't be difficult.'

'What about *my* car?'

'We'll collect it in the morning.'

'This is all completely unnecessary.' She cast me a strange sidelong look I couldn't read. 'But if you insist . . .' With that she climbed into the car.

'Let's go,' said Lucy, rolling her eyes at me as she slammed the door shut.

I got in the back, behind Daisy, while Lucy went round to the driver's door. During the couple of seconds Daisy and I had to ourselves, she said, without turning to look at me, 'How was Major Strathallan?'

She'd spoken so softly and expressionlessly that it was almost as if she hadn't spoken at all. And before I could respond, Lucy had joined us. She looked over her shoulder at me, smiling tightly. 'OK?' she asked. I nodded.

Lucy started the engine, reversed, then pulled past the bridge across the moat and away along the drive. I glanced back at the house through the rear window, at the conical roofline and the curvature of the stonework which looked, in this light and from my receding point of view, as if they might be a part of some optical illusion, a shroud, behind which the true shape of things was still waiting to be discovered.

'You ought to be aware, Lucinda,' I heard Daisy say, 'that I've told Tony everything.' I whirled round.

'What do you mean?' Lucy sounded genuinely puzzled.

'About our trip to Torquay the day your sister died. About your meeting with Cedric.'

Lucy said nothing. She drove straight ahead, her

knuckles whitening as her grip on the steering wheel tightened.

'I don't suppose Tony's mentioned it, but you may be interested to know that Cedric's dead. He died last night, in London. And Tony was the last person to see him alive.'

'Stop it,' I said, grasping Daisy's shoulder. 'This isn't the right time to—'

'Tell the truth?' Daisy half turned towards me. 'Isn't it always the right time to do that?'

Lucy braked suddenly and I was thrown against the back of Daisy's seat. With a crunch of rubber on gravel, we jerked to a halt. When I looked up, Lucy was staring at me, her eyes large and imploring. And what she was imploring me to do was to believe her. 'I don't know what Daisy's told you,' she said, emphasizing every word, 'but it was she who swore me to secrecy about the trip to Torquay.'

'That *is* what I told him,' said Daisy. 'But it wasn't all.'

'What else did you say?' Lucy glared at her. '*What else?*'

'What I felt obliged to. That we travelled back separately. That you dropped me at Newton Abbot that afternoon and left me to catch a train home while you . . . went your own way.'

'You said that?'

'I had to.'

'But . . . why?'

'Because it's the truth.'

'But it isn't.' Lucy looked back at me. 'It's a lie. She's lying.'

'Why would I be?'

'This is crazy. We drove all the way back, together.'

354

'We did not.'

'Why are you doing this, Daisy?' There was horror on Lucy's face – horror at a secret revealed, or at one invented. 'In God's name, why?'

'Because Tony has to know, my dear. He had to be told.'

'Told *what*?'

'Where you went that afternoon. Why you went there. What you went there to do. Tell him now. Tell him the truth.'

'We came back together. *That's* the truth.'

'It's too late, Lucinda. You can't go on pretending.'

'I'm *not* pretending.' She turned round bodily in her seat and grasped my arm. 'Listen to me, Tony. I'm telling you the truth, the only truth I know. I drove Daisy to Torquay. And I drove her home. There was no parting. She's lying.'

'Tony would like to believe that,' said Daisy softly. 'But he can't.'

'Say you believe me.' Lucy's grip on my arm was frenziedly tight. Her eyes were fixed on mine, and they were wide with fear. 'Please, my love. Say it.'

'I believe you.' I had to force the words out. And the quiver of shock across her face told me clearly that they sounded as hollow to her as they did to me.

'But you don't, do you?' Her mouth fell open. Her eyes drifted out of focus. 'And you never will.' Her arm fell away from mine. She shrank back. '*That's* the truth.'

'Let's all calm down,' I said, suddenly sensing that I had to defuse the moment before it blew up in our faces. 'Let's go back into the house and—'

'*No.*' Lucy's voice fractured into a scream. She swung round, shoved the car into gear and took off along the drive in a spray of gravel. 'I'm never going in there again.'

The acceleration flung me back in the seat. I fell sideways across it and, as I struggled up, I caught a glimpse of Lucy's eyes, flashing up to look at me in the rear-view mirror. They'd become the eyes of someone I didn't know – set, hard, frighteningly intense. 'Stop!' I shouted. 'Stop the car!'

'She's not listening to you,' said Daisy, still locked in her private trance. 'She's listening to her ghosts.'

'What?'

'Don't you understand?' Her blue-eyed gaze ranged back over me as the car sped towards the end of the drive, the wayside trees blurring around us like the walls of a tunnel. 'They give you choices. Then they take them away.'

I was thrown across the seat again as Lucy swung left into the lane leading to the end of the peninsula. Suddenly, I realized what she meant to do. It had happened before, in my dream at Otherways, while waiting for Matt. Before, but differently. Except that I'd prevented it. Or maybe I'd merely altered it.

'They show you things,' Daisy went on. 'But they're never what you think they are.'

'Lucy!' I grabbed at her shoulder. 'For God's sake listen to me.'

But Daisy was right. Lucy was a long way past listening. She accelerated into the next bend, clipping the verge and pitching me off balance again, then picked up still more speed as we reached the gated straight before the descent to the lake. There were the gates ahead, racing towards us, it seemed, as we raced towards them.

'Don't do it!' was all I managed to shout before we hit them, dead centre. There was a shattering of headlamp glass buried in the thumping crash of steel, then we were through, leaving the gates bouncing back against their posts behind us.

I stretched between the front seats and grabbed Lucy under the arm and around the shoulders, trying to pull her far enough towards me to lift her foot off the accelerator. But her hands were gripping the steering-wheel as if in a spasm and I could see her right leg straightening as she pressed the pedal to the floor. We raced down the slope towards the pontoon and the lake and the distant white smudge of Normanton Church picked out in the ebbing sunlight on the farther shore. It was all happening too quickly. And I wasn't going to be able to prevent it. I knew that with all the force of a remembered dream.

Suddenly, Lucy's left hand was off the wheel. Her arm swung into my face, the point of the elbow striking me hard on the bridge of the nose. I fell back and heard her scream, '*I loved you.*' She crouched forward, concentrating on the view ahead as the lake filled the windscreen. In the next moment, we were out on the pontoon, tilting as we were carried forward on the two offside wheels. The driver's window was sliding open. I saw it happening and wondered whose finger was on the control. Then we hit the water.

It was all around us, blanking out the windows, surging in past Lucy in a gout of foam. We went down fast, hitting the sloping bed of the lake with a muffled thud amidst a blinding fountain of bubbles. I was prone on the back seat. I struggled up, fighting against the shock that had engulfed me along with the water. It was suddenly cold and dark. And the car was still moving, sliding steadily forwards. I kicked at the floor and reached a dwindling layer of air near the roof. Then I twisted down to the nearest door handle and wrenched at it. It opened. I slithered out and up, swimming for the brightness a few feet above.

I surfaced and gulped in several lungfuls of air. The water around me was churning with bubbles and the after-swash of our plunge off the pontoon. The shore was only a matter of yards away, yet it seemed as remote as the past we'd left behind. I took a deep breath and dived back down.

My hands touched the car before I saw it. I thought for a second that it was the roof, then I felt the radiator grille and realized I was at the front of the bonnet. As I slid round, I saw through the windscreen into the car. Daisy had rolled forward against the dashboard, apparently unconscious. But Lucy was still clutching the steering wheel. Her eyes were wide open. It was as if she was staring straight at me. I swam towards her, hauling myself round by the frame of the open window. She didn't move or look in my direction.

I yanked at the door handle, but nothing happened. It was locked. The knob was down inside. Lucy must have locked it. She didn't want to be rescued.

But I was going to do everything I could to frustrate her death wish. I leaned in through the window and grabbed her under one arm. She was limp and unresisting – unconscious, but not yet, I had to hope, too far gone. Then I saw the seatbelt strap fastened tautly across her breast. She'd thought of everything. With my lungs straining, I pulled her towards me. But the belt held her round the waist. I hadn't enough breath left to wriggle in past her and release it. I had to give up.

I kicked away from the car and surfaced for a second time. I trod water, sucking in deep breaths. I couldn't see anyone near by, on the lake or on the shore. I dived again, straight back down to the driver's door.

My mental grasp of the sequence of events was faltering now, as my strength diminished. I reached in through the window and yanked the handle up, then pulled the door as far open as I could. Lucy hadn't moved, held where she was by the seatbelt. Daisy, who was unbelted, lolled beside her, her head bobbing in the turbulence I was creating. Bracing myself on the door frame, I stretched across Lucy and pressed the seatbelt release. The belt floated free and Lucy fell softly against me. I flinched, half expecting her to grab my arm and pull me further into the car. But though her eyes remained open, wide and staring, there was nothing working behind them. I backed out through the door, dragging her after me with my arms around her waist. My breath was nearly gone. I had nothing left. I struck out for the surface.

I'm not sure if I carried Lucy with me, or if she simply floated up beside me. Suddenly, we were out in the sweet air and clear light. I clasped her to me and swam backwards towards the shore. The floor of the lake shelved up to meet me sooner than I'd expected. From there I waded, dragging her behind me, as far as the shingle at the water's edge.

I lowered her to the ground and fell down beside her. I was exhausted, quivering and panting and beginning to shiver in my sodden clothes, but if I was to save her I had to act fast. She lay inert, her face grey and cold, her hair plastered across it, her eyes blank and unseeing. There was no breath, nor any trace of a pulse. I opened her mouth. Water and vomit dribbled out. In my mind was a fragmentary memory of the artificial resuscitation technique they taught on that first-aid course you prodded me into attending all of ten years ago. The timings were bound to be wrong, but anything had to be better than nothing. I tilted her head back, crouched over her and struggled through two mouth-to-mouth breaths, then tried cardiac compression. There was no response. I tried again. And again. And again.

Somewhere behind me, out on the lake, I heard a voice calling to me above the gnatlike drone of an outboard motor. I turned round and saw a small boat heading towards me. A man was waving to me from the stern and shouting. As he cut the engine and coasted into the shallows, his words reached me.

'I saw what happened from the other side.'

I couldn't find the breath to answer. I was on my hands and knees, struggling to control the shiver which had worsened into a quake of fear and fatigue. Lucy lay where I'd dropped her, limp and motionless, staring sightlessly into the reddening sky.

'I've phoned for an ambulance,' the man shouted as he jumped from the boat. He was a stockily built bloke in fisherman's gear, with a local accent. 'It'll be here soon.'

I looked down at Lucy. 'Not soon enough,' I murmured. Then I stretched out a trembling hand and closed her eyes.

Chapter Fifteen

I'd fled one hospital, only to end up in another. It was Leicester Royal Infirmary this time, one floor down from Matt. They said I'd have to stay in overnight for observation and I was too drained and distraught to argue. Lucy was pronounced dead on arrival, but I'd known she was dead long before the ambulance got to us, despite the paramedic's optimistic words about something called 'diving reflex'. She was dead and it was my fault and, sooner or later, I was going to have to explain that to Matt.

I was going to have to explain it to the police as well, but I was past worrying about them. They'd drag the car out of the lake, and Daisy with it, and then start trying to piece together the chain of events that had led Lucy to drive off the end of the peninsula at high speed in an attempt to kill herself and her two passengers. They wouldn't get much help from me but, no doubt, eventually, they'd get enough. By then, I'd have made my peace with Matt. Or I'd have failed to.

I couldn't face making the attempt that night. I was too tired and confused to construct any kind of coherent account, let alone answer the questions he was bound to put to me, or the accusations that might follow my answers. He was told of Lucy's death and given as much information about the circumstances as the hospital staff possessed. I didn't see him. It was an excusable evasion, I suppose, considering the state I was in, and I was too far gone to feel guilty about it. But it was only a delay. By morning, I knew I could delay no longer.

I waited until I'd been officially discharged. My clothes had been dried by then. They were badly creased and crumpled, but what I looked like was the least of my concerns. I made my way up to the private room they'd moved Matt to, still not knowing what I was going to say to him. I didn't want there to be any more secrets between us. Our friendship was the one thing both of us had left to cling to amidst the wreckage of so much else, and honesty seemed the only way to sustain it. But honesty, in this case, promised to be a brutal business. And I wasn't the only one who'd spent the night thinking about the damage it might do.

'Thank God you're here,' said Matt the moment he set eyes on me. He was still hooked up to various tubes and monitors, and you couldn't say he looked or sounded well, with a hoarse voice, a swathe of bandages round his midriff and a rash of minor wounds, a couple of them stitched, on his neck and face. He was trembling, too, and sweating slightly. But he was also sitting up and looking at me and talking. In its way, it was a miracle. But there weren't any more miracles to be had.

'I'd have come sooner, but—'

'Never mind that. Sit down.'

'Right.' I drew up a chair. 'I'm sorry I couldn't save her, Matt.'

'I know you tried your damnedest.'

'I just wasn't fast enough, or strong enough.'

'Have the police spoken to you?'

'Not yet.'

'But when they do, what will you tell them?'

'The truth, I suppose. But listen—'

'You know, don't you?'

'What?'

'That's why it happened.' He lowered his voice, as if afraid of eavesdroppers, and leaned towards me, only to wince and lean smartly back, motioning for me to sit closer. 'I've thought it through, and nothing else makes sense. If you're trying to spare my feelings, don't bother.'

'I don't know what you mean.' Had he remembered what I'd told him immediately before the crash? Or had he guessed? He'd clearly convinced himself that he knew what lay behind this latest horror and, for the moment, his concern on that score was holding his grief in check. I'd expected anguish, maybe suspicion as well, maybe worse. But I'd got none of them. Something was taking priority.

'We don't have time to play games, Tony. I realize what you're trying to do. You reckon I'm not up to hearing about it. Well, I have to be. Because we have to decide whether to involve the police . . . or not.'

'They already are involved.'

'In Lucy's death. And Daisy's, of course. But do they have to connect them with Marina's? That's the point, Tony. Do we really have to make this worse than it already is?'

Then it dawned on me. He'd asked himself why Lucy should have tried to kill Daisy and me, along with herself, and he'd come up with an answer that fitted the facts as he knew them.

'I told you about the discrepancy on the trip counter

in her car, didn't I? I was upset about it, which is probably what caused me to crash. I'd met you, in Oakham I suppose, to tell you, which is why you were right behind me when the lorry ploughed into me. I'd been wondering whether to tell you ever since Marina died. I can't remember deciding to. That must be part of the traumatic amnesia they reckon I'm suffering from. But that *is* what happened, isn't it? I've worked it out, you see, Tony, so there's no point denying it.'

And there wasn't. Because, in a strange kind of way, he was exactly right. 'I'm not denying it.'

'You confronted her, didn't you? Or you confronted Daisy.'

'I confronted both of them.'

'What did they say?'

'Matt, I—'

'*What did they say?*'

'Nothing.'

'Nothing?'

'I never got a straight answer. They contradicted each other. Then Lucy . . .'

'Drove into the lake.'

'Yes.'

'I dreamed of that happening, you know.' He thumbed the perspiration from his eyebrows. 'A few weeks back. I dreamed I was following her car in my own along the lane, at high speed. I couldn't catch up. I was right behind her. I saw it happen. Do you believe dreams foretell the future?'

'I'm not sure.'

'I do.'

'I met Lois Carmichael, Matt.'

'Lois Carmichael?' He looked blank for a moment. 'Oh God, yes. You met her?'

'I did. And I found James Milner's confession.'

'So, you know what's been on my mind.'

'Lucy didn't kill Marina.'

'No?'

'No.' I looked at him squarely, without flinching. My denial wasn't about what he or I believed might have happened at Henna Cliff the day you fell to your death. It was about the two of us – our friendship, our survival, our future. 'I'm sure of it.'

'You can't be.'

'But I am.'

He reached out a weak left fist and tapped me on the arm. 'Thanks.'

'I won't mention any of this to the police.'

'How will you avoid it?'

'I don't know. I'll find a way.'

'It won't be easy.'

I shrugged. 'The worst that can happen is that they'll think I'm holding out on them. I can live with that.'

'Thanks again.'

'There's no need to thank me. There are . . . other things you don't know. I've not been that good a friend to you.'

'I've none better.'

'None worse, actually.'

'Rubbish.' He looked at me for a long, thoughtful moment, then closed his eyes and said, 'Let's help each other through this, Tony. You can tell me these . . . other things . . . when we've buried Lucy and got the police off our backs.' He opened his eyes and attempted a smile that stretched a few of the cuts and ended in a grimace. 'If you still want to.'

*   *   *

I was hoping to leave the hospital before Matt's parents and brother arrived, but no such luck: as I got out of the lift in main reception, I found them waiting to go up. Mr and Mrs Prior were too dismayed by the loss of their daughter-in-law so soon after the near loss of their son to ask me any leading questions, but Jeremy was certain now that something was being kept from them. I could tell from the undertone of suspicion in his enquiries after my health. When he sent his parents on up to Matt's room and took me aside for a chat, I realized I was going to have to improvise a story there and then. The police were suddenly a secondary problem.

'I don't understand anything that's been going on,' he said, giving me a narrow-eyed look. 'Where have you been the past couple of days?'

'Business elsewhere, Jeremy. Couldn't be helped.'

'I didn't think you *were* in business. Lucy certainly couldn't understand your absence. We were here yesterday when that woman Nesta turned up. Lucy took off straightaway. She seemed *very* keen to see you.'

'She just wanted to share the good news about Matt.'

'So how, and why, did it end in such a bloody awful way?'

'I don't know. Daisy was with her when she arrived at Otherways. They'd been having an argument. I've no idea what about. But Lucy was upset – very upset. We were supposed to be coming here, to see Matt. Instead, she drove off like crazy in the opposite direction. It was only at the last minute that I realized what she intended to do.'

'But why should she do such a thing?'

'Like I said, I don't know.'

'And why were you at Otherways at all?'

'I'd left some papers there that I needed.'

His eyes narrowed still further. 'I find all this very hard to believe.'

'So do I. But it happened.'

'There has to be more to it. And it'll come out eventually.' He lowered his voice. 'You'd be making life easier for everyone by telling your side of the story now.'

'That's what I've just done.'

'And you're sticking to it?'

'Yes.' I shrugged. 'There's nothing more I can say.'

A short walk from the hospital took me to the busy Welford road, on the other side of which stood Leicester Prison, a majestic pile of castellated Victorian Gothic. Somewhere within its walls, James Milner lay buried, not far from the condemned cell where he'd spent his final days writing a confession only four people had ever read. And only two of those were still alive. But even we hadn't stopped rewriting the past, editing it for our purposes. Complicity is partly what friendship is about, I suppose. Honesty has its limits. The truth is never absolute. We can't allow it to be. When all's said and done, we're only human.

What should I have done, Marina? Told Matt everything? Forced him to know, even if he couldn't understand? Maybe I would have done, if he hadn't been so anxious to protect Lucy in death, just as he had been in life. One collusion had become a metaphor for another. There was a way to share secrets without spilling them, to still doubts without admitting them. That was Lucy's epitaph. And that was what Matt and I were going to have to live with.

*　　*　　*

I went to the police station and made a statement, as I'd promised I would do the previous night. It was a fuller but no more revealing version of what I'd told Jeremy. The argument I described between Lucy and Daisy served its purpose, however. It provided an explanation, though not much of one, for what had happened. And it meant I could plead ignorance where Lucy's state of mind was concerned. I had the impression the officer who interviewed me didn't know whether to believe me or not. Not that it mattered: my version of events was the only one going.

I went back to the hospital around lunchtime and confirmed with the sister on Matt's ward that the coast was clear: Jeremy and his parents had gone.

Matt looked tired and drawn. The sister had told me not to stay long and I could see why. Grief was creeping up on him as he lay there, stalling the recovery that had only just begun.

'I can't believe I'll never see her again, Tony. Never see, never touch, never hear. You know what it's like. Nothing can prepare you. Nothing at all.'

'It *will* get better. Eventually. I can promise you that.'

'I'm not sure I want it to.' He sighed. 'Jeremy's going to arrange the funeral. He's good at that sort of thing. It might be best to let him get on with it.'

'Understood.'

'Could you go and see Lucy's mother? I . . .'

'She won't grasp what I'm telling her, Matt. She still expects visits from Marina.'

'Even so, I think we should make the effort.'

'All right. I'll go. Tomorrow.'

'Thanks. And, er, there's Daisy, of course. She had no

surviving family. Not many friends, either, apart from Lucy. Somebody should contact her solicitor.'

'Do you know who they are?'

'Halfyard and Co of Oakham would be my bet. I saw her coming out of their offices once. They're in Mill Street.'

'I'll call round.'

'Thanks. I'm sorry to load all this on you, but . . .'

'It doesn't matter. Actually, I'm grateful. It'll take my mind off things. At least for a while.'

'Jeremy said you'd told him Lucy and Daisy had had an argument, but that you didn't know what it was about. Did you stick to that with the police?'

'I did.'

'Will it be enough for them?'

'It'll have to be. It's all they're going to get.'

I took the train to Oakham and tracked down Halfyard and Co – a small, old-fashioned, market-town solicitor's practice. The receptionist reacted to Daisy's name as if news of her death had already been received. She had a word with Mr Halfyard, then asked me to wait.

Ten minutes later, I was led in to see the senior partner. He was sixtyish, portly and tweed-suited, a tendency to avuncularity held in check by his professional manner. An unlit pipe was propped in a bowl on his desk. Tobacco smoke lingered in the air, blending with the must of old files. He fidgeted in his chair and looked longingly at his pipe, but left it where it was.

'I heard the tragic news this morning, Mr Sheridan. As you seem to have surmised, I am – was – Miss Temple's solicitor. Also her executor. I'll be making all the necessary funerary arrangements.'

'I'll tell Mr Prior that.'

'Please do. And please extend my condolences to him on his sad loss.' Halfyard slid the palms of his hands along the edge of his desk and drew himself up. 'The police have told me as much as they can of the circumstances, including your part in them. Mention was made of an argument between Miss Temple and Mrs Prior.'

'I don't know what it was about.'

'Are you sure? The reason I ask is that Miss Temple telephoned me at home yesterday afternoon in what I can only describe as . . .' He paused to weigh his words. 'An unusually animated state.'

'What did she want?'

'To see me, as soon as possible. We made an appointment for ten o'clock this morning.'

'But you don't know what it was about?'

'Alas, no.'

'So, you're wondering if I might.'

'The thought occurred to me.'

'I'm afraid I can't help you.'

'A pity.'

'As you say.'

'A great pity.' He leaned forward, reluctant, I felt, to drop the subject. 'When my more elderly clients demand to see me urgently, Mr Sheridan, I usually find it's because they wish to change their will.'

'Perhaps that was it, then.'

'Perhaps. But we'll never know now, will we?'

'I'm afraid not.'

'You might tell Mr Prior I'll be writing to him, by the way.'

'About what?'

'Miss Temple's will.'

'Why should it concern him?'

'Didn't you know?' Halfyard frowned at me in surprise. 'I'm sorry. I've spoken out of turn. You'll understand I can't discuss a client's testamentary dispositions with a third party. But I *will* be writing.'

I didn't try to crack Halfyard's professional reticence. I didn't need to. His meaning was clear. Matt was the principal if not sole beneficiary of Daisy's will.

I didn't believe for a moment that Daisy would have bequeathed her estate to him. But Lucy was a different matter. And with Lucy dead, whatever she stood to inherit passed to her next of kin. That's why Halfyard was going to be writing to Matt. And that's why Daisy's failure to keep their appointment raised so many questions that were never going to be answered.

I spent the night at the hotel in Peterborough I'd booked into the previous morning, when Lucy and Daisy were both still alive and the truth about Cedric Milner was still unimaginable. I phoned the hospital from there. They told me Matt was sleeping. I left the hotel and walked myself into a state of exhaustion round the airless streets of a city I didn't know. I was beyond grief, beyond shock, beyond even self-pity, sustained by instinct, propelled by inertia. I went back to the hotel and did my best to get drunk in the bar. But even intoxication was beyond me. Every sense and feeling was remote and indistinct. I viewed the world as if through a gauze, no longer quite part of it and unsure how to return to it.

I caught an early train to London next morning and went straight from King's Cross to Paddington Green police station. Detective Sergeant Harmison seemed oddly unsurprised to see me. But the change in his manner soon told its own story. Rainbird had dropped a word in the appropriate ear. The heat was off. Harmison wasn't going to be looking seriously for my assailants. But he wasn't going to be chasing me in connection with the death of William Hall, either. The post-mortem had yielded ambiguous results, he told me, in a tone that suggested it was an ambiguity he knew he'd have to live with.

I was in Bournemouth by early afternoon. The visit to your mother was a black farce. She gave no sign of even hearing what I was saying, let alone understanding it. I couldn't help envying her. Wherever she was, it was a safer place than the real world. She still believed her little girls were happy and healthy. Why listen, if she didn't want to, to the contrary nonsense spoken by a man she recognized and felt vaguely acquainted with, but couldn't quite put a name to?

I decided to head for Plymouth, where my car was well over time in the station car park. So far over, in fact, that it had been wheel-clamped. Paying and waiting for its release ate into the evening. There was nothing for it after that but to stay overnight at Stanacombe and start back for Rutland in the morning.

Unfinished business was waiting for me at the house, in the shape of Wisdom's rusty old banger and a letter from the estate agent, requesting an urgent response to an offer. It was less than the asking price, but I wasn't about to quibble. If I was capable of beginning life over again, it had to be in new surroundings. I had no plans, no expectations, no hopes. But Stanacombe was your dream, not mine. And all the dreams were over now.

As if to prove the point, I slept soundly that night and woke late. It was a sunny morning, but the grass was damp from overnight rain, the air cleansed and clear as polished glass. It was as you'd loved it most, and as I loved it on your account. But you were gone. And soon I'd be gone too – away from the places that remembered you.

I phoned the estate agent and accepted the offer. Then I called the hospital and was put through to Matt. He sounded a little stronger, which was all that could be hoped for so soon after Lucy's death. He said he was looking forward to seeing me again, which twitched up the gauze between me and the world for a consoling instant. Whatever I did next, and whatever I did after that, Matt would be relying on me. I'd betrayed our friendship once. I couldn't, wouldn't, let it happen a second time.

I didn't pass on Halfyard's message. If I was right, it could wait until he wrote. And if I was wrong . . . who'd care?

I walked down to Duckpool Beach before setting off. The sea was calm, mirror-flat, bluer than the clear blue sky. It was beautiful. But its beauty couldn't touch me. Nor could the sun warm me. I was going to have to learn to feel again. But not yet. It was too soon.

Just about the last thing I'd have expected was to find a visitor waiting on the doorstep back at Stanacombe. But there was one. And he looked none too pleased to be there.

'About time,' Wisdom said by way of greeting, squinting at me in the bright sunlight that seemed so very much not his natural habitat. 'It's cost me a small fortune in train, bus and taxi fares to get here. You might at least have had the decency to be in.'

'I didn't know you were coming,' I said, smiling at him in spite of myself.

'I didn't think you needed to. I wasn't to know you'd block me in.'

I realized he was referring to his car. I'd have to move mine before he could get his out into the lane. 'Sorry,' I said with a shrug. Then a thought struck me. 'How did you know it was here?'

'Considering you've not stirred yourself to tell me, you mean. Good question. Well, Bill did it for you.'

'Bill?'

'Yes. You look at me as if you've never heard of him, but you were doing a good impression of being anxious to find him last Friday. Which I assume you did, since this is where my car's ended up.'

'He phoned you?' Cedric must have called Wisdom in between trying Strathallan, maybe while I was sleeping on the train. It was about the only opportunity he'd had. 'When was that?'

'Saturday lunchtime, at the Top Hat.' So, it was as I'd thought. 'This was the soonest I could get here.'

'Wisdom . . .' I stepped closer. 'I'm sorry to have to break this to you, but I'm afraid the man you know as Bill Hall is dead.'

'Who was that on the blower, then? His ghost?'

'No. It was him right enough. He died on Saturday evening, in London.'

'The same day.' Wisdom nodded. He looked disappointed, even depressed, by the news, but far from surprised. 'They caught up with him in the end, then.'

'Yes. They did.'

'He knew they were close, didn't he? I could tell.'

'How?'

'The tone of his voice. It was verging on the sentimental. And he wasn't a sentimental man.'

'Do you want to know what happened?'

'No. The less I know the better. Ignorance isn't bliss, but it isn't bad insurance either.' He thought for a moment. 'You could tell me . . . if it was quick.'

'I rather think it was, yes.'

'One up to Bill, then.'

'What do you mean?'

'Well, it spared him a lingering exit, didn't it? Cancer's no respecter of dignity.'

'Cancer?'

'Riddled with it, so he told me. Didn't he mention it to you?'

'No.' I almost laughed. Cedric had joked to me about the amount of radiation he'd been exposed to. It was virtually the last thing he'd said to me. Perhaps it was his way of hinting at the truth. And perhaps it was why he'd been willing to risk walking into a trap, because, whatever they did to him, something worse had already happened. 'He didn't breathe a word.'

'He was never one to tout for sympathy.'

'That he wasn't.'

'And he always believed in settling debts.'

'I suppose he did.'

'That's partly why he phoned me.'

'Yes?'

'He wanted to apologize for not returning the car. But he said you'd be happy to reimburse me for the cost of coming here to collect it.' Wisdom grinned. 'As well as for the petrol he'd used.'

*   *   *

A few minutes later I stood in the lane, watching Wisdom drive away. As he turned the corner and vanished from sight, Cedric went with him, out of my world and back into the strange half-life of false treachery he'd inhabited for so long. He'd served their purposes for fifty years. But, in the end, they'd served his. They thought they'd got the better of him, but it was the other way round. And they didn't even know it.

I walked back to the house, unlocked the door and went in. The post had arrived in my absence and was lying on the mat. There was just one letter. My name and address were handwritten on it in ballpoint pen. I didn't recognize the writing. But when I picked up the envelope and looked at the postmark, I suddenly guessed whose it was.

Epilogue

Two months have passed since then. It's mid-September – early autumn in Rutland, late summer in Cornwall. Stanacombe is sold. The new owners moved in last week. Life, as they say, goes on.

I moved back to London. Where else was there for me to go? I thought I'd be able to talk my way back into the headhunting game with one or other agency, but my year out was hard to explain, and maybe they sensed I'd lost the heart for it. They were probably right.

It's at times like these that friends show their true colours. You won't be surprised to learn that Matt's the only real friend I've ever had, apart from you. You probably knew that all along. He didn't move back to Otherways when he left hospital. After a couple of weeks' convalescence at his parents' home, he rented a house near Melton Mowbray. It's what James Milner had expected Otherways to be: 'a so-so Midlands hunting box'. I went up there to help him unpack over the August bank holiday weekend. That's when he told me he was going ahead with Pizza Prego's expansion in the States. He needed someone to meet and assess potential franchise holders and was offering me the job. It's a six-month contract in the first instance. Not a favour, he assured me. A good deal for both of us. Well, I don't know. What do you think? I start next month.

When Halfyard finally got round to writing, it transpired that Daisy really had left everything to Lucy, meaning Matt inherited a house, a collection of sculptures and some substantial savings, none of which he wanted or needed. The house is on the market and the sculptures will be up for auction in a few months. Who knows, Daisy Temple may turn out to be a posthumous star of the art world. Matt kept one piece for himself: the unfinished bust of Lucy, which could so easily be of you.

There are quite a few things I could ask Matt, but don't. And vice versa. We share our secrets by never speaking of them. The inquest into the double drowning in Rutland Water is due to be held next week. We'll both be giving evidence. But we don't talk about it. There's no need. We know what we'll be saying. And what we won't. Least said soonest mended isn't a proverb I ever thought I'd swear by. It's never been my style. Till now.

One unasked question did get answered last weekend, though. Matt invited me up, ostensibly to discuss the American job. He'll be over there quite a bit himself, so we'll probably see as much of each other as we ever have, if not more. And we'd already discussed it pretty thoroughly. So, it was no surprise that the subject hardly cropped up. We talked about you and Lucy instead. We talk about the two of you quite a lot, actually. The things we did together, the holidays we had, and the fun. Yes, the fun. We forgot that somehow in the losing of you. But we remember it now, without flinching.

I stayed until Monday. Matt took the day off. We drove up to Lincoln to see the cathedral, which I never had before, and started back after a late lunch. Matt was driving. When we didn't take the Melton turning off the A1, I thought he'd overshot by mistake. But no, there was something he wanted to show me. We turned off at the Ram Jam instead and headed towards Oakham. I suppose I knew then where we were going, but still I didn't ask.

Soon, as we drove through Hambleton and carried on east along the peninsula, there was no need. Otherways was our destination. As Matt turned into the drive, he said, 'Prepare yourself for a shock,' and, a few moments later, the shock was there, in front of me.

Otherways was no more. The foundations were still in place, and the moat, but the house itself had been demolished. Contractors' vehicles were loading and removing the piled stonework. Glass and plaster and wood were stacked in skips. The smoking remains of a bonfire scarred the lawn. I stared at the scene in amazement. A building that had never seemed quite real now wasn't real at all. The wrecking ball and the bulldozer had smashed Posnan's subtle artifice into dust and rubble. Otherways had become part of its own history.

Seeing us, a man who looked as if he was in charge walked over to the car and spoke to Matt. 'It's not gone as smoothly as I'd have liked, Mr Prior,' he said. 'Those walls didn't seem to want to come down.' I saw Matt smile grimly. 'But we got there in the end.'

'I wondered why you hadn't put it up for sale,' I said, as the man walked away.

'I couldn't sell that to anyone.' Matt looked round at me. 'Now could I?'

'I thought it was listed.'

'So it was. That's why I've had them at it over the weekend. Less chance of official intervention. There'll be hell to pay, of course. And a fat fine, I dare say. But I don't care. It's gone. That's all that matters.'

'Did I ever tell you about Stowe House?'

'I don't think so.'

'The Grenvilles were the big landowners round Stanacombe for centuries. They built themselves a huge mansion called Stowe House in about 1680. A sequence of family tragedies followed and the male line died out. The house was pulled down in about 1740. It had stood for just sixty years. Marina read up on the subject. There was a saying about it she used to quote. "Within the memory of one man, grass grew and was sown in the meadow where sprang up Stowe House, and grew and was mown again where Stowe had been."'

'A meadow,' said Matt dreamily. 'I like that.'

'So do I.'

I thought, and think, that Posnan might have liked it as well. Otherways was his greatest work, but it was also the reason why he stopped working. He built more than a house at Otherways. He made something he grew to fear. Now there was nothing to be frightened of any more.

'I'm glad you've done this, Matt.'

'No choice, really. None at all.'

He turned the car round and headed away along the drive. Neither of us looked back. Matt didn't so much as glance up at the mirror.

At the end of the drive, he turned left and went as far along the lane as the gates Lucy had crashed through, just as he had in my dream. There he stopped and asked me to walk down with him to the water's edge.

The afternoon was still and grey, with a tang of autumn in the air. We went through the pedestrian side gate and walked slowly ahead, over the last bulge of land before the descent to the pontoon. Neither of us said anything. There was nothing to say.

The pontoon came in sight, with Half Moon Spinney to the left, fields to the right and the waveless waters of the lake dead ahead. We walked on, side by side, until we reached the last shingly yard of lane before the flood line. Lucy had died here, either where we stood or a short way out, beneath the water. This was the last piece of the world we'd shared with her.

'It's the first time I've come down here since it happened,' said Matt. 'I'd forgotten how peaceful it is.'

'I did everything I could to save her.'

'I know.'

'But she didn't want to be saved.'

'I know that, too.'

'There's something I'm going to have to explain to you,' I said, sensing that the moment had come for me to tell him how poor a friend I'd really been to him.

'Let me go first, Tony.'

'You?'

'Yes. I have my monthly check-up with the doc tomorrow. If all's well, he'll probably extend it to three months for the next one.'

'And is all well?'

'Touch wood, yes. I'll even be able to report some progress that he was predicting.'

'What sort of progress?'

'He said the amnesia would most likely be temporary. Well, he was right.'

'Your memory's come back?'

'Yes.' Matt turned to me. 'It has.' We stood there, looking at each other for several seconds. Then he went on, 'Which means you don't have to bother explaining anything.'

'I don't?'

'Not a thing.' He glanced out at the lake and took a deep breath. 'Let's go home, shall we?'

We started back up the lane. I wondered if I should try to explain, despite his assurance to the contrary. Then the moment passed and, in the companionable silence that followed, I realized how right Matt was. We were done with explanations. There were many things we could both have said. But there was nothing we needed to.

What happened at Henna Cliff, Marina? What *really* happened? You know. You must do. I can only guess – and stop Matt from guessing. The letter that was waiting for me at Stanacombe two months ago was postmarked Oakham, 12 July – two days before. But it could easily have lain in the box from the day before that; there are no collections on a Sunday afternoon. When I tore the envelope open, I found myself looking at a rail ticket, clipped in one corner. It was a first-class single, from Newton Abbot to Oakham. I don't need to tell you the date on it. You know that well enough.

I carry the ticket around with me in my wallet. I don't know why. I've often thought I should destroy it. But I haven't. Not yet, anyway. It could be a last clever piece of stage management on someone's part. Or it could be the only remaining fragment of the truth. Either way, I reckon I'll go on keeping it to myself.

THE END

CAUGHT IN THE LIGHT

Robert Goddard

On assignment in Vienna, photographer Ian Jarrett falls passionately in love with the mysterious and beautiful Marian. Back in the UK, Ian resolves to leave his wife for her – only to find Marian has disappeared, and the photographs of their brief time together have been savagely destroyed.

Searching desperately for her, Ian comes across a quiet Dorset churchyard. Here he meets a psychotherapist, who is looking for a missing client of hers: a woman who claims she is the reincarnation of Marian Esguard, who may have invented photography ten years before Fox Talbot.

But why is Marian Esguard unknown to history? And who and where is the woman Ian Jarrett has sacrificed everything for?

'A hypnotic, unputdownable thriller... one can only gasp with admiration at Goddard's ability to hold readers spellbound'
DAILY MAIL

'His best book yet, a sinuous structure of twists and traps leading to an unexpectedly sinister climax'
THE TELEGRAPH

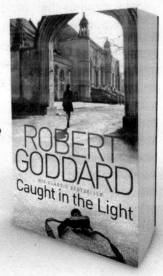

LONG TIME COMING

Robert Goddard

For thirty-six years, they thought he was dead...They were wrong...

Eldritch Swan is a dead man. Or at least that is what his nephew Stephen has always been told. Until one day Swan walks back into his life after thirty-six years in an Irish prison. He won't say why he was locked up - only that he is innocent of any crime.

His return should interest no one. But the visit of a solicitor with a strange request will take Swan and his sceptical nephew to London, where an exhibition of Picasso paintings is the starting point on a journey that will take them back to when the pictures were last seen - on the eve of the Second World War.

Untangling the web of murky secrets, family ties and old betrayals that surrounds their mysterious reappearance will prove to be a dangerous pursuit for the two men.
Because watching their every step is a sinister enemy who will do whatever it takes to stop the truth emerging...

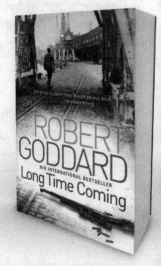

'The master of the clever twist'
SUNDAY TELEGRAPH